MORE

BOOK TWO OF THE MATATA TRILOGY

Cover: Dancing Zebras at Masai Mara concept by the Author
Photo: Getty Images: Courting Zebras, Masai Mara, Kenya
Design and art direction: Rudi Rodrigues, Avatar Inc. Toronto
Book design & layout: bookdesign.ca

Library and Archives Canada Cataloguing in Publication
Menezes, Braz
More matata : love after the Mau Mau : a novel set in Kenya and
Goa / Braz Menezes.
(Book two of the Matata trilogy)
Issued also in an electronic format.
ISBN 978-0-9877963-2-5
I. Title. II. Series: Menezes, Braz. Matata trilogy ; bk. 2.
PS8626.E55M67 2012 C813'.6 C2012-907057-2
Library and Archives Canada Cataloguing in Publication
Menezes, Braz
More matata [electronic resource] : love after the Mau Mau : a novel set in
Kenya and Goa / Braz Menezes.
(Book two of the Matata trilogy)
Electronic monograph.
Issued also in print format.
ISBN 978-0-9877963-3-2
I. Title. II. Series: Menezes, Braz. Matata trilogy ; bk. 2.
PS8626.E55M67 2012 C813'.6 C2012-907058-0

USA ISBN-13: 978-1480086333 (CreateSpace-Assigned)
ISBN-10: 1480086339
Publisher's Contact: matatabooks@gmail.com

MORE MATATA*

Love After the Mau Mau

A NOVEL SET IN KENYA AND GOA

Braz Menezes

Dedicated jointly to the memory of

Mengha Singh Juttla and Savio Agnelo Antonio Cordeiro
Born in India and Kenya
Shared High School
Through the Mau Mau years
And through a remarkable coincidence
Each passed away at an identical age of
50 years and 10 months
in Kenya and Canada

Editing Myself

Isn't life but a first draft?
Line by line
cultural conditioning written in black
religious restrictions firmly bind
create moral dilemmas
only the craving heart is
in harmony with deep desires

The adamant mind with its inhibitions
in conflict and combat with fragile emotions
What's right? What's wrong?
Who will be the judge, and why?
The temptation of a lifetime
should I really let the moment slip away
could you possibly give me all I wanted

Desire protests, reasoning pacifies
I delete the Yes and retain a No
Editing myself at this stage
is like deleting a beautiful chapter of my life
before I begin to write it
Perhaps it's in our best interest

Isn't life but a first draft?
We edit as we go along

© Zohra Zoberi (True Colours)

Contents

Prologue

As I write, the 2012 US Elections are underway, but it is the 2008 Presidential Election that is foremost in my mind.

"Please, Lando, I must see this with you," Saboti in England had asked me to wake her up as the US election results start to come in at about 8:00 p.m. Eastern Standard Time. From my condo perched three hundred feet up in a concrete tower, I gaze down at Lake Ontario, and the thin dark shadow—like a Chinese brush stroke painting—against a mottled red-orange and mauve sky to the southwest. It is the distant New York State shoreline. What happens behind that black line tonight may forever transform the way people view skin colour.

Today is November 4, 2008. This is the night the world will change. Of this I have no doubt. He is intelligent and well educated—a calm, composed candidate with a beautiful family. For me he stands tall and confident – way above the competition. Surely everyone must realise that Barack Obama is a natural born leader. He is bound to be successful. For the millions around the world who have experienced racism at first hand, it will mark a symbolic end to that chapter in our history.

But just like lake flies in a Canadian summer, swarms of gloom and doom experts are buzzing around the media. Talking heads and their invited pundits have clogged the airwaves almost to gridlock. Radio and TV stations fill in the time between mindless commercial breaks with meaningless disjointed sound bites and admonitions on the risks of the unknown. There are predictions and innuendos of Obama being no more than a black common garden snake-oil salesman peddling Nirvana.

Obama—like my friend Saboti—is of mixed race: the result of a liaison between a white parent and a black Kenyan partner. But America is not yet a colour-blind society. The pundits say many whites will vote with their eyes and not with their brain. Each ethnic minority in this alleged melting pot will be looking out for its own narrow interests. They will, in doing so, split the vote. It can go either way.

There is high tension and excitement on Planet Earth. Random polls in countries around the globe report that if their citizens could vote for an American President, Barack Obama would be their man. Eight years of the disastrous George W. Bush administration in the White House has left the world desperate, depressed and desolate. The economy of the USA and that of countries around the world is on the brink of the greatest financial crisis in a century, even as America fights two wars in Iraq and Afghanistan without an exit plan.

The minutes pass slowly as darkness sets in. I anxiously pace from room to room, trying to control my excitement or else my blood pressure will shoot through my head like a burst water pipe in the street. I glance outside into a blackness pierced by dots of lights, as the inhabitants of nearby buildings return from work to crouch with take-away dinners around their TV sets. I feel like time has stopped. It is nearly 7:00 p.m. as I press the mute button on the TV and turn to a music channel. They are playing my favourite, 'As Time Goes By' from the hit movie Casablanca --'The world will always welcome lovers, as time goes by'. How very appropriate, I think! But no… on second thoughts, not so in my experience!

It is just over an hour before the polls close. Already it is a new day in London, five hours ahead of Toronto and the part of the United States I can see from my window. I press the mute button again. The pundits are still waffling. Unable to control my restlessness, I stop by the fridge and drop a few ice cubes into my special 60-year old crystal glass, which I now use only on special occasions. I absent-mindedly place it on the table. I turn on the TVs in each bedroom—both tuned to different channels in case I have to second-guess the results projected by CNN. God help me if I have to explain to Saboti the electoral system in the USA that I know many American voters themselves don't fully understand, even as they choose a candidate who promises to fulfil their dreams.

Back in the living room, I pour myself a healthy dose of Scotch. My thoughts drift to other people's dreams and to the 'what if' scenarios if Obama wins tonight. Obama's only living relative in the USA, his maternal grandmother, has passed away only 24 hours ago. What if Obama's father, from Kenya's second most populous Luo ethnic tribe, could have been alive today to see his son complete his most unlikely and arduous safari to the White House? The older Barack Obama Sr. was of my generation. We both grew up in Kenya's colonial era, when everyone was classified by colour, race and tribe, and labelled, just like the rodents and reptiles at the nearby Coryndon Memorial Museum that I visited so often as a boy. We both lived through the Mau Mau liberation struggle. We both went to university abroad in the Sixties, and returned to do our best for a newly independent Kenya led by its first President, Jomo Kenyatta. We both were promised a share of Kenyatta's dream for an economically strong, multi-racial Kenya.

Yet, within the hierarchy of established racial barriers and privileges in Kenya Colony, our lives were so different and were shaped by our fathers.

In contrast to Baraka Obama Sr., I had a privileged childhood. My father Pedro Francisco (Chico) was born in 1902 in Goa, a Portuguese colony on India's west coast. Orphaned at the age of 15, Chico decided to follow the route taken by his two older brothers—he would seek a new life in Mozambique, Portuguese East

Africa, where it was rumoured there were plenty of jobs for young men willing to adventure into the unknown.

In 1928, a lean, handsome young man and his friends set sail on a steamer for Africa—with a deep azure ocean below and a cloudless blue sky above. But Chico and his three friends never made it to Portuguese East Africa; they jumped ship at Mombasa and settled instead in British-ruled Kenya. The small Goan community that had already established itself in Mombasa welcomed him. He found clerical work with the National Bank of India, and within a couple of months literally shot to the top—5,450 feet above sea level, to be exact—he was transferred to NBI's head office in Nairobi, over three hundred miles away.

Dad often spoke to us of that first train journey, lying awake, listening to the clanging of metal on metal; and the hissing of steam and the chatter of voices in the darkness as the steam locomotive would pull up at every station to take on more water for its thirsty boilers. He talked of the exhilaration the next morning as the 'iron snake' as it was called cut through the vast swathes of barren land and the vast panoramic expanse of the Athi Plains with its teeming herds of deer and antelope, giraffe and zebra; and finally of his first view of the blue grey hills that seemed to be intentionally placed in the path ahead; these hills that had forced the railway builders to stop and set up camp before tackling the arduous climb to the rim of the Rift Valley - the camp that later grew into Nairobi. From those early days, Nairobi had grown into a dusty, bustling town lined with a few stone buildings and many corrugated iron clad structures and wood plank shacks. This was the administrative capital of Kenya Colony.

Chico joined the ranks of hundreds of Goans who had been enticed by the British, or by relatives already in East Africa. There were administrators, tailors, clerks, cashiers, and cooks; bakers and barmen, lawyers, doctors and engineers, and they had organised themselves in community organisations and at least four clubs to fill their social needs.

One social need was harder to satisfy because of a shortage of suitable wives. Seven years after arriving in Nairobi, Chico did what almost all single Goan men did, with the help of a vibrant matchmaker network. He sailed to Goa to seek a bride. Much to the chagrin of some matrons, Chico, within a couple of days after his arrival in Goa, fell in love with the 17-year-old daughter of his host at a poker card playing evening in Margao. Angela Alice (Anja), fair skinned, with dark eyelashes and silken black hair was beautiful and intelligent. Within six months they were married and back in Africa and had started a family. I was the second born after Linda. Fatima and Joachim followed at three-year intervals, and Niven arrived after a gap of six years. Chico and Anja continued in love.

Thinking about love, my thoughts turn to Saboti and how we first met, when I was 10 and she was 7 and how we found each other again many years after-- but more of that later.

I return to watching the election results. A breaking news headline flashes across the TV screen, as I grab the remote and raise the volume: 'Agreement has been reached on the next steps for Truth, Justice, and Reconciliation Commission in Kenya.' I feel a pang of anger in my throat. Almost 55 years after Kenya's brutal conflict pitting the mainly Kikuyu Mau Mau rebels against European farmers—a violent movement that evolved into a national struggle for political independence from Britain, the country is again going through an upheaval – only now it is from within—two corrupt tribal factions fighting each other for political and economic dominance, while that beautiful country bleeds. Last December, accusations and counter accusations of fraud during the Presidential elections sparked a wave of violent clashes, along ethnic lines. Nearly 1,600 people were killed and over 300,000 were forced to flee their homes, sowing seeds of further civic unrest. Eventually a brokered peace was restored and a power sharing coalition government came into effect.

This is why the American elections have riveted Saboti and me to the news. Can a successful win for Obama help bring his message of Hope and Change to Kenya? Can America regain its leadership in the world, with an Obama win?

The channels interrupt with more breaking news. 'Somali based pirates have hijacked another super-tanker in the Arabian Sea'. Who can stop the wave of piracy now sweeping the oceans? I remember stories of how our forefathers had traveled relatively safely in dhows and steamships across the same waters for centuries that today are infested with dangerous and poverty-stricken pirates off the coast of Somalia.

I glance at the time and phone Saboti to tell her the polls will close in 10 minutes. "Lando, I was about to call you," she says. "I'm too wound up to sleep tonight." We agree to call each other every15 minutes.

At three minutes past 8:00 p.m. CNN calls Pennsylvania for Obama, as our hopes rise. Saboti and I have spoken twice. Shortly after 9:00 p.m. CNN calls Ohio for Obama. It is a close race in the early results. As New Hampshire goes to Obama shortly thereafter, I smell victory in the air. I call Saboti in London and she is screaming with joy; it's so contagious that I begin screaming in Toronto.

CNN switches scenes to a jubilant Kenya awaiting history being made by one of their own, albeit only 'partly' of their own. Change is coming to America, which may transform the world by example and leadership.

At precisely 11:00 p.m., (4:00 a.m. in London), CNN calls the results as final. Barack Obama is declared President-Elect of the United States of America. Thousands on the Chicago Lakefront explode with joy. O-BA-MA! O-BA-MA! They chant. The world stops and gasps in collective relief. Saboti and I are already choking with emotion. Words do not come out. My eyes fill with tears. Saboti says she is weeping too. We hang up.

I turn the sound off the TV; outside, every window in sight is illuminated with flickering screens tuned into the US election results. I think of Saboti as I caress the texture of the cut glass tumbler with its few surviving ice cubes. There was plenty of *matata* in our lives! So much has happened since I first met her in 1949.

As Time Goes By is humming in my head. No, the world does not always welcome lovers…not when you have to cut across racial barriers.

Those barriers played a large role in my life and that of Saboti in Kenya while we were growing up. Let me explain.

Homecoming

Plums Lane, Nairobi. November 1951.

"Lando, did you really mean to become a priest?" Linda asks me, grabbing me tightly by the wrist. Perhaps because she is now 16, she does not pinch me as hard as she used to when she wanted my full attention. Linda has always claimed it was her God-given right to pinch me, as she was three years older than me. We are sitting facing each other across the dining table – in a closed in verandah that doubles as dining room and general meeting space; its walls silent witness over the years to some of the most fiery family discussions, arguments, laughter, joy and tears. Outside, bird sounds fill the air, with occasional interruptions of frenzied yelping by Simba. I hear Mom's voice too somewhere in the garden.

I have only just returned to Kenya from Goa, where I had been sent to boarding school at age 10, only to be whisked back 18 months later when I wrote to my parents requesting a transfer to a seminary school to train for the priesthood.

"Linda, we had no choice," I reply. "Musso and I thought we would be better fed at the Seminary than at St. Joseph's. We were always hungry. Why do you ask?"

Linda pauses before replying as Mwangi, the houseboy, enters the dining room on his way to the kitchen from the backyard carrying a freshly plucked chicken. It is always fish on Fridays and chicken on Saturdays.

"I just cannot imagine you as a priest, " Linda says, "standing up there before the pulpit, going on and on, every Sunday—but Mom believed you. She made life hell for Dad. She told him she wanted you brought back from Goa immediately. She said that our uncle, Father Thomaz, had already been offered to the Church. 'One brother is enough; I don't want to sacrifice a son as well,' she told Dad."

"Would *you* offer up your brother to the priesthood?" I ask, noticing for the first time since my return how she has changed in the 18 months since I waved goodbye on the Goa docks. She has grown breasts and her hair is blacker, shiny and longer, just like Mom's the year she was married.

"Meaning you? Actually no. Not now," Linda laughs. "At least not for the next four months. Not until the Christmas and New Year festivities are over. By the way, I've already told Mom you will be going with me to a party next Saturday. Will you please come? I missed so many parties because of your being away; they wouldn't let me go alone, even to my friends' places."

The wall clock chimes the half hour. "Oh gosh. I'm late." Linda rushes out, not waiting for my reply.

I walk outside into the bright sunshine. The air is fragrant with the smell of ripe fruit, just as it was in Goa in May. I hear the cackle of mouse birds squabbling in some trees nearby, and voices coming from around the side of the house. Mom is sitting in the shade of an avocado tree, on a chair made of entwined wooden branches by local craftsmen; she seems very happy.

Simba is still yelping with excitement at my arrival. Mom looks up and smiles at me. "He too missed you terribly," she says. She is showing Fatima, my 10-year old sister, some basic knit stiches, while Joachim, soon to turn seven, also wants to learn how to knit, and struggles to look over Fatima's protruding elbow. Little baby Niven, covered by a mosquito net, is asleep in his pram in the shade of the nearby tree. The peach tree grows close to where my first dog, Jolly, is buried; the painted letters on the large rock that marks his grave now faded from a brilliant white to a dull grey.

"Do you want to join us knitting?" Mom asks as Fatima laughs at the idea.

"No thank you." I glance around. It's a peaceful scene, but somehow I feel there is no room for me in this picture. I am restless and frustrated. Fatima and Joachim treat me with some suspicion. They are too young to understand why their parents selected me at the age of ten and sent me away to boarding school in Goa. According to Linda, they know that Dad always blamed me if anything went wrong and said that as the eldest, I must set a good example, but why did they choose such harsh punishment like sending me away?

I unhook Simba's collar from his chain. The dog's movement is slow compared to the frisky, energetic and affectionate Rhodesian ridgeback I had left behind; he is still only six years old but already behaves like an old dog. Perhaps it is because he was not exercised regularly while I was away and has gained weight. I rub his neck; he likes that and is immediately more animated. He seems happy that our daily walks have restarted.

Plums Lane, with its rough, somewhat potholed compacted murram surface and shrubs of bougainvillea growing wild, looks the same on the outside, but for me much has changed. I miss having Jeep, my best friend and companion since childhood, by my side. I find myself constantly turning around looking for him, but he has left with his family to live in Delaware, where according to what his father Marco told Dad, everyone sells insurance. "It is somewhere in America. Rick Major, Marco's American boss came looking for him because he was so good at selling insurance in British East Africa," I had overheard his brother-in-law boast to colleagues in bar at the Goan Gymkhana, as I was buying a Coke.

My other two closest friends, Abdul and Hardev, still live in Plums Lane; but they too are no longer able to come out and play as we once did. Hardev is a Sikh, and Abdul a Muslim, and now they do not mix with each other because of what happened in India after Independence in 1947, when Hindus and Sikhs fought Muslims, and many hundreds of thousands on each side were slaughtered. Both Hardev and Abdul work at their fathers' shops during their free time after school. Hardev's father is a greengrocer at the Municipal Market and Abdul's father is a general trader in the Indian Bazaar.

I see Mr. Gelani's pyjamas securely pegged to the clothesline. It is clear that Mr. and Mrs. Gelani still live in their house across the lane from us. On the outside, the only visible change twice a week is the bright colour of Mr. Gelani's pyjamas. Mom says there have been no recent complaints from Mrs. Gelani about Simba's wanton assaults on those garments as they wave like twin air socks with the breeze.

But inside their home a profound change has taken place. Ahmad has gone. Mrs. Gelani has lost a very important tenant and I have lost a special person in my life. Ahmad is an engineer, a Muslim who came from Karachi as a young man to join the Uganda Railways. He had resigned after the expiry of his first contract, owing to the unfair salaries paid to Asians compared to Europeans doing the same job. A chance meeting with Dad in a store near the National Bank of India, where Dad worked, had led to a second meeting. They liked each other at first sight. Dad helped him buy a taxi and get started with a loan from his bank, and as Ahmad did not know many people outside the Railways, Dad also guaranteed the loan. "All on just a handshake!" Ahmad boasted. He was grateful to Dad beyond words.

Jeep and I too became Ahmad's fans. He was only about 10 years older than us, but very smart and strong with deeply tanned hairy arms, and a well-trimmed black moustache. He let us polish his big black Chevy Sedan every Saturday, while he regaled us with stories of his homeland, and of his daily adventures with the different characters who entered and exited his taxi. Most of all, Ahmad was to us as an elder brother, and a good friend who answered our most complicated questions, and always with good humour. But now I feared that he too was out of reach, as he has moved into his own home with his new bride.

"I can't get Ahmad to come around," I had complained to Linda about Ahmad's tardiness a few weeks ago. We were to set up the antenna for my crystal radio, (I still don't understand how that crystal magically snatched inaudible and invisible BBC news and music from the dark skies and squeezed it into sounds through my earphones.), but Ahmad had twice postponed our appointment.

"He's besotted, Lando," Linda said.

"He's bees...what?"

"Besotted...he's love-struck. But you won't know anything about love yet... besotted. Oh! I don't suppose you've learnt any new English words in Goa!" Linda snapped. "Have you met his wife, Serena? She's so lovely."

"Yes. Ahmad now just spends all his free time at home with Serena," I said.

"That's what love is." Linda had replied.

"This way Simba," I call out. He's dashing about in a frenzy, overjoyed that we can walk together again. We turn south onto Kikuyu Road towards the Gymkhana by the intersection with Forest Road. These roads define the 'Europeans only' residential area and border the zone with the stone-built European staff quarters of the Kenya Uganda Railways. Jeep and I used to take a short cut to school through this area, our hearts in our mouths, as the owners had 'Mbwa Kali' – savage, trained dogs to attack non-whites. The Parklands Sports Club to my left still has the 'Europeans Only - Members Only' sign over the entrance gate. I realize how free Goa was by comparison. Perhaps one day the government will realize we are all equal in the eyes of God. The priest at St. Francis Xavier says so.

Simba's barking interrupts my thoughts. We are near the crest of Ainsworth Hill; I can go left to the Gymkhana or turn right towards the Coryndon Memorial Museum that has a wonderful collection of stuffed animals, birds, reptiles as well as historical artifacts and geological samples. Simba wants me to take him down to the river under the bridge, where he loves to splash in the puddles and chase birds through the long grass on the banks. I hesitate. I can see a cricket match is underway at the Goan Gymkhana. Perhaps my classmates Oscar and Savio are there, since they live next door to the club; I think the match will stop soon as darkness drops like a curtain at half-past six. I decide to return home instead.

I have a lot of catching up to do in my studies, now that I am back at the Dr. Ribeiro Goan School. While at boarding school in Goa, I was immersed in the discoveries and conquests of great Portuguese mariners and commanders, including Vasco da Gama, who first reached India in 1498; Afonso De Albuquerque, who conquered Goa in 1510; and Pedro Cabral, who added Brazil to the possessions of the Portuguese Throne in the year 1500. But knowing about their exploits will not help me in British-ruled Kenya.

"Lando, welcome back," Mr. Tavares, the history master, had greeted me on my first day back at Dr. Ribeiro. "Remember you are now a part of the British Empire again. You must make an effort to catch up with your classmates." Now I am drowning in homework. I will have to learn about Sir Francis Drake, Sir Walter Raleigh and other English seamen and explorers. In addition, I must study and absorb the intimate details of a century-long war between England and France, if I am to move to high school next year.

As we approach Plums Lane, Simba bounds away with a quick yelp to welcome Dad who is getting off the bus. I wait for them at the intersection. Dad has gained weight since returning from Goa in 1950; he has been assigned more responsibilities at work, but even so, he seems more relaxed. He has eased up on his homilies to me about medicine and law as possible careers. Perhaps he has noticed how immersed I am in my homework. But I know he is worried about recent events at the school. All is not well at Dr. Ribeiro's.

"You're early Dad." I greet him. He smiles.

"Have you been to the museum? It must feel different without Jeep's company."

"No Dad. Just walking Simba. Yes I miss Jeep."

"You remember your pal Dr. Leakey?" he asks me. "I've just heard he is not a full-time curator anymore. He's now working with the Colonial Office on a secret mission." Dr. Leakey is a world-famous anthropologist, who is the curator at the museum. He lives with his wife Mary and their sons Jonathan and Richard and a pack of Dalmatians, in a small house by the entrance to the museum. One day, when Jeep and I were visiting an exhibit of a live African python, Leakey quietly crept up on us from behind and in a loud voice announced the name of the snake. My blood froze and Jeep too jumped with fright. Leakey laughed and thought it was hilarious, but he was nice to us and even got one of his assistants to show us the taxidermists' workshop. We were his biggest fans.

"What secret mission?"

"I can't say. I heard that news from a reliable source at work," Dad says. "Lando, while you have been away there has been some matata; some political problems upcountry, but you need not be concerned. It does not affect us." We arrive home.

That night as I lie in bed listening to the din of crickets outside, and awaiting the midnight hour for my regular BBC World Service news bulletin, I cannot help remembering the conversation during dinner on the SS Amra returning from Goa three months earlier with Alberto Pinto and his wife, Dona Pulquera. Alberto is a senior civil servant in the Colonial civil service, and he had kindly agreed to chaperone me back to Nairobi as I was considered a minor. I had overheard Alberto and his friends discuss rumours that many existing prisons were to be expanded and new ones built in

Kenya, and that meant the likely growth in civil service jobs at the Prisons Department. I had wondered then whether it was because the European farms needed cheap labour, as I had seen prison labour used on the tea plantations in Kericho. Later, I asked Alberto about it.

"There's a great deal of trouble brewing," he had said. "Strange things are happening on European farms. The Africans are creating serious matata for the Colonial Office." And then he had dropped his voice to a whisper. "I cannot talk about it here. Even these floating walls have ears."

I wonder if Dad was referring to the same matata, and whether this was related to Leakey's secret mission with the Colonial Office.

There has been nothing in the local papers about this. I realize how I have changed since going away. I now crave news. The trip to Goa had expanded my world, but coming back to Plums Lane had caused it to shrink again. One of my first priorities on my return had been to retrieve my crystal radio from storage. It is now working again. Every night after some crackles, screeches and a few prolonged whistles, I can usually get a good signal, the clearest around midnight.

I tune in and listen avidly to cryptic bulletins every night— 'Churchill wins General Election'—'Kiki Haakansen of Sweden who won a beauty contest for wearing a bikini at the Festival was planning a world tour'—Although I do not always understand the contents or context, I can relate to some news items. For example, when the BBC announces the King has had a lung operation, I think of my father's colleague at work, Mr. Cunha, who died on the operating table when his lungs collapsed, a week after my coming home. Dad said Cunha would not absent himself from work because he needed the money to support his family, so he postponed a visit to his doctor. By the time he agreed to see his doctor, it was too late. I know that the King, attended by the best doctors in England, will be fine. After all, we sing God Save the King at least once a month at school.

Today the BBC announces, "Six thousand British troops were flown to Egypt". I wonder if the troops flown to Egypt are heading our way to help with Leakey's secret mission. From overhearing Dad and my Uncle Antonio talk in hushed tones, I feel something is going on in Kenya, but nobody will talk publicly about it. My curiosity has been aroused. Within days I become addicted to listening to the BBC news. It is my contact with the outside world.

———•—•———

2

Under the Asian Umbrella

I t has been a chaotic term at the Goan School. On my first day
back in September after my return from Goa, Savio, who shared
a desk in our crowded classroom, pulled me to one side as we jos-
tled our way out during the morning recess. "Lando, you'll have
to decide which team you'll join," he said. "The Buffalos or the
Rhinos."

"Team? Buffalos or the Rhinos?"

"No…we're warriors really. The gangs place bets and battle each
other on horseback. You can be either a rider or a steed," he said.
He eyes me head to toe. "Gosh, you're skinny aren't you? You will
have to be a rider." I feel bad I'm thin, but I see his point. Savio is
as tall as me but bigger-boned and definitely fatter than me.

During the lunch recess, I am introduced to Maurice, the gang-
leader of the Buffalos, as that was Savio's team. Maurice is handsome and speaks with a posh accent; he always played the lead
male role in Christmas plays at the Goan Gymkhana.

We walk to the side of the brick school building.

"I suppose you've seen buffalos in Goa?" he said. "Remember
our African buffalos are wild and dangerous. Now raise your right

hand and read this aloud. You, Savio, will be the witness." I raised my hand and promised to be loyal to the Buffalos above all else. "Welcome to our gang." I felt a sense of relief; rejection would have ruined my life at Dr. Ribeiro's forever. I was so happy to be back at the school.

I could not see the sense of these mock battles, but I said nothing. Everyone had to belong. However, I soon got into the spirit of it. About six pairs (rider and steed) a side would attack their opponents at a fast pace and try and knock them over. There would be cries of victory, howls of laughter, and occasionally cries of pain on impact. I still cringe when I hear the sound of two skulls colliding, and at the scrapes and bruises that we suffer. But shamelessly, we lick our wounds; swear revenge on the Rhinos, and head back into class. The girls just snigger as we limp in. "You boys are pathetic."

Meanwhile, more than six months after a major public confrontation between the school Board, chaired By Dr. A.C.L De Souza and the Principal, there is still tension. I have seen ACL in person as he visits the school often—alone, unannounced—walking confidently along the corridors smoking thick cigars, and randomly poking his head into various classrooms. He is tall and well dressed with greying wavy hair neatly parted. His glasses with two round lens with dark rims emphasize a strict unsmiling, no-nonsense face at least when in our school. Our teachers are irritated with his visits but appear frightened when he is around. They continue frustrated as they struggle daily to teach in grossly over-crowded classrooms (my class has 47 students); and everyone agrees their salaries are low compared to teachers in other communities. The school premises cannot accommodate any more students for an expected new intake in January, which is the start of the school year. Nerves are stretched to breaking point and tempers flare at every occasion.

Savio and I, and many of our classmates, are worried about what will happen in January when we move to high school. There is a lot of uncertainty in the air. About two weeks ago a meeting was held at the school at which there were more than 60 parents present. Most of my classmates and I were allowed to observe the proceedings. The meeting with the Board had been requested by the parents of students in our class, concerned about the transition to high school in January '52. At first the mood was polite but tense, until one distressed parent kept complaining about the lack of preparedness, and pinning problems squarely on the Board. ACL exploded. "Perhaps those of you who want to, can take your brats out of Dr. Ribeiro's into non-Catholic schools."

A pin drop silence followed. A Goan child in a non-Catholic school! Blasphemy!

"I think ACL is loosing his marbles," somebody said, breaking the silence. The meeting broke up. Later Savio told me that those marbles are not the same as the glass ones with the flame design that he, Jeep and I traded regularly. I had not previously heard of other kinds of marbles.

Dr. Manu Ribeiro, nephew and son-in-law of Dr. Rosendo Ribeiro, after whom the school was named, and who had passed away 2 years earlier, is particularly distressed over ACL's suggestion to 'take your brats to a non-Catholic school'. His son Olaf is my classmate. Barely a week later, Dr. Manu invites the parents of the boys in my class, who have to make a decision about high school, to a special meeting. They are encouraged to bring their sons along to hear of a new opportunity. We are only three weeks away from the end of term and the Christmas break.

The meeting takes place at Dr. Manu's two-storey mansion with the colonnaded portico on Forest Road. There are about 25 people present: nine of my classmates with their fathers, and in some cases, their mothers as well.

Dr. Manu welcomes us and introduces two special guests, both high-ranking officials in the Education Department, Mr. Lobo and Mr. Pimenta, "who have kindly offered their own time, to discuss a new opportunity, in response to the concerns of the parents. Please understand they are not here in their official capacity; the views they express are their own." My friends and I are finding this interesting, although we do not understand some of the politics. We settle down to listen to what Lobo has to say.

"The Colonial Government's policy of strict racial segregation will stay firmly in place," Lobo informs us. "All Indian schools have been re-labelled 'Asian' schools, following the breakup of the Indian sub-continent in 1947. Government policy now is that the 'Asian umbrella' be unfolded to cover all brown-skinned people. While most Goans are nationals of Portugal, we are still visibly brown. Therefore my dear friends, if the Goan School cannot absorb your sons and daughters, they too must squeeze under the Asian umbrella."

I look around. Savio and Olaf (Dr. Manu's son) are grinning, perhaps imagining as I was, what an umbrella packed with Hindus, Muslims, Sikhs and Catholics might look like. The mood on the faces of parents is sombre. There are many questions for Lobo, and he tries to answer them.

Dr. Manu introduces the next speaker. "Mr. Pimenta is currently the Headmaster of the Indian High School in Eldoret, and has especially come down here to Nairobi to share his insights, and shed some light into this tunnel we have entered." Everyone listens intently as the professorial and balding Pimenta begins to speak.

"Many of you may remember I was the Headmaster of Dr. Ribeiro between 1942-45," he begins. "I have seen much in my time as an educationist, so I want to reassure you that although Dr. Ribeiro Goan School is journeying over a heavily potholed road, with a little time it will be fixed." He glances around the room over the rims of his eyeglasses. "But for you parents… and you boys… who are looking for a solution between now and Christmas—that's in three weeks—this is a challenging time. I know what anxiety parents suffer in selecting good schools for their children. But sadly at this time you have little choice. So I asked Dr. Manu to let me speak about an opportunity that may just flash by you, and never repeat. But first let me give you some perspective." There is a sound of feet shuffling and chairs being moved as people resettle into more comfortable positions.

Pimenta continues, "Prior to and during the war years, the white settler community, in need of cheap African farm labour, had pressured the government against educating Africans, or allowing them to farm their own land. Thus the state of African education is abysmal, and if it wasn't for the missionaries, there would have been even less progress." There is an audible rumble among the audience. Someone on my left grumbles, "I didn't come here for a lecture on African education."

Pimenta continues. "For the past 50 years, the Indian and Goan communities have largely financed themselves in the field of education. The bureaucrats at the Colonial Office in London do not frame our colonial education policy; rather it is the European settlers and their politicians here who call the shots. I live and teach in Eldoret in the heart of the White Highlands, and I know what I am hearing." The room is silent.

Pimenta adjusts his glasses and glances around at his audience; he has got their attention. "These settlers, many who are farmers and many more who are aristocrats from the British Isles, living out their lives in this beautiful warm and fertile land, very firmly wish to maintain the 'Country Club' elite white culture around Nairobi and in the White Highlands. They are fighting hard to ensure that their compatriots—white working class immigrants with artisan skills—are not welcome in Kenya, but will instead be given incentives by the Colonial Office to settle 'down-south' in Northern or Southern Rhodesia and in South Africa. Their Country Club membership will thus not be diluted."

He removes his glasses, pulls out a red silk handkerchief from his breast pocket, and slowly proceeds to wipe the lenses. The audience is attentive.

On my left I hear an angry whisper. "This bloke's lost his marbles… we didn't come here to listen to bedtime stories." Pimenta clears his throat and continues calmly.

"Since the post-war recovery our urban centres are growing. Nairobi achieved City status last year and is projected to grow rapidly. Mombasa, Kisumu, and other small towns are also growing very fast. The white community now expect there will be a shortage of skilled artisans in the country, and they argue strongly for Asians to fill that gap."

He picks up a sheet of paper from the empty chair beside him. "Let me read you an extract from a confidential report:

'The Indians are very capable fundis – artisans who can provide labour cheaply –they made possible the construction of the Kenya-Uganda railway - and God knows there are plenty of Indians around. The children of Asian construction contractors, mechanics and other tradesmen are never going to enter the professions or academia. We must guide these students towards technical trades and skills to meet this country's future labour shortage.' I have also heard such statements elsewhere. But we must be intelligent. Ignore the racism. Take advantage of the opportunity."

He pauses briefly, looks around at the impatient faces, and continues. "In January, a brand new Technical High School will be inaugurated in Park Road, Pangani. The School is the brainchild of our Education Department. It is exclusively for Asians and will include in its curriculum technical subjects such as woodwork, metalwork, draftsmanship, commerce and accounting. But these students will also study for the UK Senior Cambridge Examination."

"But where will the teachers come from?" a parent asks.

"In the initial years it will be staffed by expatriate teachers recruited in the UK, many of whom have already arrived and are getting the school ready to receive its first students. So I urge those of you who feel that you want to take a risk, and avail yourself of the dozen places or so places still available, to do so quickly. Thank you."

Pimenta is convincing and receives some applause, but doubts still remain. An irate parent yells out, "What about our religion and our culture?"

"There's still home, church and club," Pimenta replies calmly.

There are a few more questions. Some people start to leave the room. Others stay to ask further details. Savio, Olaf and I are excited at the sheer prospect of adventure into something new and unknown. We agree to pressure our dads to transfer us. Three more classmates want to think about it.

Savio and I meet the next day. "Dad says he will make arrangements for me to go to the Tech High," I tell him.

"Mine too," he says happily. Savio is the son of one of my Dad's regular card-playing friends. He lives a short distance away from me, by the Goan Gymkhana, and so we form a strong friendship, and meet often at the club for a game of table tennis. Over the holidays I tell him about my experience of boarding school. He tells me his elder brother went to boarding school, but that his family decided it was not for him.

One day Savio comes over to spend the night. We are in my room. I show him my crystal radio and tell him about the experience with Jeep and Ahmad when we first fixed up the antenna; and about the hundreds of bats that live up in the attic. Savio thinks the crystal set radio is magic too, just like Jeep did when I first got it. I tell him about the BBC news bulletins and especially about the troops arriving in Egypt. "I think they are really coming to Kenya," I say.

Savio looks over his shoulder from where he is sitting in front of the radio, and then stands up and shuts the door.

"You know my Dad works with Burmah Oil?" he says. "Funny. Only yesterday I overheard Dad tell my brother, who has just joined the company as a junior employee, that urgent confidential messages have been coming in from their headquarters. There are rumours that the Egyptians want more control of the Suez Canal. They say it will affect oil exports from the Middle East." He lowers his voice conspiratorially. "And Dad says this information is hush-hush."

"I still believe something is going on here in Kenya," I say, stubbornly, remembering the conversation between Alberto Pinto and his friends on board the steamer bringing me back from Goa.

Savio comes over again the following week. He too is now hooked on the BBC news reports. He says his dad was again discussing something over dinner with his brother, but he changed the subject when Savio arrived. We are sure something serious is afoot and agree we will find out as much as we can and share information. We will become expert eavesdroppers, as adults won't tell us anything. We decide our eavesdropping will start at the Goan Gymkhana. There are always interesting conversations going on in the bar.

Our first serious breakthrough comes later that week. Because of the many Goans employed at the district and provincial levels of government, Nairobi receives a constant stream of civil servants from outside Nairobi who need to do business with the central administration in the capital. At the end of their workday these government servants invariably drop in at one of the Goan clubs, where an exchange of news 'with one's own kind' and hospitality is guaranteed.

One evening Savio and I are playing table tennis at the club. On this particular day, two such visitors are chatting at the bar. I understand from their comments they are clerks from the Nakuru Magistrate's office.

"More cases are being reported everyday," one visitor says. "For now the authorities are calling it 'Mau Mau'. Don't ask me why."

"What Tom says is correct," his companion intervenes. "According to the police informers, persons are being forced to take oaths; they say this activity is increasing throughout Rift Valley province."

Savio and I look at each other. We do not understand what they are talking about. It seems we are not alone. "Frankly, you chaps are not making sense; what are you talking about?" a regular member asks. "Casmiro, who is forcing whom to take oaths? Are any of our Goans involved?"

The one called Tom replies. He explains the government had banned the secret society – called the Mau Mau—in 1950. It consisted then mainly of some Kikuyu leaders, who were coercing fellow-tribesmen living around Mount Kenya, Embu and Meru, to take oaths. The oath-taking and secret meetings continue. Oath-takers are required to do everything in their power to kill the *Muzungus* – the White settlers who have 'stolen' their land using Muzungu laws. "The Kikuyus must do what is necessary to regain their land, by force if necessary," Tom says.

"The white settlers are scared; they are buying guns to defend themselves," Casmiro interjects. "Many Muzungus are dismissing Kikuyu farm labour, and replacing them with other tribes. Farmers near Molo are even employing small armies of Kelenjin and Maasai tribesmen for security. Imagine what will happen if tribal fighting breaks out."

The discussion continues with more drinks served all around. But we have to leave as our dads have finished their card playing session.

The next day as Savio and I are walking home from school, we hear a loud horn and jump off the road in terror. It is Ahmad, roaring with laughter at having scared us to death. "Is this your new Jeep?" he asks, cocking his thumb at Savio. "Come let us celebrate your new *rafiki*. You have forgotten Swahili!" He gives us a short ride in his car to a kiosk by the Parklands duka next to the Police Station. The smell of freshly roasted corn makes us hungry. We sit on a makeshift bench made of a log perched on two blocks, surrounded by piles of cornhusks. Ahmad sits across on an empty wooden crate. He treats us each to a delicious roasted *mahindi*— corn on the cob.

"Ahmad, do you know about the Mau Mau?" I ask.

He turns, stops abruptly, as he is about to bite on his corn. "For many months now I have been telling your father," Ahmad says.

"At my taxi-stand in Hardinge Street, every day I see more upcountry Kikuyus looking for work. They beg me to find them a job – any job; maybe teach them to drive a taxi. It is a bad situation here." Ahmad glances at his watch. Suddenly he seems worried, nervous about something. "I must go now." He ruffles my hair as he crosses over to his taxi. He waves at Savio and accelerates away, leaving us in a cloud of dust.

3

Death at First Sight

Savio and I step off the bus at Park Road into a totally new experience. The short ride took us from the roundabout, right in the heart of Ngara—the earliest designated Asian housing area, where most government servants and Railways staff live in employer-provided wood frame and corrugated iron clad quarters on treed lots—up to Park Road, which demarcates the limit of the newer Pangani area. On either side of the bus route however, two-storey stone and cement buildings stand tightly packed with Asian-owned *dukas*; shops that overflow goods on to the street crowded with pedestrians, with the owners' living quarters above.

Savio recognises the neighbourhood of the Tech High. "The GI is so close," he points out with his characteristically big grin. I know instinctively what he is thinking. He is referring to the Goan Institute sports fields. Many of our ex-classmates at Dr. Ribeiro belong to the GI; perhaps we can meet them there occasionally, even if our parents will not step foot in each other's premises.

We don't know what to expect at our new non-Catholic school, other than a place brimming with brats. For a couple of weeks Savio and I have been slightly apprehensive about going to this place after Dr. ACL De Souza's 'take your brats to a non-Catholic school' remarks. "Does brats not mean little monsters?" I ask. "Perhaps we too will end up little horrors within a week."

We had just been to collect our uniforms the previous week from the European–owned store by the New Stanley Hotel. It is the sole supplier of official school uniforms to the Education department. We had entered the premises by a separate entrance marked 'Asians'. European customers use the store's main door on Hardinge Street. I recall feeling instantly angry with this, as I had forgotten about the colour bar during the time I was in Goa, but then I remembered about the caste system there, and assumed this was the way God intended it. "At least all us brats will be wearing the same uniform," Savio said as we left the store clutching our purchases.

The Tech High School is set back from the access road behind a gravel surfaced car park, and a strip of trees and shrubs that will grow, and in the future screen the car park from the labs and classrooms fronting onto it. As we approach the main entrance, the anxiety of what lay ahead returns. A number of boys crowd around the registration desk just inside the lobby. "Look Savio, they're dressed just like us," I say reassuringly.

Eventually it is our turn to present our registration papers and we each receive a receipt for the fees paid, as well as a set of standard rules and regulations concerning attendance, wearing of uniforms at all times, disciplinary policy, emergency and security procedures. We are herded into a large asphalt-paved quadrangle, bordered on all sides by grey-colour washed single-storey concrete block walls supporting a pitched Mangalore tiled roof. As if to atone for its excessive drabness, the architect chose to paint every alternate door either a bright glossy red, or a deep glossy blue, with all other doors painted a battleship grey. A small roof overhang over the passageways on the quadrangle side offers some minimal protection from the mid-day sun. About eight trees, grouped in pairs symmetrically across the quadrangle and set into the asphalt, provide token landscaping. There is a temporary-looking podium with three rows of chairs to one side. I notice the freshly painted lines of a volleyball court at the other end of the quadrangle.

Nearer the podium, a large number of boys are assembled like a herd of wildebeest or zebras, snorting and stomping impatiently, anxiously awaiting the slightest scent of a lion on the prowl – there are about 150 boys dressed in grey blazers trimmed with a deep blue braid on the lapels and grey drill shorts; long grey stockings with blue and white bands at the top. Many boys are sporting colourful turbans. Most are chatting with each other. "They may have previously been classmates in primary school," Savio has noticed that too. "I wonder how many of our ex-buddies will join us?" he says.

There's Olaf," I spy him first. "And look…it's Brian and Romeo."

"There's Stan." Savio says. They see us and wave back, and then walk towards us. Brian is tall but he walks with a slight haunch as if wishing to be shorter. He was one of the smartest in our class at the Goan school. Romeo is built lean, and with his dark rim glasses conveys an image of being very studious, but is a nice average guy. Then there is Stan. His dad has been part of the management of the GI for years and has done a lot to boost the club's reputation at sports. Stan is of medium height, strong, and easily the most serious sportsman among us. We greet each other with genuine relief that our ranks have swelled. We are like six fish scooped up from our Goan mono-cultural pond centred on church, school and club that we knew so well almost from birth, now suddenly transferred into a bigger well-stocked Asian pond, with which we seem to have little in common, other than skin colour. Even entering St. Joseph's High School in Goa, thousands of miles away from Kenya, seemed less strange for me.

"Do you remember Mr. Pimenta saying this school was mainly for the sons of Indian building contractors?" Olav says. "I've just met a boy whose father is a doctor; his dad knows my dad and I have met him before. I have met another boy whose family are shopkeepers. No sons of contractors yet."

"What will happen with our Catholic holidays?" Brian asks.

"I hope we don't lose our religious holidays," Stan says, "We are only six Catholics in this school."

"They're mainly Hindus, Muslims and Sikhs," Olav says glancing around.

"I just hope they don't start killing each other as they have been doing in India," I say, remembering the stories Ahmad told Jeep and me. "Maybe not."

When the school bell rings suddenly it makes us jump. It is loud after the feeble sound of the bell at the Goan school. Within 30 seconds a siren sounds briefly. We move forward towards the podium and position ourselves in the middle of the group. A procession of mainly white, black-gowned teachers and a handful of Asians, walk onto the temporary built raised dais. They all sit down and we follow. Someone announces the Headmaster will speak.

The morning sun is already warm as the Headmaster pauses for total silence before beginning his address. He radiates discipline. Mr. Stewart, tall with a strong well-built frame and meticulously groomed wavy hair, is dressed in a grey suit and white shirt, and sports a striped school tie. He watches as we jockey for a comfortable view of him. My thoughts momentarily drift to Father Mendonça at St. Joseph's in Goa, but I am brought back to the assembly as Olav whispers to us, "They're all imported Muzungus." Their pale complexions and well-groomed haircuts are a give-away.

One of the new European teachers on the dais rises and steps forward to lead us in singing the national anthem. There is total silence, then we sing.

'God save our gracious King,
Long live our noble King,
God save the King ...'

The Headmaster addresses us. He talks at length about his dream for our new groundbreaking experimental school; and about what is expected and required of the student body. He lists some initial operational procedures; after about 25 minutes he glances at his watch and decides it is time to end his discourse.

"Just before we started, you heard the school bell that will normally be used. Today you also heard a siren briefly. I hope we never have to use it, but in the event of an emergency, that siren will sound. When it does, I expect every student to stop whatever he is doing and converge into this quadrangle for further instructions." He glances over his shoulder as if to ensure the staff have heard that instruction too. He continues.

"As I said before, the whole school will respect the religious holidays for each faith represented at Tech High, so no classes will be missed. You will receive a list of all the holidays for the year. Beyond these holidays your full attendance for every day of the remaining time is compulsory, as you must make up the coursework, otherwise let me warn you now—you will not get to that final exam." There is a silence. No one speaks.

"Make no mistake," Mr. Stewart repeats. "You *will* be required to meet the exacting standards of the Unified Senior Cambridge Exam of Great Britain," he corrects himself, "...of the United Kingdom, exactly as do students at every other secondary school in Kenya." He pauses. He reaches for his pocket handkerchief and wipes the perspiration off his forehead. "Remember also, while on our school premises, you *must* speak English at all times, even to your closest friends or relatives. Finally, I want to welcome you again. Now proceed to your respective rooms to meet with your class teacher."

There is a loud buzz of relief that the assembly is over. The meeting dismissed, we move in groups towards our classrooms amid the babble of Gujarati, Hindi, Punjabi, Urdu and English.

"So much for speaking English," Savio says.

"I can't imagine why the Indians will want to switch to English," Brian says. "There are more of them than the staff and us, combined."

Our brand new classrooms are bright and cheerful compared with the Goan School. My classroom, painted with pastel green walls and a white ceiling, has wide windows and low sills and overlooks a wheat-coloured grassed soccer field, fenced on one side from the dwellings beyond.

That afternoon on our way home, Savio and I discuss the implications of the siren. We realise that our new school has been built almost on the edge of the invisible line, drawn by the colonial administrators, that separates the Asian residential area from the more congested African locations—residential areas of Kariokor and Pumwani. We speculate on whether the siren had been installed as a precaution, in case the Mau Mau ever come into Nairobi.

A week passes. As Tech High is brand new, only basic disciplinary rules and etiquette are in place. We discover that the staff are flexible and offer scope for innovation and new initiatives. We are encouraged and emboldened. Within three days we have met with every teacher. As they introduce themselves we quietly analyse and classify them just as I imagine Dr. Leakey and his colleagues might do with any new species at the Coryndon Museum. We conclude that the teachers can be divided into three distinct groups The first is the English Brahmins—the art, literature and history teachers who have been moulded in the public school tradition and further polished at Oxford and Cambridge. The second group are the 'Eggheads' – science teachers who seem to have attended grammar schools and then continued at the Universities of Liverpool, London or Manchester. The 'Fundis' – technical teachers readily confess they were recruited directly from the polytechnics. The four Asian teachers have trained in India, but have not been assigned any primary teaching roles yet.

Very quickly, we also discover our 'new Muzungus' have different attitudes from the 'old' Kenyan Muzungus. They are extremely polite and do not appear to have racist views, and none have previously lived in other British colonies so have not been exposed to such views. They quickly settle down and seem to enjoy their work.

My new classmates are an assortment transferred from various Asian primary schools, especially from Park Road Primary School, next door to Tech High. As some boys may have started primary school a year or two later, or may have been held back a year or two on the way up, there is up to a three-year age gap and a fifteen - inch height difference between the youngest and oldest students in our class. The European teachers are unsure whether there will be any interaction between the boys with such a mix and do their best to encourage this. I am told to sit in the front row, as I am among the youngest and shortest in class. The big tall Sikh boys monopolize the last bench.

"Ouch," I cry out aloud during our first history class—an introduction to the Crusades—as I feel a sharp stab on the back of my neck. It is just over a week into our classes. The missile is a tightly rolled paper, somewhat shorter than a cigarette length, folded in the form of a 'V'. I know the missile launcher is a rubber band stretched between the index and middle finger to form a catapult. Everybody laughs.

Mr. Walker, the history teacher tries to hide a smirk. "Good. I can see you are beginning to interact," he says. "Now who did that?" He glances about the room. There is a hushed silence. We are not sure what will happen next. Mengha Singh, a boy in the third row, stands up and walks to my desk and says he is sorry (in English). Mengha is the son of a contractor; he is of medium height and ties his turban meticulously like older Sikhs, but it looks strange, as his beard is young and new. He is always happy and the most outgoing of the Sikh boys, and very popular among many of his old classmates now in our class. Mr. Walker tells him to henceforth sit next to me. We soon become good friends.

About two weeks later our group of six Goans are having lunch in the shade of a flame tree by the wood workshop, when the conversation turns to our life at the Goan school and church. "Isn't it amazing how soon we begin to forget our routine?" Stan says, "And we don't see Father Butler in the passageways any more."

"I used to skirt around him when I spotted him," Olaf says, "or he would pull me up for a regular Saturday confession, whether I needed it or not."

Our beloved parish priest must possess divine hearing skills to have overheard our conversation. That Sunday after Mass, Father Butler, ambushes each of us six, individually. I am completely taken by surprise as he stands blocking my exit, his face its usual lobster red, his blue eyes staring at me through wire rims. I am a deer caught motionless in the headlights.

"Good morning Lando. You've heard of the seven deadly sins," he says. "I hear we now may have six deadly sinners in a non-Catholic school." His humour is always disarming, even if in my opinion, inappropriate at that moment. He explains: "We have established a special program of religion classes for you boys at Tech High," he continues. "We will meet at the Residence from 3:00 p.m. to 4:30 p.m. every Sunday afternoon during term time. Your parents have assured me they wish you to attend."

What alternative *do* we have? We all attend for the first two weeks. The sessions are held in a large sitting room, with windows that open into an internal planted courtyard – almost an orchard. We would rather be on the outside in that glorious sunshine. Furthermore, everyone is unhappy about losing such a big chunk of our free time on Sunday afternoons. We start to think of ways to alter the timetable.

In the meantime, the nightly reports on the BBC World Service of incidents somehow linked to the Mau Mau, become more frequent. I share this information with Savio.

One Saturday in January 1952, Savio and I decide to visit the Coryndon Museum. I tell him about the watercolour exhibit of portraits of African tribes, as the BBC had mentioned some tribe we had not heard about. Simba accompanies us as usual. We arrive to find most of the museum shuttered and a notice at the front entrance announcing a major new extension is underway. That section will be closed for a few months.

"What do we do now?" Savio asks.

"Have you walked down by the river under Ainsworth Bridge?"

"No."

"It's beautiful. Just jungle. Jeep and I used to go there often. Very peaceful."

"Let's go then," Savio says. Simba has already bounded ahead anticipating our decision. As we wander along the narrow path, brushing aside ferns, wild lantana and other growth, the sun filters through the tree branches overhead. Within the trees that cascade down the hillside we hear only the birds and our own voices and somewhere ahead, Simba's exuberant barking filtered by the heavy undergrowth. I am ever vigilant for snakes in our path. The surroundings remind me of the time in boarding school in Goa, when smitten by chronic hunger pangs, I walked through the dense cashew plantation behind the school, with my friend Musso, hunting for some ripe fruit; we heard a frantic whine in a tree; I instinctively lifted a frightened baby squirrel from its nest, even as a snake was within striking distance. I took it back to my dormitory and looked after it and Dik Dik became my companion throughout my stay in Goa. Sadly I had to leave him behind.

"I wonder if Dik Dik is still hopping and skipping about in the woods behind Grandma's home?" I say aloud. Savio has already heard about him. We arrive at the spot below the bridge where the flow of the seasonal stream has created two pebble and mud banks on either side.

"Look, someone's been here recently," Savio says. "The fire is still smouldering." We walk towards it. "Look at the footprints. There must have been at least three people here."

"Savio, I swear in all the times I've been here with Jeep, we never saw a soul." I say. "Whoever lit this fire, didn't want to be seen from above. I would have built the fire there." I pick up a twig and spread the embers and throw some sand over, to kill the fire completely. "Simba went that way. Shall we walk along the bank? Just watch out for snakes."

"Yes. Let's." Savio picks up a thin dry rod of bamboo too and walks ahead of me. I love disturbing the guppies and tadpoles in the clear puddles that form off the main stream, which is often a muddy brown. The bird sounds are now supplemented by other noises. We can hear the steady flow of running water as it negotiates the rocks and pebbles in its path; tree frogs and crickets seem to be calling to each other across the banks. There are many of the little fish and tadpoles today. A grass snake, disturbed by our arrival, slithers into the bushes. Hundreds of black and yellow weaver birds flutter around their intricately woven grass nests which dangle on the extreme ends of branches like year-round hand-crafted monochrome Christmas decorations, the birds making their usual spirited racket warning of trespassers. Two brilliantly coloured superb starlings, in shimmering deep blue and turquoise cloaks and bright fiery-orange waistcoats, skip from rock to rock, ignoring us completely.

Simba runs back towards us. He yelps and barks. He seems to have found new energy now that we have finally resumed our regular walks.

"No! Simba! Drop it!" He is holding a large frog in his mouth; it is kicking its long legs frantically. I call out to Simba again; he turns his head as if in defiance, but he only wants to play with it and drops the frog back at the water's edge. It hops away unharmed. Simba leaps forward into the shrubs and undergrowth again and disappears from sight.

Suddenly Simba's bark changes in tone. It is sharper and quicker. I climb onto a boulder and look up through the tall grass. Simba is now moving faster and faster along the sometimes-soggy bank and through the tall grass and shrubs, his nose to the ground like a bloodhound, raising his head only to bark. I see two sets of fresh human footprints and some drag marks along our path. I had not noticed them before. We are about 20 feet behind him when Simba stops. He is barking furiously at someone or something on the other bank, his front feet firmly on the ground. He is frothing at the mouth with excitement. I look anxiously at the clump of trees, trying to pierce the surrounding undergrowth with my eyes.

"What is it Simba? What is it?" I ask as we arrive by his side. Savio spots it first.

"Look there, Lando, there by the tree," Savio says. His voice trembles and fades; it seems he is overcome with shock. His hands are trembling. "It looks like an African's body. He's dead. Look at how his stomach is bloated," Savio whispers hoarsely.

I look at where Savio is pointing. I see the dark shape of a body. The grey chequered shirt seems torn and is covered in dried blood. I feel faint but steady myself. "Look at the flies swarming around the body," I find myself trembling too. I think the man has been murdered. Perhaps those were his drag marks we just passed. "Savio, we have come a long way from the bridge. Where are we?"

"Look. Isn't that the back of the Norfolk Hotel?" Savio asks.

"OK then," I say. "Follow me. I know another track up to the museum. Let's get out of here fast." I can't stop my hands are trembling—in fact I can feel my whole body begin to shake. I throw away the stick as Savio throws his bamboo cane away too and we turn and run back as fast as we can. Our path runs uphill, zigzagging its way around the trees that must have been part of the original forest that once grew here.

"Come Simba! Come back!" Simba reluctantly follows us, looking back and barking. By the time we get to the top by the Leakey residence, I can hear my heart beating with a dull thud, thud, thud. We stop near the museum, wondering what we should do. "We can't go to the police," I say. "They may think we did it. I will ask Dad."

We instinctively hug each other relieved at arriving back safely. Savio goes to his home past the Gymkhana and Simba and I return to Plums Lane. I know that I will never walk down that slope in front of the museum to Ainsworth Bridge again.

4

The King is Dead

E arly in January, 1952, the Headmaster makes a special announcement during morning assembly: "Her Royal Highness
Princess Elizabeth and Prince Philip, Duke of Edinburgh, will arrive in Nairobi on February 1ˢᵗ for a Royal Visit to Kenya. Our
school will line up along the ceremonial route along with other
Nairobi-based schools. You should each strive to look your best
in clean school uniforms and polished shoes, and of course you
will have time off from classes." The excitement at the news is
unanimous. For some boys, it is the prospect of seeing a real live
Princess; for others, it is the promise of time off from class. Even
the Headmaster seems cheerful.

I am happy too, but uneasiness lingers on over the unknown. I
am certain the government is hiding the bad news from the people,
especially after that incident when Savio and I saw that bloated
body with our own eyes. When I returned home that night, I told
Dad immediately about our discovering the body of the African
man by the Nairobi River, behind the Norfolk Hotel.

"Lando, you leave it to the police," Dad had replied. "It is their responsibility, and in any case the Police Headquarters is across the road from the Hotel." I am surprised that he was cautious.

"The smell and the flies were horrible."

"The body is decomposing, Lando. It'll get worse, but that should make it easier for the police to locate it.," Dad says. "Lando, there are strange things going on in the country. You and Savio must be more careful where you roam. Please keep away from isolated areas." That's where the matter stands. The local papers did not mention anything.

At midnight, I turn to my beloved BBC Overseas Service for comfort. There is nothing on the news of consequence. 'The King's health seems to be improving and doctors say he is making a good recovery so far. In other news, there are some British troops movements within Egypt and 20 people die in anti-British riots. The people of Kenya are finalising arrangements for the Royal Visit to Kenya.'

On the day itself the weather is almost perfect. Savio and I arrive at the school especially early, so we get to see the others actually turn up looking their best. The teachers inspect all 140 boys for neatness; some have to make last-minute adjustments. Then, armed with little paper Union Jack flags, we troop into the city, three abreast, though it is difficult to maintain that formation as footpaths are only partially paved, and that only nearer the city centre.

Mostly we walk on the road. Drivers honk and bicycles ring bells to warn us to get off, but they slow down a bit. People look at us curiously; some wave and we wave back. At the end of a four-mile trek we arrive at our 'designated area' opposite the Barclays Bank building on jacaranda-lined Delamere Avenue. The processional route is lined with flags hung on hastily erected white-washed wattle posts. Our Asian school is carefully slotted between the contingents from European and African schools; racial segregation is the norm.

We wait in the blazing sun behind a rope barrier for about three hours, periodically wiping the inevitable red dust from our shoes. At first I am slightly excited, but then exhausted; after a while it gets really boring just waiting. Then excitement. "They're here! They're here!" Cries reverberate along the processional route. A motorcade of black cars comes into view. The excitement is palpable. The royal couple are riding in a Bentley Mark IV convertible with the hood down. The beautiful 25-year-old, white-gloved princess and her handsome prince happily wave back to the hundreds of jubilant flag-waving, clapping and cheering bystanders. Following closely behind the royal couple is the Governor, Sir Phillip Mitchell, in a white plumed ceremonial hat, and his wife, (who not to be outdone, or so it seems), wears a white sunhat, embellished with dyed ostrich feathers. Another eight cars follow. Ten minutes later it is all over for us. Tired, hot and dusty, we walk back to our school. Mengha speaks for us all, when he snaps, "All that fuss just for 10 minutes?" Nobody replies. We must return to class after eating our home-packed lunches, as afternoon classes have not been cancelled.

"Lando, you want to share lunch?" Mengha asks. "My mother made extra food today because of the Princess' visit."

"Thanks Mengha. We eat under the tree by the wood workshop, not in the classroom. Will you join us there?"

"Everyone knows you Goans meet to talk about girls."

"It's because we're polite, Mengha! We don't want to offend anyone. You know Goans eat everything. But Hindus don't touch beef; Muslims don't eat pork, and you Sikhs… that's why we eat separately."

We arrive at the school and proceed to 'our' tree. Mengha brings a metal lunch tiffin. We settle down around the makeshift dining table.

"Try this," Mengha says spooning out a lentil dish from which a delicious aroma escapes. He gestures towards the tiffin, "Chapattis?"

"Um…delicious," Stan offers an opinion. Everyone concurs.

"Why do people call Goans 'Machlis-- fish-eaters?'" Mengha asks.

"All Catholics must eat fish on Fridays," Savio says.

"First take a look at what each of us have brought today," I say, "Then eat whatever you like. There's no fish. If you like our food we can bring a little extra everyday."

Mengha surveys the assortment of homemade, sliced bread sandwiches that include fillings of chopped roast chicken; ham, cheese and pickle; pork sausages and onion. He chooses the chicken sandwich. Exchanging our lunches becomes routine after that and not a crumb is wasted. We joke about how somebody else's mother's food tastes better than one's own.

Every night that week the BBC gives detailed accounts by their reporters travelling with the royal entourage of the events and activities. The first report mentions the hundreds of school children who lined the route to greet them. I hear about the formal lunches and ribbon cuttings, the Garden Party at Government House and the royal couple's mini-safari through Nairobi National Park. The reports confirm the genuine warmth for the young visitors, expressed by people of all races in Kenya.

A few nights later on February 6, I am jolted by the BBC news: 'King George VI dies in his sleep. The King is dead'. The terse announcements are repeated over and over. It is in grim contrast to the cheerful news broadcast previously: how the royal couple had travelled to Nyeri near Mount Kenya, on a trip that showed them the beauty of Kenya's white highlands and the countryside; how, on the night of February 5, they had arrived at 'Treetops', a wildlife-viewing lodge built high up on a very large *Mugumo* tree in the Aberdare Forest. Listening to the broadcast, I could imagine the details. The Princess and the Duke (and a handful of other guests) had been escorted through the surrounding forest and had arrived at a clearing. They had climbed up a single ladder into the lodge, after which the ladder was raised off the ground until the next morning. Nobody could get in nor leave. Throughout the night under bright floodlights, from the comfort of the terraces, and especially in the early hours of the morning, the royal visitors would have viewed elephant, rhino, leopard, warthog, hyena and many other animals that would arrive regularly. I could imagine the animals as they edge slowly forward as if in a solemn hierarchical Catholic procession, to a natural saltlick and waterhole immediately below the tree. Then turning around they would see the visitors. I imagine them curtsy and bow to the Royal Couple, before quietly retiring again into the darkness of the surrounding forest.

The BBC now gives more details. It reports that although the Princess had climbed into Treetops on the night of February 5, she had only heard the news of her father's death when she came down that retractable ladder the next morning. She had received the telegram on the morning of February 6, 1952, at the nearby Royal Lodge at Sagana, Kenya. She is now the Queen of England and Queen Empress of the British Empire.

My sleep is restless. The next morning as I rush through breakfast with Linda, I make the most important announcement of my life till then. "The King is dead! King George VI is dead in England."

"Shush! Lando, you mustn't joke about these things!" Mom says. "The angels may say amen."

"I don't believe you, liar!" Linda says.

"Yes, the King died at his castle," I repeat confidently. "So the Princess is now Queen Elizabeth II. You'll hear all about it later. Not everyone knows yet." I rush out, just as Fatima and Joachim come into the dining room. Dad has already left for work. I tell Savio the news on the bus; he is surprised too. As the Nairobi papers break out with the news in a special edition at mid-day, there is speculation about what will happen next. In school we hear that crowds are gathering in small groups, especially outside radio shops, desperate for further news.

The BBC was there for me again at midnight.

Within 48 hours the royal couple were back in London. A Public Proclamation announcing the accession of Her Majesty Queen Elizabeth II was made on February 8.

In an ironic coincidence, hardly have the days of mourning gone by, when our attention during history class is directed to study the intrigues of the earlier monarch, Queen Elizabeth I, especially her plan to get the Portuguese to revolt against King Phillip of Spain in 1589.

"I'm afraid this information is not something that will change your lives, " Mr. Walker says almost apologetically, "But it's something that may crop up at your Senior Cambridge exam." He glances around the room and then fixes his gaze on me. "Goan families are still subjects of both Imperial powers." The bell rings. Class is over.

On the bus home, Savio asks me: "Why did Mr. Walker say that about Goans?"

"Dunno. Maybe because we are so mixed up. So many Goans escaped from Goa's colonial system with Portuguese passports, only to work for the British colonial government. You can ask Mr. Walker to explain more during next history class."

5

Pio Gama Pinto -
A real live Communist

"Our school's policy is to respect all religious holidays, so you will have to make up the time... compensate for the fewer school days." Mr. Stewart, the Headmaster, is determined to keep up the pace. He is standing on a recently completed, permanent raised podium at one end of the quadrangle. Instead of morning prayers as at our Goan School, he uses the morning assembly about once a week to try and change the way we think. He pauses and moves his head slowly as if panning his camera across the crowd, peering at us over his glasses. "These high school years will shape the man within each of you. Don't be afraid. Think for yourself and ask questions. Analyze problems and offer solutions."

Besides the academic work, our enrolment in sports is mandatory for the first year. "We must find the best talent to build up our school teams in hockey, soccer and volleyball," The Headmaster says. We are also encouraged to enrol in other extra-curricular activities to broaden our interests and skills. This extra commitment of sports and other activities fills up our days completely. In addition, we Catholic boys also have our weekly religion sessions on Sunday afternoons at St. Francis Xavier Church.

The first four months just whoosh by until one Sunday, Father Butler abruptly stops our sessions. Savio and I are walking home together, but on the way, we stop at the club and play a few rounds of table tennis.

"Do you think Father Butler did that just because of the peaches?" Savio asks.

"Could be. Maybe we analyse and ask too many questions, and Father thinks we are not making progress." In my opinion, the real problem is that random absenteeism had set in after the first two weeks. Only three or four persons showed up, and concentration was hard in the small meeting room overlooking the little walled garden filled with fruit trees.

We bore witness to the miracle of God's creation as we watched the guava and the peach trees slowly bud, and then burst into pink and white blossoms that drove the bees crazy. Soon tiny fruit appeared and grew and grew; eventually the perfume of ripe fruit racing up our nasal caverns paralysed our brains, especially as we could almost reach and touch the fruit ready for picking outside the window. These distractions were not lost on our beloved parish priest.

"As a reward for your attendance, you can each pick a guava or two on your way out," he had said one Sunday afternoon. Attendance immediately shot back to a hundred percent. However, just two weeks later, when the peaches were ready for picking, we faced a dilemma.

"Did Father Butler mean we should pick only guavas?"

"If he says yes, won't that create a bigger problem for us?"

"Will it be a sin to pick a peach (without permission) as well as a guava?"

We analysed the problem over our lunch breaks at school until we found a solution that we thought was brilliant. We agreed that one of us in turn, would each week pick six peaches on behalf of the whole group, and confess to the sin. Thus we would avoid those heavy doses of penance reserved for repeat offenders, especially as the peach season lasted only six weeks. But this past Sunday, Father Butler had unexpectedly announced that further sessions for this year would not be necessary. He made no reference to our fruit picking skills.

Savio and I are relieved to have our weekends back. We talk about the many ways we can now spend that time. By the time we arrive at the club, there is a long line of people waiting to play table tennis, so we decide to call it a day and head home. "By the way, I talked to Dad about your idea to work together on our homework," Savio said. "He thinks it's okay, provided your dad agrees too."

"Good. You know my dad... have to catch him in a good mood. I'll try tonight. See you tomorrow."

Savio and I had been mulling an idea. Our younger siblings, both at his place and mine, are often overly distracting in the evenings, making it difficult for us to concentrate on our homework. However, our dads play cards together regularly at the club. We could accompany them to the club on weekdays and work together on our homework in the library. That way, as soon as we have finished our assignments, we could squeeze in a few games of table tennis and accompany them home when they have finished, usually around 9:00 p.m. I had a gut feeling that Dad would agree, as it is a lonely walk along a dimly lit stretch of Kikuyu Road from the club to Plums Lane. Furthermore, I knew Mom was also worried about the deteriorating security situation. "Why is it taking your father so long to get home?" she would often say after 9:15 p.m. Accompanying Dad on the walk home seemed the right thing to do.

I guessed right. Dad welcomes the idea. "Only on one condition, that if you and Savio are not up to date with your homework, we stop immediately."

It soon becomes a routine. Homework takes next to no time to complete, after which we pick up a snack of potato crisps and a

Coke from the bar. That leaves us time to play table tennis to our hearts' content.

The Gymkhana is really our second home. Two big events transform the premises every year: the Anniversary Ball in May and the New Years Eve Dance which attract over 300 members; the rest of the time it is just a nice building. To conserve electricity, the main hall is dimly lit during the week, except over the table tennis area, which has special bright lighting. An unintended benefit is that the table is placed in the centre of the hall, providing us a vantage point from which we observe the social activity of adults.

The badminton players have a daily post-mortem on the day's games as soon as sunset forces them indoors. Their corner of the hall is nearest to the bar, where under subdued lighting, they chat and argue over lemonades and beer until about 8:30 p.m. when the group usually breaks up, leaving behind only the smell of stale beer and cigarettes. On the other hand, the card players – aficionados of rummy, poker, bridge and *truuk*, who inhabit the veranda on the right, are usually at their tables long before sunset at 5:00 p.m. and do not normally finish before 9:00 p.m. Their drink of choice seems to be whiskey.

Savio and I most often just discuss a myriad of things that crop up. I tell him about my friend Saboti whom I had met on my safari to Kericho in 1949. "She told me she is from the Seychelles. She has beautiful deep brown eyes and a lovely smile, and you should see her hair. It's very curly and the colour of new copper wire, you know, like the piece we picked up last week by the gate of the Parklands Sports Club"

"Will you meet her again?"

"I would like to. She is at a boarding school for girls near Thika, but her home is in Nakuru. I wonder if she remembers me?"

"I know Thika. We went on a picnic by Fourteen Falls, and another time had lunch at the Blue Posts Hotel."

"Will you come with me to meet her someday soon?"

"Sure. Do you have her address?"

"I'll find out. I hope I can see her again."

"You mentioned Nakuru. Did you see those headlines about the two murders of Europeans near Nakuru?" Savio asks.

"Yes. Perhaps there will be something about it tonight on the BBC." From the corner of my eye, I can see Dad and friends winding up their card session. "It's time to go home."

One Friday evening, about a week later there is a break in our routine. The club is unusually busy, and as always, Savio and I are on alert for any visiting civil servants from out-stations—the ones who hear rumours of breaking news, and sometimes share useful information about the troubles up-country.

We are midway through our second set of table tennis, when a club member who we only know as 'Prisons De Souza' walks into the hall accompanied by two visitors. They make a beeline for the bar. About twenty minutes later, two regular card players – known to us as Audit Joe and JFX (John Francis Xavier) stride briskly out of the bar. They seem agitated and are talking rapidly.

"He's back here to stir trouble," we overhear Audit Joe say to JFX. Both delicately balance several drinks as they walk past our table.

"Who is he? He seems very intense," JFX asks.

"Don't you know? He's a Communist. Both are sons of Anton Gama Pinto. This boy is called Pio—Pio Gama Pinto—the other shorter one is his brother, Rosario. Good family but something went wrong." He glances in our direction, and continues. "Must have got mixed up in bad company. They say it happened in India. He got involved in politics. I believe Catholics should not get involved in politics, especially with Communists. It's against our religion."

Savio and I put our tennis paddles down. I walk around the table to Savio and whisper, "I heard this name in Goa! He was at my boarding school… at St. Joseph's High School in Arpora. I was asked more that once if I knew a Pio Gama Pinto from Kenya. Great athlete at the school but he had already left by the time I arrived in 1950."

"Let's go have a look," Savio says excitedly, as we tip-toe to the bar.

"This is too good to miss—a real Communist! And in our own club. Just imagine! We've never seen a live Communist before."

A group of men are clustered in a cloud of cigarette smoke at the far end of the bar. Tommy, behind the counter, is placing fresh whiskeys in front of each, though their glasses are still half full; he looks up as we enter, smiles, but then ignores us. The tall man speaking with his back to the wall must be Pio. He glances at us momentarily, but continues talking earnestly. He has a thick crop of wavy hair, parted at the centre, deep dark eyes. His high cheek-bones and sunken cheeks converging to a small jutting chin make him look sombre… but there is a passion in his voice.

"Yes, that's how *we* got rid of British domination in India," he says. "Now finally India can plan its future for greater prosperity. Inequalities will not exist in Goa in future if it becomes part of India; but *we* must first rid ourselves of Portuguese oppression. Everyone—even from the lowest caste—will now be able to hold his head up high in India." He stops, seemingly out of breath. His eyes dart around the room. "Nobody should have to go to bed hungry every night. Nobody should live in slums, nor have to step over shit in open drains outside their front door."

I see Fernandes—one of the members, a mild mannered man—flinch at Pio's strong words. "We Kenyans also must demand our dignity," Pio continues. "Look at the conditions that our African brothers are forced to live in at their locations…how dirty and desolate. Freedom is what we need here too. We must put pressure on this colonial government and be willing to fight if necessary." Pio stops and sips his drink.

"You talk nonsense Pio," shouts Dias, a regular at the bar, in his 50s with a patina of small pox scars on his face. "Look what a mess self-rule was and still is, in India. My God! They were killing each other! You are telling us they are happy about Independence? Is that how we behave when we are happy? I was in Bombay in

August 1947 on holiday in my sister Matilda's flat. We Catholics had to walk around with big wooden and metal crosses hanging from our necks, so that we were not mistaken for Muslims or Hindus in the street."

Noronha, a wiry man in his 40s with a Charlie Chaplin moustache, turns to address the new speaker. "Dias, what is the use of wearing crucifixes and holy medallions around your neck if you are not free? If you are surrounded by poor people and starvation, and can do nothing about it? Pio is right. Just look at the colour bar here on our doorstep. The Africans have the worst life. Indians next, but because most Indians work for themselves, they're OK. Yet we Goans in government service are happy to do what we are told by the colonialists. We have the wrong mentality. *Sossegade*! Relaxed! As long as we have whiskey and cards, our feasts and our *feni* and not to forget tombola and our dances and… and a small government pay check end of month, we're happy!" Noronha reaches for his glass and gulps down his whiskey.

"You are just a bloody Communist!" Dias shouts at Pio. "I agree the Muzungus have a good life and earn five times more than our own people who do the work. We work hard and with respect for everyone, white, brown or black. What you are saying is that you don't respect even your father who is a senior Government officer. He struggles to give you a good education. Now you come back resurrected as Karl Marx Gama Pinto to show you have been studying abroad."

I see Prison De Souza's face tense up with anger. He clenches his fist; I think he may punch Dias at any moment. I look at Savio. He nods and we creep out of the bar. It can get rowdy at times like this. A few minutes later De Souza and the two Gama Pinto brothers stomp out of the bar. I can tell from their facial expressions, and their rapid pace that they are very angry. Savio and I watch from the balcony as they climb into a green Ford sedan and drive away into the night.

I tell Savio I agree with Pio. I had seen the slums in Bombay when I visited with Uncle on holiday.

On the way home that night, I ask Dad about Pio Gama Pinto.

"He's a very clever man," Dad replies. "I hear he works at the Daily Chronicle newspaper and also with the Indian Congress."

"Some people agreed with him," I tell Dad. "Why don't more Goans speak out? Do you remember those African areas we passed by on the train?"

"So many Goans work in the Administration," Dad says, "they will not say anything against the Government, even if they agree with this Pinto boy. 'You don't eat the goat that gives you milk'… that's what they say in Goa." Dad looks at me. "Are you studying politics in school now? Better finish your Senior Cambridge exams first."

That night it's hard to sleep; I am thinking about the discussion between the adults at the club. Pio's arguments seem quite valid, but the other side also has its points. I wonder who will run the country if it is independent from Britain? I had never thought about this before now. I turn on my crystal radio. The BBC reports that the troubles in Kenya are steadily worsening, and a new Governor may be appointed in the near future.

———

6

The Mau Mau Pot Simmers

A letter postmarked December 2, 1951, arrives from Goa after a journey of almost five months across the Indian Ocean. "Perhaps it was sent by dhow," Linda quips.

Mom, Linda and Fatima are sitting around the dining table, taking turns at reading each pale blue linen textured page, written in ink. It is full of news, mainly about Mom's family, and overflowing with love and Christmas and New Year's greetings for the season now passed. Avosinha (Grandma) must have cornered each uncle to scribble one-liners—I know they are not letter-writers.

The saddest news for me is that Dik-Dik has disappeared. He was my pet squirrel that I had rescued from his nest as a baby, minutes before he was attacked and swallowed whole by a snake. Before I left Goa to return to Kenya, I had left Dik-Dik in the care of my grandmother at her home in Loutolim, where he would be safe and loved. In an earlier letter, Grandma had written that Dik-Dik had completely adapted to his new owners and surroundings. He was comfortably skipping around the garden, and sometimes he even ventured into the thickly wooded grove filled with cashew, chiku and jackfruit trees, on the hillside behind Grandma's house, but he always returned home.

"I'm sure he has finally been eaten by a snake," I say. "How could they have let him roam freely? A pet squirrel reared by humans. He would not know how to fend for itself. How could he ever be expected to survive in a jungle?"

"Lando, don't be such a pessimist!" Linda tries to cheer me. "I think Dik-Dik has met a girl squirrel, fallen in love and together they are building a nest. Soon they will take the little ones to meet Grandma. You'll see!"

"Linda, for you, being in love is the solution to all problems!" I go out for a walk.

Weeks pass. My daily walks with Simba allow me some thinking time. I am starting to believe that perhaps the troubles in Kenya are now over as there has been no news about it on the BBC. I am also surprised how few Goans at the club are even aware of any political crisis brewing in the country and seem only concerned with having a good time in the present. Nobody seems worried about the future, except maybe for a few civil servants assigned to up-country postings, where the white farmers are being threatened by some Africans. I think about what Pio Gama Pinto said in the bar. Stan and Brian told me that he had recently given a speech at the Goan Institute, and many members heckled him, especially those that work in the civil service. His ideas may raise false hopes among the Africans, they said.

A few days later, as I return from school, Linda greets me with, "Lando, please don't forget there is a Sundowner Hop at the club in two weeks' time. Mom thinks I should ask you to escort me, otherwise they won't let me go."

Yes, as I suspected, it's business as usual and the club's social activities are in full swing.

In May, the Goan Gymkhana, its hall decorated in coloured paper streamers and balloons, celebrates its 16th year with a grand Anniversary Dance. Men in pukka dinner jackets, starched pleated shirts and bow ties, drink and dance the night way with ladies in long evening gowns. Linda and her 'sweet sixteen' peers are the life of the party. Dr. Manu Ribeiro, newly elected as the Gymkhana President, delivers an eloquent speech. He congratulates the members on how well they have adapted to their life in Kenya and yet retained their traditional culture; he lauds their achievements in inter-club sports, in community organisations and educational institutions. He speaks proudly of the Goan contribution to the best civil service in the British Empire. In conclusion, he raises a toast to "Her Majesty, Queen Elizabeth II", and then, as if remembering they are all Portuguese nationals, he adds: "To His Excellency, President Antonio Salazar of Portugal." There are sounds of "Hear! Hear!" Some glasses clinking; "The Queen!" "Her Majesty!" "His Excellency!" A few groan and moan for Salazar. The dancing resumes.

Savio and I are standing in the veranda, exactly at the spot where a few weeks earlier we had watched Pio's green Ford drive away into the night.

"Savio, do you think the troubles are over? There seems to be no more news."

"Maybe, but I'm still a bit confused about what Pio was saying," Savio says. "He says Kenya must be independent but *he* is a Goan. He should fight to get rid of President Salazar, not instigate trouble against Her Majesty."

"Do you think he is speaking to Africans also, like he spoke at our club?"

"I don't know. I don't understand how can he speak as an Indian, a Goan and an African at the same time?" We go home shortly thereafter.

Late August 1952.

It is already dark as I arrive back at Plums Lane, from school, somewhat bruised after a hockey game, more convinced than ever that I have not inherited any sporting talent from my forbears. I am happy to see my Uncle Antonio's dusty BSA motorbike, with two bulging saddlebags, parked outside the front door. It usually means he has been away on a successful duck shoot on Lake Naivaisha in the Rift Valley.

Antonio is my mother's elder brother and came out to Kenya in 1937, at the age of 22. He is still single and handsome, with black wavy hair, a muscular body, and a smooth deeply tanned skin.

Uncle says he loves the open sporting life and the freedom to go duck hunting whenever the spirit moves him. But I recently heard Mom tell Linda that at 37, *he*, Antonio, should forget about duck hunting. He is now a sitting duck. The matchmaking matrons and mothers in the Goan Gymkhana have him securely in their sights. I poke my face into the living room to greet Uncle, but Dad signals me to come sit down and listen to what Uncle wants to tell us. Mom is there too. The mood is sombre. Uncle tells us he has just returned from an official business trip to Nyeri for the Education Department.

"What shocked me was my conversation later over dinner with Emerico." Uncle Antonio is uncharacteristically serious. "I was shocked to hear how organised the underground movement is," he says. "Emerico is convinced it's mainly the Kikuyu tribe that are involved. He should know. He's been years in service with the PC's office out there."

"What does he do for the Provincial Commissioner?" Dad asks.

"Everything, as far as I can tell. You know they have very broad responsibilities, but recently he has been focusing on the law and order file."

"Antonio, will you please stay for dinner?" Mom interrupts.

"Do you remember those rumours about how the Kikuyus were organising themselves to fight the government after Nairobi became a City in 1950?" Dad says, ignoring Mom's interruption. "They were convinced the Europeans would steal some of their rich land in Kiambu, Gigiri, Limuru, and all that surrounding area, and integrate it into the new city limits."

"Okay, I'll stay for dinner, thank you." Uncle Antonio says with a big grin, as if he feels he has worked for his supper; perhaps relieved that he has unburdened himself of our family friend Emerico's conversation by sharing it with Dad. He turns to me, "Lando, I see Simba is looking much better now he is getting his regular exercise."

"Yes Uncle. I also pick any ticks and brush him regularly."

Dad pours Uncle another whiskey. Over dinner they talk some more over the deteriorating security situation in Kenya. "What I cannot understand," Dad says, "is why the Government seems to be trying to keep the movement secret, especially if it so organised?"

Uncle does not reply. I am so relieved to hear Dad thinks the Government is keeping people in the dark. Savio and I knew this all the time. I excuse myself, wish them a goodnight and go to my room.

Mid-September, 1952.

It is a secret no more. The Nairobi newspapers report that Kikuyus loyal to the Government have been attacked and murdered, their cattle and goats taken away and their huts burnt to the ground. The next day, in remote parts of Kenya, European farm owners repel new attacks. The BBC also reports these stories. Although these events are taking place in the countryside and not in Nairobi and other towns, people are beginning to feel deeply unsettled at home, in school, and on the streets, and suddenly the violence has become the sole topic of conversation.

A few days later, the BBC confirms the Governor-General designate, Evelyn Baring and Lady Baring are already sailing to Mombasa. I put away the earphones and think back of my sea voyages twice across the Indian Ocean; I remember the inaccessible (to us) First Class deck. I imagine a pale-looking governor (I only know him from a recent photo in the local newspaper) in dark sunglasses and drenched in anti-sunburn protection, sipping cocktails by one of the swimming pools on the First Class deck of the P&O ocean liner. I visualize him glancing superficially at his confidential briefing notes delivered to him by the Colonial Office. They describe the dangerous situation evolving in Kenya. He places them to one side. "Plenty of time to deal with the problem when I get there," he thinks, as he turns to watch shoals of flying fish skimming the turquoise and blue ocean around him. On the other hand, is it likely they have not told him anything about his new job and he sees this job as a prolonged holiday in Paradise?

For Savio and me, this appointment of a new Governor and the increase of violence in Kenya strengthen our determination to understand what is going on. We improve our eavesdropping skills and make notes; we relish each visit by out-of town civil servants at the Goan Gymkhana. They invariably repeat the same caveats to their curious hosts at the bar: "We can't talk about it. Really! We are sworn to secrecy and cannot divulge anything to do with our jobs." Faced with traditional aggressive Goan hospitality, their alcohol-loosened tongues, especially those from Nyeri and Eldoret, give first-hand reports of brutal attacks by Kikuyu on pregnant Kikuyu women and children. They tell their friends this news will not make it into the papers, as it is officially being kept under wraps "on instructions from higher-ups". That is exactly what Emerico had told Uncle.

Soon the BBC gives more frequent "unconfirmed reports" of increasing incidents up-country as the country slides into turmoil. It becomes a topic for discussion with Mr. Walker, our class teacher who is also our history teacher. He certainly brings history to life, though ironically it is *always* about death. One time we heard about the Black Hole of Calcutta in 1756, when British officers were locked up by Indian troops in a crowded dark room for days and many died. On another occasion, he recounted the Great Indian Mutiny in 1857, when native soldiers rebelled and massacred British officers and their families, inciting British troops to retaliate by killing hundreds of Indians in revenge as rebellion spread to other cities. It was his telling of the Amritsar Massacre in April of 1919 that got many Sikhs in our class a little upset. Thousands of Indians, including women and children, had gathered at a popular meeting place for Sikhs, when General Dyer, assuming they were planning rebellion, panicked and ordered his soldiers to fire indiscriminately into the crowd when they were trying to escape the park, thus killing many thousands.

For us Goan students in the class, Mr. Walker emphasizes the tales of the constant treachery, betrayal and making good, between the British and Portuguese imperial powers over the two centuries of their shared history.

In response to our anxiety about the growing violence, Mr. Walker reassures us the new Governor-General comes from a fine family pedigree, is a member of the prestigious Indian Civil Service (ICS), and has already been widely hailed by the British press as "a leader for this time" in connection with Kenya.

On September 30, His Excellency Evelyn Baring, wearing a plumed Governor's ceremonial hat, is photographed in the stately Government House, taking over from Acting Governor Henry Potter. He stands tall; with his fine-cut lean features and a very pale face. People wonder if he will be able to contain the political situation in the country or the deteriorating law and order in Nairobi.

Mr. Stewart, the Headmaster, is aware of the stress on us, and the short time left before our year-end exams. "I know it may be difficult for many of you, but I must appeal for your total concentration on your forthcoming exams," he tells us at assembly.

Concentration proves very difficult in practice. My classmates talk about an increase in armed burglaries in their neighbourhoods, as police resources are being redeployed elsewhere. These law and order crimes in Asian areas are almost never reported in the press because they are a low priority in the English language newspapers.

About a month later, after the BBC news, I lie awake listening to the sound of barking dogs. They are louder than usual and I feel goose pimples on my body. I can never forget that night of the armed burglary in 1946, when a panga-machete blow to the side of his neck killed my dog Jolly. He had been my best friend. That night, we had heard his furious barking and then total silence. In the morning we had found him dead. Tonight it takes me a long time to fall asleep, even after the barking had died down.

Almost immediately it seems, a renewed chorus of barking dogs along Plums Lane wakes me up. At first I think I am dreaming, but I can hear Simba's furious bark and also the loud burr, burr, burr—the sound of Uncle Antonio's motorbike speeding down the potholed road. I leap out of bed; glance at the clock. It is 5:30 a.m. Seconds later there is an urgent knocking on the front door. I jump out of bed. Dad opens the door; I stand directly behind him. It is Uncle Alvaro, who along with two other bachelors, shares a house with my Uncle Antonio.

Alvaro, light-skinned, of medium height and well built, is normally immaculately dressed and groomed; his wavy hair always greased in place and neatly trimmed, his thin moustache modelled on a film star. In fact they joke about him being Nairobi's Clarke Gable. As he stands there in the doorway, he looks completely different. He is pale, sloppily dressed and very dishevelled. He has at least a day's growth of stubble, and a look of shock on his face. He is supporting his body with his left hand on the doorframe.

"Alvaro, what is it?" Dad says. "Come in. Are you OK? Is Antonio OK? That is his bike, no?"

I turn on the light as Dad takes him by the shoulder and helps him into the living room. Linda walks into the room. I ask her to bring a glass of water, as Mom comes in too.

Alvaro are you OK?" Dad asks again.

"Chico, no I'm not. Antonio I mean; he's not," Alvaro says. "Three men armed with pangas attacked him last night as he arrived home. He was slashed on the side of his face, and on his arms and legs as he tried to resist them. You know he's a fighter."

"Where is Antonio?" Mom is clutching her dressing gown tightly to contain her trembling. "What happened?" Linda returns with a glass of water. Dad takes it from her and hands it to Anja. "Come

Anja," Dad says. "Alvaro has brought news of Antonio." He turns to Alvaro. "I'll get you something to steady your nerves. He opens the glass-fronted china cabinet, grabs a glass and pours Alvaro a brandy. "This should do it." Alvaro puts the glass to his lips, leans back, and gulps it down in a single shot.

"We rushed out," Alvaro says, still a bit shaken. "Last night we were in the living room talking, when we heard this commotion—the dogs were barking furiously. You know we keep them indoors at night. I released the dogs…the gang fled…there must have been at least three of them. Jose and Tony carried Antonio indoors and tried to stop the bleeding. I jumped on his bike and went to look for someone on our street with a car to take him to hospital. Fortunately we got him there in time…he has had a total of 13 stitches and has been sedated and is sleeping. I came straight from the Shah hospital; I thought you and Anja should know immediately."

"I'll make you some tea," Mom whispers, her shocked face pale and her voice unsteady. She's still trembling as she reaches for my hand to accompany her to the kitchen. Linda follows us. When we return, Alvaro repeats what he had just told Dad.

"Both guns, the 12-bore and the .22, are secure in a gun safe; it is securely installed inside a wardrobe, so unless it was an inside job, they couldn't have known about the guns. Rumours have it that the Mau Mau are looking anywhere and everywhere for guns."

"And the police?" Dad asks. "Did anyone call the police?"

"The poo-lice?" Alvaro mocks. "It took them two hours to come from Parklands Police Station, less than two miles away. They arrived at 3 a.m. and left after 20 minutes, promising to let us know more only after talking to Antonio, who was already in the hospital." Alvaro looks at his watch. "Oh Jesus! Must rush now. Got to get to work after a clean up." We wish him goodbye.

We continue talking in the living room. The incident leaves Dad and Mom distraught. "I never in all these years worried about security," Mom says, after Alvaro leaves. "Everything always seemed to happen to other people, and somehow missed our family and friends."

"It may be to do with the Mau Mau," Dad says. "I wish the Government would do something about it, and tell us what they are doing."

The noise has woken everyone. Fatima and Joachim come into the room and Mom suggests we go into the dining room, where we have tea. Niven sleeps through it all. The next few days are spent visiting Uncle Antonio. He recovers well. A police inspector also visits him in hospital and two days later issues a signed report. Dad splutters when he sees the report. "They say this was a random case of robbery with assault. That's what it says. If it was a European who was attacked, the Governor would be calling the Queen personally, and be clamouring for more troops to be sent out."

I am more shaken by the sight of my parents in shock. Somehow I never expect parents to be more scared than me. Savio and my other classmates say their parents are also worried. They had not realised our school was located so close to the African residential areas. We wonder if perhaps we will be pulled out and re-admitted to the Goan School.

"I don't miss the Goan school," Stan says, "as I see my other buddies in my neighbourhood, though it would be nice to have girls in our class at Tech High."

"Careful what you wish for. That is sure to have Father Butler whisk us back for special religious instruction on Sunday afternoons!" I remind him. "Stop thinking of girls."

———————

7

Mwangi's Family
Moves to Town

The Ngara crossroads is buzzing with normal traffic. With four Asian schools in the neighbourhood, including the large Duke and the Duchess of Gloucester schools for boys and girls respectively, the morning peak is chaotic. In addition, all buses to the Asian suburbs of Eastleigh, Pangani, Ruiru, City Park and Parklands funnel through the intersection, as well as *matatus* – illegal sardine cans on wheels that carry mainly African fare-paying commuters from further afield to city centre.

Savio and I have noticed a recent development: open lorries and pick-up vans carrying—standing room only—labourers to seek work in the centre. Add to this mix, the hand carts transporting goods to local traders and the carts of street vendors; as well as bicycles and pedestrians from closer-in neighbourhoods, crisscrossing the five converging roads, to get to the dukas—Indian shops that sell everything from samosas to saris, spices, saucepans and sweetmeats – and newspapers.

Savio and I always cross one of these roads by the gate of The Lady Grigg Indian Maternity Home, comforted by the fact that if we are run over, there will be a couple of replacements born almost immediately.

The attraction on the other side of the road is a newspaper stall where we can catch the day's headlines on our way to school. One headline '…*near Thika*' catches my eye, just as our bus appears in sight. I grab Savio by his sleeve. "Please wait. You remember I told you about Saboti? Her school is near Thika."

We miss that bus, but get to read the lengthy story about Mrs. Wright, a European woman, stabbed to death by unknown black assailants, near Thika—that is only about 40 miles away from our school, Tech High. According to the paper, the attack was so savage that it frightens the Europeans, and sets off alarms in every direction. I feel a shiver run up my spine as I read the column, especially as it is just a few days after the attack on Uncle Antonio.

A few days later the radio and newspapers report the death of a Senior Chief – one of the many chiefs created by the British among the Kikuyu to allow the government to administer the land peacefully. According to the reports, Senior Chief Waruhiu was travelling towards Limuru Township, 15 miles outside Nairobi. His car was stopped at a roadblock by persons dressed as policemen, who asked for his papers and as soon as his identification was confirmed, three pistol shots were fired directly at him, killing him on the spot, but his driver and two passengers were spared. Just before leaving the scene, his assailants fired a few more shots into the tires of his car. The assailants are still at large. Other reports said the Senior Chief was not shot, but speared to death. I am not sure which version to believe, but it doesn't really matter. The Chief is dead.

In school everyone is talking about the brutal murder.

"Who are these Senior Chiefs?" Stan asks Mr. Walker, our history master.

"Senior Chief Waruhiu and other senior chiefs are the 'Kikuyu Brahmins' created by the Colonial Office to help them control the rest of the Kikuyus, who as you may know already are Kenya's largest tribe," Mr. Walker says. "The Chiefs have almost all been converted to Christianity and have received a good missionary-based education in Kenya and abroad. Most have been given gifts of land. In return for special privileges and other benefits, the Colonial Government expects complete and total loyalty from each of the chiefs and their followers, just as they did in the case of their selected Princes and Maharajas, during the time of the Raj in India."

"Why are they being attacked?"

"These chiefs do not support the Mau Mau, and are on the side of the Government."

Mr. Walker encourages reading the newspapers. "You will learn about what is happening around you. Today's news is tomorrow's history." I do not tell him how much Savio and I know already. In particular, I cannot mention how much we learn directly from eavesdropping at the club bar.

For the first time the Mau Mau rebellion is publically acknowledged by name in the local newspapers. The Government explains that the previous Governor Sir Phillip Mitchell had already proscribed the Mau Mau as a secret society in 1950, as its main aim was to drive Europeans from farms up-country. In addition the Mau Mau requires its followers to take oaths of allegiance to the organisation, and kill Europeans at every opportunity. This could undermine the Colonial Office's plans to actively seek more European immigrants into Kenya. The government explained it kept news of the Mau Mau secret from the public, as it had expected to finish off with the rebellion quickly.

Everyone is now aware of its existence.

On October 15, more than 30 Kikuyus are brutally killed by the Mau Mau, as retaliation for allegedly reporting to the police on oathing ceremonies taking place in their village. Telegrams, delegations, protests and pleas inundate the Government, especially from angry white settlers and missionaries. Other Senior Chiefs not wishing to meet the same fate as Senior Chief Waruhiu add their protests and appeal to the Governor.

'Your Excellency came here to govern, NOW please do something to STOP the Mau Mau.' The posters pasted everywhere around the city, scream out.

Governor Evelyn Baring takes action. A State of Emergency is declared on October 20, 1952. As Savio and I arrive at the Ngara Roundabout the next morning on our way to school, we are shocked at the sight of hundreds of police and European armed troops at roadblocks at all the intersections. More roadblocks are in place nearer our school in Park Road, as we are close to the African residential locations.

'Operation Jock Scott underway!' The newspaper headlines are explicit. 'Mau Mau suspects are rounded up!' It is a tense day. By lunchtime, all classes are cancelled and we are sent home. I meet Linda returning on the bus from her school, St. Theresa Girls School, located near the Eastleigh airport. "We had European soldiers guarding the entrance to our school today," she tells Savio and me. "I think they are based at the airport."

"But there are no European soldiers in Nairobi," I challenge her.

"There are! Saw them with my own eyes!" she insists, annoyed I would doubt her.

That night, the BBC reports on the success of a lightning predawn raid mounted by a battalion of the Lancashire Fusiliers. The British troops had secretly flown in from Egypt, where they were based, and had landed at Eastleigh Airport two days earlier. Security forces had picked up Jomo Kenyatta, President of the KAU (Kenya African Union), who, according to the news, was the mastermind behind the Mau Mau. Five other suspected leaders identified as Fred Kubai, Bildad Kaggia, Paul Ngei, Richard Achieng and Kungu Karumba, were also arrested. According to the BBC's reporter in Nairobi, all six had been handcuffed, blindfolded and led away to a secret location. The BBC report went on to explain that as many as 150 others were detained, and that the move has met with wide-spread public relief, especially from the white community.

Savio and I are at the club the next day. Having completed our homework, we are playing our usual rounds of table tennis, when we hear loud voices from the bar, and quickly sneak in to investigate. A handful of men are arguing about Operation Jock Scott. I recognize Fernandes and Dias, two regulars at the bar, among them.

"They should have code named it Operation Jockstrap," Fernandes quips, "as I see it, the Mau Mau's got the Government by the balls."

"This is no joking matter," an older member high up in the Colonial administration, rebukes him. "We have laws that must be obeyed. This is a serious matter."

"The *Kaburus* – the Afrikaners are happy," Dias says, "one of them was distributing these flyers outside the New Stanley Hotel this afternoon." He passes a few copies around. In bold letters it reads 'Finally a Guvnor with brains and balls! Thank you *Baas!*'

We leave them arguing, not sure what this means for us. Table tennis is more fun.

"Your turn to serve," Savio says. "So it's 3:2. I'm leading."

Soon after the detention of Jomo Kenyatta, the Mau Mau openly declares a rebellion to oust the British from Kenya. It is a tacit invitation for other tribes to join in.

As if to reinforce the message, more brutal attacks on whites follow shortly thereafter. In the first one, a white farmer dies while his seriously mutilated wife survives. In the other, a group of Mau Mau hack a white man to death with pangas—his insides are strewn all over the floor of his farmhouse. In an outburst of public anger, the settlers call for more British troops to be sent to Kenya. Security is the only topic of discussion at home, in the club and even in the churches. The shops begin to install more shutters and close earlier. More Europeans are seen on the street wearing guns in holsters, and the number of night-security watchmen seem to increase; church sermons call for prayers and sacrifice towards peace and appeal for funds.

At our morning Assembly the next day, the Headmaster tells us that he fully understands how the security-related events and announcements on the radio and in newspapers can be disruptive to our studies, especially at this time in the academic year; that the news should not be allowed to interfere with our normal routine and we are not to fear the future. Her Majesty's forces will prevail, he asserts. We feel reassured, as he is British and must know more than our parents about this. I join in singing God Save the Queen with great fervour.

That weekend in a highly publicised ceremony in Nairobi's City Hall, Christians and Hindus, Muslims and Jews offer prayers for re-newed courage to Governor 'Daring Baring' and for a long-lasting peace in the country. They conclude by holding hands and sing-ing God Save the Queen. The newspapers report separately that throughout Nairobi on that weekend, churches, temples, mosques and the one synagogue were overflowing with their faithful. Calm – if only temporarily—envelops the country.

At home and at the club, life seems to revert to business as usual.

Though many Goans (and Hindus, Muslims, Jews) know that British rule is racist and, in many ways, deeply repugnant, we feel it is preferable to what seems to be the alternative, namely, the end of civilization: brutal armed attacks on innocent families and com-munities, murder in the streets, utter lack of respect for human life.

By November, the jacaranda trees in Nairobi are still in full bloom and it is common to see carpets of lilac strewn over road-sides and open spaces –- wherever there is even a single jacaranda growing—and we have one in Plums Lane. It is a beautiful and warm sunny Sunday afternoon, and Linda and I opt to sit in the veranda, chatting. Mom and Dad are visiting a neighbour; Niven is asleep in the bedroom, while Fatima and Joachim are in the gar-den playing with their friends. We can hear their laughter.

Braz Menezes

"They've put up a barbed-wire (razor wire) fence all around St. Theresa's," Linda tells me.

"That'll stop those young British soldiers from breaking in, with so many sweet young things busy cramming for exams."

"Don't be funny! The nuns have also hired extra *askaris*. The Mau Mau is dangerous. I think they're worried."

The sound of Simba yelping interrupts us. We look up to see him dash to the gate. At first we think that Mom and Dad must have returned, but they are not due back for at least another hour. We go to the door.

Mwangi Macharia, our houseboy is standing in the doorway. His pregnant wife and his young son, Stephen, accompany him.

"Mwangi, what is it?" Linda says. "You are not due back till Monday."

"Yes Bwana Lando," he says, addressing me, not Linda. "You are right, but my family must live with me in Nairobi now," he says. "It is very bad for us in our village."

He explains that secret Mau Mau oathing ceremonies are taking place at night in his village near Limuru, on the outskirts of Nairobi. People who hesitate to join the organisation, or who refuse to take the oath and swear allegiance to Mau Mau, are brutally mutilated or killed, along with their family members. Their life is endangered.

Mwangi and his family have travelled by bus and on foot to get to Plums Lane. We welcome them and I take Stephen to meet the other children in the garden, while Linda goes into the kitchen to find them something to eat. Mom and Dad return soon after and there is a scramble to find additional blankets for them, and clothes for Stephen. They will live in Mwangi's room in the servant's quarters for the time being.

I overhear Dad say to Mom that the Mau Mau will soon be in Nairobi, as the troops are going after them in the country to protect the white farmers.

With the arrest of Kenyatta, it seems the Mau Mau has been defeated. The next few weeks are relatively peaceful, and the school year winds to a close.

Today is the day the exam results are announced in class. Savio, Mengha, Stan, Brian, Olaf, Romeo and I will be together as classmates again next year in January. We are seated in rows in front of the podium for a final ceremony. Mr. Stewart, Headmaster, is about to speak. On either side and behind him are the black-gowned teaching staff. Dad and Mom are out there with other parents. The Headmaster starts his address. He says he's pleased with this first year of a great experiment, and on and on...

My thoughts are at home in Plums Lane. Stephen is nearly 7, and cute, but I must find a way of keeping him out of my room when I am in school. Little boys can be so troublesome.

I am brought back to the present by the sound of clapping. The speeches are over. I escort Dad and Mom selectively to meet some teachers. Dad seems pleased with *his* decision to bring me back from Goa, and yank me out of the Dr. Ribeiro Goan School. "Soon you'll have to think about University," he says. He still wants me to be a doctor or a lawyer.

"Yes Dad," I say. "I'll know better after the second year." I am determined that I will not be pushed around anymore. Savio waves at me. We intend to enjoy Christmas and New Year's Eve celebrations at the Goan Gymkhana. Linda has agreed to teach us the waltz and the box step.

It seems the ghost of the Mau Mau has not diminished the spirit of Christmas. In Nairobi, seasonal bazaars break out like a rash, with bargains on homemade pickles, jams and spicy Goan sausages, embroidery and babywear. The newspapers are filled with photographs of European party revellers at parties along the Coast in Mombasa, Kilifi, Malindi and Lamu. The same papers report that in Nairobi, Eldoret and Kitale, the talk is about new creations inspired by heightened security requirements; fashion accessories now include small firearms for women that can provide self-protection, and will fit into cute sequin-covered purses; and for that Kenyan cow-girl look, a Masai-beaded cowhide gun belt and holster, and a slim leather (with original fur) waistcoat. Across the country, Hindu shopkeepers and Muslim craftsmen rejoice at the gift that the Christian Christmas brings to their communities, with its heightened consumption of goods and services, groceries and gifts; but only the Christians will sell alcohol.

At the Goan Gymkhana, on the Sunday before Christmas, Santa Claus arrives on a cream and dark green Kenya Bus. It is nice to see the little kids really happy. Savio and I are too old and we adjourn to the Billiards room, where we can sometimes sneak in a game if no adults are present.

Christmas Day is always special at St. Francis Xavier Church, which this year has again been decorated with beautiful floral arrangements. The church is packed, even though the six front pews are almost empty, as these are reserved only for white parishioners. The congregation is requested to offer prayers for peace; although there is no specific mention of the Mau Mau, special prayers are offered for the troops fighting 'against those who plot to overturn the course of law and order and the peaceful co-existence of our society."

It is the day after Christmas. "I don't know if we'll be ready," Linda is saying to Mom as I walk into the house. I realise the perennial ritual of my sister and her mid-teenage friends, leading to the big event—the New Year's Eve Dance—is underway.

Soon the big night arrives, and so do almost all the members at the Goan Gymkhana. I meet Savio and Olaf. Our other school friends will be at the GI. We meet our old ex-classmates of both sexes from the Goan school, but this is now our party—it is bigger. The men are dressed in dinner jackets and black trousers with a silk stripe down the legs, white starched shirts and black silk bow-ties and a black or cream cummerbund; a few in dark suits. The ladies are wearing long dresses in a variety of designs, materials and colours – generally home-tailored and sometimes hand-sewn. The club hall, already decorated for the festive season, has acquired hundreds of new freshly blown balloons, and the billiards room has again been converted into a temporary crèche for parents unable to find baby-sitters. I look out for 'Bobby and the Melodists' on the stage, but the Goan Institute must have snared them. It is 'Cooty and his Supersonics' this year – one of the many top Goan dance bands in Nairobi.

The MC takes the stage and the festivities begin. Friends meeting and greeting after months apart; dancing; drinking and dining until the MC announces the 'midnight special'. Husbands and wives; fiancés and fiancées, as well as singles getting together – all couples join arms and sing *Auld Lang Syne*. Then the countdown to midnight: 5…4…3…2…1…0. The lights go out. The fireworks and the noisemakers begin. The lights come on. Balloons float down from the ceiling. "Happy New Year" greetings, kisses, hugs, embraces galore. And then the couples dance into the New Year.

"Another year gone," Olaf says as we regroup and survey the crowd below from a balcony overlooking the hall. Savio and I recognise a few of our inadvertent informers among the dancers; out-of-town civil servants who have brought their families to Nairobi for the Christmas holidays.

As the dance winds down, Savio, Olav and I escape to the cool of the veranda in the wee hours of New Years Day 1953. Inevitably we reflect on the past year.

"I wouldn't have believed it," Savio says. "We survived our first year in our non-Catholic school."

"For me it was the death of the King that gave me the biggest shock," Olaf says. "My mom says something may be going on in London, as the Queen has not been officially crowned yet." He turns to me. "Lando, what'll you most remember?"

"Remember?" I ask, playing for time. "Listening to Pio Gama Pinto here in the bar. Secondly, I'll have to say the day Kenyatta was arrested. It was the sight of all those troops and police on the streets."

"Oh I forgot. Perhaps when Lando and I saw that dead body," Savio says. "That I'll never forget."

"But seriously chaps, what marks this a special year for the three of us is—we are all wearing suits with long trousers for the first time in our lives." I say. We look at each other and laugh.

———•·•———

8

A Star is Born

The Mau Mau sends a New Year greeting to the Government in 1953 in the form of a panga attack on a European farmhouse near Gilgil, close to where, in 1949, two *Kaburu* --Afrikaans men on horseback had fired shots at our family while we were picnicking by the roadside on public land fronting their ranch.

It had been a scary incident, hard to forget. We were driving in Ahmad's Chevy to Nakuru; we had been on the road for more than three hours, having left Plums at dawn, and so we were hungry. Famished, Ahmad pulled the car right over, well off the road onto a small grassy area, by an acacia tree with beautiful branches that created a wonderful shady spot for a picnic. We were on public land, separated from private property by a big ranch fence. Mom had spread out a tablecloth and laid out all the sandwiches and other goodies. Suddenly we heard first one shot, and then another. Earlier, we had seen these two horsemen riding across the grassland, surrounded by cattle, as well as giraffe, zebra, and other animals. It looked so peaceful. Now these same men are galloping towards us, shouting abuse at us; their bullets actually hitting the ground within a few feet of us. "*Geet* off our land, you bloody *Indiaans*," they shouted, shooting at the ground near us. Mom screamed. Then she, Dad and Ahmad quickly bundled us into the car; Dad picked up the remnants of our picnic, which we had not started on, and Ahmad drove us out of there as fast as he could. He said they were Afrikaans from South Africa now settled near Gilgil. I wonder if it was their farm that was attacked by the Mau Mau.

The Government quickly replies. It broadcasts an appeal that night on radio, and repeats it, splashed across all newspapers the next day. Europeans are asked to volunteer for special security duties and Asians are asked to form 'neighbourhood watches' to patrol their own communities against crime, as police and other security forces are fully stretched elsewhere. Africans are warned against partaking in Mau Mau oathing ceremonies, and asked to report suspicious behaviour among their neighbours.

As Savio and I arrive at school to start the new term, we are surprised to see that even our 'own' European teachers are caught up in the frenzy against the Mau Mau, 'these beasts determined to destroy authority,' as one newspaper describes them.

"Look Savio, our teachers have started carrying guns," I grab his arm. "Wait. Let him go in first."

Mr. Knight, our woodwork teacher, is getting out of his car. Slightly balding and sporting a full beard on a cheerful round face, he looks an incongruous sight with a Colt revolver tucked into a holster on a cowboy-style gun belt. He is wearing his usual khaki trousers and a plaid blue shirt. He leans into his car, tucks some books under his arm and locks the car. He pauses and looks around but does not see us, and enters the school building. We do not want to surprise him; he may just swing around and shoot first before looking. I have seen that scene often in cowboy films, although he does look an unlikely cowboy or a hunter of 'terrorists', as the government now labels suspected members of the Mau Mau.

Mr. Walker strides into our history class carrying two guns: a .38 in a shoulder holster, tucked under his tweed blazer with the leather elbow patches, and a .44 Colt on a gun belt. With his tall, slender frame, *he* looks like the Lone Ranger.

During our lunch break behind the workshop, Olav, appearing concerned, says, "Did you notice how Wally's gun holster slides on his belt right round to point at his willy? A slight accident may blast his nuts to smithereens and ruin his matrimonial prospects permanently. It would make a great headline: 'Wally shoots Willy.'"

We laugh not because that is hilariously funny, but because that's what we were all thinking. The conversation inevitably turns to the Mau Mau. "Uncle says Mau Mau are moving into the African locations," Brian says. "You know my uncle 'Prisons Azevedo'? He has been transferred on a temporary assignment with the Criminal Investigation Department, in accounts administration, but he hears things."

"The GI is going to set up a Neighbourhood Watch from next week, to patrol the area around the GI and the Pangani Goan Housing Estate," Stan says.

"You remember last October when the Government arrested Jomo Kenyatta and some others, and jailed them somewhere secret?" I ask. "Well, my friend Ahmad who drives a taxi says there are rumours circulating among the African drivers that there will be trouble as everyone knows that there's something fishy about Kenyatta's trial."

"I heard that too. Dad first heard it at the office last week," Savio said. "You remember how within days after Kenyatta was arrested, all the other tribes joined the Kikuyus to drive the Muzungus out of Kenya? They say this will be bad for us all."

"I think this Mau Mau matata is bad for everyone," I say.

Eating our lunch in the shade of a jacaranda tree by the wood workshop every day can get monotonous. Before long we vary our routine at lunch and venture further outside the school grounds. Mengha invites us to eat in a *dhaba*, a roadside food stall next to the nearby Gurdwara – a Sikh place of worship. At the dhaba we can stuff ourselves on dal and curried vegetables, and an unlimited number of chapattis, for almost nothing.

As Stan and Brian's dads are both members of the Goan Institute, we sometimes nip across to the club grounds where we picnic on our home-packed lunches, before returning in time for the afternoon session. Mengha joins us too.

Then unexpectedly in mid March, the Headmaster announces new rules restricting our movement away from the school premises during school hours because of security considerations; perhaps he has been forewarned of possible problems near our school.

March 23. I am returning home from school, when the sight of an ayah pushing a toddler in a pram with a balloon attached, reminds me it is Uncle Antonio's birthday today.

I recall overhearing Mom only a week ago, say something to Dad about Uncle going away on a secret mission. "I hope he'll be OK," Mom had said. "He says he'll be back in about 10 days."

My suspicions are aroused. I have heard it reported by the security forces that the Mau Mau are receiving supplies from unknown sources. I shrug it off. It's too absurd an idea to take any further—on the other hand, Uncle has seemed more distant recently, even absent-minded. It happened about the time he bought his 'new' second-hand car, although he still seems to prefer riding his old BSA motorbike. The car is an Austin A-40 with a spotlight mounted on the roof, and he has installed a 3-gun rack behind the driver's seat. I increasingly wonder if his mission is to do with the Mau Mau. He has disappeared twice before, but no one seems to know the details. Once, employing all my diplomatic talent, I asked him, "Where have you been Uncle?" He just smiled at me like that cat on the poster advertising Limuru milk.

My thoughts are interrupted by Simba's welcoming bark echoing down Plums Lane; but to my ears, that bark sounds more anxious than usual, as it always does when something abnormal has happened. I go straight to him, rub the back of his neck, speaking softly to calm him down. Normally, besides Simba's welcome,

I would also hear the happy sounds of two boys: Mwangi's son Stephen, 7, and my baby brother Niven, now 2 years old, playing in the garden under the watchful eye of the ayah. Perhaps they are all out on a stroll. I enter the house to find Fatima and Joachim doing their homework on the dining table. They are such good kids, I think to myself. Linda and I seem to be forever getting in trouble; perhaps it's because our parents want us to set a good example, and are always trying to discipline us.

"Shush!" Fatima greets me, holding her index finger over her lips, and pointing towards the passageway leading to the living room. There I find Mom looking somewhat worried; she is talking with Hardev's mother, Mrs. Singh.

"Come, come, come in Lando," She greets me, simultaneously gesturing with her eyebrows and rapid eye movement in the direction of the sofa, where little Stephen, dressed in an outsize hand-me-down from Joachim, is asleep.

"We have had a lot of excitement," Mom says. "But I am very worried. He's not come home yet. It's not like him."

"Is Dad not home from work?"

"No no, not him," Mom says. "He's already with his cards at the club. It's Mwangi!"

Stephen sits up, woken by the sound of his dad's name. His big black eyes dart quickly around the room. He watches quietly as Mom speaks. "Mwangi came back after walking Fatima and Joachim to school. At about eleven, he told me Wangari was very ill and had told him she was dying. I immediately went to see her. She complained of a severe back ache and unbearable pains around her belly." She glances at Stephen, as if wondering if she should continue.

"Your mother saved her life!" Mrs. Singh says.

"Of course it was obvious she wasn't well and needed to be seen by a doctor urgently."

"Your mother came running to me," Mrs. Singh takes up the story. "Thanks be to God, my driver Kamau was not asleep as usual—for nearly 15 years I have tried to change his habits—but he took your Mwangi's wife to Parklands Nursing Home for emergency." She glances quickly at Stephen who is listening intently, and turns back to me. "There are no clinics or hospital for Africans near here, but Kamau disposed them."

"What do you mean disposed?" I ask.

"He came back without them," Mom replies first.

"Where's Mwangi?"

"With Wangari." Mrs. Singh interjects.

"I don't think it is anything to do with her pregnancy, as she is not due for another five weeks," Mom replies. "I should know the symptoms after five kids. I gave Mwangi 20 shillings in case they need urgent medicines, or to take a taxi home. It is past six now, so they've been gone for over seven hours. I will go to the hospital as soon as Linda's back to stay with the children. Ayah is getting Niven ready for bed."

"You will please take my driver Kamau with you," Mrs. Singh says. "You must take Lando also. My husband says these days there are Mau Mau everywhere."

About an hour later when Mom and I arrive at the Parklands Nursing Home, there are no records of Mwangi or Wangari; they seem to have just disappeared. Nobody can help us. I remember, after Mwangi had brought Wangari and Stephen to stay in the servants' quarters, he had started telling me about the secret oathing ceremonies that took place at night in his village, and what horrible things would be done to a man and his family if he refused to take the Mau Mau oath. He had seemed frightened and had suddenly stopped speaking.

Could the Mau Mau have followed him to town? I feel scared, but I do not mention my thoughts to Mom as I can see she is worried enough. We decide to return home and wait for Dad, and then perhaps he will go to the police to report two missing persons.

Dad returns at about 9:15 p.m. and Mom tells him about our visit to the Nursing Home. While they are talking, Simba starts barking. I recognise his "good news" bark and I rush to the door. A very tired looking Mwangi has finally returned, alone.

He tells us that when he got to the Parklands Nursing Home, they were not willing to admit Wangari, as it is a hospital for *Wahindi*, Indians. But a passing doctor looked at Wangari "and said something in Wahindi language to a nurse." They were immediately taken by a hospital van to the African Hospital on the hill. Wangari had her baby early. Stephen has a baby sister!

As I leave for school the next morning, Mom is hurriedly trying to put a hamper of baby clothes together as the baby will be home in the servant's quarters within a week, according to Mwangi.

Meanwhile every day, the newspapers bring fresh headlines about the ongoing trial of Jomo Kenyatta, now in its fifth month. It is taking place in Kapenguria, a small administrative outpost about 30 miles north of Kitale and east of Mount Elgon. Visitors require a permit to enter the District. Kenyatta himself had been held in Lokitaung, an arid colonial outpost in the far north of Lake Rudolph, set up to control cattle raids among the rival bands of Turkana tribesmen, and cross-border raids from Ethiopia. He and the others were charged with being members of the Mau Mau and managing it. They all denied the charges. Jomo Kenyatta denied being the ringleader behind the Mau Mau.

———•◦•———

9

Jomo Kenyatta Goes to Jail

The trial began on 24th November and was immediately adjourned to 3rd December 1952. We were in Mr. Walker's history class that day, so I had asked him why.

"Please Sir, why was the trial postponed when it has only just started?"

"Dennis Nowell Pritt, QC!" Mr. Walker says. "He's well known in England for his anti-imperialist views. He has raised many objections about procedures and has accused the Prosecution of subverting justice. I am sure he'll give the Government a run for their money." Mr. Walker slides his gun belt around so that his revolver is not pointing directly at his assets; he must suspect this is causing a distraction. "He has a multiracial team of lawyers assisting him including H.O. Davies, a Nigerian, and Chaman Lall, who I believe is a friend of Prime Minister Nehru."

"Sir, there's also Fitz De Souza, a Goan, and Achroo Kapila," Stan says, just as Mengha's hand shoots up.

"And Jaswant Singh!"

"Yes, three bright local Indians! See? You too can be like them if you work hard now." He reverts back to his topic for the day's history class.

Back in December, Savio and I had overheard stories from our usual reliable sources —visiting civil servants at the club:

We are playing table tennis one evening as usual, when luck comes our way. A visitor arrives and heads straight for the bar.

We put our table tennis paddles down and sneak into the bar for our customary snack of potato crisps and Coke, and we stay. Till now, no adult has asked us to leave the bar—perhaps they regard us as 'regulars' too. The man is called Costa, we discover from overhearing the conversation. He is based in Eldoret and is some sort of inspector in a government department. He travels extensively. Savio nudges me. He is amused that Costa's long side locks are trimmed unevenly. He is of medium height and has a thick black crop of hair, but it is his protruding chin and the goatee beard that draws attention. I noticed he has the puffed chubby face of heavy beer drinkers.

Soon he is telling his friends about the recent invasion of foreign reporters to cover Kenyatta's trial. We understand that these reporters are not content with 'official' leaks from the Government's agents.

"They're fishing," Costa says. "They want juicy details for readers in England, and the local folk leave a lot of bait around."

"Are they talking to Africans as well?" Fernandes, a bar regular, asks.

"Yes. Even to African farm workers and not only local Muzungus in Kitale and Eldoret," Costa says.

"What about the Indian dukawallahs?"

"Not much interest. I spoke to one reporter from the Manchester Guardian. His view was that most *dukawallas* – the Indian shopkeepers – prefer to keep quiet, fearing retribution from blacks if they take the side of the settlers, and if they side with the Africans, perhaps loss of business from the Muzungus who are really their bread and butter – or should I say chapattis and ghee."

"Will local newspapers publish their reports?" Dias, another regular asks.

"British newspapers will. From their comments so far, local papers may not." Costa says, "You know how the government is censoring information about the Mau Mau."

"So finally the Mau Mau gets to whisper directly into the ears of the Colonial Office through these chaps!" Fernandes makes no effort to hide his sarcasm.

"The British public only heard the voices of settlers before," Costa says. "Of course the Colonial Office would never think of asking our opinion on the problem; we work with Africans on a daily basis; they talk frankly to us. We could educate them on how not to do things."

"And if they did ask you?" Dias asks. "What would you tell them?"

"Land! The Muzungus own large landholdings. The squatters—that's what they're called—they're mainly Kikuyus and they want their land back. They work for very low wages to cultivate the farmer's land. The Africans are given a small patch of land, in some corner, on which they must live and grow their own crops and feed their family."

Costa sips his beer; "It's just like Goa, where the landowners—the *Bhatkars* sit on their *balcão*, *sossegade*, relaxed, while the workers toil all day. At least in Goa the Bhatkars give a share of crops to the workers—and for that share and a few tots of feni, and regular mass on Sunday, they are half-way to heaven." He takes a long sip of beer.

"What about this Kenyatta trial?" Fernandes asks, "It's going on there, somewhere near Eldoret, no?"

"No. It's being held in Kapenguria, nearer to Kitale. It's a joke, if you ask me." Costa says. "They have this QC--Queens Counsel—big shot from UK. He is staying at the Kitale Hotel, but because of the colour bar the Muzungu hotel will not admit the coloured lawyers. The Asian lawyers and the black Chief from Nigeria, I am told, are staying with an Indian doctor and Goan civil servants." He sips again. "Imagine it. Fitz De Souza and these other lawyers – putting up with a drive of more than 80 miles each day, there and back, carrying their papers, from Kitale to the courtroom on a dusty, back-breaking rutted road."

"We hear the courthouse is surrounded by armoured cars and armed police," Fernandes says.

"Security is everywhere. I was up in Kitale last week on business," Costa says. "They say the Kitale Road to Kapenguria has many road-blocks with troops manning them."

The conversation turns to other topics. Savio and I move back to our game.

In the few moments each night after the BBC newscast, and before sleep comes, I think about those lawyers and their harrowing ride over red muddy and potholed roads, just like the one I had travelled over from Londiani to Kericho in 1949. We would see those dark storm clouds come rushing towards us, as they do every afternoon. Then miraculously the sky would clear, having dumped the rain around the back of the hillside. You come upon it too soon. One moment you're OK. Suddenly you're sliding all over the road, your steering wheel out of control; or you hit a pothole and the car starts to sink in deep mud up to the axle. You can never tell how deep a pothole is until you're in it. Life can be like that—full of hidden potholes. I wonder what would have happened if I had stayed in Goa?

A few days after the attack on the farm in Gilgil, Dad surprises me with "So now do you know where your friend Dr. Leakey had disappeared on his secret mission?"

"What do you mean, Dad?"

"It's all over the papers today," Dad says. "He was working on a secret mission with the CID. He was brought up playing with totos –- he speaks fluent Kikuyu and Kiswahili, so he was building up a network of informants for the Government to report on the movement of the Mau Mau, and he was making radio broad-casts in Kikuyu and Kiswahili against the Mau Mau. Propaganda... that's what they call it.

"But why did he quit?"

"Yesterday, he was so upset with the Pritt, the defence lawyer, he just quit as translator, and walked out of court. That's why he's in the news."

I feel a certain disappointment to hear that Leakey was inform-ing against the Kikuyu. After all he grew up among them as broth-ers, and now it seems he is betraying them. After all the Kikuyus are only fighting for independence, as Pio Gama Pinto had said everyone should in Goa and Kenya. On the other hand, the Mau Mau are so brutal in their attacks of innocent people. I am confused.

In late January, we hear that Leakey has returned to the court-room. The constant confrontations with the defence continue. By the end of the month, all the newspapers are filled with dire predic-tions of the aftermath of the trial, whether Kenyatta and his fellow defendants are found guilty or acquitted. The trial and its outcome seem to be the only subject of conversation anywhere – at home, at my friends' houses, in school or at the Goan Gymkhana.

On April 8, the Headmaster abruptly announces a school clo-sure at noon. The verdict had been announced in Kapenguria. Savio and I make an immediate beeline for home. The buses are packed above capacity, and by the time we arrive at the Ngara roundabout, crowds of Asians and Africans are milling around the Asian dukas. Some stores are being closed up with heavy metal slid-ing shutters. The mood seems angry and anxious. There is unusual activity on the roads, as if the peak hour traffic has been arbitrarily changed. Police begin to erect roadblocks to control movement.

I arrive at Plums Lane at about 3 p.m. to find Uncle Antonio's motorbike and Ahmad's taxi parked in our front yard. Fatima and Joachim arrived earlier. Linda has just arrived. She tells me Ahmad had picked up Dad at work, as since mid-morning the taxi drivers have been talking about the likelihood of riots breaking out following the verdict at the trial.

"Kenyatta's been sentenced to seven years imprisonment and hard labour," Uncle says, as I walk into the room.

"I must leave now," Ahmad says walking to the door. "My Serena is alone. She must be very frightened." He turns back. "Hello Lando," he says. "Be careful."

"They are saying the whole trial has been rigged," Dad says. "I heard that the Magistrate, a Mr. Ransley Thacker, QC, who is nearing retirement, has been paid a huge amount of money directly into a secret bank account in the UK, and that he will retire now and won't be returning to Kenya."

"I heard everything was going well in the defence by this Pritt Q.C." Uncle Antonio says, "But then Leakey, who grew up speaking, reading and writing fluent Kikuyu, and whom Kenyatta trusted completely as a friend, betrayed him at the trial. They say Leakey was the Court's translator and without his evidence, Kenyatta would not have been convicted."

I leave them discussing the trial and go into the veranda. Linda is chatting with Mom. She looks up. "I was telling Mom that all day yesterday, and the day before, aeroplanes were landing at Eastleigh Airport next to our school. Sister Mary told us that she thinks more British troops are being brought in to maintain law and order."

"There will be trouble," I say. "Ahmad told us and he knows because he talks to the African taxi drivers all day, and they must know." I go to my room. I am disappointed with what I had heard, as till now, I had hero-worshipped Leakey, and now it seems he has betrayed a friend. I still do not know what to make of it. I listen to the radio, but the BBC gives much the same news as had been reported in the papers – the authorities are controlling all information.

Despite the charged atmosphere, there are no major riots, thanks to Government measures including armed police roadblocks and the heavy presence of troops in Nairobi and other major urban centres. There are literarily hundreds of unemployed youth hovering around, waiting for someone to put a spark to the dry *kuni* – tinder. Nothing happens today.

But if the Government thought that putting Kenyatta and his colleagues in jail would force the Mau Mau into submission, then it was wrong. Barely a week after the verdict the Mau Mau conflict against the British escalates.

The headlines scream out the horrors wrought by the 'oath-crazed natives', 'terrorists' and 'guerrillas', as the fighters are variously labelled. The Kikuyus are angry. Thousands of young men are now volunteering to fight. A BBC report says the younger and more violent fighters have taken control of the Mau Mau's organisation and that older Kikuyus, who had fought alongside the British in Ethiopia and Burma, are now helping to train the new recruits among the rebels. Then we hear the guerrillas are collecting guns and ammunition by stealing these from European farms, houses, and police stations. An Indian police inspector is shot dead in a raid on suspected terrorists in Pangani very close to our school, and immediate new restrictions are imposed on our movement.

We are frightened, but we comfort each other that at least our European teachers are armed.

Just after mid-May, the BBC stops reporting on troubles in Kenya and transfers its attention to London. Ironically, at a time when taking oaths is a criminal offence punishable with death by hanging, in Kenya, the Queen will take an oath in London—the preparations for Queen Elizabeth II's coronation are all the news. It will be held in London in June, accompanied by great pomp and circumstance, and will be televised for the first time. We have no idea what television looks like, until it is explained to us during physics class. The next day Olaf brings in a copy of Popular Science Magazine, in which an article describes how one day, it is expected that TVs will even display colour and explains how this next generation of TVs will make that possible.

"We have yet to receive the first generation black and white TV in Kenya," Stan reminds us.

For me, the BBC news about the forthcoming events comes to life when Savio, Mengha and I are selected with others in the school to attend a ceremony in Government House to commemorate the Queen's Coronation on June 2nd, 1953.

On a cold overcast day, dressed in our grey school uniforms with brilliant glossy, polished shoes, we travel by chartered bus to Government House. On arrival at a side gate, we are herded to our designated area, and seated in groups in the usual order: the European school children nearest to the podium, the Asians next and Africans behind them. It is a colourful ceremony on the grounds of the residence, adorned with flags and marquees. I glance longingly at the flags; if only I could wrap myself up in a flag like a Masai *shuka*: it would help against the cold June breeze. There is a short parade of marching bands of the uniformed military men and the police, and a march past by the East African Women's League, the Salvation Army, and nursing corps among others. There are speeches. I can feel myself tiring fast. I look at Savio and Mengha; they too seem exhausted. Soon it is over and the guests are ushered to a Garden party complete with marquees and tents. We patiently await instructions, and eagerly look forward to the treats ahead. In the distance the clouds are gathering dark against the sky. We wonder if we will make it to the food tent before the skies open up.

The mainly white guests in dark and grey suits and ladies in fancy hats and frocks are ushered into a big tent, where sandwiches, pastries and cakes are served by black waiters wearing white *kanzus*, white gloves and red fez caps. VIPs and consular representatives and their wives, bedecked in national costumes, are invited into a separate tent for refreshments.

We are gripped by panic deep in our stomachs. "What about us?" Mengha whispers aloud, "Perhaps we will not get anything to eat." Savio thinks so too. Others in our group start to fret and grumble aloud. The sound of distant thunder reinforces the rumble in the pit of my stomach.

"Come, come! Let them eat cake!" A European lady in a bright scarlet dress calls out to our supervisors in a shrill voice. Just in time and we do!

We leave Government House very contented, each of us fondly clutching a commemorative mug with a portrait of HRM Queen Elizabeth II, proud for having been treated so especially, even if it has been a long day. Linda, Fatima and Joachim greet me as I arrive home. They proudly show off identical mugs to mine that were distributed to all schools without the fanfare of a garden party. I take my mug to my room and place it out of reach on my bookshelf.

Back at the school after the weekend, life soon returns to normal. The BBC goes back to covering news topics other than the Coronation of Her Royal Majesty. The voice of the newscaster crackles. 'First the headlines: In Egypt, the population is restive. British soldiers sent to quell trouble spots, are being kept busy. There is news coming in of fresh atrocities by the Mau Mau in Kenya. More troops may be needed.'

———•◦•———

10

Love is in the Air

June to August are the coldest months in Nairobi, with overcast skies; however today the sun is out and it highlights the new growth after the long rains. I am in the garden brushing Simba's coat after a bath, when Linda walks up to me.

"Lando, have you heard? Uncle Antonio is off again on his secret mission. Do you know what is going on?" I can see she is both curious but also as anxious as I am, about Uncle's secret trips out of town. There is no worse feeling than knowing something is afoot, and at the same time, not knowing enough.

"Stay Simba!" I grab him by the collar just as he tries to get away. "Have you asked Mom? She's more likely to tell you what she knows."

"I did, and she won't. Says it's rude to pry into people's private business. Lando, why can't you find out? You boys are so useless." She turns and walks back into the house, and I stay to finish brushing Simba's coat, as 7-year - old Stephen comes to help me. As usual, he is eager to please and full of questions. I keep him busy doing small errands; today he is trying to get me to let him touch my bike again, but I'm reluctant, because of what happened the last time. He can barely reach the pedals, but by propping himself on a rock and leaning against the garage wall, placing his right leg on a pedal through the frame, and then letting go, he can stay upright at least for a short while as the bike speeds down the sloping gravel driveway, before it crashes into a tree or something. The scratches and bruises of a fortnight ago are still visible on his right arm when Stephen brushed himself against a thorny kai-apple hedge, before hitting a tree. The front wheel and handlebars of my bike were twisted out of alignment. His big eyes convey such a message of hope and repentance that for his sake I promise to ask Dad to look for a kid-size bike for him at the weekly auction.

A few days later a different sort of bike entirely comes into the yard. It's Uncle Antonio's BSA bike, except Uncle Alvaro is riding it. Alvaro shares a house with Antonio and two other single men. Dad and Mom greet him at the door and usher him into the living room. Neither Linda nor I are encouraged to stay – on the contrary – we are told to scoot.

"Mom, why did you not want us to meet with Uncle Alvaro?" I ask, after he had left.

"Because he brought us a message from Uncle Antonio, that we are to keep secret," Mom says. "You know how tongues begin to wag!"

Within two days, we forget Uncle as a new problem arises. Dad comes home with the news that the Portuguese Consulate in Nairobi has received a clearance for him and his family to travel to Mozambique. As part of his contract Dad is entitled to take his family on home-leave to Goa once every 5 years, but as his last leave in 1949 was delayed by 18 months, he was planning to use it this year after only 4 years, and instead of returning to Goa, to take the family to Mozambique. He has not seen his older brother since 1924, when our young and handsome Uncle Nico had boarded the steamer at the docks in Goa that would take him to Lorenco Marques in Portuguese East Africa.

"But Dad, I cannot come!" Linda bursts out. "It will be my final year of high school, and I just cannot afford to miss a day. No I won't go. I'm sorry!"

Mom looks up, startled by Linda's outburst. "Wait a bit now, Linda. Let Dad finish explaining the plan that we have both discussed. You know that your Uncle Nico left Goa 29 years ago. Since then he took himself a bride, and has six children who are your first cousins. Wouldn't you like Dad to meet his only living brother, and would you not wish to know your first cousins?"

"Can we please wait a year? That's all I'm asking."

"Here's what we are proposing," Dad intervenes. "I will not be able to postpone this trip. We do not wish you to interrupt your schooling. Neither do we wish Lando to do so, as he has gone through big changes, from boarding school in Goa to Dr. Ribeiro, and from there to the Tech High, and so...."

"Can Linda and I stay behind with Uncle Antonio?" I can see the opportunities of going on safari; maybe he will even invite me to join him on his secret missions. I hope they don't change their plans.

"It may be difficult for Uncle Antonio, as I am sure he will find two of you a challenge. It would be different if he were married. Uncle Albert and Dona Pulchera have kindly offered to look after you both."

A reflex action shoots my hand to my cheek at the mention of busty Dona Pulchera. I feel a chill up my spine. "Not Dona Pulchera!" I groan. She is childless, wears the reddest of lipstick and bestows lavish kisses on any child who comes within her grasp, leaving behind bright red branding marks all over their faces. I know Albert and Dona Pulchera well, as they had escorted me home from Goa, a trip of eleven days. I am indifferent and I quite like Uncle Albert. After a short discussion Dad confirms that Mom, Fatima, Joachim and Niven will depart for Mozambique with him in early December and return to Kenya on February 2, 1954. Linda and I will stay behind – with Uncle Albert and Dona Pulchera, if no other arrangements can be made in time.

At midnight, the BBC crackles its daily ration of bad news. It seems the political problems in Egypt have escalated and taken priority over the Mau Mau troubles in Kenya. If only I could find someway of knowing what Uncle Antonio is up to on his secret missions!

Two days later Mom has exciting news for us. Uncle Antonio has returned from his trip, and will join us for dinner on Saturday.

I am waiting for Uncle, but he disappoints me when he arrives on his motorbike, instead of in his Austin A-40 that might have provided us some clues as to where he has been from the colour of the dust. The earth colour in the Aberdare Mountains is a deep red; in Tsavo to the south on the Mombasa Road, the dust would be a red-brown colour, and if he had ventured towards the Amboseli Park and the Tanganyika border, the car would be covered in grey dust. Between Savio and I we could most certainly confirm the whereabouts of Uncle's secret missions.

Linda and I join Mom and Dad at the door to greet Uncle who seems in an unusually happy mood. I look for signs of his trip to the jungle hideouts of the Mau Mau, but he is clean-shaven and looks rested. Linda and I help Mom and Mwangi get dinner to the table while Dad and Uncle chat over a whiskey. Mom especially asks Linda to light two candles to make it look romantic for Uncle. It's a nice dinner with a Goan-style pot roast and vegetables. Linda says grace. We are into our dinner, when Dad clinks his spoon on a glass for attention.

"Uncle Antonio has something he wants to tell us," he says, gesturing Uncle to speak.

Antonio grins as he shoots quick glances around the table. "I especially asked for us to be together today as I have the most important announcement to make in my life." He pauses, and glances around at each of us. Assured of our complete attention, he continues. "I have finally found a very special person that I love and I want to marry. Her name is Clara, and I wanted you four to be the first to hear it straight from the horse's mouth. I am that horse," he concludes, a twinkle in his eye.

"Have we met her before?" Linda is first off the mark. I see Mom's eyes fill with tears. Now I remember they also were tearful after Alvaro left the other day. She is so happy.

"I don't think so," Uncle replies. "Clara lives in Kampala. I have tried to keep it a secret, and you probably didn't even know I have been away often, but these past few months I have made trips regularly to see her. Last week she finally said 'yes' so I sent a telegram to ask Alvaro to inform your mother and father, before word gets around on the Goan grapevine."

"So when will you marry her?" Linda is bursting with questions. I feel myself torn between happiness for Uncle – he is so happy, it's contagious – but also a foreboding that I am about to loose a good friend, as happened when Ahmad got married to Serena. Love does funny things to normal grown men. They drop their old friends just like that! Dad is smiling through all this. Of course no one is eating, as this is exciting news.

"Linda, we would like you to be one of the bridesmaids, " Uncle tells Linda.

"First there will be an engagement," Mom says. "We will be sending out invitations next week to a few close friends. I believe that Clara's parents and her brother will accompany her to Nairobi, at the end of July, so we will be busy getting ready for them."

"But will the wedding take place during my exams?" Linda asks, "and Dad will you cancel the trip to Mozambique?"

From across the table I see Uncle suddenly lose his happy face at the barrage of obstacles being placed in his path by Linda. "Of course not, Linda," he says. "We can adjust everything to fit around your exams and Mom and Dad's holiday plans. You will love Clara. She can be very flexible once her mind is made up."

A thought crosses my mind. "Uncle, can we stay with you and our future Aunt Clara, while Dad and Mom are away?"

"Of course," Uncle says. Linda's face lights up.

The next few months seem to flash by. News of Uncle's engagement takes precedence in our household over the threat of Mau Mau. It has also triggered any number of social events, and according to Mom's lady friends, much gossip at the club. "A reluctant sitting duck gets bagged!" they joke.

The engagement is held on a Saturday evening with drinks, a short ceremony and then a big dinner at Plums Lane. Our future aunt Clara is beautiful with a fair complexion, and a lovely smile. She is so graceful and looks up at Uncle with adoring eyes, but she blushes profusely when she is introduced to his friends. Linda whispers to me that she already likes Clara, and spends much time talking with her. Alvaro and his roommates and some of Uncle's other friends turn up with an assortment of Portuguese guitars, each with varying number of strings. They sing romantic songs into the night in Portuguese, Konkani and English. The party breaks up at 3 in the morning.

On a beautiful November 7, with the jacarandas still in bloom laying impromptu carpets of purple and lilac along the route to the church, Antonio and Clara are married at St. Francis Xavier Church, Parklands, with Alvaro as the best man and Linda as bridesmaid (with two others) and a flower girl; Niven is a pageboy. The wedding is followed by a big reception at the Goan Gymkhana and then the newly married couple is off on a honeymoon. Dad and Mom scurry around to make final arrangements for the trip and Linda and I settle down to prepare for exams.

One day I meet Linda at the Ngara roundabout as she steps off the bus from St. Teresa School in Eastleigh. "They're building another security fence by our school. The nuns say the Mau Mau are closer than we think."

"Perhaps they are already in people's servants quarters," I reply. "My friend Mengha said the police had thrown a cordon around 2nd and 3rd Avenue Eastleigh last night for more than six hours."

In early December, Mom brings us good news. Linda and I will stay in Plums Lane, and Uncle Antonio and Aunt Clara will move in while they are away. We are delighted! Within a week, they move in and the rest of our family boards the train for Mombasa, where a steamer will carry them to Lorenco Marques; Dad is ecstatic. This is the trip he missed when he jumped ship at Mombasa in 1928.

It is a hectic Christmas and New Year, as Uncle wants to show off his new wife to everyone, and we go along for the ride. He takes us on a trip to the Nairobi National Park, where we see a rhino, large numbers of zebra, giraffe, bucks, and ostriches. One week we have a picnic by the Blue Posts Hotel in Thika, and even climb over the rocks and get drenched by the water cascading down the Fourteen Falls.

Love is everywhere in December. First I hear from Savio that his family has been invited to Pio Gama Pinto's wedding; then from Olaf that his family too has been invited. That same evening Uncle announces he has also received an invitation to the wedding and confirms that Linda and I will be going too. I feel sure if Dad was here he would be going as well, as Dad is a good friend of Pio's father.

Almost two months to the day that Uncle Antonio and Clara were married, Linda and I are attending Pio Gama Pinto's wedding with them. It is a much larger wedding than Uncle's was. St. Francis Xavier Church has been beautifully decorated with pink and white flowers; the red carpet along the aisle is freshly brushed and looking its best. Pio waits at the altar; he looks very elegant in formal wedding attire, but even I can see he seems slightly nervous. He looks down and flicks some dust from his jacket. An usher escorts the bride-to-be's mother who had flown in from India, to a reserved pew on the left. Pio's parents are already seated on the right hand side. Suddenly the church organ bursts forth with the wedding march and the petite bride, Emma, walks up the aisle in a beautiful wedding gown, holding on to her father's arm. The ceremony starts and eventually they are pronounced man and wife.

The church wedding is followed by a big reception at the Goan Gymkhana, with almost all the members present as well as a few other non-Goan close friends of Pio. The MC calls for J.M. Nazareth to raise the toast. Savio and I nudge each other. Goan parents use 'JM' as the role model to push their children towards the legal profession. 'JM' was born in Kenya and in 1934 was appointed advocate to the Supreme Court of Kenya, rare for a person of colour. A distinguished looking man, meticulously well groomed and eloquent, he speaks at length of Pio's family and of Emma's family too. But he spends longest elaborating on Pio's aspirations to 'shed the colonial shackles' from any nation occupied by foreign elements. For a brief moment it sounds as if JM is expressing his own political views using Pio's toast as an excuse. But he pauses, turns to the newly wed couple and wishes them a long and lasting happiness together with his conviction that the passion Pio has shown towards his work would now be partly directed to the lovely Emma. Pio responds briefly, steering clear of any political views, as if all the intensity that Savio and I had witnessed at the club bar one evening had fizzled out into naught. It does not surprise me. Love had recently transformed Ahmad and Uncle Antonio, and so why not Pio?

Savio leans over and whispers in my ear, "I can't imagine this is the same man we heard arguing about fighting the British for Kenya's independence."

"More important, love conquers all," I reply, stealing Linda's mantra. "Even communists can fall in love."

11

The Mau Mau
Outside our Classroom

"Lando, are you busy?"

Linda's face appears through my partly open door, and I can tell she is horrified at the apparent chaos in my tiny room. I have my 3-piece drum set – a surprise present from Uncle and Aunt Clara over Christmas – in one corner; in centre stage is my desk, piled high with books and gadgets, two alarm clocks, a bedside lamp made from an empty Chianti wine bottle and a shade which I have improvised from a woven cane basket; a hockey stick leans against the desk; on the floor, shoes and more books and clothes, waiting to be sorted out and put away before Mom is back from Mozambique. I know exactly where everything is, but it is not for me to convince Linda.

"Let's talk in the garden," I say, following her outside on a beautiful sunny afternoon. Uncle and Aunt Clara have gone shopping for groceries. Simba is delighted and barks up a welcome; I calm him down. Linda sits under the peach tree, and of course at that moment Stephen appears from out of nowhere, with his big, black, probing eyes.

"Do you have a cycle for me, Lando?" He is not going to let me forget my promise.

"No I have not forgotten," I tell him. "I am waiting for Dad to return from holiday."

"Isn't is amazing how fast he has learned English," Linda says. " And in only a few months too?"

"Mom is teaching him the alphabet, but at 7, she says he must be in a school."

"There are no schools for Africans anywhere around here," Linda says. "This is an Asian area."

I turn to face Stephen, "Linda and I must discuss something important. Please go and play somewhere else for a little while, OK?" He slinks away.

"Lando, I'm very worried," Linda says. "But I can't say anything to Uncle yet, as he can't do anything about it." I look at her. She seems more adult recently. Her hair is combed straight down and curls up on both sides of her face. Both of us only returned to school a week ago for the 1954 school year, so I wonder what's coming next.

"I want to run away from St. Teresa's."

"Your school?" I ask. "Why? What's happened?"

"Yes, my school. The area around it is changing so fast, and we are scared." She moves her body into a more comfortable position. "You remember when the European troops first moved in near the airport, and I told you the school was constructing a fence around the school, and you joked and said this was probably to keep the soldiers out of the school?"

"Is it not working then?"

"Lando, don't joke! Be serious for a change and listen to what I am telling you. The boys in our class told us this week – that during the Christmas holidays, some of the buildings on Juja Road, the main road leading to St. Teresa's school and by the church on First

Avenue, have been turned into brothels where the British soldiers can find African prostitutes. Of course, we – the girls – were all shocked, especially the way the boys described it. We started to look at the street from the bus, and it really is different from only a couple of months ago."

"But that area is officially an Asian residential area as well. How can they bring African girls there?"

"Yes, but who is going to bother about rules, especially if it keeps the British soldier boys happy? Remember they're here to protect the White settlers, not us."

"Linda, this is your final year. It will so difficult for you to switch schools."

"I know. There are no other choices for us as we're coloured. The Loreto nuns won't open their girls' schools to us; there's only Dr. Ribeiro's, but you know they have been having some problems, which is why Dad enrolled me here; I don't know what to do." She pulls at some grass in despair.

"What about Jean, Clarisse, Sylvie and the others?" I list her friends.

"We're all in the same boat. Clarisse's sisters are going to be transferred to the nuns in Mangu, near Thika, at the end of this term, as they are in the junior grades."

"Let's wait till Dad gets back. Meanwhile be careful. Travel together with the other girls to and from school," I say trying to console her.

Linda continues talking. "My guess is most Goan parents with daughters in the lower grades will take them out of this school, although education-wise our school is considered one of the best. What about you? How is it going after two years in a non-Catholic school?"

"Fine so far. Do you know we've almost quadrupled in size with this year's intake? Our group are still called the 'first batch', so we're used to try out new ideas; we're like the white mice in our labs. The teachers keep pushing us. We are very busy, but the area around our school is becoming dangerous, as there are rumours that the Mau Mau has infiltrated all the neighbouring African locations of Kariokor, Pumwani, and around the Racecourse area."

"I can't wait for Mom and Dad to get back, although it's been lovely with Uncle and Aunt Clara." Linda says. We talk about other things and eventually go indoors.

As I wait for sleep to arrive, I imagine what Dad might do faced with Linda's new problems and the fact that there is only Dr. Ribeiro's Goan School as the other option – and it is crowded. Dad had thought of sending her to boarding school in Goa in 1951, but with me still there sending those frequent letters complaining of my boarding school, Mom would not hear of it. Sending Linda to boarding school in the UK is likely to be financially prohibitive. It seems the problem will have to be tackled directly. I remember Pio Gama Pinto saying people must begin to fight for their rights. The priests have been preaching to us that we are all equal in the eyes of God; perhaps Dad can join up with the other parents at St. Teresa's and approach the Catholic authorities on this problem. The Goans have been among the biggest, and certainly the most fervent fund-raisers for the Catholic Church over the 50 years since the start of colonisation of Kenya. Why can't they say enough is enough? The Church must open up the white Catholic schools to all Catholics – perhaps at first, only for brown Catholics – asking for an exemption to racial laws for black ones too would be going too far for the colonial government. The White settlers would intervene and stop it, especially as they expect the Government to put down the Mau Mau once and for all; the Colonial Office would not go against the White settler demands. I think I am beginning to realise how difficult it is for parents, who might want to do the best for their children and are faced by so many barriers. Sleep overtakes me as I think about all this.

The next few weeks roll by and Linda and I talk more often as we face a new reality. It seems the Mau Mau is here to stay, and so are the British troops. Reinforcements are brought in. The

Government announces that the Mau Mau has completely infiltrated the Asian neighbourhoods of Eastleigh and Pangani, and the immediate neighbourhoods that surround our school, such as the 'African locations' of Pumwani, Bahati, Starehe and Kariokor – and almost every day it seems, partial curfews are imposed, new warnings issued and fresh numbers of casualties reported on both sides. The Government is in turmoil and people are openly frustrated that it seems to be losing the battle.

Uncle Antonio and Aunt Clara move into their own rental flat off the Ngara Road when Dad, Mom and family return at the end of January. They seem well rested and happy and Fatima, Joachim and Niven are speaking Portuguese phrases. Linda and I are interested in the 'family photo' of the two brothers and their families. There were no photos of them together before this one – the only one in the 20th century – though there is a cousin missing, as he is abroad at university in Portugal and of course Linda and I are absent. With Dad and Mom back, our life returns to a sort of normality. Within days Dad is rounding up support from other parents to deal with the problems at St. Teresa High School; it seems to drain him and we notice he has become short-tempered. One morning, Mom is strolling back with Niven along Kikuyu Road, which demarcates the boundary between the European Railway quarters and the Asian residential community of Westlands, when she spots a garden sale of used clothing and household items; a family is returning home to Britain. Among the items is a bicycle, which Mom buys for Stephen. Thereafter it seems that only surgery will separate him from his 'cycle'.

In late February, the Government reminds the population that the country is still under a legal State of Emergency. It has a special message for residents of Nairobi: Terrorists and murderers spawned by the Mau Mau are fleeing the security forces in the White Highlands and are believed to be infiltrating the urban areas. It asks all homeowners to be vigilant and regularly inspect their servants' quarters for unauthorised occupants. As unobtrusively as possible, Linda and I periodically make sure that only Mwangi and Wangari with Stephen and the baby live in their one-bedroom quarters. We know Simba is also doing a good job of surveillance.

One sunny March morning, as Mr. Walker is teaching us History, I see him suddenly tense his body. He is peering outside through the big-paned windows to an unfolding scene not yet within our line of vision, as it is happening behind us.

"Down! Everybody get down on the floor. Keep your heads down," he shouts as he unbuckles his hip holster. I put my head flat on the desk, my eyes fixated on him. He crouches and pulls out his .38 revolver, and starts edging towards the window, trying to stay out of sight, and yet still looking intently at something happening outside. All I can see is our sun-drenched playing field.

First I hear a gunshot and a split second later, clang! It is the sound of metal on metal; the sound of a bullet smashing into the galvanized metal eaves gutter and a thud as the lead drops to the ground. We now hear voices shouting. The sounds get louder. A dog barks furiously, and a man is screaming or crying for help. Some of my classmates are on the floor below their desks, but I cannot resist looking out at the scene unfolding outside just through the window. Another shot rings out… a black man runs across the sports field closely pursued by a black policeman in a dark blue sweater and khaki shorts. He has a police dog – an Alsatian – on a long leash dragging him, faster, faster. A white police officer, pistol in hand, is also chasing the black man. Two black *askaris*, policemen with rifles, follow up the rear, chasing the same man. The white officer shouts, "*Simama!* Stop! Or I'll shoot!" He halts briefly, his legs astride, and then with both hands he aims his revolver. A shot rings out. The man screams and throws his hands partly in the air. He seems to convulsively jump into the air as lead meets flesh. He falls to the ground, turns on his back. Blood is spurting from the side of his neck. Within seconds, the dog is on him, teeth bared, both front paws on the man's chest, which appears to be bleeding as well. I can almost see the terror in the whites of his eyes. We are that close to the commotion.

The school's emergency siren screams for the first time in three years.

"Please do not look out. Follow the emergency drill," Mr. Walker replaces his revolver in its holster and fastens the cover. His face is lobster red. I cannot tell whether he is frightened or angry. Why did he pull his gun inside the class? Would he have shot the man if the police didn't do so first?

Mengha and I join the line-up to the door. We stream out into the inner courtyard waiting for further instructions. About 30 minutes later, the Headmaster announces over the PA that all classes are cancelled for the day. As we are leaving the school grounds, Savio and I see the police load a stretcher carrying the man into the back of a police wagon. He is lying on his face, handcuffed with his hands behind his back. Two askaris and the dog accompany the prisoner.

The following day, we notice our European teachers, normally cheerful, appear as nervous as we are by the sudden nearness of violence. This makes us feel more insecure too. We know our parents are powerless to deal with such problems, but we always saw our European teachers as our protectors in school, and as they are British, we assume they must somehow be closer to the authorities and will ensure our safety. But now the wanton brutality and violence that is engulfing the land has finally reached us. The hitherto all-powerful omnipotent colonial government is fighting the Mau Mau literally outside our window and in broad daylight.

Until now the struggle had remained distant. The Kikuyus were challenging only the white settlers because they want their own land back; perhaps now they also want land that belonged to other tribes as well? The BBC that night, and local newspapers the next day, carries more news of violent arson and brutal attacks by the Mau Mau on African villagers loyal to the government. The reports are gruesome. Even women and children are being killed.

Some pregnant women have been disembowelled. Whole villages have been set alight and burnt to the ground. For Savio and me, this news is too much to absorb, as the reports of attacks by the Mau Mau and counter-attacks by government security forces, mix new headlines and old statistics: 'General China, the number two leader, was wounded and captured by British troops on January 15 and has agreed to ask his followers in the Aberdare forest to surrender.' 'General Katanga is captured! General Tanganyika surrenders!'

The numbers of arrests, detentions, wounded and dead, begin to lose their meaning. Rumours begin to surface that the government is lying and has set up a network of special agents throughout the land, to misinform the recently self-described 'freedom fighters', and the public at large. Attacks that were unimaginable even a few months earlier are now an everyday occurrence.

Savio and I go about our routine as if nothing is amiss. Sometimes, on our way home from school, we sneak into the billiard room at the club, play a couple of rounds and sneak out before the adults arrive. March has been a bad month.

———

12

A Long Shadow

I am on my way to school. Stephen speeds past me on Plums Lane, deftly avoiding the potholes and random bumps; he does a U-turn and greets me with a "Happy day Lando."

"You too Stephen. Remember, please do not enter my room," I say, knowing that my room no longer competes for his attention since his bike arrived. I smile to myself at the sheer pleasure that the bike has brought Stephen. I wonder what will happen if he delays going to school much longer, but then I remember that there is no school for African kids nearby, because of segregation; I feel bad but unsure what to do about it.

When I get to school, I notice the atmosphere is different. The shock of seeing a man shot in our own playground is still reverberating in the corridors and classrooms. Both students and teachers are affected. All our teachers seem more anxious to discuss the incident and the Mau Mau rebellion than to give us our lessons. Most see it as a threat to the Administration, except for Mr. Martin, the Botany teacher, who when we met in our first year, had introduced himself to us with these words: "In England they would refer to me as 'our left-leaning Commie Bastard.'" The name stuck and the boys now call him 'Our Commie Bastard.' He tells us he is not a supporter of the ruling party in the UK, the Conservatives who had swept into power in 1951, the year he came out to Kenya to teach. However, we don't care what party he supports. Regardless of who's in power in England, the same Colonial Office still runs our lives and is responsible for all our problems.

Needless to say, not much actual instruction takes place that day. After school, as we get off the bus at the Ngara Road roundabout; a number of girls in the red uniforms of St. Teresa's High School alight from the bus that pulls up behind us. Savio looks at the girls and, grabbing me by my sleeve, drags me into a store entrance away from the din of traffic noise of engines, horns and bicycle bells.

"What is it?"

"Lando, you know those problems you were telling me about at St. Teresa's Girls School? I heard my Dad and Mom discussing it last night. They're thinking of relocating my sister to the Mangu Girls' school near Thika. They will be going to see it next Saturday. Shall I say, we will come for the ride? That way you can meet your friend Saboti, and introduce her to me too."

I grab his arm and squeeze it. It is the best news I have had in a long time.

"Savio, You're not kidding me are you?"

"I swear on my honour!" he says with his big grin. We walk together to his home, and I almost skip all the way home. I am so happy at the prospect of seeing Saboti again.

As always, it is Simba, like an ever-vigilant medieval gatekeeper that announces my approach to the residents of Plums Lane. I hesitate and listen: it is Simba's 'bad news' bark, which I have often heard before. I brace myself as I enter the gate.

"Thank God you are back early, Lando," Mom, waiting in the entrance hallway, says putting out her arms to hug me. "It's Daddy. He's not well." Mom is nervous and looks pale. Her eyes are slightly puffed – she may have been crying. "Uncle Patrick brought Dad home from work by taxi. He's hot and sweating. I haven't been able to contact Dr. Manu or his partner Dr. Sorabjee. I've sent a message to Dr. Castelino with Hardev's driver. I hope he'll come quickly. I am so worried."

"What's wrong with Dad?" I ask. I'm suddenly scared but I try and not show it, while I reach out to offer Simba my hand in a delayed greeting. He has been patiently waiting, wagging his tail in slow motion. I feel his wet nose in my palm, but he too is subdued, as if he senses all is not well. "Is Dad in the bedroom?" I peek through the open living room door. I can see a candle has been lit on the table with the blue and white statue of Our Lady of Fatima.

"Yes. He's sleeping now. He has a very high fever, but he won't even touch water, won't touch anything. He's been trembling for nearly two hours," Mom says. I turn the bedroom door handle carefully and peep into the room. Mum has tidied it in readiness for the doctor; she has even placed a chair by the bed and cleared a small space for his black leather bag. The curtains are drawn to block out the bright late afternoon light that normally bathes the bedroom. A lit candle flickers on the table under the Sacred Heart on the wall. I close the door and join Mom in the living room, to await the doctor's arrival.

"Linda will not be home for another hour," Mom says. "Fatima and Joachim have gone to the Parklands shops for me. What a shock this is."

"And where's Niven?" I ask.

"With the ayah. Wambui has taken him for a stroll. I expect Stephen has joined them. He is so happy with his bike," she adds distractedly.

Eventually Dr. Castelino arrives. Tall, hair neatly combed back, and wearing a grey suit, he is the picture of professional competence. "I came as soon as I could," he greets Mom; and then glances in my direction. "Is this Lando? He has grown. They must have fed him well in Goa." I know he's joking. He follows Mom into the bedroom.

I wait, hoping at least that Linda will arrive soon so we can talk. I feel anxious, not knowing what is going on. I see her coming through the gate and breathe a sigh of relief when she appears a few minutes later. "Daddy is very sick. The doctor is in there. How come you're so late?" She doesn't reply and walks towards the bedroom but returns to wait with me.

Dr. Castelino emerges from the room with Mom in tow after about 45 minutes. Linda and I stand up. Doctors are the most respected members of our community – even more so than priests. Mom must have asked him to let us be present, because he puts his bag on a chair and faces us, Linda and I on either side of Mom.

"Chico's condition is serious as he is running a high fever," he says in a grave tone. "Not all his responses and reflexes are normal. I have ruled out some of the common ailments like malaria and so forth, although the preliminary symptoms are very similar with the high fever and the shivering…"

'So Doctor, get on and tell us,' I think to myself. 'That's why we called you.'

"I have drawn some blood samples," he continues, imperturbably, "which I will rush to the Med-Lab for analysis. We should have the results by tomorrow afternoon. In the meantime, I will leave some medication that will provide temporary relief. He must drink plenty of water. There is a high degree of dehydration – loss of water from the body – with this excessive sweating." Dr. Castelino opens his bag, leans over and fishes out two small pill containers; he scribbles the dosage of each on a tiny pad of paper, and hands it over to Mom. "I will be back first thing in the morning to check on his condition. You must all try and get a good night's sleep."

It is not what he said, but the somewhat ambiguous and absentminded way he spoke of Dad's illness, that gets Linda and me worried. We had never really seen Dad ill before – no more than a prolonged flu at worst – certainly never like this, not able to speak, eyes glazed and uncommunicative. I have difficulty sleeping that night. Linda and I offer to stay home, but Mom insists she can manage without us and that Linda should not stay home and neither of us must miss school. I feel guilty about going to school.

Dr. Castelino returns the next morning and according to Mom, he spent about 25 minutes with Dad. He returned that afternoon, saying he had received the results of the blood samples, but that he needed fresh blood for further tests. He told Mom he suspected a liver infection, but he couldn't be sure. Meanwhile, Dad was complaining of new back pains. Dr. Castelino wrote a prescription for additional medications.

By day three, there is only a slight improvement. When I enter the room, I am shocked to see how Dad has deteriorated. His skin has turned a sun-faded khaki and its texture feels like parchment.

News of Dad's illness has now spread. Neighbours, relatives, friends and other well-wishers start to arrive; they file through the house in a steady procession with generous offers of any help Mom might need. Some bring food so Mom does not have to cook for the family. Hardev's mother is a constant visitor and companion during the loneliest part of the long days; we love her as she always brings fresh and abundant fruit from their shop in the municipal market.

Goan friends turn up to find out the latest news, which they are in turn feel obliged to disseminate throughout our small tightly knit community. Nobody will say aloud what is going through their minds – that there is a possibility that Dad may not pull through. Linda and I understand that they do not wish to frighten us with such thoughts, so instead, they recount thinly-veiled stories – varied and sometimes quite gruesome – of the ways their own loved ones in Goa and sprinkled across the Goan diaspora in East Africa, have been called away from this Earth, and even as we speak are in Heaven, watching and praying over us, and for Dad's quick recovery. Some visitors will insist on staying behind after the others have left, and recite the Rosary with Mom.

On the fourth day, the results of Dad's latest blood and urine analysis begin to tell a story, according to Dr. Castelino. It is definitely a severe liver infection. He immediately stops some medications and replaces them with alternatives, and prescribes and administers a dose of injections. The fever abates slightly. More drugs are prescribed, more injections given. On the fifth day, the fever starts to go down and stay down, for the first time. A week later the doctor reduces his house calls to once a day, instead of the two daily house calls.

Meanwhile Dad, who has continued to lose weight and now looks like a pale skeleton, begins to recover. Eventually he returns to work and we begin to breathe normally again. Mom is especially relieved. She tells us that this has been the first time he has stayed away from work for more than two days in all the years she has known him.

It is a warm Saturday afternoon some days later. Linda and I are sitting with Dad in the garden. He tells us he plans to do something about the problems at St. Teresa's school as soon as he is back to his full strength. "Now please excuse me, I will go and lie down for a few minutes," he says. I take him by the arm and we go indoors.

When I return I find Mom and Linda talking. I join them. For the first time Mom tells Linda and me how Dad's own father had died.

"One day his father was brought home sick by a colleague from his Government job in Margao, just like Dad was brought home by Uncle Patrick. Just four days of a raging fever and his father was gone forever. Dad was only 15 when your grandfather passed away," Mom says. "That changed their destiny forever. Dad had to drop out of St. Joseph's in Arpora because they couldn't afford to keep him there; both of the two older brothers were forced to go out and find work. That's what pushed your Uncle Nico to seek a new life in Mozambique in Africa."

"It could have happened to us!" Linda says. "We, no, you Lando! You would have to give up school, go to work and support us all.

Imagine that!" A sly look comes into her eyes. "I bet we would all die of starvation in two weeks."

I joust back, "But we could live off your fat for about two years."

Mom raises her hand and tells us to stop bickering. "God has been good to us. Just believe in Him," she says, raising her eyes towards the sky overhead, a view obstructed by the branches of the peach tree. She looks pointedly at me, "Never mind about appearing in church on Sundays. Just have faith, and He will look after you." I wince; she has just made it known that she is aware I missed Sunday mass for the first time last week.

In my spare moments alone, as when I walk to Savio's home or back, or at night before falling asleep, I think of how Dad's illness has affected me in many ways. I realise that while he was ill, I had stopped listening to the BBC with the same obsessive discipline, night after night, and on the occasions that I did, the news was just a recital of more deaths, villages burnt to the ground by the Mau Mau, destruction. The numbers didn't matter anymore. The newspapers reported African deaths in a matter of fact way, but if a white person were attacked, or worse killed, then the Queen in London would probably be woken up in the night to be told the news, I thought. I start to believe that perhaps the British have really lost the war against the Mau Mau; just like the White settlers had begun to claim publicly.

I wonder if worry about the St. Teresa problems was partly responsible for Dad's illness. Having heard about his own father's death I realise now why he is so determined that his children will have a better opportunity at education and a better life. I make a mental note to start thinking of my own future. Linda was right, if something had happened to Dad, and I was to become the only breadwinner… I change topic. I can't deal with all those problems just yet.

On the way to school one day, during Dad's illness, Savio had told me that his father's trip to the Mangu Girls School had to be postponed at the last moment, as some relatives would be arriving on holiday from Uganda. I felt better. It would have been terrible to miss an opportunity to meet Saboti again. It is so difficult without transport and impossible while the law and order situation seemed to be getting from bad to worse.

It is already April. The pace of life seems to get faster and the days rush by.

13

Operation Anvil

April 24, 1954 will be different from other days.

It starts out normal enough – with gloriously sunny weather, the birds singing in the trees, and Stephen whizzing by me on his bicycle at breakneck speed. As usual, he brakes to a dead stop, swings the bike around and rides past again to say "Good morning, nice day, goodbye."

I leave the house together with Dad. Although he is much stronger now, he takes a bus into town instead of walking as he usually did before the illness. Today the bus is very late, so I leave him at the bus stop and walk to Savio's house. At the intersection of Kikuyu Road and Ngara Road, near the Aga Khan Kindergarten, armed British soldiers, supported by Kings African Rifles (KAR) are manning a roadblock. I can see more troops on Ainsworth Hill by the entrance to the museum. From Savio's home, just past the Goan Gymkhana, we walk towards the Ngara crossroads, where the roads coming into the city centre from Thika, Limuru, Muthaiga, Parklands, Eastleigh and Pangani, converge. This is where we catch a bus to our Park Road stop. Normally, this intersection is a bustling bazaar at any time of the day or night, but today roadblocks and barbed wire barriers have transformed the roads. Armed troops and askaris are everywhere. For the first time, British troops are present in large numbers in the city. Every car, whether driven by an African or Asian, is stopped and searched; lorries, especially those carrying labourers seeking work in the city, are pulled off the road completely, their passengers taken off the bus and herded behind barriers. All Africans must produce a *kipande* – ID card. As Savio and I walk past, we see that the detained men are mainly Kikuyus. They watch with fearful eyes from the other side of the barbed wire. Other Africans with proper IDs are permitted to continue on their way.

Savio says, "Lando! Look!" waving his hand at the 'panorama' facing us.

I suddenly realize why everything looks different. "There are no buses today!" I exclaim. I notice other differences. "Not just buses. Look, there are no *matatus* either." I say. "And all the shops are shut." Hundreds of uniform-clad children are walking towards their schools in the vicinity: the Duke of Gloucester Boys School, The Duchess of Gloucester, the Khalsa Girls School, are the main ones.

"Let's walk to school," I tell Savio. "We can take a short cut through the Asian Government quarters, all the way to school. We'll avoid the road blocks."

"But why should we worry?" he asks. "We're not Mau Mau." We decide to walk along the main roads instead, as curiosity gets the better of us.

At every crossing, the scene of the roadblocks and barbed wire fencing around temporary holding pens is repeated. We watch as each detainee is asked a few questions and directed into different groups. They are loaded into army lorries and immediately taken away.

At school, we all crowd around a wealthy Ismailia boy who has brought a battery-operated short-wave radio. It seems all the congested African areas around our school are affected. Eastleigh,

Pangani, Pumwani, and Kariokor areas are completely cordoned off. No one enters. No one leaves. Every access road is blocked.

School closes early. Savio and I are too scared today to wander and explore what is going on. The army is still rounding up detainees and putting them into holding pens. We head straight home.

I hear Simba's bad news bark as I turn into Plums Lane, and brace myself. I hope nothing has happened to Dad. I had left him at the bus stop this morning, but there were no buses today.

"Thank God you're home," Mom greets me. She is nervous and has been crying. "The police have been entering every house in Plums Lane. They are checking all the servants quarters, they say."

"Is Dad home?" I ask.

"Yes. I don't know yet how he got to work, but Dad came back early with Ahmad in his taxi. Linda did not go to school as the buses were cancelled. Dad is with Linda."

"Where?"

"They have gone to the Police Station at Parklands."

"Police Station. Parklands. Why?"

"The askaris took Mwangi away," Mom says, distraught. "They said he is a Mau Mau. They took Wangari as well... and the baby... and Stephen too. The poor boy... he was so frightened. At first he was clinging to his bicycle, watching. Then when he saw the askaris prod Mwangi with their rifle, he let go of the bike and dashed across to me. He was clutching on to my dress, crying bitterly saying he is going to be killed by the police. They are all going to be killed. He's only seven. How do kids hear these things?"

"Does Dad know anyone at Parklands Police Station?" I ask.

"No. I don't think so. But he thought they might know where the prisoners are being taken. I asked the askaris but they refused to say. 'Not your business Memsahib' they told me. They were quite rude."

"Can I go into the servants' quarters? Did the askaris search the place?" I ask.

"I don't know. You go and look. Oh my God. I hope the baby had something to eat before going. Wangari was terrified. She did not speak… just clung to the baby."

I race to the servant quarters. Stephen's bicycle is on the ground outside by the door. Inside, it looks like there has been no time to organise a getaway. The bed is tidy, but the baby's clothes are scattered on it. More clothes, along with a plastic duck, lie on the baby's cot, handed down from Joachim's days. Stephen's clothes are stacked on a shelf, along with Wangari's few possessions. It seems Mwangi has all his belongings hanging on two hooks behind the door. Someone has pulled out an old storage box from under the bed and strewn the contents, perhaps searching for evidence? An enamel bowl on the small table has the remains of porridge, or more likely corn flour gruel.

I rinse the bowl under the tap outside and place it upside down on the table. Inside, I put the contents back into the storage box, and place it on the bed; I sit on the edge. I just cannot believe that Mwangi has even a trace of Mau Mau in him. He is a kind man and has been with our family for almost seven years. In 1947 he had been a casual garden labourer at the nearby Plums Hotel. He had come to gawk with others the day after the burglary, when my dog and best friend, Jolly, was killed by a panga slash across his neck. After the police took our houseboy away, Mwangi stayed behind and dug a grave for Jolly. Three days later he enlisted the help of another labourer, and together they dragged the large rock to Plums Lane and placed it over Jolly's grave. He never asked for a cent in payment. And then he disappeared on other jobs elsewhere. He returned about a year later when he was desperate for work as he was already a father to young Stephen, and Dad took him on immediately. He may be a Kikuyu but I refuse to believe he is a Mau Mau. Nobody in my family does.

Back at the house, Dad and Linda are just coming in from the police station.

"No luck," Dad says. "They say this 'Operation' as they call it, is being handled from the top." I can see Dad is quite tired, especially as he has been ill recently.

"What are we going to do now?" Mom asks. "I keep thinking of those two poor children."

"Why don't we go to the Kingsway Police Station?" I ask as that's the closest to us in the city center. "I'll come with you, Dad."

"Eat something first," Mom says.

Linda takes my hand and squeezes it. "It's so scary. You think the soldiers will hurt them?" I squeeze her hand back.

"How would I know?"

Dad and I gulp down some food; we walk over to Ahmad's flat on the Ngara Road past Savio's house. Ahmad's taxi is not there, but I can see a light in their flat. Dad knocks on the door, while I stay well back in the driveway, so Serena, Ahmad's wife, will see me when she peeps out through the curtains behind the burglar bars. Ahmad told me that Serena always does this because she is still very nervous, as she thinks there is going to be a massacre of innocent people as happened in India and Pakistan at Independence, and she cannot get over what happened in Karachi, when Hindu and Moslem armed mobs attacked each other's communities and millions of innocent people on each side were killed and raped and their homes ransacked and burnt.

Ahmad's black Chevy turns into the gravel driveway just as Serena waves to me from her window. Dad explains to Ahmad what has happened. "I had no idea this raid had occurred when you dropped me home this afternoon," Dad tells Ahmad. We pile into the taxi and a few minutes later we are at Kingsway Central Police Station. The roadblocks are still in place at most intersections.

The Officer on Duty tells us there are no detainees there, but a Sikh Police Inspector recognises Dad from the Bank, and tells him in confidence that Special Forces from Britain are managing this operation. He says Dad may get more information through the Goans working in the Prisons Department. What he has heard in confidence from his Senior Inspector is that detainees are being held in massive detention camps located on the Mombasa Road near Embakasi, and at Manyani and Mackinnon Road, and at a temporary camp at Langata, in Nairobi. It is just after 11:00 p.m. when Ahmad drops us home. Mom and Linda are still up waiting for us to return.

Back in my room I tune in to the BBC. The news is all about 'Operation Anvil' taking place in Nairobi. According to the report, it was carefully planned on the British experience in dealing with Jewish rebels in Palestine prior to 1948. Over 4,000 British troops plus local African contingents had been mobilized during the night, without prior warning.

Savio is shocked to hear that Mwangi and his family have been taken away. His family employed a member of the Kamba tribe, and hence was not among the targets for the Special Forces.

"Funny how when you and I first heard of the Mau Mau, it was something distant upcountry, and now it's here, at school and in our homes," Savio says.

"Yes it's touching us, but it's not funny."

That evening, Uncle Antonio and Aunt Clara come with fresh news. I join the conversation. Dad tells us that the previous day British troops and Askaris had burst into the offices of the Indian High Commissioner's Office in Grogan Road, behind the Norfolk Hotel. They had ransacked the office, taken some papers and arrested all the African staff.

"Why would they do that?" Uncle asks him.

"It looks like they really want to clean-up the Kikuyus," Dad says. "Perhaps a much-wanted Mau Mau suspect is using the diplomatic cover of the Commission, though I am not sure if it enjoys the same immunity as an Embassy. I think they may be seriously after Pio."

"Anton and Emma's Son?"

"Yes. I heard JM Nazareth say that the Government is convinced Pio is a Communist," Dad says, "especially after his recent attacks criticising the Emergency Powers. The White settlers will never agree with those ideas he preaches about land reform or to anything like that. JM said that only last week Pio was warned by the Attorney General's office for again publicly supporting the Mau Mau's demands, even if Pio has made it clear he does not approve of their methods."

"But why would they attack the Indian High Commission?"

"Antonio, ever since you fell in love, you have lost touch with the news and politics," Dad jokes, while Aunt Clara blushes profusely at the transformation she has wrought. "Pio's been working for the East African Indian National Congress and it is well known that Apa Pant, the Indian High Commissioner, gave him a typewriter and stationery to set up his office. Many people believe Nehru may be funnelling funds through Pant, to help Kenya's 'freedom fighters' as they are now calling themselves, and Pio is the go-between with the Mau Mau leadership. I know for certain they won't find Pio at the High Commission. He's too smart to hang around there."

I am relieved at Dad's comment. I feel Pio is ours – Savio's and mine. He says so many things about fairness and justice that I believe are right. "Why not, Dad? Why won't the troops find Pio?" I ask.

"He works out of an office at the Desai Memorial Library on Fort Hall Road," Dad says. "He does his personal banking with us at the National Bank of India."

Mom serves dinner and after dinner Uncle and Aunt Marta leave.

That night the BBC reports that Operation Anvil continues in full swing in Nairobi. The government believes that it has finally broken the back of the Mau Mau. Many thousands of people are taken into detention; some will be released if they are above suspicion; others will be questioned further. A Colonial Office spokesman says 'these beasts that have been terrorising innocent women and children and coming in the way of progress of the nation, will be exterminated once and for all'.

Going to school without Stephen's break-neck ride and cheerful greeting is a terrible feeling. It is like death has visited our household and we must undergo a period of mourning until we find out more. Over the days following the April 24 raid at Plums Lane, Dad searches for clues of Mwangi's whereabouts, through his Goan network in the prisons and police. He tells us of his progress at dinner each night. He has met with Azevedo at the CID, and with Pinto at Special Branch. He has been repeatedly informed that everything in connection with Operation Anvil is 'hush hush for security reasons' and only a select few European officers have the facts and know the destination of detainees. After two attempts he meets up with 'Prisons D'Souza', the club member who had brought Pio and his brother to the Goan Gymkhana that night Savio and I first set eyes on Pio. I was so shocked at the news Dad gave I can only reconstruct Dad's version of the conversation:

"You've probably heard by now about Pio?" Prisons De Souza asks Dad.

"No, what happened?"

"He was picked up this morning. He asked for Fitz D'Souza to represent him. I know they're together now. It may be just a move to frighten Pio into keeping his mouth shut."

"Does Emma know? Oh my God. They've just been recently married."

"Emma has been told and a car has gone out for her," De Souza replies. "I am keeping in touch with this one. You know how close Pio and I are. Known him since we were kids and then in boarding school in Arpora for eight years."

"Won't they have to have a trial to detain Pio?" Dad asks.

"Not under the State of Emergency. The Government can pretty much do whatever it pleases, with or without a trial. They will probably detain him in one of our more remote prisons while he cools his heels and they decide what to do. The government is desperate to show results and the settlers are braying for blood," De Souza says.

By the time Operation Anvil is over almost a month later, about 7,000 troops in all were involved, we hear. Between 60,000 and 70,000 persons, mainly Kikuyus, have received intensive security screening and some have been released. At least 27,000 or more, which we presume includes our dear Mwangi and family, are locked away somewhere, without trial. The numbers do not mean anything anymore.

Within a few weeks, there is a wave of revulsion against the colonial government. Some influential Kikuyus – close relatives of the Senior Chiefs, loyal to the Government, have also been picked up in Operation Anvil and sent away. They protest furiously. *Their* relatives and supporters were not expected to be touched by the security forces.

Anglican and Catholic missions complain that some of their staff have gone missing. Within days, even the BBC begins to report about the alleged accusations against the Government's mistreatment of prisoners, the senseless beatings and physical abuse and sodomisation of male detainees; the rape and beating of females by African guards and loyalists, working under orders of their white officers. High-ranking members of Parliament in London make speeches and ask questions about the Government's alleged abuse of fundamental principles of justice and of the basic rule of law.

For me, the arrest and detention of Pio Gama Pinto, and the total disappearance of Mwangi and family, without trace or means of contact, is the last straw. I find myself listening to the Government's claims of progress in security bulletins now with some distrust, and reading the local papers with more scepticism.

Exactly a month after the launching of Operation Anvil, freedom fighters burn the Treetops Hotel near Mount Kenya, to cinders. This is where the young Princess Elizabeth and Prince Philip had spent a night during the Royal Visit of 1952 to view wildlife at a natural saltlick in the Aberdare forest. It was from Treetops that the young Princess had descended the next morning as Queen of Great Britain and Empress of the British Empire.

It was reported later that the Mau Mau fighters, unable to sustain the pressure of security forces to flush them out of the townships and villages, had fled into the forests. They had gone into hiding around Mount Kenya and in the Aberdare range. When the government declared these areas restricted zones only accessible to the armed services, and sent in troops after them, the going got more difficult. The KAR established bases inside the forests and nature reserves. When the KAR began to use Treetops as a security forest lookout to hunt the terrorists, the Mau Mau decided there was no choice but to destroy it.

I am shocked at hearing the news about the destruction of Treetops. In a way I can see why the Mau Mau had done it, but to me it was someplace special, because it was now part of history where the Princess had turned Queen. I ask Savio about it on the way to school.

"Not our history but hers." He is unusually curt, and I am a bit taken aback. "The Queen's not like the Pope, with one residence in the Vatican," he adds, "She has many palaces and country homes around the Commonwealth." Savio sits back in the bus and glances out of the window. It is not like him to make comments and then retreat into his own thoughts; he has been doing so more recently.

I shrug it off. I remember how Ahmad and Uncle Antonio also became a bit grumpy for a while when they fell in love. Maybe love does that to people. Stan had also noticed a change in Savio. "Lando, but didn't you know Savio has fallen in love?" Stan has emerged as our 'expert' in all matters pertaining to love.

"No. I never even suspected it." I decide to ask him, but Savio does not go home with me that day. Instead, he goes home with Brian to the Asian Government Quarters; he tells me they are working on a project together.

At the Ngara Roundabout, I meet Linda getting off the bus. She is bursting with excitement.

"Lando, guess what!" She says. "Do you remember about those brothels on First Avenue by St. Teresa's Church that I told you about?"

"Yeah. What about them?

"It seems Operation Anvil cleared them all out. The boys in our class told us all the buildings have been boarded up. The people are gone."

"Thank God for that," I say. "Your last few months and then it's goodbye forever. You're so lucky. I still have another year to go." We walk home together and talk about Mwangi and his family. Dad still has received no news from enquiries through the Goan network in Prisons and Police. It's always the same answer: "This is being handled by the special security forces."

14

The Enemy Within

An early morning drizzle has given way to a break in the clouds and a weak-looking sun is trying to break through, as Savio and I get off the bus at Park Road and walk the short distance to Tech High. Everything seems normal after the July Break; students stream in through the front entrance with the usual backslapping and loud greetings.

Inside the quadrangle, more students are milling around. The Hindu and Muslim students seem more excited to be back than the Sikhs and the Goans.

"Why are you so happy?" I ask Arun, one of my classmates.

"I like school. At home we have no freedom. There is always somebody checking on you – mother, father, uncles and grand-mother, all living together. Everyone wants to be boss. 'Arun! What are you doing? Why no school so long? Arun, go read your books, you must study!' Also they give you jobs to do all day. 'Arun! Come help me.' Frankly for me, school is the best place to rest." Savio's big grin tells me he's eavesdropping us.

I am happy to be back with my friends too, as only Savio and I have met during the holidays. There is a heightened buzz of conversation, which quickly dies down as the Headmaster and his entourage of teaching staff parade onto the podium.

Mr. Stewart welcomes us all and talks about the challenges ahead and the few short months before the final exams of 1954. "The recent Operation Anvil by the security forces has been a big disruption to our program," he says. "We lost some of our African workers, and many have not returned. Fortunately we can now heave a sigh of relief that the worst is over, so please try your best not to be distracted further." We are dismissed.

"Distracted?" Brian drawls in his deep voice, as we walk to our classrooms. "The old boy has no idea of what distraction is." Savio, Stan and Olaf laugh at Brian's comment. I do too. We had been discussing the distraction of puberty and sex just before school broke up for the holidays.

While the Mau Mau was encroaching on our lives from the outside, puberty had been encroaching on us from the inside, creating havoc within our bodies. Looking at each other, we suddenly realized that all of us were experiencing its awkward effects. I had felt my body grow unexpectedly, awkward and lanky. The sudden growth seemed to stretch my skin and flesh to fit over the bony frame, making me skinny with big knobs for knees, like a giraffe. Olaf's body went the same way and so did Brian's; in fact he was the lankiest. In our school uniform with short pants the knobbly knees stood out. Stan and Savio broke out in pimples, just at the time they started to sprout fine soft fuzzy beards, so they could not shave. We joked that if we looked like giraffes, then they looked like wildebeest.

Stan admitted he had discovered profuse hair growth on parts of his body, and has been having strange dreams and has had to go to confession often. We all talked about the hair growth, and what we assumed was a 'hardening of the arteries'. We had heard that it is an affliction affecting older men and yet we were definitely experiencing an unexpected and sometimes embarrassing hardening, so this must be it. These problems were never discussed at home, so we had all been to Confession it seems, and we must have success-fully avoided bumping into each other by going at odd times and to different churches, where the priests didn't know our parents.

About six months earlier, Savio and I had acquired an insatiable interest in photography at the Goan Gymkhana library. Normally we would walk through the anteroom with its newspapers and magazines, and then into a rear reading room lined with book-shelves, including a special section with children's books. There we would do our homework before proceeding to the hall for table tennis. But one day the front page of The Daily Mirror newspa-per caught our attention. It was a black and white photograph printed on yellow paper. 'Miss Bikini' was the winner of the Miss Europe Beauty contest. We studied the lines of her body, the light-ing angles; grain of the photograph, and other aspects of photog-raphy that we discussed at our Photo Club at school, albeit with less attractive subject matter. We began to look at similar photo-graphs in other magazines and newspapers. There was a big choice: The London Illustrated, Life Magazine, The National Geographic and weekly editions of foreign newspapers from Goa, India and the UK, and local newspapers like the Goan Voice and the East African Standard. Glancing rapidly through these became a rou-tine; though it was the Daily Mirror that captured our attention for the sheer beauty of the photographs, and details of salacious scandals in Britain. We would devour these and then we would go to Confession.

One of the volunteer librarians must have found us out; at some point we discovered that the pages with the more risqué photographs were being carefully folded over in both the Daily Mirror and Tidbits magazine. We found this to be a big time-saver as we went directly to the folded pages thereafter. Then we went to Confession at St. Francis Xavier Church in Parklands.

And it was Confession that focused our collective attention. We had just finished eating our sandwiches on the second-last day of the term, when Olaf opened up the subject that was clearly troubling him.

"Have any of you blokes been to Father Butler for confessions lately?"

"I have," I said.

"And was he tough? With penance I mean?"

"The usual 20 Hail Marys."

"I got two rosaries—two rosaries, can you imagine?" Olaf told us how he had inadvertently been caught fondling himself and his mother had screamed at him and sent him off to Confession. Father Butler was not amused, and besides the two rosaries, gave him the full-unexpurgated version of fire and brimstone that would immediately engulf Olaf if he ever did that again. A long discussion had followed as we all exchanged our experiences, before heading into the holidays.

Now, back to school again, we are eating our packed lunches at our usual place on a picnic table under a jacaranda tree, by the woodwork shop. Olaf is bursting with news he wants to share. "Listen you blokes. I have been researching some important information for you, which my Dad let me read from his medical books." He pulls out a paper from his pocket and starts to read: "The hypothalamus is located between the eyes and is part of the brain. It is linked to the pituitary gland by a stalk, hanging from it. Gonadotropin hormone is released to the pituitary gland to instruct it to release its hormones, which then instruct the testes to produce sperm in men and produce more hormones called testosterone that will turn boys into adults." He looks up. "In other words, it's all to do with hormones that we are having all the trouble, and we have been going to confessions, when in fact it is God who made us this way."

"I still don't understand what you read out," Savio says.

"I do. It says that men's brains are connected to their balls and we can use either one to think with." I get a laugh, but Stan brings up a bigger issue that has taken second place to our worries about the Mau Mau.

"I've been thinking…"

"About time," at least two voices interrupt him.

"Seriously. When we left the Goan School, we lost contact with our female classmates, except maybe at the club socials. Meanwhile our male ex-classmates have the pick of girlfriends and future wives. What will happen if there are no Goan girls left for us?"

There is a moment of silence as we realise the implications of Stan's comment.

"I'm OK," Savio says. "You blokes think about it." This is his first public admission of being in love.

"What about that convent school in Mangu, near Thika?" Brian asks. "I know that many of my Dad's colleagues in the civil service are now sending their daughters there, instead of completing their high school in Goa."

"Why don't we visit the school?" I ask. I am sure Saboti had said she went to a Catholic boarding school at Mangu near Thika. This would be a chance to see her again. We discuss details of getting there. Stan has a neighbour whose son has just obtained his driving licence and is looking for excuses to get as much practice as possible. It is agreed that Stan and I will visit and report on the availability of girls for our future wives.

We return to class. It has been a very intensive and informative first day.

I confess to being very excited about a trip to Mangu. I imagine Saboti now, much taller, her skin smooth and a dark olive, her deep piercing eyes even darker and more intense; her hair will probably have turned a bit redder or maybe it has bleached in the sun? I imagine her smile and I wonder if she will be happy to see me again; it has been more than five years since we first met.

About two weeks later, Gurmeet Singh, just-turned 16, drives Stan and me to the Mangu school near Thika in his two-door 1951 Ford Anglia. Gurmeet, with a 'devil may care' air about him, is carefully groomed – his beard neatly tucked into a net, and a crisp blue turban. From the back seat, I can tell Gurmeet's raging hormones are operating at their peak – not a good thing on the busy Thika Road. "Please slow down, Gurmeet," Stan also begs him to do so, from the front passenger seat.

I have a reasonably good view of the rolling landscape, still green from the recent rains. I have been on this road before and seen much of it in shades of straw beige; and patches of dried red earth, thirsty for a drop of rain. Soon coffee farms on the outskirts of Nairobi give way to clusters of grass-roofed mud huts surrounded by clumps of bananas, cassava shrubs and corn stalks that dot the countryside. Occasional bright flame trees seem to sprout into view, as do distant views of green grey sisal plantations, and closer in, a neatly laid-out pineapple plantation in its early stages of development. In the distance we see the township of Thika surrounded by clumps of trees. I feel my heart is beating faster.

I imagine Saboti's school will be something like my boarding school in Goa – white plastered buildings with arched arcades, covered with red Mangalore tile roofs and thick wood frame balconies. She has no idea I am coming; I wonder how we will find her when we arrive? I can't wait to see her again.

Gurmeet slams on the brakes. "I think we just missed the turnoff," he says. He backs the car, ignoring other traffic, and swings into a gravel road; a painted white signpost reads 'Mangu Girls Convent 1.3 miles'.

We drive up to the main entrance and park. Groups of girls in twos and three are about. Some are sitting on rough benches dotted about on the edge of the gravel; others sit on the grass in the shade. In the background girls go about their business, whatever it is, on a sunny Saturday morning; I catch a glimpse of a nun flitting between two buildings. Stan climbs out first, stretches himself to his full height and flexes his well-developed muscles, hoping, I suppose, that this display will have the girls rushing towards us.

"Gurmeet, please let me out," I remind him. He climbs out of the driver's seat, tilts the driver's seat forward and I get up and stretch. Three girls nearest to the car are watching us. One of them, her hair in a ponytail, walks towards us. "Can I help you?" she says with a welcoming smile. I can tell she is Goan.

"Hello…yes please," Stan introduces himself. "And this is Lando and Gurmeet. We are here to count the number of Goan girls…" He hesitates. The girl does not. She is already signalling her companions to join her.

"I'm Cynthia," she says, "and this is Sylvie and this is Anita." We all shake hands.

"Do you know one of your schoolmates called Saboti?" I ask.

"Saboti? Saboti who? What's her surname?"

"Surname? She never told me her surname."

"Is she Goan?"

"No, not Goan. She is from the Seychelles."

"About one third of the school are Seychellois, another third Goan, and the rest are 'nusu-nusu' you know, half and half – of mixed race – half white and half African."

"I think she has an older sister also at this school. Her name is Estelle," I feel a panic setting in. What if nobody knows Saboti? Why would she want to mislead me?

"I know," Anita speaks up. "I know Estelle and she had a sister a year or two younger. Her name was Bernadette or Grace…I think. I used to meet her in the ironing room on Saturdays. They both left the school about 18 months ago… said they were being transferred to a school in Eldoret."

I can feel my heart drop to the ground. Fortunately Stan takes over the conversation with Cynthia who is tall and seems very self-confident. She tells us there are about 13 Goan girls in all, mainly daughters of civil servants working in remote areas in the Provinces, far away from access to good Catholic schools. She invites us into the lounge, but we decline.

"Let's walk around the grounds," Stan says, "it's such a beautiful day."

Sylvie, the one with pouty lips and long, well brushed black hair, seems to know most of the girls. Her parents live in Uganda, but she had previously been sent to school in Mombasa, until Mangu opened its doors to Goan girls. She starts to recite the names of the other girls, as Stan pulls out a small notepad from his shirt pocket.

We walk along the outside of the main two-storied buildings that make up the boarding and tuition blocks, as the girls alternatively make comments.

"That's the Church. We have our own priest. He looks after our needs and those of the sisters; and that's the main dormitory house," Cynthia says. "On the upper floor are the infirmary, the sisters' quarters and eight dormitories." She points to the cement block structure roofed with Mangalore tiles.

"Here on the ground floor is the dining hall," Sylvia takes over. "That doubles as a study hall and auditorium for concerts and performances, and the restrooms, lockers and kitchen are also on the ground floor."

Anita is the one who looks most grown up. She has an attractive face and body and a mischievous tone to her voice. She walks with her back straight that shows off her profile best. I can sense she is self-conscious and knows I have been taking side-glances at her. As we are turning the corner of the main building, she says to me, pointing, "You see that long veranda that runs along the back of the dorms? That's where we sit out and study on weekends."

"I heard someone mention a basement," I say, trying to make conversation, although inside I feel a deep vacuum over not seeing Saboti.

"It's in that part of the building, under the showers. At one end there is a 'pit fire' run on kerosene. The room smells awful of course because of the fumes. There are three small irons sitting on hot metal, and you have to be fast securing a place on Saturday mornings."

"Does that mean you have all done your ironing?" I ask.

"No. It means we are waiting until everyone has done theirs." Cynthia interjects.

"Does that coffee belong to the school?" Gurmeet asks, pointing to the vast coffee plantation that seems part of the school grounds.

"Yes. The nuns run that part of the business."

"And the orchard? It seems very productive."

"That too. Sometimes a few girls will raid it, but if they are caught they get the pit latrine treatment." Cynthia says.

"What's that?" I ask.

"Cleaning the pit latrines. You don't want me to start on that. Please change the subject," she says.

"OK. What's the food like?" I ask, recalling my Goa boarding school days.

"Awful. But it keeps us going. At mealtimes we are allowed as much bread as we want, so we sometimes make sandwiches with pickles that some of the Goan girls smuggle in, and then go among the coffee bushes and snack."

As we are preparing to leave, Anita comes up to me, "So you don't remember me Lando?" I look at her. Her eyes have that sparkle of someone about to let you into a secret.

"I was your sister Fatima's classmate at the Goan School. I played the part of the Blessed Virgin in the Christmas play at the Goan Gymkhana in 1948. I was 7 then. You were one of the Three Wise Men. Remember?"

"Oh yes! Now I remember. You picked up my broomstick—my staff—when it slipped and fell on Saint Joseph."

We thank them and climb into Gurmeet's car for the drive back to Nairobi.

"You know, in my community, we are not allowed to talk freely like that to girls," Gurmeet says. "Lando, please tell me more of your Saboti girl."

"Please not now, Gurmeet. Someday later." If only he knew what disappointment I was feeling.

"Hey Lando," Stan is enthusiastic. "I have just been going over my notes. We can tell the boys we are in fine shape as far as girls are concerned. There's thirteen of them, and only five of us, if we leave Savio out as he is already in love."

"That's two each, and three to spare." I say. "Thank God we don't have that *matata* to sort out."

———•◦•———

16

A Fork in the Road

For me the trip to the Mangu School was more than an interesting day out in the country; it was a shock that went deep into my insides. I think I will never again see Saboti. She has disappeared forever with no address or contact. I feel as if I have lost a precious possession; I can't say that… I never owned her. But she was precious to me.

It is Sunday, barely 24 hours later, and I have just returned from my walk with Simba. He seems to sense I am sad and stays close, which to him must mean pushing his whole weight on me, to the point of knocking me over. I push back; I grab him by the side of his neck and massage his neck; he raises his head and moves it from side to side.

"So you want the full works!" I run my hand along the ridge of his back. He likes that.

"I wish someone would massage *my* neck," Linda has come out into the garden and has sat down with her schoolbooks. "The grass looks quite dry. Are you going to water it?" I look up. She has had her head down, absorbed in her work. It is the last term for her before she will finish high school.

"Maybe. How's it going? "I ask.

"Just a slog really. No easy way out." Linda says.

"What then?"

"Dad and Mum don't want me to go to the UK. They say it is dangerous for single young girls. And India is out of the question for me, as I'm not interested."

"I am worried too," I say. "Dad is starting that matata again about what are my future plans and why can't I make up my mind like everyone else, and am I not leaving it too late and don't come back later and blame Mom and him, etc. etc. You know what I mean?"

"Yeah."

"Linda, I went with Stan and his friend Gurmeet, to visit the Mangu School," I say. "Saboti is not there."

"What? Saboti? Isn't that the little girl with the doll that you met over the fence at Uncle's in Nakuru on the way to Kisumu, before going to boarding school?" She looks at me, bewildered, as she pulls off the band holding her hair up; the deep black locks fall down to her shoulders.

"Yes. I thought she would still be there – a little older maybe."

"Lando, you're grown up now. That's puppy love. You were both puppies then. Puppies!"

"So?"

"You're a big dog now – big like Simba. Tell him Simba!" I see him cock his ears as he hears his name and listens to Linda rant.

"Woof!" I can't tell whether he agrees with Linda, or is saying, 'you leave my friend to grieve alone'.

"Forget about Saboti, Lando – she will follow where life leads her. You must decide what you are doing with your life." She looks at Dad's watch that she has borrowed to time her prep work. "I must go back to my room."

I wait a little longer in the garden. From next door I can hear Niven's happy laughter with the little boy next door. I know he too misses Stephen. Dad has had no news of Mwangi and family. He tells us he has been given the names of various Senior Europeans to write to: Ian Henderson at Police Headquarters; Pat Shaw in Special Branch; a Robert Harrison, Assistant Prisons Superintendent, and others. Dad duly sends these letters but nobody answers – eight letters so far.

Monday morning. Another drizzly day! At school Stan reports to the rest of our group about the trip. Mengha is lunching with us. He smiles and stands up at the mention of girls. "You Goans should follow our system. It is all arranged by the parents." He walks away to join his other friends. Stan continues his report. There is an audible sigh of relief at the news that with a ratio of 2:1 girls to boys, there will be enough girls to marry one day, but for now there are more pressing problems. We discuss the latest bombshell in the guise of our revised timetables delivered earlier that morning. "We have to make up for lost 'Mau Mau days', and still compensate for all those multiple religious holidays," is how the class teacher, Mr. Walker, had phrased it.

Those of us in the "first batch" of students at the school have been divided into two different streams between those who will go into "commerce" and train as accountants, auditors and the like; and the "technical" streams for those students seeking to follow mechanical and civil engineering, surveying, construction and such like. Now within our group, we see less of each other, since Stan, Brian and I have chosen the technical stream. Olaf, Savio and Romeo are leaning towards commerce.

I have become bosom pals with Mengha, who first gained notoriety in our class, and introduced himself to me, by shooting a missile at the back of my neck during my first week at Tech High. We share stories. Once, I told him about the time Savio and I had seen the body of a dead man behind the Norfolk Hotel near the museum. "I have never been to the museum," he had said. He brings it up now.

"My parents did not take us there, all the way from Eastleigh, as my father is always working, and when he's home he wants to rest;

but I think it is because they don't speak English or maybe Dad is still afraid of the *Muzungus*."

"We can go together," I say.

A few days later, accompanied by Simba, we visit the Coryndon Memorial Museum. In the lane leading up to the front entrance, I am on the constant lookout for the pack of Dalmatians, especially as we walk past the Leakeys' residence. The old *Mbwa Kali* (savage dog) notice is there, but no sign of the dogs. I wonder if the Leakeys and dogs have fled to a secret destination, after Dr. Louis Leakey betrayed Jomo Kenyatta at his trial.

We leave Simba by the entrance and enter the building. When we enter the central hall with the high ceiling, Mengha is curious about everything; he is just like a small boy, although he tells me he is a year older than me. He was born in Punjab, and came out with his older sisters and their mother to Nairobi in 1939. We move slowly through the Mammals and Reptiles, by which time I am exhausted; but he is interested in Birds as well. I look at my watch as it is getting late and it will soon be dark. "Shall we come back another time for the rest?"

"No, no Lando – please just this last hall." It is the Botany Collection. We browse quickly past all the paintings of the plants and flowers found in Kenya. "Look." He stops at the display of polished natural woods grown in Kenya. "Elgon olive!" he says, pointing to a lightwood with deep grey veins running through it… "Mahogany, Mvuli… look, Podo". He runs his fingers over each one; he is familiar with construction woods.

Finally we leave. Simba jumps up to greet us and breaks into a little jig of happiness. I invite Mengha to the nearby Goan Gymkhana, where we buy two Cokes and split a packet of potato crisps, as we do not have enough money between us for two. We talk about his father's construction business, and he invites me to visit their workshop; finally he returns to his home in Eastleigh.

The following Saturday, Mengha takes me to his family's construction workshop off Quarry Road, a short walk from the school.

It is located in an area I would never have ventured into on my own, tucked between a dense African commercial area called Kariokor, and an industrial edge of the city centre. Numerous workshops sit cheek by jowl along this twisted, sloping road, its bitumen surface badly broken up and its shoulders littered with parked vans and pick-up trucks, broken down cars, and handcarts. Clusters of African workers crowd around lean-to corrugated roofs that provide shade to vendors of tea and roasted corn, on one side of the road. "That side is for Africans," Mengha points out. "Asians eat on this side," he signals with his thumb at a small patio serving chapattis and vegetarian dishes and chai – cumin-spiced tea – and sodas.

"The one with the big beard is called Angelo," Mengha tells me. He and the other tall one are cousins – Anglo-Indian car mechanics." We pass a 'Carpenters and Joiners' workshop. "Do you know Avtar, who is in Savio's class? That's his father's workshop." We walk past a bunch of workers welding intricate metal iron railings by a wrought-iron sign that reads 'Metalworkers and Ironmongers'. "Do you know Fazal in our class?" Mengha asks. "His father supplies glass to all the contractors around here." We pass the window glass suppliers and stand in front of a 'Plumbers and Ceramic and Marble suppliers' sign.

"I remember someone telling us that the Tech High was built mainly to receive the sons of Indian building contractors," I tell Mengha.

"Yes," he says. "I know all these sons of contractors at our school. We were together at the Park Road Primary. Only you *Machli* – fish-eating Goans – came from somewhere else." He stops and points to the sign 'Jaswant Singh and Bros. Building Contractors and Fine Woodwork'. "This is my family's workshop".

His uncle, introduced to me as 'Lachman', greets me in Punjabi and a *Namaste*, and waves us on. Mengha's workshop is a large shed-like single-storey structure, built in rough-chiselled grey stone blocks. From the timber roof structure, all manner of cables, wires, hooks and brackets hold other supplies, tools and appliances.

"Come here." Mengha leads the way to the rear of the workshop. The backspace is divided into two small offices. "The large glass panels keep out the noise of machines, and at the same time, they allow Father or Uncle to watch for visitors," he says, "and also supervise the workers." One section of the shop is framed to allow for storage of solid wood planks and plywood sheets. "Be careful there." Mengha steers me around a woodturning lathe, where a worker is turning a post of some sort. I love it here. I recognise all the machines from our school workshop, except ours are newer versions.

As were walk around an electric plane and a circular saw in a large space, a grey-bearded Sikh man walks towards us. He signals Mengha to continue the 'tour'. "We need the space here to allow for large pieces of wood to be turned around and for safety. You know what these are." He waves at two workbenches, equipped with vices and clamps, and turns around to introduce me to his dad, Mr. Jaswant Singh Juttla.

We shake hands. "Nice to meet you, Mr. Juttla, sir," I mumble. I can tell from his eyes, and the way he looks at Mengha, that he is a kind, proud father.

Mr. Juttla says something to Mengha in Punjabi. While they're chatting, I walk slowly around the store, inhaling the smells of freshly cut or planed wood. It mingles with the aroma of resin glue, which is always on the boil. Along both walls, vertical frames are secured to the wall. A series of cross pieces provide space for more hooks and clamps, against which are placed all manner of hand tools needed for the trade.

Mengha's father speaks only in Urdu and Punjabi to Mengha, and in Swahili to me, pointing out things. I reply in Swahili. He tells me that he and Lachman Singh, Mengha's uncle, came out to Africa at the age of 12, to work with Mengha's grandfather, a cabinet carpenter for the Railways.

"We have been working for 34 years," he says. "Mengha must finish school soon and help us." Mr. Juttla invites me to come back often. "Come here every Saturday. We will teach you more wood-working than you learn at school."

Mengha walks back with me to the intersection of Ngara Road and Park Road, from where I catch a bus to the Ngara roundabout.

On the bus, I mull over his father's words: 'We have been working for 34 years, Mengha must finish school soon and help us'. Father and son are in a 'chicken-and-egg' situation. Mengha cannot have a choice about an alternative future, and his father cannot retire before Mengha has finished his Senior Cambridge. Most Goans, with our parents employed in the civil service and banks, and generally working for a wage, have more choices, but only if they leave the country and go to the UK or India.

There is a college under construction in Nairobi, but no one really knows if it will open in time for us in 1956, or for that matter, what courses will be available. I know Dad is worried about my future, but so is everyone else's dad. None of us at Tech High have made firm plans yet.

The buzz of activity as the bus approaches the Ngara shops distracts my thoughts. The pavements are crowded with people, mainly Indian shoppers and African workers. It is as if Operation Anvil has meant the end of the Mau Mau; perhaps the Governor will make an official announcement about this. I get off the bus and walk home.

As I turn into Plums Lane, I am filled by sadness. It was in this spot that young Stephen would every weekday morning race his bicycle past me, brake, swing around and say, 'Good Morning, have a nice day'. I hope he is OK – I cannot imagine the life of a seven-year-old in a terrorist detention camp.

Perhaps when I finish high school, I should do something to help the Africans have a better life. I could be a politician like Pio Gama Pinto, but that would be a short career, if the British locked me up too. Simba's barking reminds me that he too is locked up. I unleash him and we go for a quick walk.

"Dad was looking for you," Linda greets me on my return. "They're out visiting the Almeidas – back in an hour."

"What about?"

"Dunno. I have my own problems." She smiles and goes back to her room; she has just two months to sit the Senior Cambridge School Certificate exam.

When Dad returns we have a little discussion on my future plans. Dad has assembled information on universities in India and England. I realise how our parents want us to have a better life, but also I am not ready to decide. "Why won't you decide?" Dad pleads. "These are good colleges from which you can choose business, medicine, law or sciences. Why is it so difficult to choose? We are willing to make the sacrifice financially."

"Sorry Dad, I am not yet sure what I want to do," I say. "Also you and Mom must look after the rest of the family too – boarding school in Goa was enough for me." I stand up. "Dad, please don't worry about me. I'll find my way in life as you did."

Dad starts to walk away. I feel a deep sense of guilt at taking such a firm stand with him, but I feel I am grown up now, "I don't want any more help Dad, thank you." I take the papers and go to my room. Later that day I overhear Dad say to Mom, "Perhaps we should have kept him in boarding school with the Jesuits – they would have straightened him out by now." I fall asleep.

At school, the pressure is on. The year is coming to a close, but I continue to visit Mengha's workshop. His dad welcomes my friendship with Mengha as we speak English between us and it helps Mengha improve his facility in that language. By November, Jaswant Singh ventures speaking English to me for the first time.

"Mengha good student Lando? He doing homework? Mengha clever boy?"

"Very clever," I reply. "He works very hard. Mengha's among the best student in class and my best friend." His father's kind and wrinkled face, beams with pleasure.

"He must join us soon here. Uncle Lachman and I are getting old."

"Only one more year to go Mr. Juttla," I reassure him. He smiles.

As I leave them, I can't help thinking that the weight of an extra year on a working life of 34 is a lot more than a year added to my life at 15.

———••——

16

Finally a Career Choice

Something is already different about the Christmas of 1954. Attendance at Midnight Mass on Christmas Eve is out of the question because of the prevailing security situation. Nobody really knows if the Mau Mau has been finally defeated. It is a crowded St. Francis Xavier Church on Christmas morning, but I manage to squeeze into a pew about five rows from the rear. The interior is inspiring as the sun outside fires up the stained glass windows casting coloured shafts of light criss-crossing over the congregation below. The Ladies Altar Committee has decorated the church beautifully with fresh flowers; and the choir fills the air with joyous Christmas hymns. The service moves on with all the solemnity of a Christmas High Mass. The congregation arises for the singing of another hymn, and as it comes to an end, we sit back to listen to the sermon that will follow. I feel a prod in my back as if someone has decided to kneel forward with hands clasped.

I turn around to apologise, "I'm sorry."

"It's okay," she says with a mischievous smile. It was no accidental prod. Anita from the Mangu girls' school is sitting directly behind me. She was the one I thought looked most grown up, meaning her tell-tale bumps were more developed than the other two girls. I remember her long straight well-brushed black hair, held back from her face with a blue band. I smile back.

Father Butler climbs the pulpit but I miss most of what he says; my concentration has been ruined and various thoughts are racing through my mind. I smile to myself when I remember Olaf's short lecture on the raging hormones that have now attacked our bodies and infiltrated our brains. I remind myself I am in church. As I look up, Father Butler is asking the congregation to pray for the hundreds of innocent people being held by the Government in detention camps throughout Kenya without trial. I pay attention. For the first time in Kenya, the Catholic Church has started to criticise the Government's treatment of prisoners. I say a prayer for Mwangi and his family. Little Stephen must be missing his bicycle terribly. The sermon over, the mass continues. I watch Anita go up the aisle to receive Holy Communion. She walks with a straight back displaying her self-confidence. As she passes my pew, she smiles. Again I feel a dig into my back as she kneels – it happens two more times before mass is over.

We meet briefly on the porch after the service. I see Anita's mother keeping a watchful eye a short distance away, but I avoid eye contact. I shake her hand. She squeezes mine. "Do you remember me, Lando?" she asks. "Will I see you at the club?"

"Yes," I reply. "Yes to both. Definitely will see you… at the club."

I am a bit overwhelmed. I used to think it was the boy that made these moves. Later, when I tell Linda what happened at church, she says, "Yes, the Goan world may be changing with the times. But isn't Anita still a tot? How old is she?"

"I haven't got as far as that yet," I say. "Ask me after the Christmas Dance."

At the dance, Anita introduces Savio, Olaf and me to her friends: Rosie, Pam and Veronica. And I also get to meet her mother. "Anita tells me you are a good dancer," her mother says. "My Anita loves to dance, and she is not even 15."

"That's more than I can do, and I am over 15," I reply. She seems happy.

We all become part of a group partying together. No one touches alcohol, as we are all under-age. Linda will be happy to hear Anita is not a tot; she is a year younger then me, which makes her exactly 14 and 7 months. Anita and I meet with the others again at the 'Boxing Day Sundowner'. This is a cheerful but modest event where club members mainly meet and greet each other. The big night is on New Year's Eve. The club hall is magnificently decorated for the festive season; hundreds of balloons have been blown and now wait patiently in a big fishing net up on the ceiling for the moment they can be set free and come floating down at midnight. I notice that this year fewer men are dressed in the traditional dinner jackets and black trousers with the silk stripe down the legs, and the starched shirts and black silk bowties. "There seem to be fewer older members this time," I say to Savio and Olaf.

"Many members are nervous to come out at night because of the Mau Mau," Savio says. But it's still crowded."

'Cooty and his Supersonics', one of Nairobi's best bands, is playing dance numbers for the younger generation, who I notice are changing the traditional dress code; the men are wearing dark suits instead of the traditional black tie. The ladies however continue wearing long dresses in a variety of designs.

Anita has many admirers, but she makes it a point of dancing more often with me. She chooses an older boy from the Goan School for her partner at the Midnight Special. As we part in the early hours of 1955, Anita promises to write often from Mangu. I promise to reply. Her mother invites me to drop in for tea anytime I am in the neighbourhood of 2nd Avenue, Parklands. "You must definitely come and visit Anita when she is home for the holidays. The poor thing meets nobody at Mangu."

I promise to do so. Things are certainly looking up for me --- but not for long.

On a perfect January day, with the morning temperature hovering at about 20° C, we are within minutes of the start of our first Assembly of 1955. The quadrangle is crowded around the podium side. With the latest intake, our school has exceeded its physical and planned capacity of 600 students. Mr. Stewart, the Headmaster, welcomes the new students in a long preamble, that we have now heard four times, and then he focuses on us, "the first batch" as we are known.

"This year is particularly important for the Tech High." He glances across the student body. "Our first batch will sit for the Senior Cambridge Examination, and for a headmaster and the teaching staff, nothing matters more than achieving the highest results possible, especially as we started as an experimental school." He pauses and for a moment seems to hesitate. "Many have been watching our progress and have agreed to withhold a final judgement on the basis of this year's results. We have discussed special timetables that will be implemented for the Fourth Form, and any student wishing to withdraw from sports and other extra-curricular activities will be permitted to do so." There is total silence; we have not heard him sound so sombre before. "We must make up for the disruptions resulting from prolonged security situations over the past three years, when temporary sacrifices and adjustments had to be made." The assembly is dismissed. I feel apprehensive about what's ahead.

Within two weeks, our workload is overwhelming and social life is non-existent. I cannot wait for the eleven months ahead to end, so we can sit those final exams and never have to study another day. We are all utterly exhausted, so much so that Savio and I have stopped getting excited over news bulletins from the BBC, or headlines in the local newspapers. Admittedly, there appear to be fewer reported attacks of whites, though the slaughter of African men, women and children, and the burning down of villages seems to go on, with Mau Mau killing their own people, according to the reports.

Unexpectedly, Governor Baring offers the Mau Mau an Amnesty. The newspaper headlines are too big to ignore. The European settlers are aghast. They scream and protest. Mengha brings in a copy of the hundreds of leaflets being distributed around the city centre, reading: "Baring, you Biscuit Bastard! (The Governor had allowed the House of Manji to name a product after him). You are an incompetent, impotent, ingratiating lover of blacks. You go back to England, but keep the death penalty here."

Savio and I are at the Goan Gymkhana when we learn the news. We had for some months given up meeting at the club to do our homework, but had turned up on this night to try to concentrate on studying for the exams. Who else should turn up but Emerico, from the PC's Office in Nyeri. He worked with Pio's dad, Anton Gama Pinto; before Anton moved to Nairobi to better pressure the government and maintain contact with his son, Pio. It was Emerico who had first told Uncle Antonio about the Mau Mau movement, about the involvement of the Kikuyu tribe and how organised it was. That was even before the government made it public.

"Look at it this way," Emerico is saying to his captive audience in the bar, "Britain is kaput. How long can it sustain being bled by a guerrilla war, which is what the Mau Mau has become? They're in the same manure here, as they were in Malaysia. Better to cut their losses, make friends with the enemy, and quietly sneak away. Let the buggers sort it out later."

"So what does this Amnesty mean?" Dias, a regular, asks.

"Since 1953, being convicted of being a member of the Mau Mau carried an automatic death sentence. Under the Amnesty – those that surrender themselves and turn in their weapons, be these pangas, semis, guns, knives and even poison arrows, will not be hanged after all. However persons may still be tried and imprisoned for their crimes."

"So what's the big difference?" A man at the far end of the bar asks.

"You get to keep your head, and serve a prison sentence instead."

Savio looks at me and we know this can get complicated, or boring. We leave and head home.

Over the next four months there is no rush of Mau Mau to take advantage of the Amnesty. In fact the killings continue on isolated farms and in small villages, and the victims continue to be Kikuyu themselves. The authorities appear to ignore these killings, just as they ignore the murders of an Indian trader in Fort Hall, and of another in Nakuru, as well as the murders of three Africans, and soon thereafter, two Asians in Nairobi. All they can say is: 'These cases are normal urban criminal activity by miscreants'. However, when two European schoolboys are murdered in April, Britain withdraws the Amnesty and ten Mau Mau activists are 'hanged by the neck till dead'. For the frustrated settlers, true British justice has finally been served on the perpetrators.

By mid-year, we students at Tech High are frustrated too. We have been inadvertently living under a form of 'house arrest' as there are restrictions on our movement in force around our school, given its proximity to the African residential neighbourhoods. Our European teachers are also for the first time displaying signs of weariness. Having arrived just over four years ago, their term contracts are running out. They seem to be comfortable about openly sharing their concerns with us, especially when we are in small groups. We are older now and understand things we didn't when we first arrived at the school. I cannot explain it, but somehow a mutual friendship and interdependence has grown between us. Our *Muzungu* teachers have crucial decisions to make about their future – especially whether they should renew their contracts for another four-year term.

Before this, it had never occurred to us that British people had normal family concerns. But one day Stan, Mengha and I are returning from a field trip with Mr. Bennet, our chemistry teacher, and we stop for a refreshment break. "The problem is if I stay away a total of eight years," Mr. Bennet says, "It is unlikely I will get back my job in England. I will have to move to Kenya permanently, or go back next year. Frankly living here could be a lot of fun; it's a beautiful country, but we have our aged parents to consider."

Mr. Knight, the English teacher, is concerned about his children losing touch with reality. "Alice wants us to return to England. She too loves it here, but we must think of the children. They are spoilt here with year-round swimming, servants, riding lessons, safaris and holidays every two years in England. We have to get them back into the real world, or else they will never make it in life elsewhere."

I ponder over what these teachers are saying. They are talking about the disparity in the quality of life here in Kenya. If you are white and a part of the ruling class, it's a privileged existence. But they don't seem to realise that at the other end of the spectrum so much poverty exists, and life is sustained on a prayer.

Mr. Martin, whom we have affectionately labelled 'our own left-leaning commie bastard' because he is always talking about social causes, is fed up living with the insecurity in Kenya, and the fact that the British taxpayer is paying for it. "Everyone lives here for years under a State of Emergency, just to protect a small privileged bigoted white community," he tells us one afternoon, looking wilder than usual with his unruly longish hair and bulging blue eyes. "People in Britain have no idea how these British folks live here in Kenya on the backs of the British taxpayer. Our brave young boys fight and risk dying to protect these few people. If I were Lennox-Boyd, as head of the Colonial Office, I would say to the future Kenya leaders: 'Go! be independent! Be like India. We don't need an Empire! Learn to take care of yourself! Go, go away now and be free.'" He speaks from his heart. We applaud.

Mr. Martin makes us think. I stay awake that night pondering his words. So true. There must be money around. What is unfair is that those who have access to power deny opportunities to others to improve themselves. Perhaps political freedom may help us all after all. Isn't that what Pio was talking about. 'Why should people have to live with shit in drains outside the front door?' he had said one night at the bar.

The European teachers are not alone in their apprehensiveness about their future. We are worried too.

"September 30, 1955 is the deadline for applications to the Royal Technical College," Mr. Walker, one of three careers counsellors, advises our class. "It will open its doors for the first time in April of 1956; it will be the first multi-racial institution for higher learning in Kenya, and will have only a few places in each faculty in the start-up years. You should think of what you want to do now. There is no time to waste." The class has a short discussion on the various options, such as mechanical and electrical engineering, architecture, surveying for men, being offered in the new College. "Go home and discuss these options with your parents, but remember you will rapidly run out of time," Mr. Walker appeals to us.

I discuss the options with Dad – I know Mom will agree to anything I choose. "You must make the best of any opportunities offered,' she says. "Just don't gamble hoping luck will solve everything." Dad suggests I might try Electrical Engineering. He now believes that I will never go abroad again, after my boarding school experience in Goa.

It is the last week before the deadline, when the applications will close. As Mengha and I walk into Mengha's father's workshop, his dad beckons us over to his office where he is looking over some complicated building plans. This past year he has often asked Mengha and me to interpret some of the more complex contract-drawings he receives from various architects. We enjoy doing it, as we both like our technical subjects and draughtsmanship. Stan is good at these subjects too. Inspiration strikes.

"Mengha, why don't we both study Architecture?" I ask, as we look at the building plans that Mengha's father is holding. "Will you do it?"

"Can't do it," Mengha says. "You know Dad wants me here immediately after school." He laughs and turns to his dad, and says in Punjabi, "Lando wants us to study together to become architects."

"Architects?" Who will give you work? These jobs are reserved for *Muzungus*," His father turns to me. "Mengha must work with

Uncle Lachman and me, Jaswant." He beats his chest as he speaks to us. "Mengha speaks good English now. He understands drawings. He will negotiate big contracts for us with *Muzungu* architects." He looks at Mengha with pride.

I persuade him to let Mengha at least apply. Then if he is accepted, they can make a decision later. He agrees. Mengha and I fill up all the appropriate application forms. Stan also confirms that architecture is his first choice. An assigned 'career guidance' teacher checks all forms for any errors or omissions. My destiny is now again in the hands of the Almighty.

At home over dinner, I tell Dad and Mom about the forms finally going out. Most important is that I have finally made up my mind. I can see they are relieved beyond words.

Two months later it is exam time. It is a terrible time of stressed nerves, sleepless nights, memorising dates, algebraic formulas, and at times, even what day of the week it is. We are all tired. I knew it would be like this as Linda had sat her exams at St. Teresa's 24 months earlier.

Then it is the Final Assembly and the speeches, prizes, certificates, sandwiches and refreshments.

Our high school days and exams during the time of the Mau Mau are over.

As we say goodbye, Mengha confides that he will travel to India in two weeks. Perhaps he will be engaged. "It is our custom," he explains. Olaf announces that his father wants him to continue his studies in the UK.

Savio, Stan, Romeo and I start to look for work just in case we don't make it into the Royal Technical. Our chances of getting in do not look good as there are rumours of the applications vastly exceed the supply of places. On the job front too, the economy is on its knees as a result of fighting the Mau Mau.

17

A Testing Time for Nerves

L inda and I are walking home along Government Road, which runs north from the Railway Station towards Ainsworth Bridge, past the Royal Technical College. It is just after 5:00 p.m. and we have another hour and half of daylight. "No use worrying about it," Linda says. "Everyone knows that postmen moonlight over the Christmas holidays delivering toys for Father Christmas. That's why other letters are delayed. You need to be patient."

"You know how patient I am," I reply, "but honestly don't you think I should have heard something by now?" We are discussing my application to the Royal Tech.

"That's a short cut to Victoria Street, down that lane, instead of walking all the way to the Nairobi Sports House," Linda interrupts me. I am so impressed with her. She had passed her secretarial training soon after leaving St. Teresa's school, and had landed a job immediately. Now she's excited showing me how much she knows her way around town. The pavements are crowded. Ladies in saris walk out of stores with 'boys' trailing them, loaded with purchases to be delivered to a waiting driver in a Mercedes Benz; while Indian clerks in suits and sandals skip about over the uneven pavement. Africans crowd the pavements peering into store windows. From their dress, I can tell most are probably unemployed; more office workers and shoppers wend their way past mainly Indian *dukas* that spill their goods onto the pavements. Askaris stand guard in doorways against shoplifters and bag-snatchers.

"There are many more people than jobs available," Linda tells me as we watch an open pick-up van, overloaded with unemployed African men and women, allow yet a few more passengers on, for the long journey home, beyond the suburbs. "They come each morning looking for work in the city," Linda says. A European steps out of Alibhai Sharif Hardware Store. He is wearing a gun belt; two Africans carrying his purchases stagger with their load to his jeep, where an Alsatian dog keeps guard and barks incessantly at passers-by, adding to the din of traffic. We stop talking, as the noise is so loud. It is quieter past the Khoja Mosque, where we recollect how when we were younger, we used to turn left and right again on Victoria Street on our way to the Blue Room for samosas and ice cream. Two over-crowded buses pass us heading towards the intersection with Fort Hall Road and the Ngara roundabout.

"I don't know why Dad won't buy a car," Linda says. "I think he doesn't want to drive."

"It may have to do with money."

"I am working now, so I can help him with cash. Do you know I am earning twice as much each month, as I earned when I first started 11 months ago?"

"You're lucky. You know you can always slip some in my direction if it's too much of a problem," I say with a grin.

"Only when you sweat for it, do you know the value of money," Linda says.

We pass the site of Royal Tech where, just two years ago, the government demolished the 50-year old corrugated-metal clad Police Headquarters to make room for the college. Across from it, the Norfolk Hotel is bustling with Europeans, drinking beer on the open patio. Coloured people are not allowed in there except to clean, make beds, cook, do maintenance. There is a line of taxis waiting for fares.

"Ahmad used to tell us how he picked up these *Muzungus* so drunk they could not remember where they lived." I say. "He would take them to the Mayfair Hotel in Westlands and park them there with the Askaris in the veranda. The guards would let them sleep, and just before their shift ended, they would wake them for some baksheesh, pocket the tips and go home. The same drunks would come day after day."

Linda laughs. "The Europeans earn so much more. It's a good way to spread it."

"Linda, do you think the Mau Mau is really over?"

"Why do you ask?"

"I just remembered… there, behind the hotel, is where Savio and I first saw a dead man. I can never forget the stench. The Government hadn't officially told us then anything about the Mau Mau. I wonder what news they are hiding news from us now?"

"Nobody knows."

We are now on a familiar stretch on Kikuyu Road, left at Plums Lane and home. Mom welcomes us with a cup of tea. "Lando, Dad left a letter. It's addressed to you. He says it looks important."

"Where's Dad?"

"Where else? At the club of course."

I take the letter from Mom. My instinct tells me I better open it in the privacy of my room. It could be from Anita. She has been sending me letters from Mangu at least once a month – very affectionate salutations and endings, but very mundane fillings between them. She tries to disguise her writing on the envelope – this one looks expensive. I hope she is not wasting her dad's money on envelopes. He is employed at a bank, just like Dad. The envelope is white and of high quality. My heart begins to pound because the letter is not Anita's. I recognise the emblem of the College. I carefully slit the envelope. It contains a single sheet of white paper. I look at the signature. The Registrar, Royal Technical College, has signed it. I sit on the edge of my bed and read the contents. 'Dear Mr. Lando Menezes, Thank you....' I skim the preamble and focus on three lines: 'Demand for places in the Faculty of Architecture has exceeded supply. Priority is given to students who have completed the Senior Cambridge up to three years earlier, and have been waiting for an opportunity. Recent school leavers will likely not receive placement in the 56-57 academic year.' I stare at the letter, and re-read the three lines. I place the letter on my desk, kick my shoes off and lie on my back looking at the ceiling – it sometimes helps me think. I am very disappointed. What do I do now?

Dad will be very upset. How shall I deal with this news and him? I sit up, slip on my shoes and go out to look for Linda. I find her in the yard reading a story to Niven. I read the letter to her.

"How do you think Dad will react to this news?" I ask. She grabs it off me, and reads it herself. Niven picks up his book and walks away.

"Of course he'll be very upset. You must try and find a job. Any job, immediately," Linda says. "Then start saving madly and go to England. There you will be able to work days and study part-time at nights. Eventually you will come out at the other end."

"How do you know all this?" I ask.

"Because I'm smarter than you, which is not difficult," I know she is teasing me to lower my tension. "But I plan on doing that myself. I've been thinking, we're stuck here. There are no opportunities for girls other than teacher training. For anything else, we have to go away."

"What about your job? You said you were doing well and you enjoy the work."

"I have a Goan colleague. She's very competent, but I can be as good and beat her, but neither of us can move beyond, because all positions for a PAGM --- sorry that stands for Personal Assistant to the General Manager—are reserved for Europeans. That will never change, so what's the point of wasting time here?"

"Have you told Dad and Mom?"

"Yes. Dad and Mom say I'm too young, impulsive and inexperienced to look after myself. But I'm going anyway." Linda leans forward and grabs my wrist. "Lando, listen to me. You better start to take life seriously. Decide what you will do, now that Architecture is not an option. Will you still want to train as an architect if you have to do it part-time? How are you going to raise funds to get out?"

Simba's bark alerts us to Dad's imminent arrival. I brace myself for an emotional confrontation and disappear into my room. I have to break the news gently.

At dinner, Dad upsets my plan for drip-feeding him the bad news.

"Lando, did you get the envelope I left for you? It looked official."

"Yes Dad. It's from the Registrar at the Royal Tech. He says I have excellent grades, but because of limited places, they have to give preference to others who graduated high school up to three years ago. It seems fair." I try to sound matter-of-fact.

Dad takes a moment to absorb the news; then he says, "Well, not much we can do. You had your chances and we were willing to make huge sacrifices. You have been dealt your hand, and now you must play as you think fit."

There is total silence. Dad looks at Mom as if Linda and I are not in the room. "We should have resisted bringing him back from Goa. We always knew there are limited opportunities for further study in Kenya. But we felt sorry after those desperate letters about going hungry in boarding school. Now he will probably spend the rest of his life hungry. What a waste." Mom knows better than to reply when Dad is so upset. Dad gets up from the table and leaves the room.

"Didn't you always say God has a plan for each one of us?" I ask his retreating figure. "Then, please, let's give Him a chance." I shove my chair away and leave the table.

I lie on the bed, reflecting that my parents may be partly right about me going hungry. I have been scouring the city for nearly two months for any possible jobs, but there is little available, not unless you know someone. I have noticed the increasing number of African job seekers coming into town as the state of emergency has driven them off farms into the urban areas where they probably know even fewer people, if anybody. In addition, the police are constantly hounding them for identification papers. I am unemployed, but the police do not harass Asians the same way. By comparison I am privileged, but that makes it more difficult, as I have to live up to other people's expectations for me.

I remember those carefree days with Jeep and our trips to the museum. Last week even the taxidermists at the museum did not have an opening for trainees. I don't mind really. After Leakey betrayed his friend Kenyatta, would I even want to work there? I hope Leakey is not still working with the security forces. We still don't know what has happened to our houseboy Mwangi or his wife Wangari and Stephen and the baby; Leakey supported the security forces.

I reach for my new short-wave radio receiver that Uncle Antonio and Aunt Clara gave me as a gift when I graduated from high school; I had offered the crystal radio to Joachim, but he sneered at it. He wants a transistor radio. The BBC news is all about growing problems with the Egyptians over the Suez Canal. Who cares? We have our own problems. I turn it off and eventually sleep comes.

The next day, I go off to Mengha's workshop to see if he has heard anything. Lachman Singh, his uncle, welcomes me. He tells me that Mengha has been taken by Jaswant Singh to Jullundur, India to meet a potential future wife. There are four families to choose from. I thank him and go looking for Stan. I know where I will find him. He and his neighbourhood buddies play daily at the 'Bhoggia Stadium' – a patch of murram behind the home of a Mr.

Bhoggia, where hockey is an obsession. It's near our old school, off Park Road,

"Yes," Stan says. "They have sent me an identical letter."

"What happens now?" I ask.

"I am trying not to think of it," Stan says. "For now I am going to enjoy my game, and beat the hell out of the other team. It may make me feel a little better."

Some days later, Linda and I are in the veranda chatting. Simba announces Dad's arrival. He is earlier than usual. His face is beaming. Mom hears his voice and walks out of the kitchen with a hot cup of tea. Dad sits down.

"Congratulations Lando. I have good news for you," he says. "The Registrar's office telephoned me today. The man asked if you're still interested in studying architecture."

"What did he say?" I ask anxiously.

"There's been one cancellation," Dad says. "You are the first in line to be asked, of six candidates on their shortlist."

"So did you say yes Dad?" I ask.

"I said you were very interested. He said your Offer Letter would be mailed today. You must confirm the Letter of Acceptance within a week."

"Thank you Dad," I give him a hug and a big one for Mom too. Linda walks up to me and hugs me too. I am so happy to see the relief on Mom and Dad's faces. "God's plan!" I smile, and give them a thumbs up, as I walk to my room and cry into my pillow with relief.

———•◦•———

18

The Barriers Begin Falling

I feel apprehensive as I arrive at the main campus of the Royal Technical College for the ceremonial Opening Session in April 1956. Only two months ago, as Linda and I had walked past, it seemed the buildings would not be ready for at least another three months, but now the signs of construction are almost gone. In the space between Kingsway and the main building, large 50-year old Eucalyptus trees, once planted randomly around Nairobi to try to drain the swamp conditions and deter mosquitos, seemed to have survived the assault at their feet. The land has been bulldozed of shrubs and small rocks and transformed into a temporary car park – God forbid that it should rain, or the ground will turn to the consistency of a molten red-brown chocolate quagmire.

Ahmad had insisted he bring us in his taxi as Dad and Mom have received gilt-lettered guest invitations. "Lando, I am very proud today," he had said as he gave me a big hug at Plums Lane before we set off. "Do you remember how I carried you on my shoulders when we came to the India and Pakistan Independence Day Parade in 1947? You and Jeep?" I see tears forming in his eyes.

"Nearly 10 years have passed. You have created so much matata – but now – good luck." I hug him back.

As we pull up before the college, he turns to Dad. "I will be back in 90 minutes. Chico, don't worry. Be happy for your son. I will wait as long as is necessary."

I walk Mom and Dad under the archway. A red carpet has been laid under the canopy over the Main Entrance. We show our cards to an usher, who points to the wide main staircase leading to the first floor. He turns to me. "You must wear your gown before you can be permitted into the Auditorium."

Mom and Dad enter the lobby where many guests are already milling around, waiting for the hall doors to open. I rush up to my locker on the fourth floor, don my bright red undergraduate gown, and like Batman with my cape flying, I am back in a few heartbeats. The doors have still not opened to the public. I see Dad and Mom are talking with their friends J.M. Nazareth, the renowned lawyer and politician, and his wife, who is clad in a beautiful silk sari. I wonder why more Goan ladies do not wear saris. Is it because they fear being mistaken for Indians? I must ask Mom about that. At that moment three sets of double doors open, and the guests and students stream in to take their seats. I enter through a set of doors marked 'Students'.

I stop to look at the scene in amazement. The first thing that strikes me is the size of the Auditorium itself. I had never before been in a hall as large, and with such a high ceiling. At the far end is a huge stage that can be used for music performances, plays, and such like. The flat floor of the auditorium immediately in front of the stage has been laid out with about 300 chairs in rows. Those chairs are reserved for us privileged students, the first to enter this multi-racial institution. It is history in the making. The remainder of the floor is built up in tiers, with fixed upholstered seats over a carpeted floor. The ushers are busily seating the visitors. I wave tactfully to Dad and Mom, who waves back equally discreetly. Mrs. Nazareth is sitting next to her.

I slide into my seat, and look around me. I am in the middle of the Red Sea, one gown in an ocean of red. The gowns are identical, but under that outer covering, we are all different. For the first time the three races, black, white and brown, are sitting side by side. I look at some of the faces. They are all strangers. I would have known more people at a packed High Mass at St. Francis Xavier Church anytime. I wonder to myself how the Royal Technical College managed this feat of mixing races in the same physical space when outside these doors, public buildings are still segregated. I see about a dozen or so white faces among the new intake. Of the rest, roughly two-thirds are African and the rest Asian.

A European man in a dark suit walks to the microphone located to the right of a row of about 12 empty leather upholstered chairs placed in an arc on the stage. From his clean-shaven, well-groomed looks, I conclude he must be an 'imported' European, like the ones we knew at our high school, and not the common - garden Kenyan *Muzungu* variety that we're too familiar with.

The audience goes quiet, but he still requests silence. There are five minutes left before the official start of ceremonies. "Thank you. I now invite members of the Academic Staff to take their seats," he says.

We watch them arrive in their black gowns, with plumage around the collars in white, deep crimson and gold. I am barely breathing, in case the slightest sound will send the whole flock in flight like the cormorants and pelicans we saw as children around Lake Nakuru. The man in black requests the audience to stand and welcome distinguished guests; this sets off a brief rustling and scraping of chairs. The Chancellor and a procession of V.I.Ps troop up the few steps, onto the stage. I am surprised to see J.M. Nazareth up there on the stage. I look back to where his wife is seated to make sure this is not just a look-alike. It's him, all right.

The MC makes brief procedural announcements and then the distinguished guests take turns in speaking.

First in line is the Chairman of the Board representing the Kenya Government. He tells us that plans to build an institution for higher learning had been initiated in 1947 in Kenya, but by 1949 has grown in concept to cover British East Africa. I wonder if my Technical High school was part of this plan. He tells us plans are underway to develop Royal Tech to University status affiliated to UK institutions.

Next, the MC introduces John Maximian Nazareth, President of the Gandhi Memorial Academy, which has made a substantial financial contribution towards the College. In his introduction, he tells us that 'JM', at the age of 8 years, was sent to India for the next 13 years, before he returned to Kenya in 1929. It is finally making sense… this is why Dad has always used JM as a role model for me, and had sent me away at the age of 10! The MC continues. "JM was an Advocate of the Supreme Court in Kenya by 1933; President of the East African Indian National Congress from 1950-52; and he served as Judge of the Supreme Court in 1953, was elected President of the Law Society of Kenya in 1954, and is currently President of the Gandhi Society of Kenya."

Phew! How can a man achieve so much and he is not even 50 years old yet? I sit up to look and listen. Of medium height and build, JM is well groomed, his hair with a touch of cream, combed from left to right. I realise he has somehow managed to cross the racial barriers set up for the rest of his kind. He stands to speak – of course I had heard him speak before at Pio Gama Pinto's wedding. They must have become good friends while Pio was working with the Indian National Congress. I wonder if he can help in securing Pio's release from prison on remote Manda Island, near the island of Lamu?

JM tells the audience that the East African Asian Community had wished to do something tangible as a living memorial to the recently assassinated Mahatma Gandhi. They had been contemplating building an institution of higher learning, and so the Gandhi Memorial Academy decided to join forces with the bigger joint project of the governments of Kenya, Uganda and Tanganyika. To do this the Gandhi Smarak Nidhi Trust had been created with him as Chairman. He speaks eloquently on why Asians see themselves as just another tribe that has a right to co-exist and live happily with the Africans and Europeans, and that studying together was an integral part of the process of co-existence in mutual respect. I look around. Some students are listening intently; others seem restless. The public are attentive.

Other speakers follow, and finally it is the turn of the Acting Principal and Dean, Dr. H.P. Gale to speak. This is a surprise for us all. Major-General Bullard, the first Principal of the Royal Technical College, whose appointment had been accompanied by a burst of publicity two years earlier, had resigned a month ago. He had had a string of initials after his name and there had been speculation as to which were academic and which were military decorations. Did the Major General view us students as the undefeatable enemy and hence resigned, I wondered.

Dr. Gale, solidly built, a 'short back and sides' haircut, dark-rimmed glasses, dressed in a well-tailored civilian suit, waits for us all to absorb his image. He makes his salutation and clears his throat.

Dr. Gale delivers an inspiring and wide-ranging overview of the future of the College, and then specifically addresses the student body sitting apparently humbled and awe-struck by his passionate performance "As we embark on our journey together into a brave new world." He pauses, pulls out a handkerchief from his breast pocket, wipes the lenses and replaces the glasses, peering somewhat over the rims.

"Who in Kenya could have dreamt even five years ago, that students of all races can study, play and live together under one roof, all equals in an unequal world?" I look across the Red Sea. Everyone is listening attentively. He speaks for a few minutes longer and concludes with, "You must each reflect in turn, on how you will share this mental wealth to make constituent countries of

Braz Menezes

British East Africa a better place for your fellow citizens." He looks around the room and specifically addresses the relatively small proportion of female students.

"To our young women I must say, you are especially privileged. Today in much of the under-developed world, girls are not even allowed to attend primary school. Even today within some Asian communities, education of girls is considered a lesser priority. The argument most often heard is that daughters will get married and go away to raise their own families. You today will prove the fallacy of that argument by your own example."

With that Dr. Gale ends his discourse with "So I say again. Welcome! *Karibuni!*" He receives a standing ovation.

I feel proud. Exhilarated. I glance around the auditorium. I have never been in such a multi-racial mix before, and I don't think anyone else in the room has either. I wonder if we will be able to live up to Dr. Gale's expectations? I realise why the competition has been so intense for the relatively few spaces in each of the six faculties. This one new institution of higher learning has to serve all the British colonies and protectorates of Uganda, Kenya, Tanganyika and Zanzibar.

The MC closes proceedings. The distinguished guests, invited guests and new students are invited to partake of refreshments in the lobby. I go to meet Mom and Dad. People mingle. I meet Arthur and Albert, ex-colleagues at the Dr. Ribeiro Goan School, and Edgar, who attended St. Teresa's but I know him from the Gymkhana. First contacts are made.

The guests start to leave. I accompany Mom and Dad to await Ahmad, who is already there. I hug them goodbye. "Thank you so much for coming. I'll see you at home." I glance at my watch. It is only 12:30 p.m.

"Okay Lando," Ahmad waves as he inches the Chevy forward. "Remember, no more matata! Kwaheri!"

I move back into the Great Court now teeming with herds of red-gowned students, each trying to find out if there is someone they know or can relate to. Funny that Ahmad should say no more matata, I think to myself. A voice interrupts my thoughts.

"Hey, Lando! You want to join us for a beer?" Skip is an Engineering student I met in line the previous week. He's rounding a group to celebrate this solemn day in our lives. This is a fundamental Goan tradition. We celebrate every event: birth, baptism, holy communion, confirmation, loss of wisdom teeth, graduations, engagements, weddings and a host of others, literally until death do us part, and even then the party still goes on.

Francis, another Goan from Nakuru, walks towards us. He already has 4 recruits in his group. We are now a total of 10 made up of 6 Goans, 3 Africans and a Sikh.

We head across Government Street to the outdoor beer patio of the Norfolk Hotel.

But the African headwaiter bars our entry, as two other waiters stop and gawk.

"We cannot admit you Sir! It is against the law!" We are flabbergasted. It seems only the *Wazungu* can continue to drink there, and Africans can only serve, but cannot drink.

"Follow me," Skip takes charge. We walk a few blocks away to Sequeira's Bar, one of the oldest bars in Nairobi, and one of the oldest stone buildings in Nairobi. It overlooks Jivanjee Gardens. It is owned by Balthazar Rodrigues, a robustly built, elegantly dressed man with the most luxuriant beard and a handlebar moustache. I had known he was Skip's dad, but had not met him before.

Skip introduces us to Balthazar. "Boys meet my dad." We file by shaking hands with Balthazar. He scrutinises each of us with sharp piercing eyes. "Your family name? Do I know your father? Are you old enough to drink?" I nod. I move along.

The interior walls are left as unfinished stone. The pride of the bar is the wooden counter, which is almost 60 years old, and is religiously polished every morning with a wood polish that is Balthazar's own secret concoction, according to Skip.

We group in a little room at the back of the bar. "If these walls could talk, " Skip says, "they would tell you more than you would ever want to know of scandals and history of Nairobi." He points to the lounge section on the other side of that screen. "According to my dad, that part was frequented by a number of 'Wazungu'. Among those that come to mind was a part-time hangman, another was a nephew of the Archbishop of Canterbury who had gone 'native' (the nephew – not the bishop) and who came on certain days to pick up his copy of the London Times."

We place our orders. When my beer comes, I sip it slowly. Although Savio and I once tasted beer hidden away from sight, and had then brushed our teeth and gargled ourselves to near death, this is the first time I am drinking publicly. I am now seventeen.

We stuff ourselves with fries, courtesy of Balthazar, and head back to the campus for further exploration. Our classes will begin the next day.

Back at Plums Lane, I am pleased and surprised to see Dad sitting back and relaxing in the garden, a beer in hand. A rare sight indeed – not the beer, but the relaxing. "Come Lando." I sit beside him and we watch Niven, now aged 5, 'repairing' his tricycle, his pockets bulging with nails, screws and beer bottle tops. Dad proudly tells me "Niven is one day going to be a great engineer."

"Yes, I think so too," I reply, pleased that medicine or law are no longer the only options that Dad has in mind for my siblings.

———•••———

19

The Spine of the Mau Mau
is Broken

"Lando, why don't you come on the bus for a change?" Linda says as we leave the house together. "We don't seem to have time to talk anymore." The packed bus makes two stops before it enters into the traffic that is crawling on Princess Elizabeth Way. By the time we reach the intersection with Kingsway, it is almost at a standstill. There is an audible grumbling in the bus. Linda, sitting by the window, strains to peer out.

"It seems your scarlet gowns have caused the blockage," she says. "I don't remember having seen this much congestion before."

I look out and realise she is right. Hundreds of students wearing gowns are attempting to cross the road. I had assumed we would don our gowns only on ceremonial occasions, or if requested, when attending lectures. Perhaps unsure of the rules, many students, rather than upsetting the authorities, are wearing their cloaks as they make their way to the college from the residences located nearby on State House Road and off Hospital Hill Road. We watch as the red gowns trickle down the footpaths towards the main campus from different directions; the trickle becomes a steady flow as they near the critical intersection with the 4-lane highway.

"I think it's making the drivers nervous," Linda says. "Look how they are dashing across the road. I'm sure motorists have not been warned of this invasion; and look, the new traffic lights have not been connected yet." Linda is right. I think the drivers were not expecting to see this phenomenon of herds of red gowns, throwing caution to the wind, plunging blindly into traffic, in a desperate move not to be left behind. "This is probably their first experience of big city traffic." Linda says.

"It's like that film we saw starring Bill Holden," I reply. "Do you remember it? It reminds me of that migration of thousands of wildebeest crossing the Mara River from Kenya into Tanganyika, in search of fresh grazing."

We are at my bus stop. "Okay, see you later. We must find time to talk." I step off the bus, and join the red gowns as we make our way past the construction debris, dodge a few potholes and puddles from the previous night's shower and arrive at the main campus. Perhaps one day there will be a proper footpath for pedestrians, I think to myself.

I make my way up a side staircase and along an open corridor that overlooks the Great Court, to the Faculty of Architecture located on the 4th floor of the Main Block. There is a great deal of twittering in the corridor below; a red-gowned student informs me that it is where the domestic science class is located, which forms the nucleus of a future Department of Home Economics. The faculties of Arts, Commerce and Science are also located in the Main Complex. The Faculty of Engineering, however, is housed across the road, next to the Norfolk Hotel.

We have 33 students in our architectural faculty, a small self-contained bubble in a much larger universe. Eight are studying fine art and the remaining 25 students are architectural students; including 2 Sikh girls; all the rest are male – 2 Europeans, 5 Goans and 6 Africans, and the rest Asians. We introduce ourselves to each other, meet the teaching staff and settle in for the long haul. Everyone seems excited to work together.

For me the speed of events is exhilarating. In just five years I have moved from a boys only boarding school in Goa, to a crowded co-ed Catholic Goan school, transferred to a non-Catholic Asian boys experimental school, and now I am about to expand my horizons into a multi-racial, multi-cultural, multi-denominational experience. Over the next few days as I see and meet other students from across the spectrum, I wonder what it must be like for our mainly foreign-recruited lecturers, as they behold what the Admissions Office has delivered. I imagine them like the fishermen I used to watch on Benaulim beach in Goa, anxiously awaiting the day's catch, not sure what the Gods will send their way. Here now is their first haul, an assortment of colours and cultures from across British East Africa: Africans, Asians, Arabs and Europeans in assorted flavours and sub-flavours including Christians, Hindus, Muslims, Parsees and Jews. In Kenya in particular many students will have come from racially and gender segregated Anglican and Catholic mission schools and from Muslim madrassas at the Coast.

Furthermore, we all come from economically diverse backgrounds. While many African students have come from the renowned black schools, such as the Alliance Boys School in Kikuyu, a few have made it from remote mission schools. Others are still nursing deep emotional scars of the Mau Mau conflict that still rages on in the dense forests of the Aberdare Hills, and in remote areas around Mount Kenya.

Only two weeks into the term, we learn first-hand about the terror it inflicted. We are sitting at Sequeiras Bar when Skip comes in, accompanied by a handsome Kikuyu man of medium height and fine sculpted features with surprisingly expressionless eyes. "Meet my colleague Kim," Skip introduces him. Kim is an engineering student. In the course of the evening, the conversation inevitably moves to the topic of the Mau Mau, and rumours of the excessive brutality by the British Forces and resultant social and economic upheaval it has caused. At one point, tears well in Kim's eyes. In the immediate silence that ensues, he unburdens himself of his family's experience. He describes the night that the Mau Mau smashed into his home and butchered his father, in full view of his terrified mother and his siblings. He describes how the family had to sweep the pieces into a box for burial. We can only put our arms around him and hug him, and hope that the emotional scars of that brutal attack will not leave him numbed for life.

Our academic and social lives begin to take shape at the campus. I assume it will be like it was at my last school –Tech High in Park Road. I will once again be part of an experiment, improvising together with our instructors as we go along. The majority of our academic staff, recruited from universities in the UK, are in their forties, energetic and enthusiastic women and men. They help us get started. Inevitably this includes mimicking the rites and traditions of universities in their motherland, like the annual fund-raising 'Rag Day' when students ride on elaborately built floats and others run alongside, seemingly amok, rattling tin cans for charitable causes.

Soon it is the end of our Introductory Term. The close of term is marked by the visit of Dr. Sarvapalli Radhakrishnan, First Vice-President of India, on an official visit to East Africa. On a blustery day in an open-air ceremony, which we attend in our red gowns, he officially opens the Gandhi Memorial Academy and unveils a life-size bronze statue of Mahatma Gandhi by the famous Indian sculptor V.P. Karmarkar. Rumours abound among the Asian community that the Vice-President has been sent as a Special Emissary by Prime Minister Nehru to seek an early release from prison of Jomo Kenyatta, convicted at an infamously rigged trial; and of Makan Singh and Pio Gama Pinto, both summarily incarcerated without trial.

Rumours among the Africans on the other hand are different. The English language press report of rumours among the African community about an Asian conspiracy, in response to rapidly escalating prices in the shops. This diverts attention temporarily from the White settlers and the land issues that the Mau Mau rebellion is all about.

"Indian dukawallahs are up to their tricks again' the head-lines scream out. But in reading the headline stories, I realise it is the trouble in Egypt that is reverberating thousands of miles away. Egypt's President Gamal Abdel Nasser is fighting for greater control of the Suez Canal, and Britain and France are resisting, creating mounting pressure on commercial shipping and severely threatening the smooth flow of trade. Now I finally begin to com-prehend those early BBC broadcasts about British troop move-ments in Egypt, that I had picked up on my crystal radio years ago. The trouble has been building up for almost 5 years.

By July, we are all fully tuned in to the radio and newspaper headlines. Kenya is making its Olympic debut and has fielded a team to the Melbourne Games of 1956. A number of Asians are also included in the delegation; Alu Mendonça and Anthony Vaz, both ex-colleagues at Dr. Ribeiro are on the predominantly Goan and Sikh hockey team, and Mendonça has the honour of being flag-bearer for the Kenya delegation.

There is little else to do until College restarts. I call on Mengha. He is back from India and helping out at the workshop. He con-firms that all the preparations had gone well; he has met his future bride, who must complete another year of school before they can marry, perhaps in 1958. He says he likes her family very much. We go together to visit Savio, who is working in an accounting firm on Government Road, and doing some further training. He is sitting in a corner room, files piled up high. "I miss the good old days," he confides, puffing on a cigarette. "But I have a good boss. By the way Lando, I have suggested your name for the social committee at the Goan Gymkhana. They need new blood in management."

"Savio, when did you start smoking?" I ask him, but he just grins, puts a cigarette to his mouth and blows me a smoke ring in the air.

"We're counting on your help," he says.

"OK, but I must warn you that my life will be busy in a couple of months when College resumes."

The official term starts with a bang, so to speak. On October 24th, HRH Princess Margaret, on a Royal Tour of Kenya, officially opens the Royal Technical College at a short ceremony in the Great Court. She talks about the special role we will each have in developing "this most precious corner of the British Empire, that I have grown to love so dearly."

There is a short tree-planting ceremony in which a magnificent yellow-barked thorn tree is placed a short distance from our bronze Gandhi. Dr. Gale and a couple of dark-suited men escort Her Royal Highness to the front entrance of the College, where she tugs on a cord to expose for the first time the College's Emblem, secured to the wall high above the Main Entrance, and thereafter unveils an engraved marble Foundation Stone. The College is born.

This event is followed by a real big bang, albeit some distance away. On October 26th Israel, in collusion with Britain and France, attack Egypt whose military forces counter attack; within a short while more than 40 ships are sunk, and the Suez Canal is made un-navigable. The repercussions are felt throughout Kenya. There are immediate shortages of foodstuffs and goods as a result of the interruption of trade. The Indian shopkeepers are accused of hoarding. Crowds ransack Indian shops in Kisumu and Mombasa. In Nairobi, Nakuru, Eldoret, Kericho, the presence of heavy troops weeding out remnants of the Mau Mau, seems to limit escalation of the attacks by Africans on Indian shopkeepers.

Back at the College race relations are moving along nicely. Roland Cooper, an Englishman in his late forties, has been recruited to be a Student Advisor as well the Warden of the Men's Residence. His mandate and personal motivation is to promote a full schedule of social, cultural and sporting activities that will draw the students together and help break down the racial barriers in the first truly multi-racial institution of higher learning in the country.

A Student Union is formed and the process of electing office bearers begins. Eventually Francis Noronha, a lanky Goan in the Faculty of Arts, who has campaigned with great passion, is elected the first President of the Student Union; Nathaniel Asalache, an African architectural colleague is Vice-President, and Mahendra Shah, an Indian Arts student is elected Secretary. These are early days yet and the calm within the student body on the campus is still subject to the ebb and flow of political events outside.

It is January of 1957. We are in a design team working in groups of five, each on a different design project, when Dennis Pimenta speaks up. "Hey chaps, Cooper want us to form a band." We laugh. We think he is having us on as we have been teasing him about his non-stop whistling. He can make music whether he is exhaling or inhaling. Dennis is a solidly built chap, a receding hairline, and with a big chest to house a big heart and a strong pair of lungs.

"No seriously," Dennis says. "I'm not fibbing. You know how Cooper walks around the residences after dinner, checking if the men are generally obeying rules? Well yesterday, I was in my room practising the trumpet. I had rolled my towel tightly and placed it against the door to stop sounds getting into the corridor. But he heard me. He knocked on the door and I had to let him in."

"So what did he say?" I ask. "Wow, you could be a one-man band – that was very good!"

"No. He told me that the previous week he was doing his routine walk after dinner. He was walking through the grounds, outside the block next door on the side overlooking the sports fields, 'when I hear the sounds of a clarinet blowing melancholy notes into the night air over the sports fields'... his words"

"That must be Eddie," Romano says. "His room is in that block. Hey Eddie, come over here, quick." Eddie is also an architectural student. He confirms that Cooper had heard him play and had told him he would scout around for more musicians.

That's how the College Band was born. Dennis on trumpet; Eddie on clarinet; Romano on the box bass (an up-turned plywood crate that once held the finest Ceylon tea attached to a stick with a single taut string. The idea came over from Britain with Lonnie Donegan and other skiffle groups improvising on different instruments) and Lando – me – on drums. The next day we scout around among the Engineering Faculty, which we figured must have the biggest pool of potential talent. We recruit Edgar and Rodosakis on lead and bass guitars. We start practicing that same weekend, playing whatever comes naturally: soft jazz, Latin American and European dance music. We have not heard any African music yet.

On February 18, the Government announce that General Dedan Kimathi, leader of the Land Freedom Army – formed to carry on the struggle the day after Kenyatta was arrested in October 1952 – was hung by the neck until dead at the maximum security Kamiti Prison, where he had been detained since his arrest last year. He is buried in an unmarked grave in an unknown location, so that his followers will not turn him into a martyr. The colonial authorities considered Kimathi to be the most dangerous of the leaders of the Mau Mau movement.

The Campus is tense again as racial tensions, always close to the surface given Kenya's history, could erupt in Nairobi. The newspapers give out the whole story, not previously divulged:

Ian Henderson, a Kenya born and raised European, had formed a number of small head-hunter cells to track each group of terrorists still roaming the forests around Mt. Kenya and the Aberdare forest range. (I recall that Henderson was one of the people that Dad had been told to contact after the police picked up our houseboy Mwangi and family in Operation Anvil in April 1954.) Henderson and one of his cells of Mau Mau hunters had finally succeeded in tracking down and bringing to justice their most desired trophy – Dedan Kimathi.

According to Henderson, some members of the Mau Mau of lower rank had betrayed Kimathi; they had been disgusted with his ruthlessness against his own people, including pregnant women, children, the aged and the infirm. Another newspaper claimed loyal Kikuyus led Henderson to his prey. Kimathi was detained, tried and sentenced to death by Justice O'Connor, while Kimathi was still lying under heavy armed guard in Nyeri African Hospital nursing gunshot wounds. The Europeans rejoice and declare the movement is now leaderless. "The spine of the Mau Mau has been shattered," reads one headline.

———•◦•———

20

My First Blind Date

For all practical purposes it is just another day, except that there is much anticipation and a full turnout of students; the room is alive with multiple conversations like an acacia tree loaded with weaverbirds nests at sunset. Mr. Baron, the Head of the Faculty of Architecture, has requested the presence of every student to talk about 'Blind Dates'. We speculate about what he has in mind. Has he noticed how outnumbered the women are with a ration of 23 men to 2 women?

Mr. Baron, fiftyish, greying hair, clean-shaven and sporting an Omar Sharif-like moustache, walks in. He glances around the drafting studio and grins, presumably at his own genius in luring a full attendance. I think if he were a tad taller, he would cut quite a dashing figure – a man always in a hurry. But it's too late for him to grow any taller.

"It is almost the end of our first academic year and I have good news," Baron says in his usual no-nonsense style. "We've had a good response to my letter. We have a larger number of architectural firms willing to offer you vacation employment than we have students. Your stipend may vary by firm."

"What does that mean?" I venture to ask. He looks me in the eye.

"You may be paid nothing," He glances around at the packed studio. "Not just Lando. You all must understand the employers will be exposing you to invaluable practical experience in the real world. They must have the discretion to pay you what they see as your value to them."

"What happens if I am unlucky and get a bad employer?" Dennis asks the question that I would have asked.

"Tough. Life is a lottery," Baron replies. "You have been allocated firms on a random basis. That's why I've called it a blind date. Over time you'll each find firms you prefer to work with and vice-versa. We are testing the waters this first year. This is not an arranged marriage. Both sides will have a choice about working together again; that is the understanding I have reached with the Association." He clarifies a few procedural questions and returns to his office. Before the session we were all curious and amused. Now Baron has introduced some apprehension.

My "blind date" takes place on a drizzly day at the end of May. I make my way along Government Road, turn left on Duke Street and right again, to the address I've been given on Victoria Street. The office is on the 7th floor of Sunshine House. 'Europeans Only', the painted sign by the main entrance directly off the street, is explicit. An arrow indicates Africans must enter at the rear of the building by the goods delivery gate. I find a side doorway that says 'Asians', and I am surprised when it opens into a small common lobby shared with Europeans. The walls are finished throughout in a speckled beige-and-brown coloured terrazzo that amplifies every sound because of the hard surfaces (I've learned that much at least in my first year). A curved staircase in pink terrazzo with a plastered balustrade and a wooden handrail is on the right of the lift entrance. A moment later, the elevator arrives at the ground floor and two sets of collapsible metal gates clang and clatter open. An elderly European walks out as five younger white men enter. One of them, with an overgrown head of red hair, signals to me to enter, but another, already in the elevator, glances at his companions and points at the notice above the elevator gates that says 'Lift for Europeans only'. I race the elevator to the 7th floor and I have to lean on the handrail for a few minutes to catch my breath. On a door facing me, a brass engraved sign reads 'Cecil Oliver-Smith, A.R.I.B.A, Chartered Architect.' I see someone move behind the wire-glass panel on the dark wood door. I knock gently and enter.

An engraved chrome sign, 'Patricia Atkins, Receptionist-Secretary', identifies the elderly lady who looks at me over the rims of her glasses.

"Good morning, Madam," I greet her cheerfully.

"Good morning," a frigid Miss Atkins asserts her authority. "Please wipe your shoes on the mat. Sit there. Mr. Cecil Oliver-Smith will be with you shortly. He is expecting you."

"Thank you," I reply, mortified. I look down at my shoes and feel stupid; here I am on my first day at work with muddy shoes, despite having spent a big chunk of my life polishing my shoes because Dad is obsessed with clean shoes. How could I have forgotten, today of all days? I scrape my shoes furiously on the coir mat.

Oliver-Smith's room is to the right. Straight ahead is a big room with four European men bent over their 'double-elephant size' drawing boards. I see no black or brown people, but I was warned it is a small practice. Miss Atkins stands up and ushers me into her boss's office. A man is sitting behind a heavy desk. Behind him is a long chest with two sets of drawers for storage of maps and plans; to my left is another heavy-looking wood meeting table about the size of a dining table for eight, but it has only four chairs.

Cecil Oliver-Smith stands up, a big man with stooping shoulders and a pudgy tanned face with heavy jowls holding it together like bookends. We shake hands. "We've been expecting you," he says, gesturing for me to be seated in the leather armchair across the table from him. He tells me how happy he is to respond to the College's request to practicing architects; how everything he learned of use, he learned only after he left his college in London in the 20's. I cannot help noticing that his teeth and fingernails are slightly stained – this is a man moulded by weather and a life nurtured by alcohol and tobacco. He stands up. "So forget what you learn at the Royal College," Cecil Oliver-Smith says. "Life will teach you what you need to survive, and by the way, always remember: in practice, the theory is always different. Now, let's go and meet the staff."

I let him lead the way into the room with the European architects. "Richard, Chris, Andrew and Geoff," He waves his hand. "You will work directly with Richard, who will be your mentor during your stay with us."

I shake hands with each person in turn as he introduces them. Richard is the young redhead who had invited me into the elevator. His handshake is firm and welcoming, compared to the flaccid handshakes of the other three.

"By the way, you too can call me by my initials – Cos - they all do," Cecil Oliver-Smith says, "Now, come this way, Lando." We walk through a doorway into a smaller drafting room packed with five work tables and three Indian draughtsmen; they seem to freeze at the unannounced arrival of their boss.

"Good morning, Sir," they recite in unison. I reply, but Cos manages only a grunt in response to their salutation and introduces me.

"Lando will be with us till August," Cos says, as he glances around, sees an empty workspace and continues. "He can sit there. This is Surgeet, careful with him, he gossips a lot and will get you in trouble. Shanti - study his drafting style and lettering, it's very good. This is Ajit. He is a good worker if he didn't sneak off early on Wednesdays and Fridays to play hockey at his Sikh Union club." Ajit is visibly shocked that the boss knows all about his activities and attendance. I have already noticed the mirrored window on the wall that provides Miss Atkins a view of this India enclosure. "Where is Kumar?" Cos asks.

"Sir, he's at City Hall checking on plan approvals, Sir," Surgeet replies.

"And this is Mwendwa but we call him Jeeves – it's much easier." Cos has entered an annex to the drafting room. An African with a kind gentle face, dressed in a navy blue tunic and shorts, and wearing sandals made of cut-up used car tyres, is standing at attention. I can tell he is from the Kamba tribe. "Without Jeeves this office cannot function. I will leave you now," Cecil Oliver-Smith departs while I stay behind and familiarise myself with my new colleagues and the office.

Mwendwa's—I cannot bear to call him Jeeves—room is the office nerve-centre for print-making, office cleaning, and tea/coffee preparation. It is small and cramped, with a printing machine and a plan-cutting table, a counter top with a small enamel kitchen sink and above it, a rack of cups and supplies. On one side is a chest of drawers for storage of large plans. A small cupboard is reserved for office cleaning equipment and supplies. Within a few hours, I see how Mwendwa is capable of making endless blueprints, unperturbed by the ammonia fumes from the plan-printing machine, made worse by inadequate ventilation. The Asian staff and Mwendwa, and, as of now, I, work mostly in this under-ventilated space, inhaling ammonia fumes. Opening the rear door leading to the fire escape would improve the flow of fresh air, but this has to be kept shut at all times, on instructions from Cos.

Mwendwa makes coffee and tea twice a day; he ruthlessly controls the issue of sugar cubes to reward or punish staff who treat him or each other with respect or fail to do so. I do well with Mwendwa's sugar awards.

Within four days of reporting for duty, I am on a project with Cos himself. He drives me to the Kenya Meat Commission plant in Athi River. I remember this plant very well from the time I was ten; it was the source of an awful stench on my first train ride to Mombasa in 1949, bound for my boarding school in Goa, and then again on the return voyage 18 months later.

"Lando, I want to be out of here within an hour," he says aggressively, as he pulls into a gravelled space by a sign marked 'Reserved'. "You must move fast, so don't expect to enjoy the scenery." I really have no control on that, as it is my first job, but I keep my big mouth shut. As far as I know we have to measure the existing structure and the location of equipment that cannot be moved, in order to make improvements and some extensions.

"COS stands for Crazy Old S**t," Richard had warned me the previous day, when I told him I had been asked to accompany Cos. "He can suddenly turn nasty. Unfortunately, the abattoir must keep operating as it has big contacts for supplying meat products to British troops in Egypt and the Middle East, so it won't be fun." As we drive to Athi, I listen to Cos rattling louder than the 1953 Ford Zephyr we are riding in. He is furious with his architects as none will assume design responsibility for this commercially lucrative, if unpleasant, project, and so he is handling it himself.

We enter the abattoir; Cos informs a supervisor what we are doing and starts work immediately. He hands me the tape.

"Lando, you call out the numbers," Cos says, "I'll make notes."

I pull out a short section of the tape from its leather and brass shell. "It's a little hard to read the numbers, Sir," I say timidly.

Cos explodes. "That tape was a present at my architectural graduation in England in 1927," he informs me with a sneer.

The practical implications of a barely legible cloth tape in a steamy abattoir seem irrelevant to him. Nevertheless, I climb the slippery metal stairs; the railings are also coated with grease and congealed fat, and steam is everywhere. I stop at each landing to read out measurements. I realise that years of neglected maintenance have left the stairs dangerous; I dare not touch the slimy pipe handrails, either. My *Bata* rubber soled canvas shoes feel slippery.

I shout out the numbers to be heard over the din. There is noise of hissing and gurgling from the giant steaming vats, and more hissing from the partially leaking steam pipes that connect them.

In addition, the employees are yelling instructions or telling jokes to each other in Swahili and in Luo, and it's hard to not follow the thread of the languages.

"For God's sake speak up, Lando! Nobody is likely to overhear you," Cos screams at me. Richard had predicted that Cos's temper would be inflamed by the added indignity that he—Mr. Cecil Oliver-Smith—famed Architect of Kenya Colony, is personally writing down measurements that in Cos's own words, 'any half-brained idiot can do' and 'God knows I have a number of them on my payroll.' From my vantage point I see vats of freshly butchered bloody meat being rolled in. I try and look the other way. I cannot stand the sight of fresh blood. I look towards where the workers are grouped.

Almost all employees have stopped working and are clearly being entertained by our spectacle. A big white Muzungu with his frail pet assistant at the other end of a leash (the measuring tape)—that is what we must look like. The Muzungu shouts instructions and his pet jumps into action.

I am not even holding the handrails; they're so gruesome. Who can blame the workmen for preferring to watch us over working? Their own monotonous routine is limited to loading raw meat, and unloading cooked guts from the conveyor belts to and from the steaming vats. They are now witnessing world-class live theatre.

Up on my perch, I feel a little queasy. The sight and smell of fresh blood and steaming intestines is overpowering. Everywhere is reeking with the stench of steamed flesh and tissue guts of cattle. This I understand is the stage before it is converted into canned products. Dad had told me once that during World War II, cans of corned beef were shipped out of this factory to feed British soldiers and African Carrier Corps in Abyssinia and Burma.

Suddenly the queasiness gets stronger; everything begins to swirl around me. My knees feel wobbly. I grab for a handrail, miss and I slip. I slide on my back. With lightning speed I hit a landing and manage to slow my descent. The grease has made it easy to slide on the metal staircase. I feel no pain. I crash into the metal railing and pass out. As I am coming to, I hear voices shouting '*daktari*' and 'doctor'. Black people in bloodied white aprons surround me; I hear someone ask Cos whether I should be carried to his car.

"No, you cannot use my car. Get an ambulance or a Commission truck if an ambulance can't be found. Damn!" I turn to catch a glimpse of his red and angry face and feign death as he turns to look at me. Suddenly there is silence. I overhear the Africans say 'Bwana D'Souza *amekuja*.' 'D'Souza has come.'

"My driver is outside, take him to our clinic. Please use my car," says a new voice, presumably that of 'Bwana D'Souza'.

I remain at the clinic for about four hours, while Cos returns to the office and sends Richard out to fetch me. While I am waiting for Richard, Bwana D'Souza pays me a visit; he is the Chief Accountant at the abattoir. "I know your father well," he says. "Our accounts are with the National Bank of India."

"It must have been the sight of fresh blood as well," I explain to Richard when he arrives. I tell him about the time many years ago I had fainted at the sight of fresh blood, when robbers had broken into our house in Plums Lane and slashed my dog Jolly with a panga; how I had seen him lying in a pool of blood and had fainted. "That is why I can never be a doctor, as my father had wished. Architects are not expected to see fresh blood."

Two days later, that incident begins a series of recurring nightmares. In one, I hear voices at first, and then see people running towards me to help. A big heavy-built African picks me up like a baby and carries me out of the cutting room where the floor is wet and hard. My eyes struggle to focus. His face is shiny. Now I am lying on the wet terrazzo floor surrounded by black faces attached to ghost-like gowns. There are only 11 of them. Were there not 12 apostles at the Last Supper? They have fresh bloodstains on their snow white gowns and some are wearing gloves holding fourteen inch-long kitchen knives and they look shocked as if they have completed a ritual killing in a trance. I realize to my horror that they are Mau Mau. But then I feel confused; they cannot be Mau Mau, the Government announced a few months ago that with Dedan Kimathi dead, the Mau Mau was gone. But maybe the Mau Mau have turned against the defenceless Asians instead, because Britain will do nothing to protect us. It's a mistake, I shout. I am a Goan student, not one of the Indian dukawallahs who have taken your copper coins for cigarettes, salt and soap. I feel a warm dampness and see my bloodstained sleeve. My arm is bleeding; they are killing me!

"Good Morning. This is the Kenya Broadcasting Service. The time is seven o'clock. This is the morning news, read by Jonathan Short." My new short-wave radio alarm comes on. I sit upright in one movement, sweating but relieved. I slowly get out of bed, glad to be out of the nightmare but not looking forward to the daily nightmare that is my job.

It is only 5:30 in the morning; the household is still asleep. I sit on the edge of my bed. So this is what Baron meant by 'blind date?' I know mine is a sad and dismal office. The Indian draftsmen feel trapped too. "We are supposed to finish work at five, but always we get message from lady Atkins that the boss wants to discuss our work before we leave," Surgeet (the talkative Sikh) had told me a couple of days ago when we had a little office gossip.

"Yes! By the time we finish it's six or six thirty, maybe later. There is no overtime," Kumar adds. The others nod their heads in agreement.

"Sure we'd move, if we found other work," Surgeet says, "but the Muzungu firms know each other and they control our wages."

I am by now also disillusioned by the 'Cos brand' of design, uniformly applied to all projects - a blend of Victorian utilitarian architecture with Cosmetic touches of European Art Deco. Back at the Faculty, we have the latest imported architectural magazines; they bring to us full page photos of modern architecture and trends in urban planning. Brasilia, the future capital of Brazil, rises out of the red earth; Le Corbusier's new town of Chandigarh in India.

Modernists are flourishing in the USA and Japan. Luigi Nervi, Oscar Niemeyer, Frank Lloyd Wright, Kenzo Tange and Paolo Soleri among others, are names that inspire. I decide Cos is going nowhere and that's not the destination I have in mind. I will do something about it.

Outside, bird sounds fill the air. I draw the curtains apart—another beautiful Nairobi morning. I get off the bed, get dressed, down a quick breakfast and catch the early bus with Dad. I do not whisper a word to him; he has enough on his mind and this is *my* problem, and I will deal with it.

Richard is my 'Sir Lancelot' – my white knight in shining armour – and he is fun to work with. He graduated in England and landed in Kenya, following short-term working contracts in Hong-Kong, South Africa and Rhodesia. He mixes freely with everyone and treats us Asian staff and Mwendwa with respect.

"Lando, you okay for a beer after work?" he says after our second week together.

"I won't be served in Muzungu bars," I tell him. "Let me show you some good Goan watering holes around here." We pop quickly first into one and then another, both located behind the National Bank. They are crowded and noisy, so we end up at Sequeira's Bar.

"Lando, about what you went through with COS at the abattoir," Richard says, "I want to say I'm sorry. I refused to take on that project as I have enough on my plate."

"Was Cos upset when you refused?" I ask.

"He huffed and he puffed and said he'd do it himself," Richard says. "'That's a good idea,' I replied, and suggested he take you to help. So again, sorry, Lando."

"That's okay, Richard. The experience opened my eyes," I reply. "In fact, I'm thinking of chucking architecture. I think it was a mistake. Problem is, there aren't many options for me now, unless I go overseas to study."

"No, no, you mustn't do that!" he interrupts. "This firm's not really about architecture," Richard says. "Look at our big projects—a pork products factory in Limuru, a milk pasturing plant in Meru, a tea leaf drying warehouse, a sugar factory – it's hard to produce architecture with that."

"What about the soap factory in Nakuru? Surely that was a wasted architectural opportunity?" I joke.

"I've told Cos what I think, Lando." Richard says. "He's pretty upset with me."

"Aren't you worried he'll fire you?" I ask.

"I'd love it if he did. You see, if I go of my own accord, I have to pay him four months' back pay," Richard explains. "On the other hand, if he sacks me, he only pays me up to the time I work, and has to show proof that I deserved to be sacked. I can't wait."

"If you go, can you promise to take me with you?" I ask.

"Listen, Lando," Richard looks at me intently, "life usually happens when you're not looking — opportunities come from nowhere. You have to learn how to recognise these. I will find something for both of us. I promise." We order another round.

Barely four days after our 'heart to heart' Richard confides he has found us both jobs, starting just as soon as he can get fired.

"Fantastic. Let's both work on that," I joke.

Mwendwa's tea has three sugar cubes for me, instead of the standard one cube, so altogether I am feeling great. As luck will have it, the frigid Miss Atkins reports in sick the next day. Richard tells me to sit at the reception desk; these are Cos's orders; Richard will help me when necessary with the important clients.

The telephone rings at about 11.00 a.m. It is Mrs. Oliver-Smith calling in with her routine daily shopping list for the European Butcher in Hardinge Street. Normally Miss Atkins takes notes and calls in the order, and Mwendwa will go across and collect the order at 4.00 p.m. so it stays refrigerated at the butcher's until the last minute. I take down the telephone order. Richard walks by as I put the phone down.

"Here's Cos's meat ration," I tell Richard. "Shall I just leave it on Cos's table?"

"No. Gimme it. Thanks. I'll handle it," Richard says.

That afternoon, a very red-faced and agitated Cecil Oliver-Smith confronts Richard. His contract is terminated, to take effect within a week, "to allow for an orderly transfer of on-going projects." Cos leaves the office early, slamming the front door after him. Richard is jubilant; he invites the Indian draftsmen into the European Architects' space. He then gleefully recounts the story of what he did to get sacked.

"I took the meat shopping list that Lando gave me, and added items to the list, including 'three pounds of kidneys, three pounds of freshly washed intestines, and as many hearts as you can spare'." Richard is beaming. I can see how happy he is at being sacked. "I substituted the telephone number of the butcher with that of the City Mortuary, and added a scribble, 'note new telephone number', and left the note on Cos's desk." Everyone is rolling over laughing.

"You know Cos, like many well-established bullies, is afraid of no one but is terrified of his wife. So he comes in after lunch, and calls the number, and ends up being insulted by the African man at the Mortuary. He knew I had done it as it was my writing."

Within a week, Richard and I are working with another firm of architects that is progressive and friendly. I get a varied choice of work, and a lot of travel to building sites. By the time the vacation apprenticeship is over, I am invited to come back the following year and given a nice 'stipend'. I am looking forward to the start of the new term.

Braz Menezes

21

Less-Academic Matters

S tarting the new session at the college is like being a non-
swimmer thrown into a pond, being immediately submerged
and then threshing furiously to stay afloat. I find myself overwhelmed by a myriad of activities that have to be woven into a
an un-stretchable fabric of 24 hours: lectures, design studio, field
research, organising socials and special events with Francis, Skip,
and the others, and attending selective sports events to support
our college teams. The college band begins to attract a small fan
club, so we squeeze practice time on weekends, especially after we
pick up some paid gigs outside the college. On top of all that, Savio, my high school buddy, has taken on some responsibilities with
the Social Committee at the Goan Gymkhana and wants my help.

Let me not forget the time I have to devote to Anita and her
obsessive letter writing. I first met Anita at Mangu Girls School
when I went with Stan and Gurmeet to look for Saboti. She had
reminded me later that our paths had actually crossed before that:
at the Christmas Play at the Goan Gymkhana in 1948 when she
was 7 and I had just turned 9. I was one of the Three Wise Men

and she the Virgin. After our encounter at Mangu, we had met a few times whenever she was home for the holidays.

Anita taught me new dance steps on a linoleum-covered floor between her kitchen and dining room at her home in Parklands, under the ever-watchful eyes of her mother, an aunt, a curious little sister, and an adoring little brother. For the past two years she has been bombarding me with letters containing such romantic phrases and ideas that my 'raging hormones' as my school friend Olaf described them, were woken from their normal dormant state. Now 16, Anita will graduate before the Christmas holidays.

In November I receive another letter from her. One sentence catches my eye: "You must perfect the cha-cha-cha and tango, and by the way, you're already booked for the 'midnight special' with me on New Year's Eve."

I am really excited. She is the most sought after dancing partner by my friends, and *she* has chosen me. I have been patiently waiting for her to get through high school, because if for any reason she didn't make it through the Senior Cambridge Exam, I would be blamed for leading her astray, and I don't need any more guilt to cope with. In the meantime, I concentrate on working with the boys at the club on planning the Christmas decorations and other events.

And soon the season is upon us, bringing with it the Christmas Day Dance at the Gymkhana followed by the Boxing Day Sports Fair and dance. Anita is as popular as ever at both. She tells me she misses dancing with me more often and how she is looking forward to New Year's Eve.

Finally it is the day of the big dance of the year. Anita makes a stunning entry into the hall, accompanied by her parents. She looks gorgeous with her olive skin set off by a flamingo-pink cocktail length dress and high heels. A brilliant red rose is tucked casually in her long silky black hair. I remind myself she is still a mere schoolgirl of 16. I go to greet her; her mother is especially friendly and warm towards me and I feel she approves of our friendship.

After the first dance, other boys surround Anita; soon she is booked three or four dances ahead. I sense there is something bothering her; perhaps it's because we have seen little of each other this past year because of my own busy College schedule.

Savio is standing next to me in a smart dark suit; he notices the attention Anita is receiving. "Lando, just look at how these blokes hover around your girl like humming birds."

"Not humming birds," I say. "Bees."

Anita and I dance the midnight special, we join hands with others to sing *Auld Lang Sang*, and we usher in the New Year with more dancing. It is 2.30 a.m. in 1958 when the band pauses for a break.

"Lando, please can we sit out in the veranda and talk," Anita says, squeezing my arm gently. "It's too noisy in here."

"Perfect! Come this way." We find a quiet corner, illuminated by reflected light through the French doors. Outside a thousand stars perforate a black sky and the gentle fragrance of her hair mingled with a slight tinge of perfume fills the immediate air. I take hold of Anita's hand, but she gently pulls it away; She seems preoccupied.

"Is something wrong?" I ask.

"I can't decide what I should do after high school," she says. "Lando, you are lucky that you are studying architecture. There is nowhere for girls to study in Kenya besides teacher training and nursing."

"Have you looked at the courses now offered at the College— Royal Technical…?"

"Yes. Nothing there," Anita interrupts me. We talk some more— she does the talking and I listen; we cover a range of unconnected topics. About an hour later, her brother comes by to say their parents will go home soon.

"Okay, I'm coming," she tells him and turns to me as he leaves. "Lando, there's something more I wanted to talk about," Anita says, "but we didn't get round to it." She stands up. I reach for her hand; she seems comfortable with that.

"What is it, Nita?" I ask, still holding her hand.

"I won't be seeing you again," she says. "I'm just confused. I can't explain now but I'll write to you, I promise." I feel her body go tense as she tries to pull her hand away. I am shocked over what Anita has just said, but I know a reaction from me will provoke a public outburst of uncontrollable rage, her usual reaction when confronted. My mind is racing.

Should I kiss her instead? I wonder. She had taught me to kiss for the first time; although it was more a clumsy fumble of lips. I look at her. Anita loves drama and this is a moment for it. I remember a line from 'Gone with the Wind' starring Vivien Leigh and Clark Gable, when Savio and I sneaked into a matinee at the Empire Cinema on Hardinge Street one recent Saturday afternoon.

"'But first you should be kissed and often, and by someone who knows how,'" I quote. I feel her body relax as we say a passionate goodbye. "Okay, I'll wait for your letter."

"I hope we will always be friends though," Anita says, adjusting the rose in her hair, as we walk back to her family.

"Of course," I reply. I greet her family, 'A Happy New Year again'. I watch as they leave the hall.

Savio is standing nearby; I put my hand on his shoulder. "Come Savio, let's have our first New Year drink together." We adjourn to the bar.

Back at college, the pace continues heavy, and we pack as much in as possible. The Government's 'State of Emergency' is still in place and security forces are very jittery, as we soon discover for ourselves. One night in February, a few of us take on a wager with the girls to penetrate the highly touted security of the Women's Halls of Residence. A colleague, Arthur and I, being smaller in size are chosen to climb in. An apparently sleepwalking Assistant Warden hears the slight click of a window catch and dials the police emergency number. It seems as if all the armed forces in the country have been camping outside the Women's dorm. Within minutes police sirens sound as we disperse into the grounds in various directions. The security forces surround us; four of us are cordoned off, and with our hands up, hustled into the back of a police wagon. It is awful inside the van: musty and strong smells of sweat; an open metal grille separates an Alsatian police dog with very bad breath; I can see his teeth, and his amplified bark is deafening. "What happens now?" a nervous Arthur whispers to me. "See, I'm trembling." Arthur is an engineering student and an ex-colleague from the Goan School.

"Not sure. I just hope my Dad doesn't hear about this." I reply, as I feel a slight tremble too.

"Yeah! What a damned mess!" Arthur says as he leans back and closes his eyes.

"Do you think we might be dismissed?" asks George, another Goan colleague from Dar es Salaam.

It is a very long 12 hours wait in the temporary prisoner holding cells at Kingsway Police Station. Eventually, with the intervention of Francis Noronha, president of the Students Union, and someone from the College administration, we are all set free. No charges are laid.

We meet about a week later at Sequeiras Bar to lick our wounds. We decide against such night-raids in future; instead we plan new events. Someone proposes that we must begin to put pressure on the bars around the College, including the Norfolk Hotel, to ease their colour bar, at least in the beer garden. Our group is now a multi-racial group of friends and we might make tangible progress. We have been hearing more about the civil rights movement in the USA.

Back at the college's architects studio another challenge has emerged that needs a solution. "Hey Lando," a grinning colleague, Asalache, calls out to me, "We need you here."

The problem is this: Throughout the week, especially on Monday, Wednesday and Friday mornings, and Tuesdays and Thursday afternoons, the cooking smells originating in the kitchens of the Domestic Science Department waft in through open windows into our Studio. The odours are so mouth-watering, almost pain-causing delicious, that they are distracting.

"Let's hold Lando upside down and lower him to the next level. He can tell them we are offering to taste some samples," Dennis suggests.

"Let's send a message through their window instead." I suggest. Agreement reached, we paint a huge S.O.S. (Save our Stomachs) banner that is lowered slowly to the window below: 'Discerning tasters available at short notice – Quality desirable, but not mandatory during training period. Call in person at Architects Studio. Room 5-155'.

A few days later, two attractive students in neat gingham aprons and white caps respond to our banner. Christina, an African girl, introduces herself and Juliana, her Goan colleague. "We received your message," Christina says. "Our group would like to invite up to four students every Monday and Thursday. You will each have to fill in a form, so your comments will be in writing."

"By the way, it was quite clever lowering a banner down that way," Juliana says. "Whose idea was that?"

"His," Dennis replies, pointing at me. "My idea was to hold Lando by his legs, as he is the lightest, and dangle him outside the window upside down, so he could deliver our message personally."

"I see," Juliana says. They take their leave and skip away. Thereafter, I keep bumping into Juliana all over the College; we exchange small talk, and before long I ask her out on a date. I am still nervous. I cannot help thinking of Anita's abrupt rejection.

Meanwhile a new practical problem emerges on the home front. Mom begins to fret about Linda and me. Linda has bought herself a Vespa with her earnings. But it is often already dark when her scooter comes tooting along Plums Lane. My hours are more erratic. Linda and I have a chance meeting one evening and the issue comes up.

"Lando, Mom stays up every night, watching the clock and listening for the click of your key in the lock." Linda says.

"I think you are the bigger worry," I say. "Goan mothers worry more about their daughters."

I understand it is difficult for mothers to know when to stop being mothers. When is the best moment to stop worrying? The work of a parent is never done. It is similar to an artist who keeps dabbing a bit of paint here, a stroke there; or an author constantly reworking a novel; the work is never really done.

"How can I convince Mom that my life, my days, my hours have irreversibly changed?" I ask. "We are no longer children"

"I don't know, but we must find a way to stop her worrying." Linda says.

One day in May 1959 an opportunity comes. Robert Marshall, a leading architect in Kenya, is the guest reviewer for the design portfolio. We are all tense as we await his comments, which will form part of our year-end evaluation. I am hoping he will find my design for transforming housing in African locations innovative and of great merit.

Following the two-day session he approaches me with a proposal. "Lando, I am putting together a small team to make a submission for an International Architectural Competition for Liverpool Metropolitan Cathedral. I am impressed with your drafting skills. Would you like to join us?"

"Thank you. Yes, please!" I am very excited at the opportunity.

Over those 10 weeks in mid-1959, I earn a stipend that I hope will buy a TV set. The windows of electronics stores are full of TVs, as black and white television has just arrived in Nairobi. Kenya Broadcasting Services has just launched its first ever TV broadcasts from a transmitter in Limuru. The reception is not perfect, but so what? Nothing is perfect. I trot off to see Pius Menezes, a namesake and owner of Mini-Cine Films. Pius is a big, charming man who started life modestly in Uganda. He migrated to Nairobi and set up a small radio store, later imported 16 mm films, and with his projection equipment, he would travel across British East Africa, bringing films to Goan clubs and other small communities.

He greets me like an old friend. He tells me that B&W will soon be out of date; in Europe everyone is switching to colour TV.

"Don't worry," I quip. "With our colour bar in Kenya, we will be with B&W for a long time." I cannot get it out of my head, that our three recent attempts to bust the colour bar at the Norfolk beer patio have not yet been successful.

Pius and I make a deal. I will still owe him some money, but I promise to settle his bill within 90 days. "Please don't ever let Dad know about this. He will never buy anything if he hasn't the cash already in the bank." I hand him my full paycheque of ten weeks.

"It will be delivered at Plums Lane tomorrow at about five," Pius says. "Claude, my assistant, will hook up the set as the station opens its daily programming."

My plan works. During the evening hours previously devoted to worrying about Linda and me, Mom watches the BBC reruns, long past their prime time debuts in England. The icons of British culture at the time, such as Sid James, Hattie Jacques, Benny Hill and Ken Dodd, are intended primarily to elevate the spirits of Kenya's white community from their despondency, after seven years of battling the Mau Mau.

As I imagined, Linda's appreciation for my brainwave is immediate and tangible. She pays off the balance of my debt with Pius, as with Mom sufficiently distracted, the pressure on Linda eases too. Her Vespa has transformed her social life. She seems happy at work and has postponed her plans to go to England for a year, although she assures me she will still go to study nursing at Guy's Hospital in London.

At the Goan Gymkhana, the pace of 'Socials' continues as if the Mau Mau conflict never happened. Leo, Darrel, Freddy, Archie and Vince, our Goan beer-drinking colleagues, tell us that this is indeed the case in the Goan Institute in Nairobi and in Mombasa, Kisumu and Nakuru.

"As long as so many Goans receive their pay check from the Government, Skip says, "the Mau Mau has not affected them; it won't unless the Government is overthrown."

"That explains why Pio Gama Pinto used to get so red-faced and angry, when he used to argue in Goan clubs," I say. "He used to say the *sossegade* –relaxed—attitude of the Goans would keep them in slavery for all time."

The new session in September brings a fresh crop of students to the college. I am in the cafeteria overlooking the reflecting pool one afternoon, when one of the new girls smiles at me. With her smooth tan, dark hair and general physique, I guess she is Goan, and introduce myself. She tells me that her name is Vera from Uganda, but that she has only recently returned from Goa, where she had been sent at the age of 7, with her older sister, 9, to study in a convent in the village of Siolim.

"I know Siolim," I tell her. "It is just a few miles west of Arpora, where I was a boarder at St. Joseph's High School."

We compare notes of our lives in boarding school: the deadly loneliness of being separated from our families and siblings; the near-starvation meals and how we were always hungry. I tell her how my friend Musso and I used to go around in the woods behind the school looking for cashews or anything to stave our hunger.

"My father also had to beg the nuns to give us an egg or something with breakfast," Vera says, "but they refused, until my parents made extra donations to the local convent." She seems happy to talk.

"Were you not scared going out so young?" I ask.

"I had a terrible time. It's easier for you boys," Vera says. "I was scared mostly at nights, as the nuns would turn off the lights early. We had this long dark corridor to walk through to go to the toilets at night. There were only one or two small oil lamps placed in alcoves in the walls, and as I walked down those corridors, I would see those flickering lights and shadows." She looks around to see if anybody is eavesdropping.

"It's okay," I say. "No nuns here to listen in." She continues.

"I would imagine ghosts, but there was a sister who they said was a bit funny up here—she twirls her finger indicating 'mental illness' – she used to walk the corridor talking to herself and praying. One time I was so frightened, I just did what I had to in the corridor, and went crying back to the dorm. The nuns punished me for a week with special duties and extra prayers."

We talk a little longer and then part company, agreeing to meet again soon. I think Vera is good fun to chat with.

It is about two weeks later when I see Vera again. I get the impression she has been evading me, so I go up to talk to her. She smiles as if happy I came over.

"So Vera, have you been avoiding me?" I ask.

"I have to," Vera says. "I have been warned."

"Warned? What are you talking about?" I ask.

"Lando, you remember that nice conversation we had two Fridays ago?"

"Of course. I enjoyed it immensely."

"At about 11:00 a.m. that Saturday, I was lying on my bed reading, when one of the girls came up to my room, " Vera says. "She said they were having a surprise party for one of the new girls and could I come down immediately with her? So I go. When I get to the place behind the Women's Dorm, you know by the little structure where the gas cylinders for the kitchen are stored, these three girls attack me. They have cakes of wet mud in their hands; they slap these on my face. One of them pulls my hair and two others drag me down into a puddle, which they must have filled with water from the garden hose. They roll me in the red mud. I am screaming for them to tell me what's going on. At first I thought it was a joke, but one of them really hurt me. So I punched back. I may be small but I learnt in convent school to defend myself and I can scratch back like the best feline in the world."

"And then one of the girls put her hand up. Everyone stood back and she spoke. She explained that Juliana and you had been 'coupled' as a pair suited for each other about a year ago, and that I as a newcomer, should remember that what the 'matchmakers of the Women's Dorm have put together, no one should dare pull asunder. We girls must stick together! Now you have been warned."

"Vera, I cannot believe what I am hearing." I say.

"That's your problem to deal with." Vera collects her things, throws them into a bag, and says goodbye.

I am dumbfounded that a bunch of self-appointed matchmakers in the Women's Dorm can 'couple' folks and then exercise such strong-arm tactics. I realise I have a lot to learn about the ways of women. On the other hand, I quite like Juliana already, and she is such a good cook; charming and I just love the way she plays hockey. I have already been to watch her team play on three occasions in the past six weeks. Vera remains elusive for the next few weeks, but once I did see her from a distance, and she seemed to have found a companion – a tall handsome Architectural student. Perhaps the infamous 'matchmakers' have already coupled them.

Soon it is the end of 1959. On the social front teams are working on organising the Student Christmas Dance. It is the week before the Dance when the police are summoned for the second time. Darrel and a team of volunteers have inadvertently cut down a twenty-foot tall pine from what they—and the Warden who authorised them—thought was college-owned land; this was to be the featured Christmas tree in the Taifa Hall. Only it transpires that the tree was on an unfenced part of Lady Delamere's estate bordering on the college. The police respond to the alarm within minutes. Fortunately nobody is killed, hurt or detained. Lady's Delamere's kind gift is publicly acknowledged at the Christmas Dance.

———•·•———

22

When The Wind Blows
the Cradle Will Rock

On February 3, 1960, I am sitting in the college's crowded, tension-filled cafeteria at lunchtime. The newspapers that morning stated that an announcement from the United Kingdom was imminent and that it would have deep repercussions in Kenya. Except for the rasping metallic-sounding voice of the broadcast being relayed from South Africa, through about a dozen transistor radios, the silence is palpable.

Prime Minister Harold Macmillan is speaking to South Africa's MPs in Cape Town. He has just announced a fundamental change to Britain's colonial policy, under the banner 'The Winds of Change'—"to create a society which respects the rights of individuals – a society in which individual merit, and individual merit alone, is the criterion for a man's advancement, whether political or economic." There is a momentary silence, as if no one can believe what they have just heard, and then a loud cheer erupts up from the assembled students.

"The foundations of the British Empire in Africa have begun to tremble," says a loud voice from across the room. It is Joshua, a Luo student well known for his fiery speeches at the Student Union meetings. As soon as the broadcast is over, there is excited chatter at every table; everyone it seems has a view of the future. Twenty minutes later outbursts of cheers continue to break out from individual groups. Now finally the government may lift the colour bar—our campus will no longer be a multi-racial aberration. The newspapers scream out the headlines with special afternoon editions, which explain the ramifications of this latest decision from the colonial government.

We feel the shockwaves in Kenya immediately. My first thoughts are about Pio Gama Pinto and how happy he must be at this news; I wonder whether he even has a radio at Kabernet, where he is under house arrest.

Over the next few days, the papers and radio report the impact of these momentous decisions on various segments of the population. The white settler community is outraged beyond anger. 'Traitors', 'Irresponsible f*****g bureaucrats' and worse epithets are hurled at London and at the Governor General. White businessmen, on the other hand, see opportunities opening up, but white civil servants are in a state of shock, as most will have to repatriate from the privileged lives they have enjoyed in the remaining colonies, especially in Africa. A few Goan civil servants acknowledge their futures are inextricably linked to their white counterparts and they too will have to leave. They are unprepared. Suddenly, it seems we are all discussing politics during our lunch breaks. The Asian community is divided too, as many think their contribution to fighting colonial laws is not being acknowledged. "We had A.M. Jivanjee and M.A. Desai who from the '20s fought against the colonial government's racist laws," Dhalla, an engineering student, says.

"The East African Indian Congress and many Indian publishers in Kenya provided so much support to the independence movement," another student says.

"My personal view is that the Indian dukawallahs in small towns upcountry will suffer the most." Vinod, a Gujarati student says. "I spoke to my Uncle in Kitale. He says the Muzungu settlers are their principal customers and when they leave, that's it."

"I think all Indians rely completely on the government for the maintenance of law and order especially in the cities," Mansukh, an Arts student says. "It is the Indian shops which are always broken into, ransacked and looted, whenever there is a lapse in security, which is bound to happen when the Muzungus leave."

How will it affect us Goans, I wonder? One evening on my way home, I go to the Goan Gymkhana bar, where I have habitually sought wholesome native wisdom. The 'regulars' did not wait for me to arrive; a discussion is already underway, as I imagine it must be every night. I order a Tusker, and perch myself on a stool.

"Of course independence will affect all Goans in the civil service," Dias says. "The question is what will happen to our pensions after 30 years of service?"

"I believe many will be asked to stay and train Africans," PWD Joe says "Personally speaking, we have worked hard and have had a good life here. But it is their country and we must leave if we are no longer welcome."

"It's okay for you to talk like that," a middle-aged man replies. "Many youngsters have been born here. My children have never been to Goa ever. They must have a right to live here, too."

"Personally speaking," Joe butts in again, "I know the British believe in fair play, and they will do the right thing by us."

"What do you mean?" Dias asks.

"We must not bite the hand that has fed us all these years," Joe says. "We must be on the side of the British; they will treat us as we treat them." He turns around to face a man with a thick flock of wavy grey hair, at the far end of counter, blowing smoke rings into the air and quietly listening to the arguments.

"What about you, Tom?"

"Me? I am happy to call it quits," he replies. "I will go back to Goa, live the simple good life with fresh fish, *chourico*, mangoes, coconuts and a few tots of *feni* daily, and Sunday Mass to meet people. Live *sossegade*. Let the children find their own way in the world. They have had a better education that we ever did."

"Everybody relax," Joe speaks again. "You know nothing moves fast in government. This process to independence can take 10 years to resolve."

I decide I have heard enough. As I walk home, I find myself agreeing with Tom. Perhaps Dad (and Mom) will retire to Goa as he has always dreamt; and Linda, I and the other siblings will adapt to an independent Kenya. As I approach Plums Lane, I hear Simba's welcome bark: at least he does not have to make any big decisions.

I see the flicker of blue light behind the translucent fabric of the drawn drapes in the living room. Mom is watching TV. I go instead into the dining room, where Linda is sitting, clasping a hot cup of tea. "What brings you home so early?" Linda asks.

"I stopped at the club," I reply. "This Winds of Change stuff is really causing an upheaval. Folks don't know whether they'll stay or go."

"I know what I'm doing," Linda stays. "I have reached as high a scale as I can be promoted here. My boss says I would be a Godsend to his London office, so I am cogitating that idea. That worry you brother?"

"No! But I've been worrying recently about Mom watching so much TV." I confide my anxieties to Linda. "Mom stays hooked watching Dr. Kildare, and the reborn Frank Sinatra. I'm sure all this TV viewing is not good for Mom."

"What are you talking about?" Linda sounds angry.

"You know how tired she has been lately? She has always been slim, even skinny." I say. "Now she just sits and watches TV every night and she's put on so much weight."

"You must be an absolute idiot," Linda says. "I've told you before, but God only knows where your brain is these days. Mom is expecting a baby in April – that's in two months time, and it's nothing to do with TV watching."

I confess to being somewhat shocked at the news; that would make Niven nine years older than the new arrival, who would be 20 years my junior. I retire to my room.

And I really never even suspected it.

Our little baby brother arrives in April 1960, 'on time and on budget', without, it seems, any apparent complications, even though Mom has just celebrated her forty-third birthday. Dad is proud. His father-in-law, Granddad Joachim, sired his last son, my Uncle Armando, at the age of 56. Dad is 58 years old. I shrug all thoughts away; after all, weren't we taught from a young age that having a baby is always a miracle and part of God's plan?

Linda and I go to inspect the new arrival together. At the hospital we are ushered into the Maternity Wing. Mom is glad to see us; she looks happy and well. A nurse shows us a little room where about eight babies are lying in cots. A big label identifies our new baby brother; the nurse invites us to go in. Everything—nose, eyes, ears, fingers, toes and squirting device—appear to be in working order, although 'baby' sleeps through most of our formal inspection. We interpret this as nothing less than the arrogance of being the baby in the family. Within a month, after Mom's return home, and after following a democratic name-selection process by all the siblings, he is baptised 'Frank Agnelo'.

Frank's arrival must have been the signal that Linda was waiting for to pursue a career in nursing. Within a month, she sells her Vespa, and three months later takes off for Heathrow, London, from the newly opened Nairobi International Airport at Embakasi.

I am going to miss her terribly. She has been my big sister, friend, confidant and occasionally partner-in-crime.

As if on cue, the winds of change sweeping Africa seem to have caught up with my personal life. Juliana and I are on a date – the first in about three weeks. Her cryptic answers to every question or comment I make, should have alerted me that it was not going to be a fun dinner. We are at the Swiss Grill on Salisbury Road and I want it to be a special birthday dinner for her. I had put aside some savings from our paid band gigs to pay for today. I still need to get her home before her 11 p.m. curfew.

Juliana looks lovely in a blue dress and a simple necklace, which, she tells me, was a gift from her maternal grandmother in Goa. The restaurant is about half-full and the dance floor is empty. We skip the starters and both order the evening's special 'Canard a L'Orange.' "What four-letter word rhymes with 'duck'?"

"Lando, please don't be stupid," Juliana snaps at me. "I'm in no mood for jokes."

"Luck. L-u-c-k! I feel lucky tonight," I say. Juliana lets just a tee-niest sign of a smile escape. I see her eyes are moist. I know there is something waiting to come out.

"Lando, we need to talk," Juliana says. "You know I will gradu-ate in four weeks time, but, you still have another 18 months to finish."

"I know," I say. "I have been thinking of it too."

"Well? Are we going to get married?" I almost fall off my chair, as the waiter arrives with the wine. He pours a little in a glass and hands it to me. I sip it. The price tells me it must be better than av-erage wine, and anyway I do not have much experience with wine. But my mind is racing. I wonder what has brought on this urgency in Juliana's voice. The waiter leaves us alone.

"You're not pregnant are you?" I ask. It's a very unlikely pos-sibility as an immaculate conception is very rare. In any case with her very strict Catholic upbringing since primary school, she made sure that if there was to be any s-e-x – she even refuses to utter the word – it would be only after there was a ring on her finger, placed there in Church in front of a priest, a ring through my nose, and a noose around my neck, for good measure.

"Of course not," she snaps. "It's just that we haven't talked about it, because we are both always busy. With all this talk of independence, Goans are nervous. People are starting to leave the country for Goa, UK, Portugal and India. Where will we be? You and I?"

"I will be here. I am not going anywhere. I only have a birth and a baptism certificate. No passport, so I am not leaving. What about you?"

"Lando, I'm not pushing you. You understand? It's just that we're both getting old. Damn it. You are already 21. Are you going to wait until you are 35 to settle down, just like your Dad did?"

Fortunately our duck arrives. I now feel I'm really being pushed against the wall. Surely she would have learned that about me by now? How I will never be pushed if conditions are not right. And yet I am very fond of Juliana. Our initial 'arranged coupling' by the self-appointed matrons at the Women's dorm had gradually morphed into affection and evolved into a sort of love during a time of great uncertainty and shifting sands.

"Juliana, I need time to think." I say. "Marriage is not something we can rush into. I do not have two pennies to call my own. Please let's talk a bit more about it."

"Okay Lando. I am willing to wait for you, but not more than two years. Is that clear?"

"Clear. Now please eat your dinner. This was meant to be a special evening. Happy Birthday!" We clink glasses. She is teary. I am choking inside, but manage to keep myself firmly in control of my emotions. Funny thing – boarding school trains you to drain yourself of emotion. We finish our meal. We dance, eat dessert and dance again. I kiss her goodnight in the shadow behind the concrete screen wall by the front entrance – not too far from where the police hustled me into a police van about a year ago.

Juliana and I spend hours and days discussing the choices open to us. Love is like cement that binds bricks together, but we are sorely missing the bricks of economic stability and now political stability. I remember how Ahmad suffered being separated from his new bride in 1947 for nearly three years, as she didn't have the correct papers to travel to Kenya. I do not wish for either of us to suffer and live with the anxiety of the unknown.

We meet about two weeks later in a small cosy restaurant off Sadler Street, a small elegant place renowned for its ambiance and good food. It is almost our last meeting to once more work through the list of 'should we?', 'can we?', will we?' and 'must we?'

It is time to part. We have exhausted ourselves with the endless discussion. I am holding her close. I can feel her tears.

"Lando, I'm sorry. I suppose what made me panic was the realisation that I might miss the boat. My mother was married at 16," she says.

"A couple have to think of the wherewithal they need," I reply. "What kind of future for the kids? The St. Vincent de Paul Society cannot support everyone."

We reluctantly agree to part to go our separate ways. It is a very painful experience for both of us. But right at the moment the practical realities we have to face are monumental. So much is happening all at once.

I lie awake for hours that night waiting for elusive sleep. I can't help recalling the gentle refrain of a lullaby Mom sings to Frank: 'Rock a bye baby on the treetop; when the wind blows the cradle will rock.'

The Winds of Change are indeed blowing, not just for the settlers, but also for me.

23

Adeus Salazar. Namaste Nehru

Like the wind that sweeps over the African plains and builds up into a powerful dust storm, throwing everything into turmoil, I can feel Macmillan's winds of change engulfing the country and me. With the stroke of a pen, the colonial government lifts the strict segregation laws. It feels like a window has blown open in a strong gust and has let fresh air into a dank and musty storeroom. The impact seems instantaneous. The Norfolk Hotel bar and other bars, restaurants, hotels, nightclubs and cinemas are suddenly overflowing with people of all races, albeit those patrons who have money to spend. These include almost all Europeans, a large number of self-employed Asians, and a number of Africans who are in well-paid, high visibility positions for foreign firms. For the rest, salaries and wages are still race-based and inadequate, or non-existent. At the same time, as Africans start to venture into non-African establishments, their music starts to first infiltrate the Goan clubs through Goan bands who have quickly picked up the rhythm of catchy Afro-rhythms of Kenyan, Congolese and Senegalese music; these bands transform themselves into Afro-music vectors in hitherto 'Europeans only' dance establishments in the city. Our own college band has renovated itself as some members have graduated and left; while new talent has arrived, including Donald Dias, a brilliant pianist from Daresalaam. The music covers the range from swing, jazz and the new afro-beat.

In October 1952, the colonial Governor General had described Jomo Kenyatta as 'an evil man who would lead the country to death, disaster and darkness'. In April 1960 a petition with over a million signatures was submitted to the Governor General seeking Kenyatta's release, and even while that matter was receiving consideration, Kenyatta was elected President, *in absentia*, of the Kenya African National Union on May 14, 1960. Political ploys and vicissitudes are moving at a break-neck speed. On all fronts the momentum of change spins almost out of control and many people are becoming nervous at the pace of developments. The months fly by. The balloons floating down at midnight on December 31 at the Goan Gymkhana confirm it is already 1961.

By May we are all glued to the TV watching events unfolding in America where the bloody confrontations between the Freedom Riders and the Ku Klux Klan in Alabama are being transmitted live. The black versus white conflicts are now being brought right into our living rooms, and into the streets of Nairobi in TV store windows. Europeans and wealthy Asians watch at home behind locked doors and drawn curtains. Africans and some Asians crowd around storefronts to watch images of the racial violence engulfing the most powerful nation on earth. Can it happen here in Kenya, we all wonder?

I spend the long vacation of 1961 in the office of Graham McCullough, one of Kenya's leading architects. Graham is a charming man in his mid-fifties. Of medium build, with steely blue eyes and a large receding forehead trimmed around the back and sides with a flock of silver-grey hair, he cuts an impressive, professorial figure. Graham has been a regular 'design resource' at the Architecture Faculty and a lecturer on professional ethics and legal aspects of practice. He insists architects should know all aspects of office operations as part of their basic training.

"Lando remember," he smiles, "To teach a dog tricks, you've got to know more than the dog." He knows I didn't expect to be making copies after four years of college, but I take it cheerfully in my stride. It is a nice office to work in.

"It's okay, I'm the dog," I grin back, as I continue turning the handle of a 'Gestetner' duplicating machine. It is slow and messy. The text is first typed on waxed stencils, which are then cranked over a well-inked roller; finally the copies are manually collated. I daydream that Kenya's independence will bring Xerox to Kenya. In a recent architectural magazine, I read what an incredible breakthrough Xerox has been: it has transformed office technology in the USA since 1959. I wonder if I will one day get a chance to visit America.

"Shush, chaps!" An architect calls out in an attempt to hush the Punjabi chatter among the mainly Indian draftsmen. "The Governor General is about to speak."

"Why today 21st August?" I ask. We crowd around a transistor radio. The Governor-General, referring to the same man who only nine years earlier in 1952 was described as a 'leader into darkness', proclaims Jomo Kenyatta as 'a very good man – a forgiving, honourable and wise man – a great natural leader who will take the country forward in peace and prosperity'. Kenyatta, now 71, had been released from prison the previous month and placed under house arrest. The GG confirms that all restrictions are removed and that Kenyatta is at that moment travelling in a ceremonial cavalcade to his home in Gatundu, outside Nairobi. He returns as a national hero. I welcome the news, as we all knew that Kenyatta's trial had been rigged. The rejoicing over Kenyatta's release is widespread, and so is the anxiety about the future.

On my way home, I drop in at the Gymkhana bar to meet Savio. Everyone has a view on the day's big news. "It's how Britain creates leaders, first it imprisons them," Costa, a bar regular, says. "Gandhi, Kenyatta, so what. They have lost the battle with the Mau Mau."

"Didn't they also have a state of emergency in Malaya?" Dias, another regular, asks. "I remember hearing something about a Chinese rebellion like the Mau Mau. My sister-in-law's family moved there after India's independence. They couldn't stand the way things were going on in Bombay. Good jobs depended on whom you knew."

"If you ask me, I think Britain is handling this carefully," Audit D'Souza says. "They must have promised something to Kenyatta," he rubs his thumb and index finger to indicate cash, "to be nice to the Muzungus after independence. It is we buggers that will be shafted." An older member of the club walks away in disgust at the language used by the speaker.

The topic changes to the ongoing racial conflicts in the USA. I realise we have all lost count of the combatants; the Freedom Riders in Alabama, the Civil Rights Movement, Black Power, Latino Labour, American Indians and others. It seems the armed retaliation and violence of the authorities has shocked everyone in Nairobi, and has become the topic of everyday conversation, just as the Mau Mau was in its early days. Perhaps it is because of the impending political changes ahead.

As I arrive home Dad and Mum are watching the TV news. I greet them.

"Any news from Linda?" I ask.

"No. Maybe we should trade in the set," Dad says. "There is only bad news."

"Everyone at the club is discussing the violence by whites on blacks in America,"

"At least they are not beating up on Catholics and Jews anymore," Dad says. "I think watching TV will simply frighten folks here. Not everyone will know why the blacks in America have to respond so violently to the way they are mistreated."

Meanwhile, African leaders agree to take part in the Constitutional Conference that has been convened by the Colonial Secretary in London to work out the details and timetable for Kenya's Independence. The rumours of possible inter-racial violence grow. But a number of smaller tribes are frightened too. They are worried about the two biggest tribes, the Kikuyu and Luo, becoming too dominant in an independent Kenya; so these smaller tribes form a new political party to negotiate their interests. Tom Mboya, a Luo, and a charismatic, well-educated ex-trade-union leader, takes a lead in calming all parties. He had addressed the students in the Taifa Hall at the College on his return from the USA and could not leave because of the long, standing ovation. He is intelligent and eloquent, a man of the new world, skilled at bringing people together for a common cause. Soon rumours circulate. The Kikuyu and Luo have made a secret deal. Tom Mboya will be the natural successor to Jomo Kenyatta. The prospect of tribalism and racial conflict begins to fade. Times are changing even faster than Joe at the Goan Gymkhana bar had predicted.

It is the week before Christmas – Monday, December 18, 1961 to be exact. My team and I must complete the hall decorations by Friday, but the well-used and much abused family Peugeot 203 is spluttering. It has survived two previous owners, and during our brief ownership has had multiple organ transplants at the hands of Mechanic Lobo of Chambers Road, Ngara. Despite all the tender loving care, it barely reaches the club gate. Then, like a drunk who makes it to his room and then flops onto his bed, the car coughs and lurches forward across the last few yards, onto the compacted murram patch we call the car park and the engine dies.

Merde! I race up the terrazzo steps.

The main hall is dimly lit to conserve electricity, but lights at the far end confirm the card players are alive and well. I head for the source of the loud voices instead.

In our youth, the Gymkhana bar functioned as our 'newsroom'. Savio and I had eavesdropped our way to adulthood selectively picking juicy morsels of rumour and gossip that we would chew on until they eventually translated into a real story. Now that we have reached drinking age, we sit on those same bar stools and exchange real news. My helpers are all there: Savio, Gerson and Ferdie, among others. "One Tusker (beer) for Lando," Savio says to Ben behind the bar, "and one for this man." He gestures as Edwin walks in behind me, clutching a sheaf of papers. Edwin works for one of the daily newspapers.

"Hey chaps! Hot off the press!" Edwin says, "Look at what's happening in Goa. Just fresh off our teleprinter."

"What?" Savio asks.

"The Indians have invaded." We crowd around the printouts. Gerson, recently graduated as a schoolteacher, reads the startling headlines aloud: *'Finally Freedom for the Oppressed'*; *'Indian War Mongers Invade Goan Peace Lovers'*; *'Vassalo Vacillates – Governor hesitates in offering Total Surrender'*.

The dispatches, datelined Bombay, India, 18 December 1961, tell the story:

'India has launched an armed attack on the Portuguese enclaves in India.'

'Goa will be liberated,' says a Government spokesman. 'The army, navy and air force are combining operations. Tanks, warships, bombers and ground troops are involved. It is expected to be a quick operation. It has taken the Portuguese by surprise. Their troops are hopelessly outnumbered and their defence is almost non-existent. Portugal has indicated its agreement to negotiations. India ignores their response'.

'Goa airport's single runway in Dabolim has been bombed out of action. Goan radio station in Bambolim is silenced.'

Mr. JFX (initials used on his scorecard) in his late fifties, puts down the two whiskeys he has just paid for. I see him stiffen and quickly turn pale. I fear he may be having a heart attack.

"Please, please let me see those," he says. "Back soon." JFX strides out of the bar clutching the news reports. Minutes later all sixteen card players that make up the four tables try to squeeze into the bar. I realise my father's generation is most affected by the news. Edwin suggests we move into the main hall. I can see the shock and nervousness on most faces. Savio and I exchange glances; our whole team goes out into the hall and quietly observes, as JFX motions us to pull our chairs around. He emerges as the self-elected chairman.

"This is a very serious situation," JFX says. "Before we decide what to do, we must assemble our views. I want you each to speak frankly. Say exactly what you think."

"Who asked Nehru to liberate Goa?" someone shouts.

"Yeah, who did?" There is loud applause. The spontaneity is electrifying.

"Politicians don't do anything for people," a man says. "Nehru must have an ulterior motive."

"What'll happen to our culture?" L. D'Cruz asks. I know him well as Dad's friend. He was one of the original members of the Goan Overseas Association with Dr. A.C.L De Souza, and a Founder Member of the breakaway Goan Gymkhana in 1936, and a member of the Goan Academic Circle. He is a good friend of J.M. Nazareth. "And what of our Catholic religion, our music, literature? Our special way of life is still the…" He is interrupted by Costa, a bar regular.

"Please do not interrupt. Everyone must be heard," JFX appeals for order.

"There have been Goans outside Goa, fighting for freedom ever since India's Independence," Costa says. "You remember Pio? Anton Gama Pinto's boy? He already told us it would happen. He said one day the Goans would run their own country. He said freedom fighters in Bombay have been organising for this day."

"Even if I agree with freedom," Audit Pereira joins in, "this is not the way to do it. Not by violence. Goa is a peaceful country. What happened to Gandhi's thinking and preaching?"

"We came to Africa for jobs, remember?" It's Dad voice. "Perhaps now we can return and develop Goa peacefully?" Many people shouting interrupt him.

My friends and I can just listen in awe as our parents' generation erupt with a passion we have never witnessed before. They are bitterly divided for and against the invasion. The emotion is palpable.

"Nehru has been trying to negotiate peacefully since Independence," Costa shouts, "but Salazar will only listen with a torpedo stuck up his backside."

"Negotiate with *military force*?" Dad asks. "What sort of negotiation is that?"

"No Chico! Nehru offered to make it a peaceful transfer – even to guarantee that Goa's culture will be maintained intact," Rego, another supporter joins the discussion.

"But we Goans are different," D'Cruz says. "We have embraced our Catholicism and blended Portuguese culture within our bones. Our cultural masala flows in our veins after nearly four and a half centuries. We have our music, our literature, our special cooking. We never were purely… we are not Indian."

"Rubbish!" Rebelo, the bearded man shouts. "Before the Portuguese came and converted our ancestors by force, they were all *pukka* Hindus, so that makes you Indian too!"

"Maybe some were even Muslims," Audit Pereira says. "Can't you see how dangerous this type of talk is? Look around. Even after 14 years of independence Hindus and Muslims are still killing each other on the sub-continent."

"But how can we live as part of India?" Gomes speaks up for the first time. "Are we ready to give up drinking? All over India there's prohibition. In Bombay, Poona, Calcutta… everywhere people are distilling homemade liquor *chini-chini*, illegally. If you're caught, you are thrown in jail, until you agree to bribe the policeman, and even his boss for the rest of your life!"

"Maybe that's what their motives are, their so-called *liberating Goa*," The grey-haired man who opened the discussion speaks up. "The politicians want to be *liberated* to take charge of the smuggling trade from Goa to India – Just see what we can buy freely in Goa – liquor, medicines, tobacco, watches, Van Heusen shirts, imported cars and nylon socks. India has had so-called independence since 1947, and you still can't buy foreign goods in the shops there as freely as in Goa."

"But the smuggling in Goa is not done by Catholics," D'Cruz says. "It is already mostly in the hands of Hindus. They have the expertise."

"That's not true!" Dad says. "For over 400 years the Church and the Administration officials controlled all the permits and licences for trade, shipping and land sales. They traded money and favours and became very rich themselves working with Hindu and Arab traders. Corruption is not a new idea and is not an Indian monopoly."

"Chico, the Indians will steal all the jobs from Goans," Jovito, a Chemist, has joined in the discussion. "The price of everything will shoot up. I have just returned from home leave to Goa, and by the way, spent a week in Bombay. Everything is more expensive in India."

"Let sleeping dogs lie," Gomes says. "In my opinion Goa should continue under Portuguese rule because we are a long way away from Lisbon, and mostly they ignore us anyway. Our people enjoy a peaceful life in the villages. There is always fish in the sea and fruit falls off the trees. It is stupid to fight for freedom. We must say to Nehru, no thanks, we are happy with the present arrangements."

"What about freedom to speak and write?" Jovito asks.

"Every Goan has equal rights as any citizen of Portugal," Dad says. "It's been so since the eighteenth century, when the Marquis de Pombal abolished the colour bar and other restrictions in Goa and all overseas territories. In fact…"

"What nonsense! All that has changed," Rebelo, the bearded man interrupts him. "This bloody dictator Salazar in Lisbon has reversed everything. Since 1926, there is censorship of newspapers. Informers send secret reports to the government. They have a file on each one. Has anybody holding a Portuguese passport tried to get a visa?"

"Yes. I went to Mozambique in 1953 to visit my brother Nicolau," Dad replies.

"And please tell us how long did it take to get a visa, Chico?" Rebelo asks.

"About nine months." Chico replies.

"You see what I mean? Even with a Portuguese passport, it is so difficult to visit another Portuguese territory," Rebelo says. "With Goa being part of India, all the travel restrictions will be lifted. Now travelling to Bombay from Goa, you have to change trains at the border, carry your bags across a no-man's land, and connect with a train on the other side. All that will change. Just imagine how fantastic that will be."

"In my opinion Goa will change for the worse," a loud preacher-like voice booms for the first time. It's Fernandes, a man with angry eyes that have darted from speaker to speaker all evening, "Our beloved land will one day become one big slum. We will have filth and rubbish everywhere. Our clean towns will become just a few more dirty Indian cities. The politicians will steal the money meant for schools, drainage, trash clearing and roads. You mark my words! I have spoken at this club on 18th December 1961." He makes his point and slumps back into his seat.

"I think they should resolve this conflict peacefully," JFX says nervously from the chair. "Perhaps our Goan Overseas Association should be involved. Let's wait and see what the great world powers say about the invasion."

"The so-called great powers have already spoken," D'Cruz says as he holds up one of the teleprinter messages being circulated. "Let me read it to you: 'Prime Minister Harold McMillan has appealed directly to Nehru to negotiate, and is rebuffed'. In America, 'US Secretary of State Dean Rusk met urgently with his top aides. A statement was released shortly thereafter. It stated 'This is a classic example of the use of force by one of the most moralistic members of the Neutral Bloc'."

"And what was Nehru's response?" JFX asks.

"This!" D'Cruz makes a rude sign with his hand.

The meeting breaks up. Chairs scrape the floor as people leave. I take Dad's arm. "Let's go home, Dad. It's late," I feel Dad's arm trembling. His eyes are teary. Savio offers us a ride home. I will pick up the Peugeot in the morning.

At home, we bid Savio a good night, as Dad puts his hand on my shoulder for support. "Lando, till today, I never realised how one is attached to the soil of one's birth," he says in a soft barely audible voice. "Now you children may never really know your heritage, and the glory that was once Goa."

We enter the house; I pour Dad a peg of Johnny Walker. He says he wants to sit alone, quietly in the living room. I recount to Mom in a few words what happened at the club.

"It was his dream one day to return to Goa," Mom says. "That dream is gone."

I go off to my room. Sleep is evasive as I replay in my mind the scene at the club. I feel guilty. Perhaps if I had stayed on in boarding school in Goa and remained behind to make a life, Dad would have returned sooner to Goa, and lived the last years of his life as happily as he lives in Kenya. On the other hand, perhaps the doomsday scenarios predicted for Goa about filth and slums and corruption will never happen. Who is to know? Only time will tell. I toss and turn and punch my pillow into different positions. I cannot understand why Dad was so happy in 1947 to carry me on his shoulders to watch the Independence parade when the British left India, and yet now he's so sad to see Goa become a part of India. I wonder if Pio Gama Pinto will return to Goa to live, now that he has been released from prison in Kenya? If he does, who will continue his work in Kenya?

The next day it is all over. 'Goa has been liberated' is splashed across the front page of the local newspapers. That evening, back at the club with my decorating team, we hear that a similar reaction to the invasion had taken place at the rival Goan Institute. As many members were in favour of the invasion, as against. It appears several members who had been born, lived and trained in British India, had migrated to Africa within five years of India's independence. They were the angriest over the invasion. A fist-fight resulted in one black eye, two broken chairs and a smashed windowpane of their recently opened clubhouse.

The Christmas season's festivities at the Goan Gymkhana are subdued. Too many folks are waiting for news of loved ones at home, as the invading forces have imposed a blackout on news from Goa. It is over 12 days now since the invasion. I attend the New Year's Eve Ball but it feels especially different for me this year, with Linda away, and no girl in particular holds my attention.

'The Scorpions' band, led by Henry Braganza, an ex-classmate from the Goan School, look stunning in their black trousers, white tuxedo jackets and bow ties. Many of my parents' generation have stayed home, but there's no shortage of energy on the dance floor by my age group. The place is swinging. I spot Anita in the crowd; she's now older, and in the subdued light, looks a wee bit heavier. She is whirling gracefully in a long red gown in the arms of a young man who is expertly guiding her past the slower moving traffic of the dance floor. She taught me to dance. Savio notices my glance.

"She has a new one every year," he says, "and a new dress as well."

"Hey, Savio," I say, pretending not to hear. "Want to take a stroll around this joint? See if anything's changed? Do you remember when we went round together in 1949? Let's pick up a drink first."

"Sure." He's still grinning at his joke about Anita, as he adjusts his bow-tie.

The bar is packed as usual, except that now a couple of women, drinks and cigarettes in hand, are comfortably chatting to men in the bar. The billiard room has again been temporarily converted into a crèche, only now the infants sleep in their own carrycots; not like the early days when a mattress was placed over a rubber sheet over the green baize. The ayahs still seem more asleep than the infants in their care. "Most folks now have babysitters at home," Savio explains. "At least, both my sisters do."

"Things are finally changing around here," I say.

"Lando, talking of changes," Savio says, "What do you think is going to happen to us Goans now with the British leaving Kenya, and the Indians forcibly taking over Goa?"

"I don't know," I reply. "Dad and Mom and my uncles are worried and confused. It's been almost their only topic of conversation this Christmas."

"Mine too," Savio says. "They say we now belong nowhere."

"Come on. Let's go and find some partners for the midnight special," I say. "These problems can wait until 1962."

———•———

24

A Chance Meeting

It is four months later. From my first floor picture window at the Mount Kenya Safari Club, Nanyuki, I am staring directly at Mount Kenya –*Kirinyaga* – from where, according to the Kikuyu legend, *Ngai*, God, came down from the firmament. Thick puffy white clouds, tinged with grey, speed across the bright blue sky, creating moving shadows across the gently sloping green lawn in the foreground. In the centre of this visual frame is the jagged blue-grey, multi-peaked mountain, its glaciers defining each of the peaks, the tallest of which, Batian at 17,057 feet, is the second highest in Africa, after Mount Kilimanjaro. I am here with Graham McCullough, with whom I have previously spent working summers. At Graduation in June of last year Graham had offered me my first full-time job. "After two years of practical experience," he had explained, "you will sit a professional qualifying exam for full membership of the Royal Institute of British Architects." And now that experience is coming fast and furious.

Later today, Graham and I will meet again with film actor Bill Holden; he is here on a final shoot of his latest film, 'Lion' with co-star Capucine. "Holden first came out to Kenya on holiday in 1959, fell in love with this location and bought the hotel," Graham told me over breakfast. "Then, with his two friends that we met yesterday, the American Ray Ryan and Carl Hirschmann, the Swiss banker, they embarked on a plan of renovation and expansion. This is the second phase."

We meet with Holden on the patio overlooking thick cloud that has now engulfed the peaks of Mount Kenya. "Sorry Fellas," he drawls. "They had me out of this joint in the pre-dawn. Ready for sleep, so be careful." He flashes a big friendly smile, drags his chair back and before he sits, shakes Graham's and my hand. "How's that again?" he still grips my hand. "Lando as in Or-lando?" I nod. "Gottcha!" A big man, almost 6' tall, with a muscular built, he looks very handsome in his khaki Kenyan Safari outfit. I cannot take my eyes off his slightly bristly look. His photo in the hotel lobby shows a meticulously clean-shaven face. The meeting goes smoothly. He knows what he wants. Confirms answers to queries that Graham had sent in writing, and seems happy to work with me as the 'gopher on the job', which I take as a compliment, not having met a gopher yet. And then the meeting is over and he goes off to bed.

Later at the nearby Nanyuki Airstrip, as Graham completes pre-flight procedures – he uses these trips to build up his flying hours – I reflect on how destiny has suddenly carried me on a wild uncertain ride, like a piece of paper by the roadside, swept up and tossed about in a sudden gust – the winds of change. Before this year I had flown only twice, now I am frequently in the air, on frequent trips in single or twin-engine Cessna planes from Nairobi's little Wilson Airport, to skinny compacted earth and gravel airstrips in remote corners of the country.

Soon after graduation in June, my Class of '61 exploded like seeds in a dry pod, and scattered to the winds. Almost all my African colleagues received leadership scholarships to Britain and the USA, to prepare them for key administrative roles in an independent Kenya. Some Asians with financial means pursued further studies abroad. A handful of Goans go abroad also to study, and the remainder seek local employment.

With the Mau Mau effectively routed and racial barriers lifted, economic activity resumes, bringing in a burst of investment, especially in tourism infrastructure, for which Graham's firm has received many design commissions, so I am in the right place.

Finally, under a relatively clear sky, we take off and barely 20 minutes later, we're cruising over the heavily forested mid-slopes of the mountain. I imagine it was here that Henderson of Special Branch and his handpicked team hunted out the last fugitive bands of the Mau Mau freedom fighters.

"Hang on to your stomach," Graham jokes, as our Cessna drops suddenly into an air pocket. I know he is a relative novice at flying but hide my anxiety, even as I discreetly sneak a view of the controls, in case I have to second-guess him. His sharp steel-blue eyes under bushy eyebrows are focused on the gauges. "Oops! Sorry!" he says as my stomach plunges a second time. "Katabatic winds! The cold air is heavy so it rushes down the mountainsides at great speeds, especially in those valleys between the peaks."

"Are they dangerous?" I ask.

"They can easily flip this plane if it takes us by surprise," he says.

"That'll ruin my evening," I reply. "Have to be at my club tonight."

Soon we are over Ruiru on the outskirts of Nairobi, and the glinting corrugated aluminum amid a quilt of rusty brown roofs on the edge of Mathare Valley. I press my head against the window to get a better glimpse. "I hear the farmers are employing fewer Africans since the Mau Mau troubles, so they're flocking to the cities," I say. "I wish we could design better housing for them."

"Our mayor is against doing anything about it, " Graham says. "He says they are occupying city land illegally." I feel the plane begin to tilt. "Okay! Belts! We're coming down," Graham says, as air control gives its okay. He taxies the plane to a stop. We unload our belongings and head off to the car park.

"Lando, it is important that you involve yourself in Architectural Association affairs," Graham says as we drive back to the office. "It's a good way to meet your professional colleagues and also familiarise yourself with the practical and legal issues facing our profession."

"Will do," I say, though I'm sure Graham knows well how busy he keeps me.

My first Association meeting a month later is at the Norfolk Hotel. The nametags in front of each office-bearer list the crème de la crème of the architectural and quantity surveyor fraternity in Kenya. On a table to one side, a young woman is helping administer membership renewals and other logistics support for the meeting. I peer at the name tag.

Grace is a severe distraction for me, with her dark olive skin, deep brown eyes, and well groomed, if somewhat crinkled, hair. I assume she is Goan – they are the most sought-after secretaries. I know she is not a member of the Gymkhana, so I assume she must be from the rival Institute, but then I would have at least remembered her from my pre-high school days at Dr. Ribeiro's Goan School. I wonder whatever happened to her hair to have got it so curly? I remember Linda telling me that some women use beer or even cold tea to set their hair. I resolve to make her acquaintance after the meeting. However about ten minutes before the meeting draws to an end, Grace glances at her watch, collects her things and discreetly leaves the meeting room.

It's as if God intends us to meet. The next morning, Graham hands me a package of folded plans. "Lando, can you please deliver these documents to Roger personally? He must have them by 10 a.m." Roger, I had found out last night, is Grace's boss.

When I get there, we introduce ourselves and she tells me she is extremely busy, but she soon realizes I am persistent.

"Okay, thanks Lando," she says, "give me a minute, but I must be back in twenty. Deadline today for a big job." We take the elevator down to the ground floor.

"How about the Thorn Tree Café?" I ask. "It's open for us non-whites now."

"Lando, that's expensive. It's in the New Stanley Hotel," she says.

"Don't worry," I say, "First impressions count." The café gets its name from a large yellow-bark thorny acacia in the centre of the patio. It is an old tradition for residents and tourists to leave messages for their friends by piercing them to the long thorns.

"Okay, I'm very impressed." Grace says, as a waiter pulls her chair back.

Grace is even more beautiful today at close quarters, in a pink blouse, a beige long skirt, open sandals and a double string of Maasai beads wrapped around a slender neck. Her eyes are sparkling as if happy to have been asked for coffee.

"Grace, thank you for making this time," I say awkwardly. "Meeting went well yesterday… everything worked like clockwork. Congratulations."

"It's nice to meet you too," she says with a big, warm smile. "I overheard Roger, that's my boss, say to his partners that you're a good addition to McCullough's office."

"I'm sorry, yesterday, staring at you like that," I blurt out. "Very rude of me."

"I know," Grace replies. "Embarrassing for me too, as each time I sneaked a look at you, I found you were watching me."

"I just could not take my eyes off you," I reply. "Are you Goan?"

"With a name like Grace Hunter-Brooke?" she laughs heartily – an infectious, disarming laugh that puts me at ease. "I'm Seychellois. I know some Goan girls though."

"Are you from Nairobi?" I ask, as an American tourist in a loud Hawaiian shirt, and an even louder voice, spikes an envelope on one of the three-inch long thorns.

"No. Born in Kitale but really I've lived in Nakuru… well almost all my life," Grace says.

"Nakuru? What a coincidence!" I say. "Must be many folks out there from Seychelles. I met a little girl once from your community in Nakuru. I was ten years old then. She said she was seven then, must be older now. Boti... Her name is Sa-bo-ti."

"Lando, that's me... Saboti. I'm Saboti!" Grace shrieks jubilantly, waving her arms about. I put out my hand to try and calm her as I am not used to such an exuberant public display of emotion, and worse still, every white patron and black waiter is looking at us – the only two browns with glowing red ears in embarrassment.

"Quiet Sabo... Grace, or they'll bring back segregation," I mumble.

"Yes, Yes. I remember now," Grace says excitedly. "You poked your nose – gosh you have grown too– through the fence. I showed you my doll, Dusi. Remember?" She glances at her watch and stands up ready to return to her office. "You showed me two used bullets, but left the next morning and I was so sad the next day and the next."

"Why did you change your name? I like Sa-bo-ti," I ask.

"The nuns at the Mangu boarding school said I must have a good Catholic name as it would be easier to find a job," Grace says. "So I'm Grace now. Lando, I really must go."

"Why did you leave Mangu?" I ask.

"Lando, I really must dash. You ask so many questions," she says.

"Okay. Just one more then," I say. "Can you prove you are Saboti? You had a scar here," I indicate, moving my finger across the front of my right shoulder. Grace's scar is of course discreetly covered by her pink blouse and I imagine will be just above her now well-developed right breast, below the shoulder.

"Gosh, you're cheeky, Lando. I'll have to report you to McCullough."

"Fine, but please can I call you Saboti?" I ask. "I love that name."

"Only in private, otherwise everybody will be confused," she says. "Gosh, isn't it exciting to meet after so many years?" We agree to try and meet over coffee the next week. We walk back to her office.

Roger hands me an urgent package for Graham. As I walk back to Graham's office at Solar House, I can't help thinking a messenger's job is fine by me, as I will see Saboti more often.

Meanwhile, my Technical High School education is paying off. "Lando, as you understand construction well," Graham says, "Would you like to be responsible for the supervision of the Lutheran Church near Arusha in Tanganyika and the Baptist Church on the Ngong Road?"

"Yes, Thank you," I reply, although I am worried. When will I see Saboti?

Saboti and I manage to meet every two weeks for coffee, during which she gently asks questions; she probes my past life with such elegance and precision, that I answer her questions before I realise it. She hears about my Catholic upbringing and of the Gymkhana, and of my visit to the Seychelles. She smiles as I tell her of how desperately I looked around at all the passers-by, hoping I would see her or her close relatives in the Seychelles. "I was 10 then." I explain, embarrassed by her smiling.

"But you have not spoken about the real you," Saboti says. "Surely in more than 20 years, your big heart has had a flutter from time to time?"

"Flutter? Yes," I reply truthfully. "Flutter and a couple of hairline fractures in my heart." I tell her how Anita taught me to dance, and then quick-stepped out of my life so abruptly. She quizzes me in detail about Juliana who was so close, and loved cooking; yet ironically, it was bread and butter issues that brought that relationship to a standstill.

Saboti divulges little about herself; as she had said I ask too many questions, I am reluctant to probe further. I can only speculate the obvious: that she has acquired her English surname of Hunter-Brooke in the British-ruled Seychelles, in the same way as we adopted Portuguese surnames, or that she might be married? But then I did look for a ring and did not see one. I can't wait to meet her again.

25

Dinner with Saboti

In mid-April, Saboti finally accepts an invitation to dinner. My heart seems to beat faster with excitement. I have been trying so hard to get Saboti to say yes. She is considerate and knows I do not earn a 'European salary', so insists we dine at a modest Ismaili-run restaurant near the College. I park my newly acquired, much-used VW 'beetle' under a street lamp; the family-owned Peugeot couldn't bear to go on living and must have just taken its own life according to Mechanic Lobo. With Saboti on my arm, looking lovely in a colourful blouse and long skirt sewn from a *kitenge*, a Masai beaded necklace and long earrings show off her beautiful neck, we walk a short distance.

A waitress, in a neat black and green uniform, takes our order, but cannot hide her curiosity. It is only very recently that the colour bar has been lifted. Saboti tells me she does not drink alcohol, so I order a mango *lassi* too. "Saboti, tonight I want to know more about *You*." I say. "Please?"

"You'd better eat first. You cannot listen to my story on an empty stomach," Saboti gives me her usual disarming smile. We make some small talk until the food arrives.

"Oh good, tum was growling," Saboti says. "Lando, if you are a good boy and finish all your dinner, I'll tell you a story, okay?" She bows her head, says grace, sips her mango *lassi*, and we eat, interspersed with chat, some jokes, until we're almost done.

"Excuse me," she says and goes to the restroom. When she returns, I notice her eyes seem to have lost their usual sparkle. I excuse myself in turn as I instinctively sense hers may be a long story. In the meantime, Saboti has regained her poise, though her dark eyes emit a sadness that I had not seen before. She is waiting for me to say something.

"Saboti, first please tell me why you have refused so many of my dinner invitations over these many months?" I say.

She looks directly at me and starts to talk in measured tones.

"Lando, about six months ago," Saboti says, "I swore I would not go out with a man until I was absolutely sure about him." She proceeds to tell me why. "When I started my new job here, I didn't know anyone socially in Nairobi. One of my co-workers, fixed me up with a friend of hers on a blind date."

She moves her cutlery around.

"Quite a handsome bloke, really," Saboti continues. "So we met at the Capitol Cinema for the afternoon matinee, as we had agreed. Terry - that's his name - seemed surprised and uncomfortable; my colleague perhaps forgot to tell him I was not white." Saboti's eyes are teary.

"We bought our tickets and Terry insisted we enter the auditorium immediately. Terry was fidgety and kept looking around, as if he was hiding from someone. Then it seemed his nightmare came true. A group of boys from his ex-high school had arrived. He pulled his jacket over his head, grabbed the arms of his seat, and slid down low on the seat as if to hide from them."

"I'm sorry," I say.

"I realised what was happening,' Saboti continues. "Terry was ashamed to be seen with me – a non-white. At that moment the cinema went dark and before the MGM lion roared three times,

I ran out of that bloody cinema." Saboti's tears cannot mask her anger. I take hold of her hands across the table. She pulls them back in a rage.

"Please don't touch me," she says. "Can you even imagine what it feels like to be treated like a leper? As if being coloured is some terrible contagious disease that will instantaneously spread on contact to all white people. It is not my fault that I am a different colour!"

"Where did you run from the cinema?" I ask as she moves her hand away. "Nowhere," Saboti says. "I first ran down Government Road. People were staring at me like I'd gone mad. I stopped by the palm trees at the intersection with Delamere Avenue, as I was hot and exhausted. A kind Indian shopkeeper at the sports shop on the corner told his boy to fetch me a glass of water. Nearby, two African men were watching me all this time; I felt uncomfortable, so I half-walked and half-ran all the way down Delamere Avenue, past the post office and all the way to my flat behind the pink Delamere Flats."

I put out my hand to console her; I can feel she is very upset. She continues.

"I slammed and locked the door and rushed to the bathroom. My stomach was churning, and I felt better after vomiting, but I just couldn't stop crying for almost a whole day. My eyes were swollen and I just wanted to die. I decided I did not want to live with this racism the rest of my life. But where can I run? I did not choose to be born this way."

Saboti is distraught. I hesitate to react, as she had pulled her hands away the first time.

"So I decided I would never go on a date again and face the same experience," Saboti continues. "Now I lead a quiet life; I enjoy reading and sometimes I play tennis with my few close friends."

Her eyes convey only pain. I feel like I want to hug her and assure her that not all the world is cruel, that there are people of all shades who are working to rid us of this curse of racism. I place my hands on the table, palms facing upwards. She leans forward.

"Lando, can I trust you? I mean *really* trust you?" She places both her hands in mine and I squeeze them gently. "I know I must talk to somebody. Okay. Now listen!" She leans forward again.

"I have been living a lie all my life. I didn't start it, but it's a lie all the same." She pauses for a few seconds, looks into my eyes as if demanding my full attention.

"I am not Seychellois, but Aunt Mena and Papa are both Seychellois. Aunt Mena told me when I was young that I was also Seychellois, so I believed her. But it's a lie. Do you believe me?"

"Tell me more," I say, not quite sure yet where she is going.

"I'm a *nusu-nusu*, a *chotara*, a half-caste. My mother is Elgon-Masai, and my father is an English aristocrat, known among the settler community as RC," Saboti says, looking straight into my eyes.

"Roman Catholic?" I ask, hoping I am successfully hiding my shock at her news.

"No, no. Dad's initials," Saboti says. "Probably Robert Cromwell or something. Your guess is as good as mine. No one will tell me, but I will find out one day."

"Who knows the truth?" I ask. This time I am looking into her eyes to see if my line of questioning troubles her.

"Basil Gordon – we call him Uncle Bas," Saboti says. "Found this out recently. He took care of some things for my father while he was away. Dad was an Army Major fighting in Burma in the war."

"How did they meet?"

"Who RC and Uncle Bas, or RC and Mum?" She asks.

"Both."

"According to Uncle Bas, they both came out separately from Britain around 1939 as 'agricultural pupils' – they received a small wage from the government while they worked on white-owned farms in Rumuruti. They were only 18 at the time, and became friends." She takes a sip of water. "A year later, both enlisted in the Kenya Regiment and were sent up to the northern frontier with Abyssinia for six months. RC decided to live permanently in Kenya and requested that his siblings remit his share of the family estate to him. With the money, he bought a farm near Kitale, where Bas had already settled."

"So did your dad - RC - marry your Masai mother in Kitale?" I ask.

"No, no. My father did not marry my mother," Saboti says. "I'm both a bastard and a half-caste." Her tears have dried up and she is recounting the story dispassionately.

"Uncle Bas told me that my father was re-commissioned into the Army again, this time to lead a regiment into Burma. RC needed to leave the farm with someone reliable while he was away. Uncle Bas suggested RC contact Hugh Hunter-Brooke, who owned a large farm next door. Hugh invited RC to stay for dinner and they had drinks, and then some more drinks. RC had gone over to Hugh's on horseback and it was now too late to return, so Hugh invited my father to sleep over, and enjoy the hospitality for which he was renowned - the companionship of one of his 'Bibi ya Jikoni'- kitchen wives. RC stayed the night, woke up with a hangover and spent another night, and then, according to what he told Bas, after a hearty breakfast of eggs, roasted deer meat, jam and toast, he rode home. A week later RC was on his way to Burma with a contingent of British troops and African soldiers from the Kings African Rifles. I was born when RC was still in Burma." Saboti stops for breath.

"So where were you born?" I ask. "Who looked after you?"

"Kitale. Uncle Hugh made sure my mother received proper care up to the time of my birth," Saboti continued, "and took care of us after that – Hugh already had a daughter of his own, Geri - Geraldine - with one of his Bibis. He even gave me his name: Hunter-Brooke. When I was five, Geri and I went to live in Nakuru together, until I was seven, and then we were both sent to a boarding school in Thika. I have never met my father."

Saboti sits back without blinking an eyelid, her big eyes now again showing a sign of sparkle. It reminds me of our first meeting. She was about seven, proudly showing me her pink plastic doll 'Dusi' with those big blue eyes and eyelids that opened and closed as she moved the doll into a sitting and then a sleeping position. Now here she is 13 years later, and I have grown accustomed to her skin –darker than mine, and her crinkled hair makes her so beautiful. It's my turn to stare at her in disbelief.

"Saboti! This is one of the most bizarre stories I have heard in all of my lifetime of 22 years," I say. "Let's be serious please. Are you saying you were conceived just like that over drinks, dinner and…and…dessert?"

"Yes, exactly that!" She replies. "Lando, do you think adults even imagine the consequences of their actions on the next generation? Do you think anybody even stopped to think about what it would be like for me, and others like me, to be born and grow out of wedlock? A bastard and a half-caste - where neither community will acknowledge your very existence?"

I am speechless for a reply but Saboti continues to speak. "Even in school, we children of mixed race have to be extra smart just to get on. We work twice as hard at lessons and at sports and at everything!"

"Saboti, you say you only recently found out all this?" I ask, "Surely Uncle Bas wouldn't have known details of what happened at Hugh's house?"

"About two years ago. After I finished high school, I was determined to know more about my past," Saboti says. "Nobody should have to live without an identity, so I asked Uncle Bas first, and then confronted Uncle Hugh."

"You confronted Hugh?" I ask.

"Yes, I did."

"Did your father ever find out about you?"

"Yes. According to Hugh, when RC returned from his tour of duty in Burma, he went to see Hugh. I was still a toddler in Hugh's household."

"What did RC - your dad - say or do, when he was given the news? I ask.

"According to Hugh, RC - my dad - seemed surprised, but not unhappy," Saboti continues. "He might even have happily accepted me. However, when he came back from Burma, he had almost immediately betrothed himself to an English woman. When she was confronted with the news of my existence, she would have nothing to do with it. RC told Hugh that he would assume full responsibility for his actions, but that he did not know how to deal with the arrangements and settlements that would have to be made."

I sense she is haunted by her story. "Lando, just imagine the scenario," she says, cheering up a bit:

"Act One – enter RC facing Hugh (holding Scotch on the rocks in crystal tumbler): 'Look here Hugh old boy, you helped get me into this f*****g mess in the first place, now please help me deal with it. I want to do the decent thing by the woman and the baby, old chap. See what she needs by way of compensation. Then let's find a proper adoption place for the girl – by the way – does she have a name yet? Eventually let's get her into a decent school.'

"Hugh (removing cigar from mouth): 'there's a place near Nairobi, which the dear nuns put up to take all the illegitimate Catholic babies of those Italian POWs. Do you remember Bob something or other at Endebess? Old boy had a similar problem - blind passion with black girl - English wife didn't suspect a thing. Little girl is now with nuns.'

"RC: 'Oh, what would we do without these big-hearted Sisters! So my dear Hugh, just do me that favour. Money is no problem. Just handle it and let me know from time to time how we're doing. Thanks, old chap! Cheers!'"

Saboti pauses like a diva waiting for applause before continuing with her lines.

"So there you have it, Lando! Act One. Curtain drops. Audience stands up and gives a standing ovation! The story of a not-so-immaculate conception!"

"Bravo," I gesture applause.

Saboti has not finished her lines.

"So, Lando, my dear Goan boy, I am nothing but a little half-caste bastard. Now that I am grown up, nobody wants to go out with me - not even to the bloody cinema!"

Saboti stands up. "Imagine listening to this story on an empty stomach. Please take me home now, Lando. Thank you for being so kind and patient. I feel better, now that I have told someone the real truth. Up till now, I thought no one will listen and I'm very tired. Please can I go home now?"

"Saboti, what can I say?" I blurt out. "I am shocked and feel angry as well. Until today I had not really thought about what it must be like to be born without an identity – to be born of mixed race and having to constantly search for an identity and acceptance." I pull my chair back. "Also I just never imagined how painful raw racism can be in such a situation as you experienced. We grew up accepting it as if God preordained it. I am truly sorry." I hold out my hand. This time Saboti takes and squeezes it gently.

"It's OK, Lando. Thank you for listening. I'll survive now. I talk too much. I've taken so much of your time. I must learn to talk less," Saboti smiles again as if a heavy burden has been lifted off her shoulders.

We were so engrossed with each other, that we did not notice the restaurant is completely empty. Even the waiters have gone, except the Ismaili owner of the restaurant. "I'm sorry. We didn't realise you were waiting to lock up," I say. He lets us out.

I am shocked by Saboti's story, as I have never even imagined anything like it. I instinctively take her hand and place it under my arm. We walk back to the car and I drive her home. I walk her to the door of the apartment building.

"Saboti, can I see you again?" I ask.

"Are you sure?" she asks. "Yes, that would be nice Lando." She shakes my hand.

"Perhaps we can go out to dinner again?" I say. "I want to hear more. I will call you as soon as I am back from the Masai Mara. Goodnight Saboti."

"Goodnight Lando. Thank you for listening."

I wait for her to enter the lobby, close the door and then drive home to Plums Lane.

———•◆•———

26

The Dancing Zebras

Saboti has infiltrated my mind like nothing else before. Asleep, awake, at work, or travelling to a job in a remote part of the country, I just cannot stop thinking of her, of our incredible chance meeting after 13 years and her amazing story. Her words 'Lando my dear Goan boy'; 'my not-so-immaculate conception; 'nothing but a little half-caste bastard', reverberate inside me and raise questions I had not even imagined.

When I asked her to go out again, she had replied 'Are you sure?' Did she know what a big leap this would be for a 'Goan boy', from a well-respected Brahmin family at that? Did she expect me to be repulsed by her story; perhaps take a step back? Why should I? It's not as if I plan to marry her or something. That phrase she used, 'nothing but a little half-caste bastard', is exactly how many Asians (and Goans) would describe her, with their caste-obsessed culture. But I *will* see her again. Nobody will tell me what to do.

Miscegenation outside marriage seems so cruel and unfair, and yet it is inevitable in a mixed society. After 500 years of Portuguese colonisation in Goa, have we not all become mixed anyway? Was it not the Portuguese who invented words like *mestico* and *mulato* to describe persons resulting from sexual liaisons between different races? And what is the Church's position in the 20th century on miscegenation, I wonder?

Saboti's story helps me to realise how my friends and I grew up happily in a segregated society, protected by parents and community, in which we accepted the political and social hierarchy as if God ordained it. She has woken me up not only to the politics of race, but to the injustices and hypocrisies of religion and colonial society… and the great vulnerability and enforced powerlessness of women. I must ask Saboti about her mother. For the first time, I am aware of the unfettered freedom the white man enjoys. The right to take all and consume at will, to exploit cheap labour, and even lust sexually and gorge himself at will. Such is the corruptive use of colonial power. I find myself now looking forward to Independence from colonialism.

A month later, Saboti and I meet for dinner again in the same restaurant. The waiter remembers us well. Like the first time, we are among the first patrons to arrive and will be the last to depart.

Saboti is bubbling with happiness and wants to hear about my trip to the Masai Mara Game Reserve.

"Lando, thank you for the photograph of those dancing zebras. It was so sweet of you to remember me," she says. "I'm dying to hear of your adventure."

"It certainly was an adventure," I reply. "This project is for the tourist lodge at Keekorok that I had told you about the last time we met. It's finally happening. There's nothing there now. Only the general area for the future lodge has been demarcated."

"What does that mean?" Saboti asks.

"The final site for the lodge must be surveyed and deeded only after further studies. Graham is giving me major design responsibility so I'm very excited."

"That's wonderful, Lando," Saboti says. "Did you go alone?"

"No. My assistant Balbir Singh — he's a Sikh. He was a year behind me at the Tech High school – and I drove in my VW beetle,"

I reply. "It has 135,000 miles on the clock and no problems, except for a flat tyre near Hells Gate and a flying pebble that cracked the windscreen. Thank God the glass didn't shatter."

"I know Hells Gate," Saboti says. "Our class went on a day-trip in our final year at high school to see the geo-thermal geysers bubble sulphur-smelling steam, and I remember we had samosas and tea at Narok. The Masai gathered around chattering excitedly. They were curious to see me with a class full of white girls." Saboti's eyes are sparkling as she speaks.

"Did you see the wildlife down in the base of the Rift Valley?" I ask. "It was just teeming with herds of zebra, giraffe, antelope, and herds of Masai cattle as we drove past."

"Yes it was fantastic," Saboti says. "Our teacher said some people believe the Valley is the original Garden of Eden, mentioned in the Bible."

"Anyway, because of our flat tyre and some rough patches of roadway, we arrive at our destination with only an hour to go before total darkness," I say. "The nights in the Masai Mara Game Reserve are really black with just a brilliant starry sky above, but that's not enough light to see anything, and it is dangerous to walk about in the dark. That's when the animals come out to the river, so we have to move fast. Balbir and I spot a flattened area of grassland and hurriedly pitch our two-person tent. We collect kindling, and some dried leaves and get a fire going. We're rushing against the clock remember. By the time we are finished, we're both exhausted, so we eat early and bed down in our sleeping bags."

"Weren't you worried about snakes creeping into your tent," Saboti asks.

"No. Our tents have sewn-in ground sheets," I explain, "We only have to make sure the opening is zipped tight. It was unexpectedly cold that night because of the clear sky, so we spread our clothes over our sleeping bags and fell asleep."

"I'd be very scared sleeping in the open," Saboti says. "Even in a tent."

"We were too exhausted to be frightened," I say. "Now, for the really scary part. At about 3:00 a.m. I hear a pounding sound - it seems to be coming from within the earth below us. Balbir also sits up, woken by the same noise. The tremor gets stronger and louder."

"Was it an earthquake?" Saboti asks.

"No. We hear animals, mainly zebras barking; the occasional trumpeting of an elephant somewhere in the distance. Soon there are other sounds and these are suddenly very close. We are terrified. I am holding the flashlight but am too frightened to turn it on in case it attracts something in our direction. Balbir is muttering under his breath… could have been his last prayers. I whisper to him but no sound comes out, as my throat is dry with fright. It seems all the animals in the park have come to greet us and we are in the middle of some sort of stampede. The next moment, two of the tent's guy ropes are pulled down; then another – the tent collapses on us, as the sewn-in ground sheet has been tightly pegged all around the base to keep it in place."

"And then what happens?" Saboti asks, her big eyes getting even bigger. She stretches out her hands across the table to touch mine.

"Balbir and I lie absolutely still, while a herd of elephants pass in procession, within a few feet of us. I might not have made it tonight for dinner, but God was looking after us." I say. "We could have been trampled to death. Now we have the tent on us and need to get out, but we don't know what's out there and we can't get back to sleep anyway."

"Isn't it dangerous to be outside anyway?" Saboti asks.

"Yes it is," I reply. "We just prop the canvas up, so we don't feel suffocated, and lie still, talking until about 4:45 a.m., then creep out as it's almost morning. It is the most beautiful experience at sunrise. First the sky turns from a deep grey to purple, then to shades of pink, followed by a bright orange. Finally, the sun makes a grand entrance over the horizon. It is absolutely magnificent, Saboti, and more beautiful when you've spent half the night thinking you might never see it again."

The waiter brings our order and departs.

"Oh Lando, I'm glad you came back safely," Saboti says. "How scary that must have been for you both. You are so brave. What exactly is your work on site?"

"Our job is to survey the topography, the landscape and other physical features," I explain. "We must use the absolute minimum land for buildings, and their final location must respect the natural environment. We must also not disturb the natural paths taken by wildlife in search of grazing, water and salt."

"Is there no safer way to locate the paths of the animals, than pitching your tents anywhere and having elephants almost trample you to death? " Saboti asks.

"Funny! We were just ignorant and hasty. Of course there is. A professional wildlife expert will also prepare a 'wildlife-tracks' plan, which will plot the established paths of various species of wildlife to the natural water hole and salt lick, and to the nearby swamp, where a herd of hippos come ashore every night. With this information and our own surveys, we must then determine the most advantageous location on the site, to ensure the best views for the tourists in the public areas and from the bedrooms."

"Oh gosh, it sounds very complicated," Saboti says.

"It will be. After the tent crashed in on us, we quickly moved our tent to what seemed a safer spot – where the grass had been less trodden. The next day the Masai Park Ranger and Duncan, a European wildlife 'expert', arrived at about 9:00 a.m. in a Willys Traveller Safari Wagon – not many of those around. We had planned to meet on the site. We told them what had happened to us. The expert has two Maasai game scouts who work with him. One of the two Masai scouts walks in the direction of the spot where we had pitched our tent. He signals to his colleague and they both discuss something, pointing to the ground. They return and one of them says to me, 'The *ndofu* – elephants – herds walk to the water here. Next time, you both may die'. I thanked him for his prediction."

"Please don't say such things," Saboti says. " Did you get to see animals in daylight?"

"Yes we did. First we were driven around in Duncan's Safari Wagon, to view the park immediately around our site. The plains were teeming with wildebeest, zebras, deer and antelope. I wish you could see them. At one spot we stopped a bit longer right in the middle of a herd of zebra to watch a ritual dance of courting zebra. They just seemed so happy, almost dancing. The shorter one, being the female, tries to jump up and kiss the male on the lips, the male raising himself on his hind legs playing hard to get, staying just out of reach – that's where I took the photograph that I sent you. We visited a nearby swamp. A herd of hippos, their nostrils just above the water, snorted very loudly at us for disturbing their peace. The previous night, Balbir and I had listened to their snorts and belching all night. Have you heard hippos belch? They're very loud."

"Lando, I really love that zebra shot. I have pinned it up where I can see it every day. Thank you." Saboti reaches out across the table and squeezes my hand. "Your hippo belches can't be worse than my Uncle Hugh," Saboti says. "Before I left Kitale to live in Nakuru at the age of six, I was very frightened of animals."

"Why?"

"As children, we used to huddle around the fireplace on chilly evenings. We needed that fireplace. The houseboy used to place big logs of *kuni* that burnt all night, and we never ran out as farmers were always cutting trees to grow crops. The dry *kuni* was stored under a lean-to shed by the house. Geri and I used to roll on the animal skin rugs, because Hugh and his friends used to go shooting often. Most of these rugs had the heads of the animals still on. They lay spread-eagled on the floor with enormous glass eyes that stared back at us, blank and helpless, as if *we* had killed them. Although we felt sorry for them, sometimes we used to scare ourselves, imagining that some of the eyes were actually moving and following us around the room."

B r a z   M e n e z e s

"Who is Geri?" I ask.

"Oh, Lando, I'm sorry," Saboti laughs aloud. "Of course you must be confused. Geri is Hugh's own daughter with Sinawe, her Masai mother. So Geri – her real name is Geraldine - is *nusu-nusu*, like me. But Sinawe did not live with us. Soon after Geri was born she left Hugh and went back to her Maasai 'husband' with whom she had previously had one son. On her return to the *boma*—that means the Maasai settlement– her husband cut off her ear as punishment for giving birth to a white man's baby. I met Sinawe only once, when she came with my mother, Siron, to see Geri and me at our boarding school in Mangu. That's when I noticed part of her ear was missing."

The waiter arrives at the table.

"Please Bwana," he says, his hand outstretched with the bill, "We are closing now."

I hand him some money and turn back to Saboti. "Please, please finish this story about why you were frightened of animals."

"There were many mounted heads in Hugh's house – bucks, antelopes, gazelles and a warthog with its round tusks. So the eyes were also on the walls – our every movement was being watched. The farmers used to shoot animals to feed their dogs and provide meat for their farm labourers. Once we heard them say that a whole antelope will only last two days. Hugh had a friend in Nakuru - a taxidermist - who used to prepare the skins and mount the heads. Geri and I went there once – a very smelly place."

"We must go to the Coryndon Museum together," I tell her. "I live near it. I even thought I might work as a taxidermist one day. Instead, I trained as an architect."

'Thank heavens!" she exclaims, "somehow I cannot imagine you as a smelly guy going out with normal people after work. As an architect building lodges for tourists, thousands more will enjoy seeing the animals alive. Taxidermists deal with dead ones." She stands up to leave. I see the waiter reflected in the mirror, returning with change.

Saboti takes my arm. It feels such a normal thing for her to do. I am glad she feels comfortable with me now. There is a light drizzle outside. "Shall we make a dash for it?" I ask.

"Yes Lando." She runs ahead of me. In a few minutes the Beetle delivers her at her apartment. We say goodnight with a hug. "Thank you Lando," Saboti says. "I am fascinated by stories of your world. Till the next time."

"It's *your* world I am interested in," I reply. "I'll call as soon as I return from Keekorok in about three weeks."

———•+•———

Braz Menezes

27

Hoof Marks, Paw Prints and Dung Droppings

The following week I am travelling again, this time to the dry arid landscape of the Samburu Game Reserve, north of Mount Kenya. We must make a quick appraisal of the feasibility of extending a small existing lodge on the banks of the Uaso Nyiro River. Graham and I, along with Peter, an engineer, will spend two nights at the lodge. The pilot will return to Wilson Airport, and pick us up when we're done.

The drone of the twin-engine Cessna 301 and the conversation of the three occupants do not interfere with my thoughts. I pull out a little pocket book in which I jot the various sightings of birds and wildlife.

The most recent notes were of the last trip to the Masai Mara. I peruse the list: crocodiles, hippos, zebras, two black-eared lions, one cheetah, giraffe… and so on. I flip over to the back and insert a note to myself, under a heading: 'Questions for Saboti': If she was taken from her mother, who looked after her as a child? Was she sold to her foster parents in Nakuru? Did the nuns baptise her a Catholic?'

Graham turns around from the passenger seat beside the pilot. "Lando, I see your jotting down some questions."

"Exactly that," I reply. I flip to a page of recent bird sightings: 'hornbills, waxbills, bulbuls, crows, warblers, orioles, superb starlings, kingfishers, African green pigeons, ox-peckers, egrets and the sacred ibis, and more'.

"Will you please add 'Check water levels at Buffalo Springs? Check on age and condition of generator and capacity'?" He turns around.

I flip to my Saboti page and scribble: "Was Hugh looking after S because he felt guilty sharing his bibis with RC? Was he just 'milking' her father (RC) for money?" I put the book away. Saboti has penetrated the inner crevices of my brain. I could have asked her all these questions earlier, but after her comment that I was too curious, I was afraid of losing her.

We manage to get all our work done in two days, and are expecting the pilot back any moment. We wait by the airstrip in the shade of a clump of acacias. It is very warm even in the shade, with almost no breeze. Mirages appear in almost any direction I look – I know to our north there is dry arid countryside, yet it appears a big lake separates us from the purple hills beyond; on the west, it is similar.

I whip out my notebook and make an entry I almost forgot. I add 'Gerenuk' to the list - a long-necked antelope that stands on its slender hind legs to feed off tender new growth atop stunted trees. It is special to this park. I turn over the pages. There is too much wildlife and I think I have almost 200 birds. I decide to abandon further additions in future.

On our return to Wilson Airport and the office, Balbir confirms that all logistics for our next trip to the Keekorok in Masai Mara are in place. Because I must finish some work on our Samburu trip, I leave him completely in charge of preparations. He even has my car keys. Two days later, after a dusty drive along the floor of the Rift Valley, my VW beetle delivers us safely to Keekorok.

"Hey Balbir, what's the deal with two tents?" I ask, as we unload at our campsite.

"My grandfather lives with us and he's 75," Balbir explains. "It was his idea. He insisted that we 'must sleep in separate tents to confuse the lion.'"

"What lion?" I ask

"Never mind," Balbir replies. "The one in his head. He still remembers the lions near Tsavo, attacking railway workers when he was a young man."

"I remember that, Balbir. We were travelling to Mombasa on the train on our way to Goa. Dad told me that story of how on some nights, man-eating lions would sneak silently in the middle of the night into the railway construction camp near Tsavo River. How the lion would pick an Indian worker for its dinner and drag him screaming and screeching into the blackness and disappear without trace, and how it took more than two years to hunt and kill them. I was so scared I sat up all night praying, and on the lookout out for lions. Aren't you scared of lions?"

"No, but I will be now, if you don't stop repeating these stories," Balbir says. "Shush! Listen!" We both hold our breath and listen for sounds in the tall grass. "My mother said if I do not respect a *wazee's* venerable wisdom something bad will definitely happen, so that's why I changed our order for the tents at Low and Bonner. Your friend Ferdie, the Accounts chap, said there would be no extra charge as we are their good customers."

We eat early and from our vantage location, sit and admire the incredible beauty of the landscape. Against a deep-orange sky we watch the gently rolling savannah, isolated acacia thorn trees in silhouette dotted around and clumps of concentrated woodland along the river, where animals seek water and shade from the blazing sun during the day. I want to tell Balbir about Saboti, but I can't as I have pledged her total secrecy.

There are no lion attacks that night; just sounds of occasional roars and coughs; of zebras barking and hippos belching; hyenas laughing hysterically against the constant buzz of crickets. Occasionally, night owls will add their hoots to the constant nightlong lullaby that only fades with sunrise, when a chorus of screaming monkeys screech out the joy of another imminent sunrise.

As dawn breaks, Balbir and I cradle our enamel mugs of freshly brewed hot tea, and study the herd of hippos emerging from the long grass by the bank. They waddle around, like giant blow-up vinyl monsters, each with a glistening wet dark brown upper side, fading away to a bright flesh-pink underbelly all supported on four legs, which seem very slender for the weight they are carrying. Nearby, crocodiles lie motionless on the riverbank for hours, their mouths gaping, as if expecting food to drop from the sky.

We hear the sound of the engine first, and then see the cloud of dust that follows the dark blob driving towards us. It is Duncan's Safari Wagon bringing him and his two Masai scouts, Ole Lengai and Olitip. They park in the shade of an acacia near our tent. Duncan proceeds to unfold a map on the hood of the vehicle, as we walk to meet them. We exchange greetings. Ole Lengai is the tallest. His red-brown skin glistens in the morning sun and his hair has been cut. He seems incongruous in his khaki outfit, with his deep pierced earlobes and string of beads knotted around his strong neck. Olitip is more sinewy and smiles often as if to display the spaces between his otherwise perfect teeth. He has a 35mm Kodak film canister balanced in one ear lobe. I imagine when he is not tracking, he poses for tourist photographs dressed in his native red shuka.

"Okay, here it is," Duncan says. "The paths of every mammal in this park."

"*Every?*" I ask.

"Yes. Every," Duncan says while Lengai and Kip nod their heads. "The whole alphabetical spectrum - from the aardvark, antelope, buffalo, cheetah, to the wildebeest, warthog and zebra."

"How do you do this?" I ask. I can see Balbir is also impressed.

"Hoof marks, paw prints and dung droppings," Duncan says.

"Dung droppings?" I ask. "Even for the little mammals?" I see Kip walking off searching the ground. He picks something up and brings it back to us. It is a 'dung beetle'. It measures just under a half inch long, and it is still hanging on to its prize - a small olive-size ball of dik-dik dung.

Duncan spreads out some black and white photographs over the maps.

"You don't want one of these to land on your foot," he says, pointing to a heap of elephant manure. Other photos are of hoof-marks and dung of different animals.

"Here along the right," he explains, "are listed the different animals. Just follow the lines." We study the amazing patterns of criss-cross lines. Balbir brings out our site plans drawn to the same scale, where he had plotted the alternative site layouts based on our earlier survey of the physical features of the site.

"Thank you Duncan," I say. "And to you too Lengai and Kip. This is a very impressive piece of work. I can see we're going to have to make some adjustments to our earlier layout."

"When does Graham get here?" Duncan asks.

"In two days time," I reply. "We've received the drilling results on the soil samples, and the boreholes for water quality samples has also been completed, so we're making good progress. Graham will be in touch with you – he handles the cash." We shake hands and they depart, leaving Balbir and me to get on with re-drafting alternate site layouts.

"Tonight we're going to tempt the lion," I say. "Let's make one tent our design office." That night I sleep lightly. I know from experience that often my parents would warn me about something and later when it went exactly as they had predicted, I would hear the words 'I told you so'. We won't have much of a chance if a lion does visit us tonight. Fortunately nothing happened that night nor the next morning.

Two days later, Graham flies in with Peter. The two of them and a pilot are booked into a posh, tented safari camp about three miles up-river. We spend another two days going over all the material accumulated so far, examine the two alternative site layouts, make further adjustments, and are almost finished with this phase. We now have every rock outcrop, dry-weather streambed, bush and tree, plotted and superimposed over the animals' tracks.

We know that the lodge will be built in timber and natural stone from the area. A potential quarry site outside the park boundary has already been identified and negotiations are underway between the client and the local authorities. On our return to Nairobi, I will work on the detailed design over the next month, assisted by Balbir.

The next day, we dismantle camp and pack up, make sure no embers are still alive; kick more sand over the campfire site, and we are on our way back to Nairobi. As I glance around this paradise of wildlife, I say to Balbir, "Do you realise that thousands of tourists will visit Keekorok Lodge in the future, and we will be able to say we were there before there was a lodge?" He doesn't reply. I swerve to avoid a pothole. Balbir wakes up.

"My grandfather will be glad that the lions did not pay us a visit this time," he says.

We get back safely to Nairobi without any major adventure.

I must ask Saboti those questions that are still buzzing in my mind.

28

Saboti's Early Years

I see Saboti more often now. Linked by her secret, we have become friends, and slowly through meetings over coffee or a snack, or occasionally through a walk in the recently- named Uhuru Park, she opens my eyes to a world completely different from my own. I know her well enough now to ask some of the questions that came to me the first time she told me about her history. She seems comfortable talking about her childhood.

It is a November Saturday morning; everyone works a half-day. Nairobi is awash with jacaranda blossoms under a perfect blue, almost cloudless sky. We drive to the higher ground by St. Mark's Anglican Cathedral from where we can view the fast changing city centre skyline, preparing to debut for the biggest party of all – Independence Day - projected for December 1963.

We sit on a rock and take in the scene.

"Look there Saboti," I say, pointing to the clock tower of the Legislative Council that dominates the view. "Immediately behind they are building the new Office of the Attorney General, and look, the Hilton Hotel is already obstructing the view of the Headquarters of the National Bank of India. That's where Dad started his first job in 1928." Beyond Princess Elizabeth Way, there seems to be construction everywhere in the city in readiness for *Uhuru* –Independence.

"Let's sit over there," Saboti says. She has made some sandwiches. We get to our feet and pick a quiet, shady spot under a willow tree, still overlooking the city centre. We lean against the thick tree-trunk.

"So please tell me how you ended up in Nakuru," I say.

"I was only six. I was frightened. 'Mama-Sankau' – she was a tall, young Nandi woman about 17 years old, was one of Uncle Hugh's bibis and that's what I called her – 'will the *Nyangaus*, the monsters—come for me tonight?', I asked. 'Of course not, my little baby, I am here with you.' She sang soft and gentle songs in her own language, which I didn't understand, but the music was sweet."

Saboti pauses for a moment.

"When I woke up the next morning, I was given my bread made of *posho* and milk. Hugh drove me to Nakuru where I was placed in Aunt Mena's care. Her name really was Philomena. She ran a kindergarten as well. Her husband was a nusu-nusu, half-Indian and Seychellois. I called him 'Papa' as that's what their one real daughter, Angela, called him. Hugh's daughter Geri was already there."

"Geri must have been happy to see you," I said.

"Yes. She was very happy and I was too, as I could now play with a real girl, instead of with Ambrose, Geri's black half-brother. Then Hugh, Aunt Mena and Papa talked for a little while. Hugh made them both sign some papers, which he took from a brown envelope. He counted some money, then he gave this to Aunt Mena, and she signed another paper. She then showed him another letter. He took some more money from the envelope, and gave it to her. Hugh then turned around looking for me. 'Where are you my Black Beauty?'– He often called me that – he said there was a children's story of a famous horse by the same name too. He then hugged me, promised to see me soon, and left. But it was nearly a year before I saw him again." She turns to look directly at me. Saboti's eyes are both fiery and moist as she talks about Hugh.

I feel my eyes moisten just listening to her. I try and imagine what it must feel like to be suddenly taken away at the age of 6, and left with someone you have never heard of before. Even when I was left in Goa, Dad and Mom had prepared me for it, and I had my Grandmother close by. Surely God didn't wish this on her?

"Was Mena a Catholic?" I ask. "Did *she* have you baptised?"

"No, Papa was. Mena was Anglican. About a week after Hugh dropped me in Nakuru, Papa, Aunt Mena, Angela, Geri and I, go to Our Lady of the Holy Rosary Catholic Church in Nakuru, and that Sunday, I was baptised, just like that." Saboti snaps her fingers. "I was given the names of Bernadette Grace Saboti Hunter-Brooke. Both Papa and Aunt Mena had told me, 'You must become a Catholic to go to school with Geri'," Saboti continues. "I practiced saying my night prayers about five or six times a day 'so the nuns can see you have been a Catholic since birth', Aunt Mena said, and a week later I was at the Thika School. I did what the other girls did. Mostly I followed Geri around and learned from her. There were black girls who were orphans, and there were also many '*nusu-nusu*'– half-caste children, like me." Saboti stands up; stretches, swings her arms about, and stamps her feet, to get her circulation moving. I remain seated.

"Did all the girls come from around Thika?" I ask. Saboti sits down again.

"The orphans came from the Thika area," She says. "The *nusu-nusu* like Geri and I came mainly from the White highlands. Most of the girls had a black mother, but white fathers, mainly English, *Kaburu* (Afrikaans), or Italian. There was one half German whose parents lived in Tanganyika and a half Indian from Eldoret. Around 1953, the school started to admit Goan girls, who had both fathers and mothers who doted on them, and brought them homemade pickles and cakes, they had a normal family to go home to during their holidays. That's how I know many Goans."

I know that this is true as the only choices especially for civil servants in the districts was to send their darlings to Goa or India. The nuns charged high fees to the Goans to help pay for the black orphans. I am curious how Goan families reacted to their daughter's coloured friends.

"Did any of them invite you to their homes for the holidays?" I ask.

"No. You know Lando, it's funny looking back now, how we were all Catholic, but we never thought about these things when we were young," Saboti says. "The nuns were super really. Strict, but mostly kind. I could have completed my Senior Cambridge Certificate there."

"Why didn't you?" I ask.

"When Geri left," Saboti says, "she was two years ahead, I was suddenly whisked away from the nuns, and transferred to Nairobi. Nobody asked me. I had no choice, but I enjoyed it there too. Our new school had been an exclusive European girls school, but since 1957 they took a handful of non-white students as an experiment to prepare for the future. I imagine that not everyone was happy with the presence of a nusu-nusu, but times were changing."

"Saboti," I say. "I still don't fully understand. Are Papa and Aunt Mena your legal foster parents?"

"No. They are a Seychellois couple with a child of their own called Angel, who calls him 'Papa'. To Geri and me, it was a guest-house where we stayed during school holidays. They received money from Hugh, who received it from my real father, RC."

"How old were you when you first met your real mother?"

"My earliest memories of my real mother are of two visits to Kimilili, a small village about ninety miles southwest of Kitale. I must have been about four. Namelok, a friend of my mother, and one of Hugh's three Bibis, took me there. I remember a small river and the mud hut with a grass roof where my mother, Siron, said I was born. She hugged me and gave me a gift of a stuffed doll but

Braz Menezes

one day it burst and all the cotton wool spilt out and the dogs fought over it and I cried and cried."

"That must have been horrible," I say. I hold out my left hand, and Saboti clasps it. I do not know how to react. I open the sandwiches and offer her one. She bites into it. I do the same and for a few minutes we chew our sandwiches gazing at the scenery. My mind is craving for more information. "Did your Mom say how you landed at Hugh's?"

"Yes, she only told me that when I was in boarding school," Saboti replies. "She came with Sinawe, a Masai, another of Hugh's bibis, who was Geri's mother. Sinawe left Hugh and went back to her Masai husband, remember? Siron told me that Hugh offered to take care of me, and he gave her some money to improve her hut and a small 'stipend' as he called it. But soon after a Muzungu came and took me away to Hugh's farm, where I was treated just like Geri. We were both registered with his surname. On my original birth certificate where it says 'Father's Name', it reads 'Unknown', but by its side, 'Given Name: Saboti Hunter-Brooke' is printed."

"Why did Hugh agree to do that? What was in it for him?" I ask.

"I really don't know," Saboti says. "But I have been trying to learn more about my background ever since. When I was about 14, I heard from Uncle Basil, do you remember him? He was the one who was already farming in Kitale and had recommended RC go and visit Hugh, about looking after his farm while he was away in the army. Well Uncle Bas told me that Hugh was always short of money, so my father, recognizing that he was now indebted to Hugh, had promised to provide him financial help, if he should ever need it. Hugh, now bankrupt and needing money, wanted to hold my father to that promise – but that's another story for another time," Saboti says, looking at me with a mischievous smile and squeezing my hand.

"So which of the three bibis was really mother to you?" I ask.

"Namelok, the Kelenjin, especially loved me," Saboti says. "She was my mother's friend after all."

"Saboti, you have mentioned so many names," I say, sitting up and adjusting my back on the tree. "How big was Hugh's farmhouse?"

"As a child, it seemed enormous," Saboti replies. "It was built of stone with a corrugated metal roof - it's probably still there. It had a big rectangular living room with a huge fireplace, a few pieces of furniture and a bookshelf with no books, only odds and ends."

"Saboti, you said *probably* it is still there," I ask. "Isn't Hugh still living there?"

"No. When I was about 15, we heard he suddenly disappeared to South Africa and married a white woman there. He just left all his bibis behind. He didn't tell me he was going. He didn't even tell Geri, his own daughter. That's when Uncle Basil stepped in and helped Geri and me."

"Hugh doesn't sound a very nice man," I say.

"Worse than that," Saboti's eyes fire up in anger. "Uncle Bas told me that just before Hugh did a bunk, he had told him that my father, RC, had set aside a sum of money to send me to England after high school, and this was deposited into a special fund with Barclays Bank. He even asked Uncle Bas to write down a confidential bank account number, and only approach the Bank when I had a Senior Cambridge Certificate to show them. Guess what? When the time came, it turned out that no such account existed. Hugh ran away with my education money as well."

"Saboti, I'm sorry," I say, reaching out to touch her hand. She gives it a gentle squeeze.

"Lando, do you mind if we don't talk about Hugh now?" Saboti says. "I have blanked him out of my mind, otherwise I could never move forward." She smiles. "But let me finish telling you about the house.

"The living room was generally quite bare of furniture, because of his parties – Oh, except for one thing. At one end there was a real church pew – without the kneeler – which he had bought very cheaply. Hugh said God was good to him, as the bench turned out to be a good deal, with the large number of people who usually attended his parties. Hugh felt guilty and wanted to make a donation to the local church, but some white women who were angry about his friendship with black women put pressure on the church folks not to accept his gift."

I imagine the Goan congregation at St. Francis Xavier would have reacted the same way, but I say nothing. Saboti lets go of my hand, and continues talking.

"The wall opposite the fireplace had a row of French windows opening out onto a veranda, that encircled almost three-quarters of the house. Geri and I would lie on the low parapet-wall gazing at the sky and watching the clouds move and make magical shapes. When we were on the veranda, if any of Hugh's Muzungu friends came to visit, we were told to run and hide until they left, otherwise the *nyangaus* (monsters) would come for us at night, and take us away.

"We could see Mt. Elgon almost straight ahead, and to the right of it were hills. Hugh told us these were called the Cherangani Hills. Whenever there was a storm, the whole sky would first turn a dark grey with only a thin outline of the hills visible against an almost black sky. There would be horrible lightning and thunder and we would be frightened. Even the dogs, which otherwise were afraid of nothing, would put their tails between their legs and run in, whimpering, and sit by the fireplace."

"Where did you sleep?" I am drawing a plan of the house in my head as Saboti speaks.

"When we were tired, we just curled up anywhere we liked. One of the women would pick us up and carry us to their room; sometimes they just let us be till the morning. In the living room, one door led into a corridor, from which another door opened into a dormitory of about six to eight beds. This is where Hugh's women-his *Bibi ya Jikoni*, who provided for his every need, slept. On the left side, doors opened to a couple of bathrooms. On the right hand side, a door led into Hugh's own bedroom and bathroom with a very large bed in the centre. Hugh's favourite amongst the women was the Nandi girl Sankau.

"As part of the household, we ran around half feral, like pet animals, with no enforced discipline, no rules and nobody specially appointed as 'mother'. After Geri left for Nakuru, her half-brother Ambrose became my constant companion. All the women loved us, and while they did not particularly fuss over us, we were extremely happy, and had all our needs met. The centre of our universe was the kitchen, which was attached to the house by a covered passageway. We had no shoes and only wore clothes if we were being taken somewhere special, where clothes were expected. We ate when we were hungry and slept when we were tired. Nor did we have our own designated room or bed, with the result that I would quite happily fall asleep under a bed, as on it." Saboti stops for breath, but she has left me breathless.

"Lando! Just look at the time," Saboti jumps up and pulls me up with a jerk. "You said you must be back at work at 2:00 p.m."

I stand up.

"That hulking concrete frame is the new Catholic Holy Family Basilica," I say, pointing. "You see how it dwarfs the quaint church with its slender steeple, and the small parochial school by its side? The Irish and Goan community built them both about 50 years ago. It was in that school that my violin accidently crashed onto the cement floor and prematurely ended my possible career as a musician at age eight."

"At eight I had not even seen a violin," Saboti says. "I didn't even know what a violin was until my boarding school near Thika." She giggles.

My Catholic upbringing has left me shocked at Saboti's story, which has stirred deep and conflicting emotions. I wish she hadn't told it me in such detail, and yet I wanted to know everything. Who am I to pass judgement on Hugh's life of apparent debauchery? But I cannot detach myself from feeling protective of Saboti, the innocent victim, born out of wedlock, without dignity, possessing it seems, a birth certificate with a blank space, and a baptism certificate with five names, of which she can use only one, and yet without an identity she can claim her own, as neither side, white nor black will accept her. I resolve to do what I can to make amends. That too is Christian. I will be the best friend she can have; for now it will be better than no identity. I drive her home. We part with a hug and promise to meet again as soon as possible.

———•—•———

29

A Time of Instability

About two weeks later, I am meeting with my high school buddies, Savio and Mengha, who, although a Sikh, has enrolled as a member at the Goan Gymkhana. It has been at least three months since my last visit. I love checking the conversation in the bar; it is my barometer on my Goan community in the uncertain political environment that prevails. My first impression is that nothing has changed from the other Fridays I have known at the Gymkhana. The card players are there en masse; the badminton players are engaged in après-match post mortems; the billiards room is packed.

Savio and Mengha are waiting for me in the bar. Someone is smoking a cigar, and the air is unusually thick with smoke.

Savio leans across to me and whispers, "Lando, it's just like old times." He's referring to our teen years when we eavesdropped on conversations to learn about the Mau Mau. Today, I sense an air of foreboding.

"In our department alone," Jose, in his mid-thirties says, "at least 20 Goan account clerks have been laid off."

"Four persons have received a letter in my group," Audit Pinto says. "It's part of the political change ahead. I spoke to Abreu in Admin. He is adamant that he can't help."

"They say it will soon get more difficult to move," a visitor from upcountry says. "Britain is tightening visas and entry permits, though I hear it will honour its obligations to civil servants who have served her so faithfully."

"Better to go sooner rather than later," Ben says. "I hear Canada and Australia may be changing their immigration rules. Some Goans are already there and they seem happy."

"We Goans can be happy wherever we go," Audit Pinto says. "We are willing to work hard and we don't meddle in politics."

"In my opinion," Ben says, "we have served our colonial masters so faithfully, that we are as much a guilty party – partners in the crime of colonialism."

"How can you say that?" At least two of the previous speakers pounce on his words. "We did not make policy. We just carried out instructions."

Savio gestures to me and we leave the bar. Mengha joins us, "I must leave now," he says. "Lando, where are you lost these days? You have a girlfriend? Gurvinder from Central Plumbers saw you." He laughs to see me taken by surprise. Savio grins.

"Okay Mengha, goodnight. You'll be the first to know," I say as he leaves us. Savio and I run over the plans for the dance hall decorations for the forthcoming Christmas season, and I take my leave.

I get in my Beetle and drive home to Plums Lane. I realise that the conversations I have been overhearing at home between Dad, Uncle Antonio and their friends who drop by, and at my encounters with friends in town, are true. A large number of Asians are preparing to leave, many because they will not find alternative jobs, because of the process of Africanisation that has already been initiated. It is going to be hard at the personal level for many Goan families. On the other hand, my Dad's generation of workers have paid their dues and earned their keep; they deserve a country that will let them eventually retire peacefully and enjoy their modest pensions. Their adult children will make their own choices.

I have been thinking of the future and have decided to stay in Kenya. Colonial rule is the ultimate form of human abuse, I believe, and as more stories of the colonial government's brutality and the treatment of alleged Mau Mau prisoners in the detention camps, start to leak out, public attitudes begin to change.

We never did hear back from anyone in authority about what happened to our houseboy, Mwangi nor Wangari, Stephen and their infant child who disappeared without trace. Although the violence used by the predominantly Kikuyu-based Mau Mau movement against its own people has been despicable, many of my generation now start to view the struggle, in retrospect, as not such a bad thing for Kenya after all, as it has shaken the colonial structure at the foundations. Thank God that change is in the air; the situation can only get better for all.

What will happen to Saboti after Independence, I wonder? Will she be considered British after her father, who she has never known, and be allowed to emigrate to the UK, or Kenyan, after her African mother? Or will both the white and black communities reject her? I must ask her about her plans.

A week after my visit to the Gymkhana, I return to the office from a site supervision visit. "Lando, this message is for you. It's from Roger's office." The receptionist hands me a small envelope marked 'Personal'.

"Thank you." I tear open the envelope. It is a brief message: 'Lando please can we have lunch or dinner (on me) next Friday? There is something urgent that I want to talk about. Please can you make a reservation at somewhere of your choice? (signed) Saboti'. I am both excited and nervous. Excited, as Saboti has never made such a request before; and nervous, about what 'something urgent' might mean. Perhaps she is just reminding me that we haven't met for three weeks as I have been away so much.

I make a reservation at Alan Bobby's French Bistro, a restaurant with everything French: food, wine and prices. I don't mind. Saboti is already so much part of my life, that I actually miss her very much, especially when I am travelling.

Standing in the lobby of her block of flats, Saboti looks radiant. She is wearing a beautiful long printed cotton skirt, with a Masai-red on black design, a pale terracotta coloured blouse, and a necklace of amber and turquoise beads. Her crinkled hair has been specially worked to make it stunning. Instinctively I know I want her to be with me at the New Year Eve Dance at the Gymkhana. I will ask her later.

I open the car door for her and she lets herself in elegantly – not an easy manoeuvre in a VW Beetle. "I hope we are going somewhere special," she says.

"You never said what we're celebrating," I answer, "But I am sure you'll like it."

We arrive at the restaurant. A waiter shows us to our table. The décor is predictably Parisian cliché. Saboti accepts a glass of red wine; it's her first time drinking wine. For her entree, she selects a *Demi-Poulet a l'Estragon* and I, a *Tajine de Volaille*, which for all we know, could have been two halves of the same chicken; hers was a garlic marinated roasted half-chicken served with a tarragon sauce; the *Tajine* was chicken braised with Middle Eastern spices, almonds, dried fruit and couscous. She is so happy, and seems relaxed and carefree, which makes me very happy. The waiter brings the wine; I taste it. He pours a glass for Saboti and then mine and leaves us alone.

"So what are we celebrating?" I ask her.

"Just being alive and knowing each other," she says. "Lando, I want to thank you for making me feel a person again. You have no idea how low I had sunk before I met you, and then suddenly you come along and listen to my miserable tales and self-pity, without showing any signs of boredom, despair or disgust. So I just wanted to say thank you. That's all." Her eyes are sparkling. I am very happy to see the transformation.

"Maybe you just needed to cough it all up anyway. That's what shrinks do, I'm told, when you lie on a couch and rattle away." I say. "But your story will one day be part of our colonial history under the British. I wish I was an author – I would love to write about it. Of course, I will have to ask you permission first." Saboti's face is glowing. "Lando, perhaps you will make a better shrink!"

"Cheers! *Affyia!*" I reach for my wine; we clink our glasses. Saboti takes a sip and a deep breath almost simultaneous. She closes her eyes. I think she is about to splutter it all across the table. But she manages to take control of herself, swallows it and opens her eyes. "Wow. That was a bit of a shock. I didn't know what to expect. It's quite nice really." I smile, feeling almost guilty enjoying the show. "Just take smaller sips."

I decide I will pop the question.

"Saboti, do you like dancing?" I ask her. "Will you be my guest for a New Year's Eve Dance at our club?"

"Lando, I adore dancing. Mind you, I haven't done much except at school dances."

"Well here's a chance to catch up then," I reply. "Will you come?"

"Lando, you are so impulsive," Saboti says. "You know Asians are, as a rule, racist towards Africans, and it is understandable, given their own cultural biases with caste and all that. I can't imagine Goans are less so."

"Oh, I know it will raise a few eyebrows," I say, "but I believe it will test our community's claim to Catholicism and its dogma, that all people are equal in the eyes of God. In any case, that's how we can begin change in the world. Please say yes?"

"Then it's yes, if I am still here," Saboti says, "Lando do you remember I wanted to tell you something urgent?"

"What do you mean?" I ask, as a waiter interrupts. Our meal has arrived. We pause for a few moments to sample it.

"Mine's delicious," Saboti says. "How's your *Tajine?*"

"Delicious! So what do you want to tell me that's urgent?"

"Uncle Bas called yesterday," Saboti says. "We had a long chat. The Bank's investigations have confirmed that Hugh and his white South African wife have absconded with RC's funds set aside for my education. I am determined to one day get to England for further studies, so I must start to save more diligently. So I need a job that pays me better."

"I can see that. But you are happy in your present job, no?" I find I am raising my voice to be heard. I turn around and realise the restaurant has filled up with patrons.

"I must also get out of Nairobi. Lando, I haven't told you this earlier, not to worry you." Saboti says. "But for the past two months, I have been receiving phone calls in the evening. Mine is an unlisted number, because it's Uncle Bas's apartment. It's an African man's voice. He says the Government wants me to work in the President's Office, to convey the image of a young, dynamic country after Independence."

"Do you have his name?" I ask. I can see it is worrying Saboti.

"Uncle Bas says the man is a charlatan. If it were official business he would call during normal office hours," Saboti says. "The man only gives a title, and a phone number to call back. I have passed that to Uncle Bas. He has friends in Special Branch and will track him down." I see Saboti's face is now serious. "Uncle Bas thinks I will be safer in Eldoret, and has actually confirmed a job for me, if I want it." The buzz of voices is irritating. I lean forward.

"Up north in Eldoret in Settler country?"

"Yes," Saboti replies. "It's not so bad; I have worked there briefly before. The woman PA working for a British Manager of a multinational British company based there, is returning to England with her family."

"You will leave Nairobi then?" I ask. The reality is finally sinking in.

"Yes, Lando," Saboti says. "I am frightened living here alone, especially as you travel so much, and I seldom meet other people after work, or want to."

"How long is the job for?" I ask. I feel a panic attack coming.

"Forever," she replies. "Uncle Bas says with Independence, jobs that were previously reserved for Europeans will be done by us coloured types."

"You sound happy to be leaving," I say, although I notice her eyes are teary.

"Just relieved," Saboti says. "The uncertainty of the future is eating me up on the inside."

"And *Uhuru*?" I ask. "What do you think of our coming independence?"

"That's it really," Saboti says. "We don't know what to expect. Before coming to my job here, I worked in Eldoret. I would over-hear my African colleagues discuss it among themselves. They were horrified by the violence of the Mau Mau against its own Kikuyu people. If the Kikuyu can do this to their own people, what will they do to us weaker, smaller tribes when they are in power? That's what my colleagues would speculate about."

"There is something in today's paper," I say. "Another Conference will still take place next year at Lancaster House in London. It's all politics."

"Is it affecting your work?" Saboti asks.

"We're very busy," I say. "Do you remember me telling you about Treetops Hotel? The original Treetops was burned to the ground by Mau Mau terrorists in 1954, and was rebuilt in 1957, very close to the original tree. Now we're involved in new extensions."

But my mind is still whirling around to figure out a happy ending for Saboti's story. "Do you think one day you'll marry an African or a Muzungu?" I ask, "Or maybe even a Goan?"

Saboti bursts out laughing loudly. "Are you proposing to me or something?" Again she chortles - that inimitable and conta-gious laugh. "You'll kill your folks with shock, and just imagine the scandal in your Goan Gymkhana club." She glances at her watch. "Gosh, Lando! You've done it again with your interminable questions. We're going to be locked inside here. Everyone's left."

"Excuse me, Bwana." It is the waiter with the check. "We must close soon."

As I let Saboti out at her front door, she grabs my hand and squeezes it tightly. "Lando, as soon as I know from Uncle Bas whether I am to report before or after the 1st of January, I will let you know about the New Year's Eve Dance. Lovely dinner. Thank you again."

I put my arms around her and kiss her on the mouth for the first time. She doesn't resist. Instead she responds with passion. "Good night Lando. Go safely."

I get behind the wheel and wipe the tears from my cheek. They may even have been her tears as well.

For the next few days, I am in a daze. I cannot imagine what life will be like without Saboti in Nairobi. I pack in the work hoping to soften the pain. A solution, albeit temporary, comes from nowhere. I am at a construction supervision meeting at the Baptist Church on Ngong Road. As the meeting terminates a pastor walks in and introduces himself as the Rev. Njenga of Eastleigh Community Centre.

"I came especially to meet you," he says. "We are in need of some technical help but we cannot pay for it. Our Centre is located next to St Teresa's Catholic Girls School, overlooking Mathare Valley and there is a growing community of homeless people who have occupied land without the legal permission of the owners – the City Council."

"I know it," I reply. "And I know the Mayor wants to demolish the temporary housing."

"Exactly! The Nairobi City Council is emphatic that it will not provide even basic water, sanitation or electricity to any illegal settlement, so it is left to social and religious-based organisations to help the local community. The people are very poor and their shelters are constructed with only scraps of wood, plywood, cardboard and plastic. Can you please help us plan this basic sanitation?"

"Of course," I say. "But I will have to clear this with my boss. I'm sure he'll agree to it, but remember I can only work on Saturdays."

"Thank you," he smiles. "It was Graham McCullough's idea that I should ask you."

He leaves happy. I am overjoyed too as I can contribute something tangible to improve housing for Africans. From the time I first saw the terrible conditions of African housing from the train, in transit to Goa in 1949, I have wanted to do something about it. Now I suspect I have just made my life even busier.

At the very least, it will fill up some of the emptiness I will face with Saboti gone. I am still living at 'home' in Plums Lane, except that for the past two years Dad has converted the garage as my sleeping quarters and Studio, but I avail myself of Mom's cooking and occasional access to the TV in the main house.

———•◦•———

Braz Menezes

30

The Year of 1963

I return to Nairobi on a Monday in early December after an unforeseen delay of two days in Arusha. There is an envelope marked 'Private' waiting for me at the office. It's in Saboti's handwriting. Inside is a brief message scribbled on a page torn from her diary from the previous Friday.

Nairobi, December – '62.
Jambo, Lando!
I was praying you'd be back to tell you personally. I heard the news about the job ten days ago. Came by to say goodbye, as I am leaving Nairobi on Sunday. Uncle Bas is coming down and will drive me up to Eldoret. I will write soon with full address in Eldoret. I will miss you and our talks! Please don't work so hard. Keep safe and well,
Saboti.

It is as if the katabatic winds are bringing down my plane over Mount Kenya; my stomach plunges. Over the next few days the emptiness is painful. I will not be able to fake happiness, so this year, for the first time since I returned from Goa in 1951, I skip going to the season's festivities and the New Year's Eve Dance at the Gymkhana.

I meet Savio for a coffee. He wants to persuade me to attend the various events. I tell him about Saboti. "I suspected something was afoot, Lando," he says. "But now she's gone, won't you start looking for someone?" He seems lost for what to say. "Maybe find someone among the girls we know? Do you remember the list of girls at Mangu that Stan had prepared? What happened to that list?"

"He never really shared it. He is studying engineering in Portsmouth and has taken that list with him," I say.

"Lando never mind, but please come to the dance. Aren't you at least curious to see if Anita has a new dress and a new dance partner?" I sense Savio is taken aback by the fact that Saboti is non-Goan and of her mixed heritage and does not know how to react.

"No!" A few minutes later we return to our respective offices. Alone with my own thoughts I reflect on Saboti's anxieties over the future. I inexplicably begin to feel nervous over what 1963 and Independence will bring. My work is useful therapy for my solitude, and I am glad that I have to leave Nairobi again to work on Keekorok in the Masai Mara and at Treetops in Nyeri.

Unlike in Nairobi, dusk in the wild stops physical work, but the brain thinks on. Every evening, as the campfire crackles in the night against the background chorus of the cicadas and tree frogs, and the chat of colleagues dies down, private thoughts come to the fore. I stare into the dying embers and wonder how Saboti is doing in her new job. I long to hear her voice and her happy, contagious laugh, again, even if it is over a static copper telephone wire, but I know long-distance calls are very expensive. It's the same every night. I watch the hundreds of twin specks of eyes glowing in the darkness, with no way of telling the wildebeest from zebras or deer; I kick some dirt on the fire, and retire into my sleeping bag, after zipping the tent tightly to keep the reptiles on the outside.

Braz Menezes

Back in Nairobi, I scan the newspapers daily for any news from Eldoret; but there are only reports about the rising cost of fertilisers, weather conditions, food prices and of the big forthcoming Agricultural Show after Independence.

One day a notice on the front page of the East African Standard catches my eye. 'The Independence Celebrations Directorate has launched a public Design Competition for street decorations. The contest is open only to registered and practising members of the East African Institute of Architects. However, recently qualified, but not yet registered graduates of the Royal Technical College are also eligible to enter.' The prize is a token 'One hundred Kenya pounds'. I read it carefully. Saboti and I had talked about doing something special for Independence, but now I cannot reach her, I still do not have her new address. I'll do it. Although I am very busy, I decide to submit a design.

As if by telepathy, a letter arrives the next day, postmarked 'Eldoret'. I recognise Saboti's handwriting and on the back is her new address.

Eldoret, January –, 1963.
My dear Lando,
I hope you will be happy to hear from me. How are you? I have settled well into this job with Uncle Bas' friend. I want to stay put here for a while. I'm glad I moved out of Nairobi, as living alone, I feel much safer here, and the cost of living is more manageable, especially on rent. I can put savings aside to eventually go to university in England. This past week I was invited by another English company here to work with them. For now though, I'm keeping my options open. Lando, I cannot ever forget our 'last supper' at Bobby's Bistro, but for some unexplained reason, I keep remembering that time we walked through the Park and you talked so seriously about the significance and opportunities for our generation after independence, when normally you are always telling funny stories. It set me thinking on how I too may contribute to our country. Have you started work at Mathare Valley? Are you keeping safe? It will make me very happy to hear from you

soon, with your news. Unfortunately I do not have a telephone at home and the one at work is too public. I just dream of hearing your voice again.

With warmest regards,

Saboti.

I feel my heart thump loudly as I fold her note. 'Warmest regards.' Really? A flesh-eating monster is consuming me from within, just worrying about her, and that's all she can offer? 'Warmest regards'? Perhaps she has more English blood running through her veins after all – the English are cold in matters of the heart, or so I've heard. That evening I sit down to reply. I have a long list of news items I want to share - but those will run into 20 pages. I will not rush things. I must restrain myself or I may frighten her away.

Nairobi, February—, 1963

My dear Saboti,

What a welcome surprise it is to hear from you after all these months. Your timing is perfect. The loneliness I now feel in Nairobi without you is killing me. I survive by immersing myself in work, and am gaining much experience. Almost every day out on the job is proving an adventure. I have had some scary moments recently on the extensions to the Treetops Hotel near Nyeri. You remember it? Treetops' advertising slogan is 'She went up a Princess and came down a Queen.' As a result, tourists from around the world have booked every night for the next five years, so it cannot be closed even for a night during construction. My job is to provide instant design solutions to the construction team, since it is all constructed in rough-cut poles and planks, and at least two trees grow right through the building. The cabins are small and cosy, almost like the ones on the ship that I sailed to the Seychelles and Goa in 1949. We stop work daily at 3.30 p.m. – that's just before a fresh batch of overnight visitors arrive, and we start at 8.00 a.m. as soon as the guests depart in the morning for breakfast at the nearby Outspan Hotel. The crew have to work fast, clear up and exit the site, without being seen or heard by incoming or outgoing guests and without disturbing any wildlife, though there are no rules for the wildlife disturbing us.

Last week, a troop of about 15 baboons came up to the rooftop viewing balcony, and perched themselves on the railing of the balustrade that encircles the rooftop viewing terrace, which is 50 feet above ground. They have been doing this every day since I've been there, and have been relatively calm, picking each other's fur for lice, and occasionally screeching with delight like teenage boys sharing rude jokes. And they watch me work away at the drawing board. At other times, they resemble a bunch of old men, wrapped up in thick furs in the tropics, just hanging out with nowhere else to go.

I normally eat a sandwich inside the lounge, except that last Friday was so beautiful; I took my lunch to the terrace. Suddenly I noticed that the whole troop had formed a circle around me and were approaching too close for comfort. I realised with some disappointment, they were more interested in my egg and lettuce sandwich than in my architectural sketches. I grabbed a roll of tracing paper and waved it at them, and then they got nasty. They started to growl, screech, snarl and bare their evil looking fangs. I was scared. Fortunately, Kulwant, a Sikh carpenter, re- alised I was about to be attacked and shouted to the other work- men, who rushed to my rescue. They made a lot of noise and eventually shooed them away. I was warned against bringing my lunch out on the terrace. I was told the baboons, however tame they may seem, can suddenly turn violent, so we have to be careful how we shoo them away. I have taken many photos and I will send you some. I will be returning to Treetops for the finish- ing touches in two weeks. Boti, I must finish now. I hope we can write each other on a regular basis and stay in touch. That will make me very happy.

Warm regards,

Lando.

Within three weeks another letter arrives, postmarked 'Eldoret'. Saboti expresses her concern for my safety, provides elaborate

details of her life in Eldoret, and most important '...*your letter brought joy and yet also frightened me, because I feel an affection for you like I have not felt before with anyone. You made me feel stronger and my anxieties melted away like an ice lollipop in the noonday sun.*
Affectionately,
Saboti.

And so an exchange of correspondence starts. While Saboti's letters grow in their intensity of expression and depth of emotion, mine grow in length and expand on detail, and much to my surprise, become more emotional, more affectionate. The words come from deep within my heart. I start a journal of events to share with her, and so when I sit down to write, the stories pour out.

Nairobi, March --, 1963
Dear Saboti,
My last letter could literally have been my last...

I recount my latest adventure.

Balbir and I were travelling to the Masai Mara, and on a rough gravel stretch of road, a stone pierced our petrol tank, just to the side beyond where a protective guard had been welded. We were stranded without petrol, in a no-man's land just outside the park boundary, where the wildlife roams free. We slept in the car; the windows wound up with only about a half-inch gap for ventilation. At about midnight we heard a lion roar very close by. The next moment we felt the Beetle being rocked. In the dim moonlight we could see a lion scratching its rump against the VW bumper. Eventually, its itch relieved, it left us alone. The next morning we saw the lion's footprints where it had circled the car a couple of times before dealing with its itch.

Saboti writes back almost immediately expressing her concern, and recounting the minutiae of her life in Eldoret. Her letters are now unmistakably those of a woman in love. Soon my letters too are warm with more affection and oozing emotion I cannot contain.

One day near the end of March, I return home as the late night TV evening news is winding up. Mom's gone to bed. Dad looks up. "Looks like a deal's been struck at Lancaster House," he says. "Kenyatta for Prime Minister and Odinga Odinga as the Deputy."

"And what about those ex KADU members representing the smaller tribes?" I ask. "You know who I mean… the Kelenjin, Masai, Turkana and Samburu?"

"They got nothing," Dad replies. "These British are smart at negotiations. They know if they have the two largest tribes happy and in power, those two will sit on the rest and lick them into shape."

"I overheard a discussion at work today between two of the English architects. One was saying Colonial Office just wants to ensure a peaceful transfer of white farming land to Africans. His folks are farmers upcountry. He thinks there'll be tribal war. The Masai complain that most of the land upcountry was originally 'illegally' purchased by the British from the Masai and the Kelenjin, and resold to white farmers. With Kikuyus holding power, most of this land is likely to go to Kikuyus. He thinks there is a lot of tension, and things may get nasty later."

"People will always spread rumours," Dad says. "Personally I think with Kenyatta and Odinga at the top, it should be a smooth handover." I stay and watch the rest of the news. Nothing there.

"Goodnight Dad." Then I go off to dream of Saboti.

In mid-April I am summoned to a Press Conference at the Ministry of Works. Amidst a flurry of publicity, the results of the Architectural Design Contest for Independence Celebrations are announced. I am declared the outright winner. Overnight, I am transformed into a minor celebrity. The press perceive my reluctance to say much and my state of chronic exhaustion, a consequence of overwork, as 'shyness and reclusiveness'. As I arrive home Dad and Mom are reacting to the announcement just beamed over the evening news. They had heard from me earlier in the day and now were glued to the TV.

"Of course I am very pleased," Dad says to Mom. "It was a good idea to bring him back from Goa when we did."

"So now you will stop worrying about him," she says. 'It's his life to handle."

I knock gently and enter. "We're so proud of you Lando," Mom says as I hug her.

"Well done," Dad says. "We are so glad finally you are doing something you enjoy." We chat for a little while, but now I am too wound up to stay still. I go up to my room and write a note to Saboti. I wish she was here to share this moment.

The next day, a new reality hits home. The publicity in the newspapers and TV brings instant benefits. For example, shop-keepers recognise me and offer me credit without the need for a guarantor. But success brings more demands on my time, as I must now prepare detailed designs and supervise prototypes of main ele-ments of my project before mass-production can start. This time is volunteered as my additional contribution to Kenya's indepen-dence. I feel swept off my feet.

This giddy pace of work and travel comes at a price. My social life is now non-existent. Without intending it, I have severed the umbilical cord with the Goan Gymkhana, which has nurtured and sustained me since boyhood; my world has changed completely.

I make efforts to stay in touch with friends, but by now the whole country is on an exhilarating roller-coaster. *Uhuru*, the promise of 'Freedom', albeit nearly eight months away, has intoxicated the land. My world too, is spinning faster than it did only a year ago. Meanwhile, many of my community are leaving the country *en masse* - leaving because they were part of the colonial civil service, and have been told they will not be needed in future. They must start their life somewhere else. We have grown up together and suddenly our futures are diverging in opposite directions, with un-identifiable tensions appearing where none existed before.

One day at the end of June, my phone rings just after I dash into the office, drenched from being caught in a freak afternoon thunderstorm.

"Hello! Is that you, Lando?" A man's voice asks.

"Yes, it is Lando," I reply. "Who is it?"

"We have never met," The voice says. "My name is Basil... Basil Gordon. I am a friend of Saboti who currently lives in Eldoret. I am in Nairobi and I have brought a letter for you. But more important, I must talk to you urgently. Can you please join me for dinner tonight at my hotel... the Norfolk?"

"Oh yes," I reply. "I've heard of you... you're Saboti's Uncle Bas, aren't you?"

"Affirmative. See you then, Lando. Seven o'clock. Meet you in the lobby."

I am full of apprehension over his 'I must talk to you urgently' comment. What now? I wonder. I hope Saboti is okay.

I park close to the hotel, and walk the short distance to the entrance lobby. Upon my arrival, Basil walks up to greet me. Not a difficult problem, as I am the only brown face in a sea of white guests and black hotel staff. Basil, in his early forties, looks like I imagine any white up-country farmer must look. Well-built and well-tanned, well-trimmed hair and wearing a tweed jacket over a checked cotton shirt that doesn't match his jacket or tie. He guides me into the formal dining room.

"Stuffy joint," he says. "Borrowed this jacket and tie. Doesn't do much for my physique."

He hands me a sealed envelope. "Read this first, then we'll talk." He raises his hand for a waiter and orders drinks. I open the envelope with my hand trembling just a little. Is Saboti going to tell me it's all over between us? Has she found another man close at hand?

Eldoret, June — 1963
My dearest Lando,
Uncle Bas will explain what's going on. I have confided in him and Aunt Maua, about my feelings for you. I know this is crazy, but I want someone to know in case we do not have a chance to meet again. I am very frightened now. Please try and meet me before I go… a chance to see you one last time and tell you all the things I cannot put into a letter. You have understood me like no one else. Just listening to your voice will help me deal with the future calmly. Please will you do it, Lando? Thank God the nuns taught me to pray - I do a lot of that now - I don't know when, and if, we will ever meet again… so please just come and see me one last time, OK?
I love you so much Lando,
Saboti.

Basil briefly tells me about himself (of course, I had heard most of it from Saboti) and explains the reason for Saboti's sudden change of plans.

"Although I am paid by Her Majesty's Government to disseminate 'facts' to the media and among the native population," he says, "I also work closely with Special Branch on gathering intelligence. I don't believe the Colonial Office is telling our people the truth."

"*Our* people? Do you mean the Europeans?"

"No no! I mean Africans and *we*, Europeans and Asians who intend to remain in this land we all love."

"In what way is the Government lying?" I ask.

"That it will be a peaceful transition to Uhuru," Basil says. "The situation is tense in the highlands. Many white farmers have in the past recruited assistant managers and headmen in Central Province, because they are better trained and are good workers. Now there are rumours circulating that white-owned farms will be transferred to these Kikuyu employees by their owners, or by a Kikuyu-dominated Government. The Kelenjin, Luos and Masai are not happy about this at all. There is talk of forcibly taking back, if need be, what is rightly theirs."

"So does Saboti feel she will be caught up in this chaos?" I ask.

"Yes. I think so. It could be dangerous for her, and I have advised her to leave," he says. "It will be difficult without proper papers, but I will figure a way to get her a British passport with our boys in Special Branch."

"Will she get an Entry Permit for Britain?" I ask. "Many Goan families are finding new rules have been brought in to keep non-whites out."

"We've discussed that. One of Saboti's British managers is returning with his family to the UK, after 15 years in Kenya," Basil explains. "Bill agrees with me that there may be all manner of rioting, looting of property and even rape of women, that will accompany Uhuru. He will offer Saboti employment as a nanny for his two children, and that will enable her to get an Entry Permit into England. But she must leave in less than a month."

I thank him for being such a good 'foster father' to Saboti. I am distressed and overcome by the turn of events, and shocked at his view of the possible breakdown of law and order. The colonial government was not making this information public, but for now it is Saboti who will have priority.

"Please tell Saboti I *will* see her before she leaves for England," I say.

We make some further small talk on general topics. Basil informs me that he and his family will be moving to Nairobi by the end of the year, and invites me to meet his wife too.

I am traumatised by the sudden turn of events – as if Eldoret is not far enough already! How can I bear it with her in England? That night, in my room, I can only stare at the calendar. I have been so submerged in my job, that I have lost direction in my personal life. I scribble a reply to Saboti.

Nairobi. June –-1963.

Dear Boti,

I will leave Nairobi on Friday 19th and hopefully will be at your office in Eldoret by 2 p.m., and we can leave together almost immediately. Will you be able to take Friday afternoon and Saturday off, so we can spend the maximum amount of time together? I will make a reservation at the Kericho Tea Hotel. Do you remember I was heading for Kericho with my family in August 1949 when I first set eyes on you and your doll, Dusi? I still cannot believe you are leaving. I was thinking that with Kenya's Independence, we could have a new life together. I intend to make up for all you missed in life so far. You will never again have to look for an identity. We will talk about that when we meet...

Fondly, till we meet.

Lando.

The next morning I stop at the post office and have it registered for fast special delivery.

31

Independence Arrives

My VW Beetle is purring. I can tell she is happy to be out alone with me in beautiful open country, instead of always having Balbir and loads of camping equipment to weigh her down. She is responding to the affection and attention suddenly lavished on her after months of total neglect. She has four brand new tyres, a new fan belt and a full change of oil: there is no room for delays on this trip. We cruise north, past all the familiar landscape and landmarks of rich Kikuyu farmland, past Limuru, the Escarpment, and the panoramic views across the Rift Valley, up to the turn-off road west to Narok and Keekorok. This road she knows so well.

But today I point my beloved Beetle towards Naivaisha township and Nakuru, where I first set eyes on Saboti 14 years ago; and from there it will be full speed north for Eldoret. As we approach the town I can see the lake to my left, bordered by a pink and white edge – the pink from the millions of flamingos feeding on the algae in the lake, and the white, the soda deposits reflected in the sun. I recall the sound of millions of birds tweeting, honking and squawking, all at the same time. How amazing that some memories remain etched in the mind. In Nakuru the Beetle and I take a quick swing by the street where Saboti used to live. It means nothing to me now that she is away. I pull the sliding sunroof shut to block out the blazing heat.

For the first time in a long time, I feel the strength of a lion – *Simba*—but coupled with this strength, I feel compassion and an overwhelming sense of wanting to protect my dear Saboti. I want to feel she belongs with me, and forget the rejection of being of mixed race.

Many thoughts rush through my mind as if propelled by the breeze that is buffeting against the windscreen. I feel a sense of guilt that I am actually meeting Saboti; it is guilt shaped by my Catholic upbringing. It seems love, hope, charity are virtues preached by the church, provided they are put in compartments. All people are equal in the eyes of God, provided they stay in their respective boxes of race, colour, caste and creed. 'These are the governments rules' is how the Church explains its practice of reserving the front pews for white Catholics. But now I've just heard Basil tell me the Government also lies. Did it not rig Jomo Kenyatta's trial? And does the government not take innocent people away like Pio Gama Pinto and lock them up without trial, or like our houseboy Mwangi, Wangari, Stephen and his baby sister, and have them just disappear? Do the people in government responsible for these crimes ever confess? I smile at the thought of the whole government lining up for confessions.

Why should I feel guilty about meeting Saboti like this? I know we are both virgins. I recall when I asked her about whether she would even marry, she had laughed; one thing led to another and perhaps anticipating my next line of questioning, she had convinced me she would wait to have sex until after she was married. I remember her good naturedly joking about it. "The older girls in high school used to say that the nuns only used a 23-letter alphabet – the letters e, s and x did not exist." She had said.

Of course any boy who dates a Goan girl automatically faces enforced celibacy before marriage. Now Saboti and I are both about to spend two full days together, consumed with conflicting emotions – but the one that matters is the strongest one – I realise that I have found my true love.

Saboti is waiting at her residence and eagerly gets into the car with her little overnight case. As we head south towards Kericho, taking the Kapsabet Road, she reaches out and rubs the back of my neck, as I move my head around to ease the stress of driving.

"Lando, I'm so sorry to have disrupted your routine," She says. "I just can't help it. I've never before experienced such a surge of emotions. I know I have only this short time to let you know how I feel and I cannot lose this precious time thinking serious thoughts. That can come later."

"Me too," I stretch my left hand to touch her, only to grab the steering wheel again and swerve violently to avoid collision with a herd of warthogs racing across the road.

Two and a half hours later, we arrive at the Tea Hotel in Kericho. It is a fine two-storeyed structure, built in natural stone and plastered blocks, with a red tiled roof, and set in beautifully manicured gardens. In every direction the view overlooks the rolling scenery of a tea plantation in those innumerable shades of green.

There is an awkward moment at the hotel reception desk. I assume they have not seen a brown man with a mixed-race Masai woman before. "Yes sir, here it is," The clerk has found my reservation. "Mr. and Mrs. Yes?"

"Just married," I say with a smile and a wink, while Saboti, cleverly avoiding eye contact, looks away at the scenery.

"Then you must have our special Honeymoon Suite," the African assistant manager says. "It will be at no extra cost, and with our compliments. Congratulations." A bellboy takes us to our room.

The discreetly located suite overlooks a private garden and the most expansive view of the plantation, but it does not hold our attention for long. Saboti enters the room first. I drop the latch in the door and pull her towards me in an effortless move as our bodies are like powerful magnets instantly drawn to each other. I feel the softness of her dark milk chocolate skin for the first time.

"Now will you tell me how you got this scar?" I ask her, gently stroking the scar. Saboti laughs. "Now you have a right to know. In our culture, when a beautiful girl is born, the mother makes a special disfigurement on the baby, to ward off the evil eye, and to protect her forever from evil spirits. That's the small scar of the cut Siron made."

That weekend we discover that colour, caste and creed get blown out of the water when there is an underlying feeling of true love at its purest and most passionate. Saboti and I are in love, and that love is not going away no matter how many obstacles lie ahead, and we will find a way to deal with it.

As we head back for Kericho on Sunday after a late breakfast, we both know that this rendezvous has turned both our worlds upside down. Our hearts will now take over and shape our destiny. After this meeting, nothing can stay the same. We vow we will always be part of each other, no matter where we finally end up. As I bid my beloved Saboti 'bon voyage' in Eldoret, I know I have finally met the girl I am able to love with all my heart. I feel strong enough to overcome all impediments in my way.

About three weeks later, I return to Nairobi from a delayed trip to Keekorok. There is a note from Basil waiting for me. In it, he confirms that Saboti embarked on one of the many BOAC charter flights carrying émigrés from Nairobi's Airport to Heathrow Airport, London. I missed her by 48 hours. His note said he had managed to get her a pukka British passport after all – not one of those new ones with letter suffixes. It continues...

'I had to certify that Saboti's father was personally known to me, and that he was of unblemished British descent – so she's home and dry on that count. Bill and family will take good care of her up to London at least. Maua and I will drive back today. If you

hear news first from Saboti, please let us know she has arrived safely and is well.
With warm regards old chap,
Basil.'

Eventually Saboti's first letter arrives.

Penge (Near London), July 17, 1963
My Darling Lando,
As I sit here, I am reminded of Nakuru when I was young. Aunt Mena had a whole lot of chickens running around in all directions, and we had to catch them one by one, and put them back in a bamboo coop. I have more thoughts than those chickens and they are also all over the place, so I will deal with them in the order I catch them, as I don't know where to begin'.

Saboti's is a long and passionate letter of longing and loneliness, and wish to be together again; of her excitement on boarding the plane and her arrival in England; and of her first impressions of London.

'Here white men sweep streets and do jobs that are the domain of Africans in Kenya.'

She writes of her landlady, who cannot do enough for her to make her feel welcome, and hints of new anxieties.

'Now that I am so far away, will you look for somebody else, someone of your own kabila – your own kind – to go out with? I wish I had squeezed you into my trunk, and that I had brought you to England, but that would have been difficult considering you still don't even have a passport. I hope you will come soon. With you here, I will be in heaven.
I love you,
Saboti.'

I reply with my news, and meanwhile another letter arrives from Saboti.

'Here in England we live without the colour bar. The white people here are completely different from the Wazungu in Kenya. Lando, when you come no one here will stare at us, or notice we are different, or our skins are a different colour, or that my hair is curly. Lando, please write soon. It is agony to be so far. To not know what you are thinking, or doing, every minute of the day. My address is on the envelope. Please keep it and use it often.
Yours forever, and more deeply in love,
Saboti.'

Saboti and I continue to correspond. While her letters are packed with the minutiae of her arrival, survival and revival in London, my letters tend to deal with an update of events in a Kenya now moving at a feverish pace towards Independence.

I tell her of the work at Mathare with the Reverend Njenga; of re-planning the lanes between the shacks through which we can bring in sanitation and drainage; I write about the stench and smoke from grilled goat meat on charcoal jikos; of the smells of open drains and rotting matter among the cardboard, plastic and corrugated shacks of the transient community in Mathare; of how the Reverend is successfully raising funds through donations and help from Christian charities abroad; and how we are making visible progress in some areas.

I share with her the irony of my schizophrenic experience. I spend my weekdays supervising the new self-contained cottages at the Mount Kenya Safari Club – with their sunken baths, glazed with the most exquisite glass and ceramic mosaic tiles imported from Turkey and Morocco; with gold-trimmed bathroom fixtures from California; and wall-to-wall fitted sheepskin carpeting. On Saturdays I am working with the poorest of the poor in the slums of Mathare Valley

In mid September I receive another letter from Saboti. She sounds melancholy. She talks about black ghettos in Brixton, and the growing 'paki-bashing' that is targeted towards people of Asian origin from India and Pakistan and hints that it will not affect Asians from East Africa.

'Lando, you need not worry. Even I can tell the difference between Goans and the other Asians from East Africa and those from India and Pakistan.'

I do not reply to her letter immediately. After all, what philosophical advice about racism can I offer her, which she could not think out for herself after her life in Kenya? I am swamped in work and I cannot keep pace with her letters, so I send only the briefest, selected news. I tell her that I have taken up a paid part-time job, working evenings with an American architect for the Opus Dei Mission. They are planning two higher education schools in Nairobi and Graham gave me permission to moonlight, as he knows I am saving to come to England to persuade her to come back here to me in Nairobi. Of course we hadn't discussed this before she went as everything has happened so fast. I am beginning to think more about a future with her, so it is important to discuss her plans.

Soon it is November of 1963. With less than three weeks to Independence Day, the air we breathe is a blend of jacaranda blossoms and sheer excitement. The early partying has started.

I take a break from working to celebrate a co-worker's wedding anniversary with my colleagues at Graham's office,. We are at the Swiss Grill in Westlands – a moderately priced restaurant with decent food and a small dance floor, which is crowded with dancers as an African Band belts out the latest afro-rhythms. Saboti and I had dinner here, but dancing is only available on weekends.

It is just after midnight. Suddenly the band stops playing. The happy buzz of conversation fizzles. A European man, of medium height, in a dark suit comes to the microphone and stands for a few seconds as an eerie pin-drop silence engulfs us.

Reading from a piece of paper, he says "Ladies and Gentleman," he pauses and adjusts the height of the microphone. "I have a very sad announcement which I will read out. '*The American President, John Fitzgerald Kennedy, has been assassinated. A sole gunman attacked the Presidential motorcade in Dallas, Texas. The First Lady Jackie Kennedy is unhurt. People across the globe of every skin colour are in shock. The world outside has come to a standstill*' This message just came over our telex printer." A loud collective gasp goes up from the crowd.

"When?" Somebody asks loudly but with a shaky voice.

"Today." He looks at his watch. Remember it is still November 22, 1963."

With news of the assassination, the nightclub empties within 20 minutes. That day in Kenya, people of every faith and race organise services in their churches, synagogues, mosques, temples and other places of worship and communion; flags on public buildings are flown at half-mast; sports events are cancelled. The Voice of Kenya (VOK) cancels most programs, and continuously relays the transmissions of the BBC and VOA for the next 48 hours, until after the funeral held on November 25.

Our Goan community is devastated. The first Catholic President of the USA inspired hope and held so much promise – we had seen Kennedy's presidency as a new direction for a country rife with racial hatred. He represented a hope for world leadership. At Sunday Mass the sermon is about death, hope, redemption and resurrection. We pray that Independence, now only just over two weeks away, will redeem us from our own shameful past, and resurrect our adopted country of Kenya; that the new government of Kenya will be blessed and fulfil the hopes of thousands for a peaceful transition; and that the forces of death and destruction (as still prophesised by some people) will not materialise on December 12, 1963.

Meanwhile, there has not been a peep from Saboti for over two months. I know I owe her some replies, but it is not like her to retaliate. She has always been so respectful in the past. But she did mention changing jobs. I assume she is busy with her new job. Perhaps she is caught in the frenzy of the festive season in London.

I sit down on the morning of December 12, and tell her that Independence has finally arrived, and how I wish she could have been by my side at the formal handover ceremony.

Nairobi, December 12, 1963
Dear Saboti,
I hope you are well. I am very worried that I have not heard from you for a while, and neither has Uncle Bas. Is all really okay at your end? I hope you have received the special Christmas Card I painted for you. I am sorry that I have been inundated with work, and have thus not been able to respond to all your letters. I just had to write today. It is 5:00 in the morning.
Yesterday, Independence Eve, dawned under a blue, cloudless sky. A few clouds gathered and then dispersed in the late afternoon. Mom said that was a good omen. Throughout Nairobi, special arrangements were in place to control traffic and security was very tight. Police cordons and GSU contingents were tactfully deployed, for 'crowd control', as they called it. All day, crowds of jubilant supporters arrived in Nairobi on foot, bicycles, buses, lorries and matatus and naturally all roads to Uhuru Stadium in Nairobi West were congested. I feel proud to have personally made a contribution, albeit small, to this great day in our history, as every major intersection in Nairobi had my street decorations, all carried out in accordance with my winning design. I just wish you were by my side; I think you would have been proud and I would have been very happy. The traffic roundabouts along the renamed Uhuru Highway were crowded with tourists and special visitors in safari attire, competing with happy locals for the best spots from which to photograph the decorations, and to record both on film and tape every aspect of this momentous day in Kenya's history. Adults and children wanted to be photographed

against the background of the decorations especially at the traffic roundabouts. Of course, in order to do so, they carelessly trampled on, and destroyed, some of the most beautiful landscaping, so painstakingly put together over the years, by Peter Greensmith of the Parks department. But they got their photographs, and that's all that matters.

I had received an official invitation with two tickets to attend the Independence Day ceremony. One would have been yours. Do you remember Mengha, my high school classmate that I told you about? He went with me instead. We parked the car about a mile away, on Whitehouse Road, now renamed Haile Selassie Avenue, and walked about a mile and a half to our designated entry gate, and up to our seats on the bleachers in this rapidly constructed Uhuru Stadium. With our technical training, both Mengha and I could see so many unfinished details in the construction. We were worried that there might even be an accident, which would be a terrible tragedy and leave a permanent scar in our memory. Fortunately, all went well.

His Royal Highness, The Duke of Edinburgh, represented Her Majesty. He spoke for a few minutes. Precisely on the stroke of midnight, the Union Jack was hauled down, and the new flag of our now Independent Kenya was unveiled and flew for the first time. You should have seen it! It is as if the wind was waiting quietly for it to unfurl. Exactly at the precise moment, a gust of wind came on, and the flag just fluttered open, it seems in happiness. Someone next to us said that was the last puff of the 'winds of change' that Harold McMillan gave in Cape Town in February 1960. Ironically South Africa is still not a free nation. If anything, segregation laws in that country seem to have become more savage.

All around us a loud cheer went up. Thousands of voices shouting and screaming 'Uhuru'– 'Freedom' – followed by clapping. Can you imagine it? The end of almost seventy years of colonial rule? Everyone now equal irrespective of colour, race, tribe or religion. I had tears running down my cheeks and so did Mengha.

The National Anthem was sung, and then Jomo Kenyatta, the first President of the Republic took to the podium. Gosh he can speak for a long time! He told us Kenya was destined to have a long and prosperous future. It will be a country where the rule of law will prevail and no one will be left behind; where all races will unite and make the country strong; and most important poverty will be eradicated forever. He said every Kenyan could henceforth hold his/her head up high. The crowds just cheered.

Mengha and I left with the crowds in the early hours of this morning. It was wonderful to feel the happiness radiating from everybody. I could almost feel their hearts, as were ours, beating proudly and warmly, even marvelling at the smoothness of the transition. Thousands of people around the country, and Dad and Mom at home watched the official handover ceremony on TV in the cities. In small towns and villages, according to VOK, hundreds crowded around radios, some holding transistor radios to their ears. Our Kenya Nation is born. I expect the celebrations will continue for days, the flags will flutter for months and the euphoria, it seems, will last forever. I just wish you were here by my side. We will be able to do so much for the country together. We have the rest of the week as public holidays, but I will have to go in to finish some work. I hope when you can you will send me some news too. Can't wait to see you again.

I love you and I am missing you very much,
Lando.

I drop the letter through the slot, realising it will be a week before anyone clears the box. I don't expect Saboti will receive my letter before 1964. I am glad 1963 is almost over.

32

Off to London
to Meet My Queen

I n mid-January I receive a telephone call from Basil.

"Lando, Maua and I were wondering whether you have heard from Saboti recently?" He says. "It's not like Saboti to stay incommunicado for so long."

"No Basil. I've been worried too. I had no way of contacting you. Are you fully resettled in Nairobi?"

"Yes, but no telephone yet. I will drop in at your office later this week and leave our new address and hopefully a phone number. You must come over and meet my wife, Maua. Please let us know when, old boy, will you?"

"Basil, I am still worried. I even convinced myself that she's probably switched to sending her letters by surface mail, as the cost of air mail is so expensive now." I say.

"That's true," he says. "In which case we may not hear for some weeks yet, with all that Christmas mail that's always late. Okay thanks old boy. Just give us a call if you hear something first, won't you?" He hangs up.

Another week goes by and the worry is killing me. Is she sick? Did anything happen to her in those race clashes with the police? But she is too smart to go near those areas. Is she too busy with her new job, but then, surely she would drop a brief note to her Uncle Bas or me about it. Could she have given up on me and found someone else? No, that will not happen.

I cannot bear it any longer. I must go and meet Saboti in London. I will beg her to marry me immediately, and we will return to Kenya together. I explain the situation to Graham, who is very sympathetic.

"Roger and I knew there was something cooking between Grace and you for a long time," He says with a grin. "Of course you must go and make sure she is okay. Persuade her to come back with you to our beautiful independent country."

"Is the first week of March okay then?"

"February is better, as we are expecting a green light on that Samburu job. It's always the same – clients take their time to make up their mind, and then they want everything by yesterday."

Over the next two weeks I rush to get a passport and my papers in order. The line-up at the Immigration Office at Gill House is horrendous. Hundreds of Asians line up soon after dawn on the pavement, long before the offices even open. They want British passports. There are only a few applying for a Kenya passport. I sign a sheaf of papers placed in front of me and pay the fees. I am promised a passport within three weeks.

I mull over how to break the news to Mom and Dad. I can almost guess what Dad's reaction will be. It's a particularly awkward time to talk with the siblings too: Linda will hear all about it when I land at her doorstep in London. My sister Fatima, 21, is currently on holiday in India where she is meeting the family of her fiancé, Dom Luis Pimpao. My brother Joachim, 18, is away at university in Dar es Salaam. I decide I will first go and see Basil and Maua instead at their house in Hurlingham Roadand get their blessing for my plan.

I hear a dog bark hysterically as I approach their front door. I press the doorbell to the townhouse, one of a block of six recently built units. I feel the frenzy in the barking and visualise the dog's teeth and froth around the mouth. I used to walk to school and back past a battery of these *Mbwa Kalis*. How could I imagine with Kenya's Independence all the dogs would be repatriated with their owners? I take a deep breath and heave a sigh of relief as Basil opens the door wider, holding his Alsatian tightly by the collar.

"It's okay Lando," he says. "He'll only sniff you. He's already been fed. But he's a *kali* one; so never pop around when we're not home. Please come in." Basil leads me into the living room. It is sparsely furnished; I know they have recently moved in. A beautiful African lady walks in from the kitchen in a long kitenge gown. "Lando, this is Maua – my flower," he says.

"*Karibu*, Welcome," Maua says with a big welcoming smile. "Please sit down here. I will bring you drinks." Maua goes into the kitchen, leaving me a bit confused. Saboti never talked about Basil's wife. I was not expecting a black wife. Is she a *Bibi ya Jikoni*, like Hugh's 'kitchen wives'? I wonder.

"Well, any news of our dear Saboti?" Basil speaks first.

"No Basil. So you have not heard either?"

"No. *Hakuna habari kabisa*! Absolutely no news," he says.

"Basil, I plan to go to England and persuade Saboti to come back with me."

"Lando, please wait a minute," he interrupts me. "Maua must hear this. Maua! Please come join us." Maua returns with a bottle of Johnny Walker Whiskey and three glasses, a jug of water and a bottle of soda water. She places it carefully on a small round table in the middle of the room. Basil pours two whiskeys and offers me one. He pours a glass of water for Maua and then tops my glass with soda. He drinks his neat.

"Cheers, old boy!" He takes a sip. "Now please start."

I am grateful for the scotch. I take a big sip. "You both know Saboti and I have been friends for some time?" I ask, as Maua sits, hands clasped in her lap.

"Yes. Saboti told us all about you. But you must be properly married," Basil says. "There is no other way for both sides to make a lasting commitment. We would like you to be properly married, just like we were – especially for the children's sake. The children must have an identity."

Maua is smiling coyly as Basil continues. "When I decided to make Maua my wife – she is the same tribe as Siron, Saboti's mother – I went up to the Elders, the *Wazees* of the tribe, in Kiminini. I asked what would be a fair bride price for her, if I were not a Muzungu. They told me what would be demanded, and I paid up. Here, pass me your glass. Let me top it up with a *chota* (small one)."

"I bet she must have cost a bomb," I say. Maua beams happily at the compliment.

"Yes, she didn't come cheap. They demanded five cows at 100 shillings each; one sack of maize meal; one *bomba* – a canister of chewing tobacco for her father; and a new axe for her mother to chop *kuni* --firewood. The ceremony was performed in Kiminini. That was in 1944. Later, we got married again in a Catholic church in Thika, where I was briefly stationed. We will take our three children to England for their education. Children of mixed race will have no opportunities here in Kenya after Independence."

"Then I have your blessing?" I ask.

"Of course, old boy," Basil says. Maua clasps both hands on mine.

"You have made us both very happy, and I know you will be a good man indeed for our Saboti." She embraces me.

I glance at my watch. "You're not going anywhere, old boy," Basil says. "Maua, do we have enough to feed Lando?"

"Of course! In 10 minutes." She goes into the kitchen.

"Basil, Saboti had told me you would be coming to Nairobi after Independence…"

"Oh gracious yes!" he interrupts me. "And what a relief – I was glad to pack up my job up-country in the services of Special Branch. Imagine being paid to lie on behalf of Her Majesty. I suppose my job is related to the whole Mau Mau matata in a way."

"What do you mean?" I ask.

"Well, to ease the transition to Independence and give Jomo Kenyatta something to reward his freedom fighters in the Mau Mau, the British government concocted a plan, where the government would buy land belonging to White settlers, sub-divide it into very small lots, and then parcel it out to these poor landless types. They will each be given, in addition, the equivalent of about one hundred and fifty pounds sterling, in cash, as well as a starter kit of a *jembe*, *panga*, cultivation tools, a wheelbarrow, and other odds and ends – with that the Colonial Government expects them to feed the whole country and the world."

"And how do you fit into this plan?" I ask.

"Oh, me? I am officially the chief statistics officer for this land resettlement project," Basil says. "But my real job was to see who were the 'big fish' that were likely to play an important role in future Kenya. Sooner or later, we knew that JK's closest henchmen were going to surface and want to sniff out their take. I would be the person the 'big fish' would talk to in confidence."

"I don't understand," I say. "Maybe be I missed something?"

"It's not going to work. These bloody bureaucrats who thought up this scheme don't understand the culture or farming."

"In what way?" I ask.

"My prediction is that these ex-Mau Mau fighters will first blow the cash on *pombe*—you know local liquor," he says. "Then sell their piece of paper, title, to one of the Kikuyu 'big-fish' that are already prowling around, and then end up sleeping in the slums of Mathare Valley and on the streets of Nairobi during the day, looking for work. Meanwhile the Kelenjin, Masai, and others will be even more pissed off than they already are." He pauses as Maua summons us to dinner. "Just a minute, my flower," he continues,

"These tribes see this as another Muzungu project, transferring their original tribal land, which was trickily acquired from them, by the British, to someone else. After independence there will be a bloodbath between the tribes. It will be based purely on land, and settling old *fetinas* (feuds) over land. Farm labourers are concerned for their future as well. Living alone in Eldoret, Saboti was frightened about the future. That's why I helped her get away to the UK."

"I believe it's going to be okay in Nairobi," I say. "Kenyatta said so in a very convincing and moving speech on Independence day."

"I hope so. Please come to the table now."

We have a simple dinner of sliced pot roast, served with boiled potatoes, *sukuma weeki* (kale) and French beans. After dinner, we talk a little longer, before I take my leave.

"I will come by in the next two weeks before I depart for the UK." I promise them.

I cannot postpone sharing my plans with Mom and Dad any longer. The next day, I return home at noon, when Dad is at work and Niven in school. I tell Mom what I propose to do. She receives the news calmly. Fortunately, Mom has met Saboti once and thinks she is a nice girl. Her anxiety is over Dad's likely reaction. We agree that she will break the news to Dad, so he has time to blow up, calm down, and blow up again with lesser intensity, when I turn up. That way he is not blinded by rage, and will have a little time to reflect over his position.

As luck will have it, that night they are arguing as I arrive home. I am in the entrance hall and their voices carry from the dining room. It is well after their dinnertime. I know they are talking about me as I overhear a part of it.

"This is madness. How did it ever get to this stage? You should have nipped it in the bud earlier."

"And what is the father's responsibility? How can Lando hear a man's point of view from his mother?" Mom asks.

"No! I won't approve it," Dad is livid. I feel myself getting tense. I want to rush in and tell him I am not a 10-year old anymore.

"Approve what?"

"Him – Lando marrying that black girl."

"But Chico, she's not black! She is a *mestico* – mixed race – like us Goans," Mom says. "Saboti is half Masai and half European. I don't see how that makes her different from Mr. Joseph Murumbi – such a wonderful man. He's half Goan and half Masai. You can't just disown Lando."

"*He* has disowned *us*!" Dad says. "Ever since he came back from Goa." I nod in approval. He got that one right.

"So what will we say to him this evening?" Mom asks. "Lando wants our blessing."

"I believe we parents have a duty to stop this whole thing," Dad is adamant. "Apart from the moral aspects, there are biological factors involved in such a relationship."

"Chico, what nonsense you talk!" Mom says. "There are more serious biological factors when related families marry into each other, as they do in Goa, just to keep property within the family. You and I know of so many cases like these."

"Anja, please listen to me for once." Dad is trying to negotiate. "We risk becoming the laughing stock of all and sundry. The social stigma is very definitely to be considered. What would we say if something like this happens in another Goan family?" I am angry. He should know better than argue about these issues. Look at how the Goans are divided into clubs by class and caste and it has interfered even with the running of the Goan School. Everything balanced on keeping up appearances.

"Forget about what people will say," Mom says, "Just look at the problems we create for our children. That Costa girl finally had to run away from her family to marry her non-Brahmin boyfriend and people still talked. How hypocritical we Goans are - Catholics on Sundays, and practicing a Hindu caste system the rest of the week!"

"Look here, Anja. I don't object to his friendship with that girl," Dad says. "Friendship's fine. There will be mixing of the races in the future I'm sure, but for Lando to become romantically involved is nothing but total stupidity – it is irresponsible!"

"Why?"

"How can he be in love when he doesn't have two shillings to rub together? I waited until I was 35, and had enough savings to come and look for you in Goa."

"Chico, times have changed. Lando works hard," Mom pleads. "He is responsible – he got that quality from you – they'll manage."

"I don't understand this generation," Dad says. "They don't take advice. They go to the cinema, hold hands in the dark, come out into the light, and want to get married. Hollywood is destroying their brains. You wait and see – the next thing – Lando will have two or three wives like Clark Gable. Then she'll have five husbands like Elizabeth Taylor. No! I won't approve it." I smile at the thought of having three wives.

"So what are you going to say to him?" Mom asks.

"Leave it to me, Anja," Dad says. "I will be firm with Lando and give him my views. He will have to decide for himself where he goes from there, and then live with the consequences."

I quietly turn the doorknob and discreetly leave the house and drive to the Gymkhana, where the place is deserted, except for a couple of hard-core regulars at the bar. I down a quick peg of Johnny Walker and return home about 20 minutes later. Dad is waiting up for me, as the evening news is finishing.

We have a discussion. In summary, his view, as expressed to Mom, has not changed. Neither have my plans. The debate ends.

Ten days later, Mengha drives me to the re-named Jomo Kenyatta International Airport. I am about to fly to England for the first time. I clutch my brand new Kenya passport numbered in the low hundreds, as I am among the first non-Africans to apply for citizenship. Mom and Dad said their goodbyes at home, so only Savio and a few colleagues from work are with me.

"We're expecting you both back in two weeks," Mengha says. "I will come personally to pick you both up at the airport."

"I'll be back," I assure him.

I wish I could somehow get into Saboti's brain to know what she is thinking. Perhaps she'll agree, or she may decide she is better off in England with the ample opportunities for further education. Perhaps I will have to make a decision and be willing to move to the UK. Maybe we will both be happier that way.

The final boarding call blares out over the PA system. Goodbyes over, I complete formalities. The immigration and customs officials are all so polite, helpful and efficient. I am so proud of our now independent Kenya. "This way, sir." The uniformed officers points to a group of fellow passengers heading into the departure lounge.

Saboti is not aware I am already on my way to London. She will be surprised to see me. I am so elated, that my feet hardly touch the ground, as we walk across the tarmac and up the steps to the plane. Inside, passengers jostle for luggage-bin space. There is so much to squeeze in: Canvas and leather bags, briefcases, plastic raincoats, sheepskin jackets, umbrellas, diapers and toys, wooden carvings and tourist bric-a-brac picked up in the airport curio store and of course duty-free whiskey and cigarettes, imported from Britain, that we feel compelled to buy and return to their country of origin.

Love, joy, excitement and inadequate oxygen inside the plane are a heady mix. We fasten seatbelts, and some passengers extinguish cigarettes, after the fourth announcement from the cabin crew. In the seat in front of me, a sari-clad woman appears intent on extinguishing her screaming toddler with a pillow as well, while a BOAC stewardess holding a glass of orange juice, looks on helplessly. We are finally ready for take-off. I am already too wound up to be further excited about anything around me, having embarked on a single mission: to be re-united with Saboti, the love of my life.

I am travelling economy class, which includes an aperitif, dinner, wine and a chocolate bar and liqueur served with compliments of the airline. Then an extra blanket is offered for anyone who requests it before the cabin lights are dimmed. I wonder what it must be like in First Class.

As I sip my liqueur, I think about, and then dream of my first meeting with Saboti at that architectural association meeting in the Norfolk Hotel three years ago. She was a stunning distraction, like a powerful magnet attracting my eyes, as if they were loose ball bearings. Each time I looked in her direction, I noticed she, too, was looking at me, and as our eyes briefly connected, she would turn abruptly and look away. I must go straight from the airport to see her. I wonder if Linda received my telegram and if she will be at Heathrow Airport to meet me?

33

With Saboti in London

My sister Linda, now a five-year London veteran, meets me at Heathrow. I almost don't recognise her. She is much slimmer than she was when she left Nairobi. Her dark brown hair has been dyed jet black and styled in a sophisticated cut. She is stunning in her London winter look with leather jacket and high boots. She spots me first as I exit the customs hall. I would not have recognised her among the sea of faces all peering anxiously for someone they are expecting, and in many cases probably have never met before.

"Lando, I want you to meet David, my friend," she says, expecting me to be quite surprised to see her with a white friend.

"Hello, friend," I greet David; a tall rather distinguished looking man.

"You can call me David," he says in a soft gentle voice. I can tell he is not sure of my comprehension of his language. "Is that all you are travelling with?" he reaches out and picks my bag. "The car is parked on the next level up. Thataways," he gestures with his left thumb, picking my bag at the same time. A pukka Englishman carrying my bag is a bigger surprise, but I say nothing. Why spoil a good deal? We are moving with the flow of newly arrived passengers, pushing loaded luggage trolleys to their various transportation points.

I pull out a paper on which I have scribbled Saboti's address and show it to David.

"David, will we be going anywhere near this address?" he squints at the paper and says, "Thataways," he points with his thumb over his shoulder. I have lost my orientation as we have done a double dogleg turn inside a tunnel. David must have sensed that.

"Thataways is Grimsby-speak for 'that way'. Have you heard of Grimsby in Kenya?"

"Not if it hasn't been on any of the comedy shows on TV. Peter Sellers? Sid James? Benny Hill?"

"Lando, it will be better if you first rest and recover from the flight," Linda says. "I remember I just collapsed with exhaustion after my first flight, and needed a rest. We can point out some landmarks on our way home." She turns to David; "Please can we just drive past Buckingham Palace on the way home?" We arrive in Central London; I am fascinated by everything I see, especially as it is a beautiful sunny day. David pulls up the car by the Buckingham Palace gate and Linda and I step out.

"Ten minutes is all you got. I'll just circle the block." At the palace gates, the sentry with the red jacket and black bearskin hat refuses to talk, but a fellow tourist informs us that Her Majesty is preparing for her imminent Royal Visit to Canada, and may not appear on the balcony as she usually does.

That evening, I tell Linda and David everything about my romance with Saboti, and of Dad's strong reaction.

"Well, it's tough for his generation to understand love and romance, and to accept change," Linda says sympathetically. "Theirs was such a different world, especially coming from Goa. And remember, it's barely five years since the colour bar was removed. Before that, everything was racially segregated, and everyone followed their funny unwritten rules with caste, class and race and those funny customs. You'll see how different it is here in England."

Monday morning is a beautiful sunny day. The clean lines of steel and glass towers springing up all over the London skyline stand in sharp contrast with the more charming lines of traditional stone and brick architecture. Signs of an early spring are everywhere, especially the tulips and daffodils in bloom. Newsagents and florists spill onto the pavement and the streets are clean. The flowering verges and green spaces are trimmed, giving the impression that people are proud of their city.

I study the map and the scribbled directions that Linda left behind before she went to work. I take the London Underground to a station closest to the address I have for Saboti, praying she still lives there. I have this horrible feeling that she had mentioned perhaps moving soon. I hope I'm wrong. I wish she hadn't stopped writing so suddenly in September. At least she should have kept Basil and Maua informed, especially after all that Uncle Bas did for her. I hope she is well. I wish I had replied to all her letters and kept her close.

An older lady answers the doorbell at a semi-detached bungalow that matches the address I have. I am shocked and disappointed to find out that Saboti has indeed moved, and worse - the landlady has not been given a forwarding address. "You may wish to try her place of work," the landlady suggests.

I hail a taxi on the street to take me to her last place of work – I have that address. I instinctively make the sign of the cross. Thank God I remembered to include that one.

"Grace no longer works here," Sally, the receptionist tells me. "I think it must have been last October, or was it September, since she left?"

I am frightened and shocked that Saboti has just disappeared into thin air. I stop and ask people arriving for work if they know Grace. I cannot believe that there is absolutely no one who may know her, or would not remember someone as distinctive as *my*

Saboti – *their* Grace. In Nairobi, people make it their duty of sticking their nose in everyone's business; everyone knows everyone.

I am not willing to give up easily. Eventually, my persistent efforts at interrogation of anyone and everyone pay off. Sally, perhaps moved by the disappointment she can plainly see on my face, beckons me to her desk.

" Here Love… try this number," She says. "Grace said it was to be used only in emergencies. Do you know London?"

"Just Heathrow Airport and Buckingham Palace and my sister's flat. I arrived on the weekend," I reply.

"Good idea to get one of these," she says. "An A-Z road map. Let's see if we can find out her address." She opens the book. "Here it is – should be around here. It's relatively close by."

I thank her and go out into the late afternoon sun. I find the familiar red phone box on the corner. With a shaking finger I dial the number given. A sweet, somewhat huskier voice than I remember, responds.

"Hello, this is Grace – may I help you?" I *hate* that name now, as I want to know her only as Saboti.

"Boti, Saboti, Grace, is that you?" I am breathless. I can feel a pounding inside my chest; I pull my jacket tighter, in case the heartbeat gets so loud that she cannot hear my voice. I speak but I can hardly get words out, as my throat is dry. A few seconds go by, followed by total silence. I think I have been disconnected. "Boti, Saboti darling, it's me. Lando! Are you still there? Please say something! Can you hear me? I'm here at last. I'm in London." This time a softer, very hesitant but familiar voice, answers.

"Yes, I can hear you, Lando."

"Saboti, where are you?" I plead. "Please. Quickly, I am running out of coins and I need your address. I must see you now, right now. Is everything all right? Why did you not tell me you had moved?"

Again, a slight pause and then "Lando, I thought you were never coming, after my letter in September. Then, as I heard nothing, I began to give up hope of ever meeting again."

"Saboti, can we please talk face to face? Just tell me where you are. I think I'm going crazy, where *are* you?" I hear a click and a loud dialling tone. She has hung up or I have been cut off. I rush out of the booth to the corner newsagent and buy the Guardian newspaper with a ten-pound note, and ask for all my change in coins. This time, another voice answers. It is not my beloved Saboti.

"Please, help me, madam," I plead. "I need to speak to Grace, urgently."

"I am sorry," she says. "Grace has left for the day and will not be back until tomorrow."

"Then please tell me where you are located," I say. "I have arrived from Saboti's hometown in Kenya, and have a parcel for her from her family." She gives me the address. I realise it must be her new workplace. As it is now almost 4 in the afternoon, I return home to Linda's flat. I am distraught at the thought that another night must pass before I can even hear Saboti's voice again.

The next day, I wait till mid-morning to call her; that way Linda will have left for work, and it will allow enough time for Saboti to get to work. This time my call goes through directly to Saboti. "Boti, I know where you are located. This is just to confirm that I'm on my way to see you."

"No. No. Please, Lando!" she says. "Please do not come here. It's better we don't meet again. Please, Lando."

"Boti, have you gone mad?" I ask. "Is something wrong?"

"Lando, please believe me, it is best this way," Saboti says. "Please don't try and see me. All this is very difficult for me, Lando. I thought you could never be happy in England and I have moved on with my life. You must do the same, please!"

"Saboti, my darling, I can only move on with you by my side. I will be there in an hour."

"Lando, this is not a good idea, please try and understand," she says.

"I said I'll be there, I cannot wait to see you again," I reply.

"Okay then, Lando," she relents. "But please do not come to my place of work. There is a little bistro round the corner here in Holland Park. Do you have a pencil and paper? We can meet this evening. Let's meet there, but it can only be between 6 and 8." I take down the address, and as I replace the receiver in its cradle, I feel my heart pounding so hard again that I pull my jacket tighter around me, as if it will stop my heart beating its way right out of my chest. I can hardly breathe.

I sit down for a few minutes and inhale deeply, as Ahmad my taxi driver friend, had taught me to when I was a boy. He breathed this way whenever he was too excited over something and it would calm him down.

I make myself a cup of tea; chop a banana deliberately and spoon the pieces into a bowl of corn flakes. It helps me calm down. I take out the notes I have assembled for Saboti - the plans and ideas I have for us, when we return to Kenya. Basil and Maua have given me fifty pounds sterling as a gift for her, as well as a family photo with their three sons. I select some random photos from Kenya's Independence celebrations. Now I must be patient, as the next few restless hours drag by.

It is late afternoon, as I scribble a note to Linda to say I will be back at about 9 p.m. I put on my warm jacket and a corduroy cap, and step into the street, pulling the door shut after me.

Now on the pavement, it seems everyone is rushing somewhere, in every direction. I am again engulfed by panic. I pop into a pub, down a peg of whiskey, walk out into the street, and hail a taxi. The whiskey helps. I am calmer now, and feel silly about my panic. I am not a habitual drinker; the whiskey has raised my confidence. I am filled with the joys of spring, as I pass the street florists with their abundant displays of tulips, daffodils and other early spring blossoms. I pick a bunch of six red roses.

I arrive early at the bistro and notice its beautiful hanging flower baskets. For good measure, I order another shot of scotch, which I sip very slowly. I am now ready to take on the world, my whole world – in the shape of Saboti. I just cannot imagine what madness has overcome her.

It is calm inside the restaurant. A trickle of early diners starts arriving.

I imagine I am hearing the sound of violins. I think it must be the booze. Then through the arched opening into the next room, I see the two violinists. I signal them over.

"I'm meeting someone very special," I tell them, "in about 35 minutes." I look at my watch again. The older looking of the two looks up at the grandfather clock in the corner and nods.

"When she walks in, can you play a tune for her? Here she is, so you recognise her when she walks in." I show them Saboti's photograph, taken outside our room at the Kericho Tea Hotel on our last meeting.

"Do you know the tune 'Malaika' – 'My Angel' in English?" I ask.

"This one?" They play a few chords. "Yes, yes. We have heard it sung by Miriam Makeba and Harry Belafonte."

Done. I hear them practice it in the adjacent room, as they go around the guest tables. I am deliriously happy and deeply and thoroughly in love. Whiskey is such an energiser and morale booster.

My watch says its seven minutes to 6. I pat down my hair and move my chair to get a good view of the doorway. I see her first peep through the etched glass door panel. Saboti enters, glances around, sees me and very hesitantly walks towards me.

Instead of walking to greet her, I stand by the table, my arms outstretched. The violins start to play; I have tears running down my face, helped somewhat by the whiskey and the waiting. My beautiful Saboti is finally here with me. She is looking so lovely, so vulnerable, and so tender. Her hair has been straightened into Afro 'corkscrew curls'. A deep blue velvet band highlights her slender neck. She has never looked better.

I impulsively hug her, as she removes her coat, and I almost fall back in shock. Her face looks strained. Am I imagining it or could she be pregnant? Perhaps ever so slightly, though it barely shows. I steady myself on the table edge. Surely there is no situation where a girl can be half-pregnant! The violinists continue to serenade us, blissfully ignorant of the unfolding drama and the turmoil within us.

I take Saboti's coat and help her sit down. She has tears streaming down her face. We cannot take our eyes off each other; Saboti reaches for my hand, takes it to her lips and kisses it. By now the violinists have finished their serenade. I reach for my wallet and hand over two notes. Perhaps I have overpaid them; they offer to repeat the performance, for no charge. I am still choked, so I gesture them away. They give a gentle bow and amble off into the next room. We are finally alone. We both start to speak at the same time, and stop. An awkward silence ensues.

"What were you going to say, Lando?" Saboti speaks first.

"Ladies first," I reply, as she grasps my right hand tightly with both of hers.

"Why didn't you reply to my letter last September?" she asks. "I wrote about the paki-bashing… the growing racism against people from India and Pakistan in Britain?"

"I remember the letter well," I reply. "But you didn't say you were directly affected, so I wasn't worried. I was very busy. I had just started on this part-time job, to save money faster, to come out here and be with you."

"Lando, you live with your head in a cloud," Saboti says. "In my letter I explained that I couldn't in good conscience expect you to come to live in England, and face more racism after growing up with it in Kenya. I love you too much for that."

"But Saboti, a few bigots in the UK are not going to trouble us," I say. "I beg you to come back with me and live as my wife in Kenya. We can do so many things together."

"I can never live in Kenya again," Saboti says. "I was always frightened there. Then there was always news of you from my Nairobi ex-colleagues. They sent me newspaper cuttings of you in the Daily Nation and East African Standard. I read of your success with the designs for the Independence Street Decorations, and I am so proud of you. I always knew you would do it, but it made me realise how far removed from my little world you really are, and of what little use I can be to you. How can a half-caste *nusu-nusu* girl like me hope to win and keep a fine, successful, strictly brought up, Catholic Goan boy? What chance do I have? I thought you might be pressured to put me aside, and find someone else, more in keeping with your family's wishes and your Goan community's traditions and customs."

"Why did you stop writing so suddenly?" I ask. "We could have sorted this out earlier."

"I couldn't," Saboti says, wringing her hands helplessly. I notice she is wearing a ring, but I think nothing of it, as she wore one that weekend we were together in Kericho.

"As I thought of a future without you," she continues, "I found it harder and harder to bear. I started to look around and see if I could patch the big hole you had left behind in my heart. At first it was so hard, then one day at work, this kind, caring Englishman came over to talk to me. He said he was drawn to me because, although I smiled often, my eyes were always sad. He asked if I would give him a chance to put the light back into my eyes. Lando, it was so easy to give in, as he came to me at just the right time."

"Is that his ring?" I ask. I can't believe what I am hearing.

"Yes, we were married last month, on January 6th," Saboti says.

"That's the feast of the Epiphany in the Catholic calendar," I say. My brain has stopped working and I cannot think of anything else to say. "It's also the feast day at my Dad's village in Goa."

"Lando, although I will never love him the way I did you, he has helped me with my recovery and little by little, I have started to laugh and have fun again." Tears are streaming down her cheeks. "At first, I thought I would never be able to carry on without you, and now here you are, and it feels like we have never been apart, and all the love I was trying to forget is back in full force again. What have I done to us, Lando?"

Saboti grips my hand so hard that her knuckles are turning white.

"Why did you – could you not at least, tell Maua and Basil?" I am still not speaking coherently. "I … I was so busy… I was so exhausted… I took on extra jobs, Saboti… to save faster for my trip to England…"

I am squeezing her hand now. I feel I am clinging… clinging for dear life. Clinging to the only woman I have worked so hard to get to, and now here she is – and she belongs to someone else – *my* special Saboti is suddenly someone else's wife. She will give birth to his child in a few months. I can see her lips moving, but I cannot hear what she is saying; suddenly I hear the words "…the baby is due in mid- July."

I stare aghast. I realise then that all my dreams, my aspirations, my plans, my heart's desire, but most of all my true love, have been taken away and are now lost to me forever.

"Lando, I want you to have this back," Saboti pulls out a photo from her purse. "I kept it by my side ever since you gave it to me. It helped me through so many difficult moments." She places it on the table and slides it towards me. I see, through my own tears, her tears drip onto the photograph of the two zebras doing their courtship dance.

What a cruel twist life has taken. This pain will be something that will stay with me for the rest of my life, I think.

I cannot recall much more of that tragic evening, except I hear Saboti say she will always love me and I will never really be out of her heart. I too mumble words to that effect, but when I take her into my arms one last time, I know it is time to let go.

She stands up, looks at the bunch of roses; hesitates, and picks them up. "Thank you for these, Lando."

I help her with her coat. We walk out to the street. "I go this way," she says.

"I think I have to go this way," I say, pointing in the opposite direction, although it's a lie.

I wanted her to know that she is free of me. I must find my way alone.

Epilogue

I have just one day free in London before I am due to fly back to Toronto. London basks in the warmth and sunshine of late July.

I had walked from St. Paul's Cathedral down to the Victoria Embankment on the north side of the River Thames, and across the beautifully engineered and magnificent Millennium Bridge, which had been opened eight years before, as the new century began. I am on my way to the special Street Art Exhibition at the Tate Modern on the south bank. Like the other tourists I stop frequently and turn around to look back at St. Paul's and click a few more photos – the view of the cupola and dome from the Bridge is by far the most impressive.

The Tate Modern Gallery, a converted power plant from the Industrial age, never ceases to impress me with its architectural creativity. The street art exhibition featured six artists from Barcelona to Sao Paulo. Predictably, it was crowded. After an hour I decide that I have had enough. I have been meaning to visit the London Eye and ride in those high-tech pods. Today I will do it, as the weather is what Londoners describe as 'rave quality gorgeous'.

I am standing on the steps of the Tate, clicking yet another shot of the city, when I sense someone standing by me. She is dark-skinned, with a slightly salt and pepper, coiffured hairdo. She smiles and says hesitantly, "Excuse me, you remind me of a friend from Kenya. You are not Lan…?"

Her eyes are the giveaway.

"Saboti! Saboti! It's you!" I give her my camera to hold, so I can hug her with both arms.

It is the first time we have met in 44 years, since that night at the bistro in February of 1964. Saboti tells me she lives in an apartment just around the corner, overlooking the Thames, and often pops into the Tate for a quick update.

We walk together along the Thames Embankment, westwards towards the London Eye. I scarcely notice anything – the river, the people, the Embankment, as we talk, sometimes walking, sometimes sitting, but always talking.

Later we have dinner. She tells me all that has happened in her life. Her husband passed away a year earlier. She talks about their two boys, graduates of the London School of Economics and Harvard; and Oxford and Columbia. And she tells me of her daughter with the UN in Indonesia; and of her three grandchildren.

I tell her about my family and me – and of my current single status. Inevitably though, we talk about Kenya and the bloody inter-tribal conflicts that erupted in that beautiful country after the elections of December 2007. We talk about how the world is losing hope especially as the USA is now fighting wars on many fronts and seems to have lost its global leadership role – and the hope that is being placed on Barack Obama.

"Lando, you must promise me," she says grabbing my hand over dinner, "that we can watch the results on Election Night together. Wow! Just imagine what it will do as a symbol to ending all that bloody racism across the world!"

I smile at her contagious enthusiasm. "I promise I will call you."

The next day I leave from Heathrow, for Toronto. Of course all I can think of is Saboti and how her destiny has led her to where she is. I reflect with admiration on how given an opportunity and a willingness to work hard – and of course an element of luck – almost anyone can make it in a free society, liberated from the shackles of colour, race, caste and tribe.

From my condo I look out at the flickering lights of TVs in the adjacent towers. A lot of people are watching history in the making this night. The texture of my crystal cut glass whiskey tumbler feels almost sensual. There was something very special, almost magical, about sharing this moment with Saboti.

Toronto, October 2012.

Acknowledgements

I am deeply indebted to a large number of readers of *Just Matata – Sin, Saints and Settlers*, whose messages encouraged me to bring out this sequel as soon as possible.

I particularly wish to single out for gratitude: Saboti (UK) for permission to share details of her early life; Basil Gordon (who sadly recently passed away after a short illness) who provided me with details of his double life during the days of the Mau Mau in Kenya; Canadian Emma Gama Pinto, widow of the Late Pio Gama Pinto—Kenya's most famous Goan in the fight for political Independence-- for filling in some gaps in the narrative on Pio.

I also want to thank Roland Francis (Toronto) who patiently read through the draft of *More Matata, Love After the Mau Mau*, and has provided steady encouragement; as has my daughter Sasha Menezes, who is a source of inspiration that keeps me writing. A number of people provided details to some stories, and many have consented to their names being used understanding they appear as fictional characters only, in this novel.

This book would not have materialized without the guidance and support of my close friend and mentor, author Victor Rangel-Ribeiro (USA), who had reviewed early drafts of this manuscript; however he must not be held responsible for my shortcomings. I also am grateful to author Mervyn Maciel (UK) who has generously shared his knowledge and experience in Kenya's Civil Service.

In turning this manuscript into a book I am particularly grateful to my friend and Editor, Terry Lavender (Vancouver, BC); Jim Bisakowski (Book Interior Design); Rudi Rodrigues (Design and Art Direction, Avatar Inc. Toronto) and Getty Images (Cover Photo). Once again, I could not have survived this solitary task without the support of my partner Norma

Starkie, who patiently checked the final draft, and most important kept me supplied with food rations and water during yet another long final stretch of solitary confinement. And finally readers—Thank you for your support in buying this book.

Your comments will always be welcome at matatabooks@gmail.com

Author's Note

Just Matata[1] – *Sin, Saints and Settlers* and *More Matata -
Love after the Mau Mau* are part of a Trilogy.

Goa is today, India's prime tourist destination and projected
to grow. It has been an integral part of India for over 50 years,
yet most people are unaware of its special culture, that now forms
part of the greater Indian mosaic. In December 1961, Indian
Armed Forces invaded Goa, and liberated this tiny territory from
the Portuguese, who had ruled it for 451 years since 1510, when
Afonso de Albuquerque first stepped ashore and claimed the territory in the name of the Portuguese Throne. During this period of
occupation they imposed their own religion and culture on people
creating a distinct blend of Indo-Portuguese.

In the early 20th century the British began to colonize Kenya
following the massive effort by thousands of Indian skilled tech-
nicians and labour, who went out to build the railway line from
Mombasa to Lake Victoria.

Soon the rulers of British East Africa were desperate for administrators and accountants; bartenders and bakers; cooks and
clerks; musicians and mechanics, engineers and tailors, doctors
and doormats.

The people of Goa fit the bill perfectly and they created no
matata. They spoke English, wore western attire and drank Scotch
whisky. They played card games and cricket. Although they gyrat-
ed to the m*ando* and *dulpod*, and they also danced the lancers, the
waltz and the foxtrot. They were Catholics and were considered
reliable to handle the purse strings. They stayed with their faith

---

[1] Matata means 'trouble' in Swahili

Braz Menezes

and never strayed into politics. They did what they were told and were always loyal and docile. Above all, when compared to the cost of British labour, they could be had cheap--very cheap indeed. They flocked to East Africa by the hundreds.

Reknowned authors like M.G. Vassanji have covered much of the Indian history in East Africa. However, there is a gap in the Asian history of Kenya that needed to be filled – how a small community from Goa, played an inordinately important and quiet role in the administration and the services economy of British East Africa, and when it was time to leave Kenya many went. Others stayed behind in the land they loved. In all the novels written, previously by European authors, especially those set in Kenya; the Indians and Goans were merely 'props and shadows' in other people's stories.

That is how The Matata Trilogy was born.

———•+•———

Glossary

Swahili words

Affyia	cheers, good health
askari (s)	guard, watchman, watchmen, policeman
Bwana	Sir
chini-chini	underground dealing/under the table deals
dhow	sailing vessel
duka, dukawalla	(Indian) shop, shopkeeper
fundi	artisan, mason, carpenter, repairman
Goan	person from Goa (Portuguese India) usually Catholic
Kaburu	White Afrikaans (South African) settler
kipande	I. D. Card
Karibu, Karibuni	Welcome
Kwaheri	Goodbye
mara moja	hurry, quickly, this minute
matata	trouble
matatu (s)	pirate taxi (s), informal transport
Mbwa kali	Savage dog (warning sign)
murramred	laterite soil used for road surfacing
Muhindi	Brown person (any Asian)
Muzungu	White person (any European)
Nusu-Nusu	mixed-race

Common Abbreviations

CID	Criminal Investigation Department
D.C.	District Commissioner
GSU	General Services Unit
PWD	Public Works Department
KADU	Kenya African Democratic Union
KAR	Kings African Rifles
P.C.	Provincial Commissioner
POW	Prisoner of War

Change of Names
Countries and Cities

Abyssinia	Ethiopia
Bombay	Mumbai, India
Margao	Margaon, Goa
Panjim	Panaji, Goa
Lorenco Marques	Maputo, Mozambique

Street Names (Nairobi)

Ainsworth Bridge	Museum Hill Bridge
Delamere Avenue	Kenyatta Avenue
Government Road	Moi Avenue
Kikuyu Road	Ojijo Road
Whitehouse Road	Haille Selassie Avenue

The Coryndon Memorial Museum is now The Nairobi National Museum

————•••————

To see Reviews and Readers' reactions on
Just Matata-Sin, Saints and Settlers,
please visit website: matatabooks.com

Made in the USA
Charleston, SC
26 May 2013